No Justice:
No Victory

The Death Penalty in Texas

Susan Lee Campbell Solar
Edited by Susan Bright

Plain View Press
P. O. 42255
Austin, TX 78704

a collaborative project

Anomaly Press
P.O. Box 3138
Austin, TX 78764

Copyright Plain View Press, 2004. All rights reserved.
ISBN: 1-891386-99-9
Library of Congress Number: 2004097294

Cover and title page photos by Susan Lee Campbell Solar. Thanks for help with cover production work to Annie Borden.

Family of Odell Barnes (cover) receiving the worst news a family can receive.

For information call: 512-441-2452, 512-444-1672.
Email: sbright1@austin.rr.com
Websites: plainviewpress.net, gift-economy.com

The Legend of Josefa "Chipita" Rodriguez

An epic poem written by Rachael Hebert of Corpus Christi spread the tragic fame of Josefa "Chipita" Rodriguez. After a trial in English, a language she did not speak, Rodriguez was hung from a mesquite tree on the banks of the Nueces River in south Texas in 1863. She is reported to be the last woman executed in Texas until Karla Faye Tucker in 1998.

Rodriguez was accused of gold theft and the ax murder of an Anglo Confederate horse trader named John Savage, who reportedly stayed at her inn. Several days after his stay, Savage turned up dead with an ax blow to the head, his body thrown into the river and wrapped in gunny sacks. The process from indictment to execution of Rodriguez for the murder reportedly took four days; the trial itself was accomplished in one morning. From the gallows, the aged roadside café and inn operator proclaimed her innocence: "No soy culpable."

A Scripps-Howard report in the *San Angelo Times*[1] reported that "women in the town were aghast" at her sentence. The sheriff left town to avoid responsibility, leaving the execution to a hired hangman from out of town, and he had trouble commandeering a wagon to carry her to her death.

Geraldine McCloin of Corpus Christi said that her great-grandmother donated a dress for Chipita to wear to her hanging. She described the hanging as "pretty grisly" because Chipita's slight frame wasn't heavy enough for her to choke quickly. She thrashed and strangled for quite awhile before her body was cut down, then she was buried in a cypress coffin beneath the mesquite tree from which she was hung. Legend says her ghost is still seeking justice along the banks of the Nueces River in San Patricio County, where Savage's dead body was found.

The story of Rodriguez became legendary when, after her execution, a man made a deathbed confession to the crime for which she had been tried and convicted. Another story spread that the gold reportedly stolen from Savage had been found, and in fact had never been stolen, thus removing the assumed motive for the murder. Yet another version of the legend arose, maintaining that Juan Silvera, a man convicted with her and given a sentence of only five years, was her son and actually the guilty party, and that she had died to protect him.

According to a column by Murphy Givens in the *Corpus Christi Caller Times*,[2] the sheriff of Corpus Christi served on the grand jury that indicted her, and was a buddy of the foreman of the trial jurors, which also included four men convicted of felonies, one for murder. Givens wrote: "It looks now like Chipita was found guilty based on who she was (a Mexican), rather than for what she did."[3]

At least Rodriguez had some semblance of a trial. A useful compendium on Texas justice, *Lone Star Justice*,[4] relates the 1863 hanging by an angry mob in San Antonio of a white cowhand acquitted by a district court judge of drunkenly firing his guns in the street (apparently causing no injuries). Between 1889 and 1942 there are long lists of lynchings of men often merely accused, never tried in court, the blacks mostly in East Texas, the whites mostly further West and listed as outlaws. In 1890, for example, 18 men, all black, were lynched for reasons as incomprehensible as accusations of "racial prejudice," gambling and larceny, though the majority were accused of rape or murder.

One cannot help thinking that old-fashioned frontier justice, raw and unfair as it was, at least never claimed to be anything it wasn't. Recent state sanctioned killing sprees, cloaked as they have been in institutional and bureaucratic rhetoric and law, are alarmingly hypocritical.

The legendary Texas Congressman Bob Eckhard, longtime opponent of the death penalty, is reputed to have quipped, "If we're going to keep this institution, we ought to return to hangin' in the public square."

Special Thanks to Genevieve Vaughan

Since the early eighties, Genevieve Vaughan has supported feminist, peace and justice projects both individually and then as the Director of the Foundation for a Compassionate Society (1987-1998). Susan Lee Campbell Solar worked for Genevieve in the Foundation's sister organization, Feminists for a Compassionate Society, doing antinuclear and feminist activist work during the nineties. Genevieve purchased the motorhome Susan Lee outfitted as a museum, painted with blue sky, clouds and named: *Earth and Sky Women's Peace Caravan for a Nuclear Free Future*. Susan Lee drove the museum tirelessly throughout the United States to educate people about the dangers of nuclear weapons, dumping and nuclear energy. This work was instrumental in blocking the plan, supported by George W. Bush, to dump nuclear waste near Sierra Blanca, Texas.

After Susan unexpected death in February of 2002, Genevieve was one of the first of her friends to suggest we finish the death penalty book, and she offered to fund it, which she did throughout the long technical journey to a finished book. Genevieve's support, along with contributions from Susan's family, sustained the project.

Josepha "Chipita" Rodriguez, it turns out, was probably buried on the land belonging to Genevieve's ancestors, the Dougherty family, on the Nueces River in San Patricio County, in South Texas, and one of her relatives gave Chipita the dress she wore to the hanging. Genevieve, at our first advisory council meeting, told us about the area, which she had visited often, "There are spirits all over that place. I think Chipita really does want justice," she told us.

Genevieve's own work has been a life long pursuit of social change, both as an activist and as a theorist. Her theories about the gift economy present a radically different paradigm based on women's values. Her book, *For-Giving: A Feminist Criticism of Exchange*, is available from Plain View Press and Anomaly Press. The book in its entirety as well as numerous articles can be found on her website at www.gift-economy.com.

This book exists because of Genevieve's support both of Susan Lee Campbell Solar's initial work on the book, and then after Susan died, of many months of editing, community input and documentation by Susan Bright and many others. We gratefully acknowledge this gift, and the underlying gift paradigm her theories have expressed.

Contents

Introductory Notes
    The Legend of Josefa "Chipita" Rodriguez   3
    Special Thanks to Genevieve Vaughan   5
    Foreword, by Steve Hall   9
    Editor's Notes, by Susan Bright   12
    Introduction and Gratitude, by Susan Lee Campbell Solar   17

Chapter One: A Tilted Playing Field   21

Chapter Two: Innocence in the Lone Star State   43

Chapter Three: Appeals, The One Way Door   71

Chapter Four: Gary Graham (Shaka Sankofa)   89

Chapter Five: No Clemency, No Mercy   105

Chapter Six: Larry Robison   119

Chapter Seven: Anthony Graves (Part 1)   135
    Crime and Conviction
    Anthony Graves (Part 2)   167
    Railroad Justice
    Anthony Graves (Part 3)   181
    Post-conviction Chances

Chapter Eight: Remedies   209

Chapter Nine: Reconciliation, Not Retribution   219

Chapter Ten: Pablo Melendez, Jr.   227

Chapter Eleven: Michael Toney   255

Chapter Twelve: Odell Barnes   271

Endnotes by Chapter   285
Bibliography   315
About the Author   325

Susan Lee Campbell Solar on her land on the Perdenales River near Austin, TX.

Photo by Annie Borden.

Foreword

by Steve Hall
7/18/04

To meet Susan Solar was to experience a mature activist in full bloom. When she saw a problem, she wanted to fully understand it in all its ramifications. Then, she wanted to focus attention on the problem and its solutions. Mostly politely, but with great persistence, she then worked to educate others and push for change and reform; almost as a force of nature.

She turned her attention to Texas' application of the death penalty at a time when only a handful of journalists and writers were beginning to appraise how broken the state's criminal justice system was when it involved capital punishment. This book is an historic document that captures the state of an accident in mid-occurrence. Susan was watching it a bit earlier than most.

Texas has carried out more than one-third of the executions in America since reintroduction of the death penalty in 1977. The volume and the relentless pace of executions sets Texas in a class by itself. Numbers and pace, so far removed from any other state, have forced people to focus on Texas.

After years of analysis by journalists, legal scholars, legislators, and others, we know that systemic problems exist in virtually every step of Texas' application of the death penalty: flawed investigative techniques that lead to misidentification; wide discretion by prosecutors in when to seek the death penalty and resultant geographic disparities in its application; police and/or prosecutorial misconduct; inadequate resources for indigent defendants, meaning virtually everyone charged with capital murder; the use of junk science expert witnesses; a partisan and elected judiciary that especially skews the postconviction process; and finally, a clemency process that in the past 25 years has failed to meet its historic responsibilities.

Each one of the systemic problems identified has the potential to call into question the integrity of the criminal justice system. Taken together, they are a powerful indictment of a deeply flawed system. The worst, most dreaded outcome is the wrongful conviction and execution of an innocent person.

Since reintroduction of the death penalty, at least seven men have been exonerated and released from Texas death row. These exonerations came about, not on the basis of some legal technicality, but because the wrong person was convicted and sent to death row. More damning is the fact that many of these exonerations came about, not directly through judicial review or the clemency process, but because of the work of journalists and others.

As this introduction is being written in the summer of 2004, three separate cases are receiving judicial review over actual innocence. Nationally, 114 men and women have been exonerated due to actual innocence.

Increasingly, Texans are concerned about this danger. In 2002, the Scripps Howard Texas Poll found that 69% of the respondents believed the state has executed innocent people, an increase of 12 percentage points from a previous poll taken in 2000. Former state district judge Jay Burnett, who presided over capital cases in Harris County and strengthened requirements for attorneys appointed in death penalty cases in the county, has stated that he has no doubt that the state has executed an innocent person. Sam Millsap, the former district attorney of Bexar County and San Antonio, has said, "Our system in Texas is broken. Until it is fixed and we are satisfied that only the guilty can be put to death, there should be no more executions in Texas."

The American Bar Association, the nation's largest group of attorneys, has called for a moratorium on executions by jurisdictions with capital punishment until ABA standards for the appointment, performance, and compensation of attorneys in such cases are adopted, as well as safeguards to protect the innocent from wrongful conviction. The ABA, which does not take a position on the death penalty per se, adopted this resolution at its annual meeting held in San Antonio in 1997.

Since Susan Solar began this work, all the major Texas daily newspapers, and many smaller papers, have editorially endorsed a moratorium and reforms. So have many religious organizations, the League of Women Voters of Texas, and others.

In the time since this work was originally written, some positive changes have occurred. The 2001 session of the Texas Legislature passed the landmark Texas Fair Defense Act. For the first time, the state appropriated limited funding to assist in the appointment of lawyers for indigent defendants, and mandated that standards for attorney appointment be developed. This law applies to all criminal cases, including death penalty cases. Another law established a procedure for postconviction access to DNA testing in an effort to discover wrongful convictions in cases where DNA evidence might be available.

In 2002, the U.S. Supreme Court ruled in the case of *Atkins* v. *Virginia* that it was no longer constitutional to execute offenders with mental retardation, a lifelong condition marked by limited intellectual capacity and diminished adaptive behavioral skills. In March 2004, Governor Rick

Perry, acting upon the recommendation of the Board of Pardons and Paroles, commuted the death sentence of Robert Smith to life in prison. Smith was found to have mental retardation. A number of other death row inmates are known to have mental retardation, and others require screening and access to attorneys for a thorough review.

In several legal cases, the U.S. Supreme Court has criticized the Texas Court of Criminal Appeals and the U.S. Fifth Circuit Court of Appeals for failing to properly apply past Supreme Court rulings in death penalty cases.

The Texas Board of Pardons and Paroles has been reorganized and reduced in size from 18 members to seven. Some observers hope that this will lead the board to give more thoughtful and active consideration of clemency petitions in death penalty cases.

Steve Hall is the director of the StandDown Texas Project, which advocates a moratorium on executions, a state sponsored study commission on Texas' application of the death penalty, and needed reforms.

Editor's Notes

by Susan Bright
8/15/04

The first time I met Susan Lee, my first husband and I climbed the steps of the rambling two-story house on Wheeler Street, near the University of Texas, where she and Hoyt Purvis lived with their two daughters, Pamela and Camille. It was a wonderful old southern house, long porches, screen windows, high ceilings and a wide staircase, strewn with books, laundry, and children's toys. We'd come to a Sunday *New York Times* party, a weekly gathering she and Hoyt began in the tradition of the salon — a time for people to discuss ideas, politics and the news. It was 1974. Susan Lee was making black beans and tabouli. Children were racing about, strewing debris far and wide. Susan Lee and I became fast friends, working together, allies at cascading levels, sisters, mothers, artists, activists. When I wrote her obituary I checked my own resume to get the dates right.

Not unlike the effect she had on anyone, she was always pushing my thinking off a ledge. She was a leader of activists, a primary change agent, the one who understood the problem first and set off to remedy it. The day Susan Lee died a spontaneous gathering of friends held a memorial at Austin's beloved Barton Springs. People began to talk about getting the death penalty book finished. Logically it came to me — one of her oldest and closest friends, an editor and publisher.

I wasn't sure I wanted to do it. I'd worked with her in the jails in Travis County in the late 70's. We'd published a book of inmate poetry. I hated the oppression and vowed to have nothing to do with prison work again. In Rottenberg, Germany I'd seen medieval torture chambers underneath the Berger's house. The jail behind the woodwork of our county court house wasn't vastly different. I saw junkies going cold turkey on a sleep inducing flu syrup. I saw whole families in jail — mothers, daughters, sons, brothers. It was evil through and through. I didn't see a single way to make it better. But she did.

It is incredibly ironic that I ended up working for two and a half years to finish her book about the death penalty in Texas. In the first place, I am a poet, not an attorney, or a Texan. In the second place, prisons, particularly in Texas, make me ill. I opposed the death penalty because I was raised to believe killing is wrong, not because I understood the depth of oppression and corruption capital punishment manifests, particularly in Texas, and I didn't want to look at it. So it took me several months to realize that finishing her book was something I could, or wanted to do.

When Susan Lee Solar ran for Governor of Texas, as a Green Party candidate against George W. Bush in 1998, her first scheduled press conference collided with a weekend she'd chosen to spend in minimum security jail. She'd been arrested protesting a plan to dump nuclear waste at Sierra Blanca in West Texas. I was trying to get her to do community service, but she didn't have time. It was easier to spend a weekend in jail, so that's what she did. I worried all weekend about her safety. When, several years later, she embarked on the death penalty book, I was busy with other things. Of all the projects she worked on during our thirty some years of friendship, this was the one she spoke to me about the least, which is not to say she didn't tell me what I eventually needed to know.

One late summer night six months or so before she died, she stopped by to tell me about the book. She told me about the interviews, that she wanted to tell the stories of people on death row who she thought were innocent. She wanted people to understand the traumatic impact on families of the condemned and their communities. She told me about victim's families who chose alternatives to retaliation. She said the death penalty was the tip of the iceberg of a system of institutionalized injustice and oppression that was at the center of what was destroying our country and the world. I said she should tell the stories. She said she had begun to think there were two books — one about justice and the other about mercy.

Ralph Yarborough once said Susan Lee had the metabolism of a flying squirrel. Her energy was boundless. I never met anyone who could keep up with her for long. In order to accomplish the work of finishing her book I gathered an advisory circle of friend and experts. Quite simply the work would not have occurred without them. Ric Sternberg commented, after reading a few chapters, "she never took a breath." Annie Borden was the first person to separate the death penalty tapes and papers from the rest of Susan's archives. The Center for American History at the University of Texas at Austin wanted her papers. Annie said we had to keep the death penalty papers until the book could be finished — 30 boxes of papers, tapes, dozens of books, and hundreds of computer files.

My job was to read those 30 boxes, find (with Tony Switzer's help) the latest electronic versions of her chapters, listen to a hundred plus interviews and decide what should be included in the final manuscript. There wouldn't be two books. There would be one. I had to come up with a new outline. And then my job was to edit the multifaceted sentences and paragraphs that spun out of the vast intellect of someone with the metabolism of a flying squirrel.

I wanted to change her voice as little as possible. I called on the advisory circle time and time again, asking for multiple reads. Every chapter got at least eight reads. I tracked down sources, attorneys, people she had communicated with to be sure what ended up in print was correct. I was intimidated by the fact that there were lives at stake, and cautioned by the reality of liability law. I was able to find materials that may turn out to be critical evidence in the Anthony Graves case, and pray they make it into court.

Of course, Susan Lee left much of the documentation until the end of the project. Everything we needed was in those 30 boxes, tapes and computer files, but what a long search it was to put the pieces of the puzzle together, which is how I finally experienced the project — as a vast puzzle. Ted Applewhite, an attorney who works as a carpenter, in that Austin tradition that has Ph.D's driving cabs and international students who are members of their country's elite running convenience stores, tracked down the legal citations.

Susan Lee ran for governor against George W. Bush because she thought he was dangerous. When she first encountered him, he wanted to use Texas as a site to dump nuclear waste which indicated to her that he was uninterested in protecting the environment. He presided over the execution of more people than did most countries in the world during his time in office, which indicated to her that he didn't mind killing people. He came to power on a tough on crime platform that was an early manifestation of the politics of fear, as did his father. He worked to fast track habeas appeals because he thought habeas corpus law, which guarantees a citizen's constitutional rights, was a waste of time. His take on clemency was the result of a complete misunderstanding of tripartite government. It didn't bother him that people were condemned to die without evidence of their innocence ever making it into court. He didn't much care about evidence. It didn't bother him that his state executed people who were under age, mentally ill or mentally incapable of understanding their situation or crime. It didn't occur to him that prosecutors, judges and investigators should be held accountable if they contributed to wrongful convictions. George W. Bush believed the system which had elevated him to office worked just fine. Susan Lee didn't.

She wanted to finish the book before the 2000 election, but the scope of the work was overwhelming. When I began work on it in the summer of 2002, George W. Bush was in office and 9/11 had scared America senseless. We closed our eyes as he fast tracked trade agreements that sent our jobs overseas. The Patriot Act made short work of the constitutional rights of many Americans. Non-military combatants were being held in Guantanamo Bay. Arab Americans had been arrested and held without being charged, no word to families or friends, all over America, and George W. Bush was clamoring to invade Iraq, which has to date resulted in the death of between ten and thirteen thousand civilians and a thousand American soldiers. When the Abu Ghraib prison scandal hit the world press, it read to me like the next chapter in Susan Lee's book.

Now that I have arrived at the end of what seemed along the way to be an endless work, I realize the stories Susan chose to tell in depth were harbingers. Gary Graham (Shaka Sankofa) thought of himself as a political prisoner. The world saw Odell Barnes in the same way, not because either of them were above fault or started out in politics, but because they were black, poor, on death row and spoke out about their situation. Michael Toney was convicted of a terrorist bombing just after the 1998 Anti-terrorism and Death Penalty Act. Evidence against him was primarily hearsay, later contradicted by facts yet to make to before a jury. Pablo Melendez was a gang kid so messed up from sniffing paint he didn't remember whether he did the crime or not, but it was good politics to get gang members off the street. Larry Robison endured the devastating mental illness we call paranoid schizophrenia and slipped through the holes in the Texas mental health system, which ranks last in the country. He was violent only one day in his life, the day he killed six people, for their own good, because the voices said to do it.

What links these men condemned to die in a system George W. Bush braggs about, to the fundamental horror of American foreign policy under his administration is that in both circumstances people die from state sanctioned retaliatory acts of vengeance which result, with alarming frequency, from incompetence, racism, and/or because of an astounding disregard for evidence and human rights.

Thanks to Susan's family for contributing to the cost of finishing this book and to Genevieve Vaughan for continued financial support. Thanks to our Advisory Circle of friends, family and experts who shared expertise, lent encouragement and helped me scope the dimensions of the book: Camille Purvis, Pamela Purvis Hatcher, Sarah Campbell, Wilda Campbell, Genevieve Vaughan, Tony Switzer, Annie Borden, Ric Sternberg, Glee Ingram, Molly Bean, Bill Reid, Suzy Reid, Thomas Torlincasi, Roy Greenwood, D'Ann Johnson, Gary Taylor, Jennifer Long, Walter Long, and Pam Murfin for being part of that circle. Thanks to Genevieve Vaughan, Sally Jacques and Gary Dugger for helping me house Susan's papers while I worked on the project. Thanks to John C. Andrews, Daryl Andrews, Nick Crews, Megan and Anne S. Bright, who have arranged their lives frequently in honor of my work. Thanks to Ted Applewhite for clarifying legal citations; to Roy Greenwood, Richard Burr, Jay Burnett, Lois Robison, and Rob Owen for verification of various sections of the book; to Roy E. Greenwood for many helpful explanations of legal processes; to Steve Hall for helping me identify photographs and for writing the introduction; to Andrew Hammel for checking the veracity of the first part of the book; to Frieda Werden, Glee Ingram and Kimberley McCutcheon for proof reading; and to the Center for American History at the University of Texas for housing the Susan Lee Campbell Solar Death Penalty Papers and other records of her lifelong work as an activist.

Susan Bright is the author of 19 books of poetry, the publisher of Plain View Press and publications coordinator for the Center for the Study of the Gift Economy.

Introduction and Gratitude

by Susan Lee Campbell Solar
January 29, 2001

In January 2000, determined to pursue a full time job so I could build my dream green home of straw bales and earth (cob) on the Pedernales River, I got caught up researching and writing about a really grim, even grisly theme: capital punishment in Texas. The original idea, proposed to me by a good friend who intended to write a book for Spanish-speaking audiences on the same topic, was to focus on George W. Bush's role in an execution assembly line that left some victims and their advocates feeling justice was finally being served. But it left human rights advocates around the globe gasping at the breathless manner with which we dispatched people condemned as murderers. In 2000 Texas executed 40 people. In the entire year of 1990 Texas had strapped down just four men to the gurney in the small turquoise room behind the high, dark, redbrick walls of the Walls Unit in central Huntsville, in East Central Texas, the heart of the Bible Belt. The rush to kill was gathering attention at every level, from local to global.

Between 1982 — when Texas resumed executions ending an 18 year informal respite after which the electric chair was replaced by lethal injection, a method considered less brutal because it didn't leave the smell of charred flesh behind — and 2001 when this book was begun, the Texas Court of Criminal Appeals, the federal district courts, the Fifth Circuit Court of Appeals in New Orleans, the U.S. Supreme Court, and finally, the governor and his or her Board of Pardons and Paroles sent 247 men and 2 women to die — before witnesses they chose and others they didn't, including the media. That figure represented more executions than all but four other countries. Texas, with a tenth of the country's population, boasted a third of the executions committed in the United States.

The presiding judge of the Texas Court of Criminal Appeals said in the last year of the last decade of the last century in the last millennium AD that the Texas system of capital punishment "is a model for the nation."[1] There were many others who agreed with Texas Attorney General John Cornyn who said it was the last throwback to a savage age.

As I researched, I learned that Bush was not the beginning and the end of this rush to vengeance. The record of his Democratic predecessor Ann Richards (not to mention her Democratic primary opponents) was nothing to brag about either in the halls of justice or mercy. I found both Bush and Richards perpetrated a tradition where politicians, in some cases cynically, used capital punishment for professional gain.

I learned about the historical roots of the tradition in 19th century days when lynchings in town squares were the *mode du jour*. When these displays of public gore were replaced in 1924 with centralized electrocutions, Texas was considered a national model for progressive reform. I attended events and interviewed stakeholders who would consent to be interviewed in 2000 and the first few months of 2001 as the legislature considered a plethora of bills dealing with different aspects of reform for the death penalty system. By March of 2001, I sensed some kind of turning point had occurred as I'd stood on a parking lot across from the Walls Unit watching Odell Barnes, Jr.'s forlorn family and their European and North American allies standing in horrific vigil, waiting for word of his execution. European parliamentarians and ordinary citizens had become emotionally embroiled in the life and fate of a death row inmate most Texans had never heard of. The world was watching, and while international condemnation of the death penalty didn't save Odell Barnes, it might stop the Texas death machine eventually.

The book that follows was provoked in part by George W. Bush who threw down the gauntlet to the national media during his presidential campaign with his repeated claims that the judicial system works in capital murder cases in Texas, and that no innocent person had been executed on his watch. Here's to the stellar disregard for justice and life exhibited by the 43rd president of the United States during his stint as governor of Texas and to the international spotlight it helped focus on the Texas death penalty.

Thanks to many friends, old and new, who provided shelter, listening ears and research assistance along the way: my mother Wilda Campbell and our friend Dorothy Tice in Houston, who always support me, no matter what wild project I've espoused (although Dorothy forbade me, and her son, to discuss capital punishment, which she supports); my firstborn, Pamela Renee Purvis [Hatcher], who gave me *Dead Man Walking* for Christmas when it first appeared, provoking a sleepless, tearful night and the resolve to not read any further on the topic; my daughters Camille and Pamela Campbell Purvis; my sisters, Sarah and Wilda (Gilda) Campbell, who provided support from D.C. and from Delhi; and Sarah's daughter Emily, who sent me reams of newspaper articles from the Library of Congress. Thanks to my mother Wilda Wells Campbell, whose support and love has always given me strength and endurance. Lynn Gilbert inspired re-writing and re-organization of a section of the book and the addition of the introductory chapter; Linda Dunbar Kravitz who thoughtfully critiqued my outline and introduction from afar, and Troy Jones from closer in, and other D.C. and even more far-flung friends who inspire and encourage me always; to Genevieve Vaughan whose family foundation, the Dougherty Foundation, made an initial contribution to the research of the book, and who wholeheartedly supported my anti-nuclear work for years, and whose own serious, disciplined effort to change values as a thinker and author with her book, *For-Giving: A Feminist Criticism of Exchange* served as a role model for me.

I must credit also old friends Suzy and Bill Reid, who shared their collection of bound *Texas Observer* articles from the seventies and eighties; Joyce and Mac Hall and Rita Clarke in Dallas, hosts and activists par excellence; Howard and Sally Phillips of the Phillips Hilton in Houston; John Washburn in his writer's/philosopher's/poet's retreat on Possum Kingdom Lake west of Fort Worth; and Kathleen Sommers, Grace Love, and George Thompson who shared their organic farm south of San Antonio when I needed a place to hole up away from Austin's distractions; Tony Switzer, my "research slave," encourager and special friend; Annie Borden and Ric Sternberg, who sustain my spirit with laughter and creativity in their strawbale home on the Pedernales; and Charles Alverson, who wittily shares his writer's tribulations and encouragement by email from Serbia.

Because I am not an attorney, I am especially indebted to those who patiently explained many technical, historical and political aspects of the Texas legal system. Thanks to Gary Taylor, who opened his files and big bubba heart and store of knowledge about the Court of Criminal Appeals and the process of capital appeals in the state and federal courts, and specifically the Odell Barnes, David Soria and David Stoker cases; and to Catherine Haenni, the Swiss-born attorney in Taylor's office who exposed me to the role of Europeans in Texas death row cases; to Houston attorney Gerald Bierbaum who critiqued early drafts of background chapters; and to Doug Robinson, a commercial attorney-litigator in D.C. who spent hours detailing his experience as a volunteer lawyer struggling to free two Texas death row inmates with innocence claims; and to Steve Latimer, another East Coast attorney, who labored long and gamely to save David Stoker's life.

Thanks also to the several victims of prosecutorial misconduct in Burleson County, who stepped forward to share the insights and clues they'd garnered through efforts in their own self-defense, some directly relevant to the Graves case, such as Thomas Torlincasi, Richard Surovik, Ralph Hatfield, Allan Spence, and those who from fear wished to remain unnamed; and to former prosecutors Stephen Keng, Judge W. T. McDonald, Brooks Cofer, and Roland Searcy who shared insights about a D.A. run amok and a state ill-equipped to rein him in; and the often humorous and insightful and surprisingly idealistic defense attorneys who battle for their clients across the state and sometimes from outside Texas, occasionally without pay, because they still believe justice should be served. And to those attorneys who've always followed the path of public service like James Harrington, Walter Long, Eden Harrington, Maurie Levin, Jim Marcus, Mandy Welch and Dick Burr; and to Judge Charles Baird, all of whom granted long interviews from their busy schedule, as did SMU Southern historian and human rights professor Rick Halperin.

Finally, thanks to the people who've inspired me with their stories of recovery from traumatic loss, the murder victims' family members who managed to climb out of depression, anger and grief and move toward reconciliation with offenders and even sometimes to become their advocates. I deeply appreciate the words of those recovering from the trauma of wrongful imprisonment on death row, Andrew Mitchell and Kerry Cook, who welcomed me into their homes in Tyler and Plano and told me their maddening and yet hopeful stories of life on death row and after release. Deep gratitude goes to those still caught in that wrenching anxiety, the family, friends and allies of Anthony Graves, Pablo Melendez, Jr., and Michael Toney; and to those who are grieving loved ones (Gary Graham, David Stoker, Larry Robison, Odell Barnes Jr.) who were executed. Thanks goes to inmates themselves whom I came to know through interview visits and letters. All of these provided important clues and information and shared their emotions about their own experiences with the lethal institution I was studying.

Here's to all those who engage seriously in this debate, no matter what side you're on, for it is of urgent matter to the soul of our community that it be considered in depth.

Chapter One:
A Tilted Playing Field

Rally for Gary Graham (Shaka Sankofa).

Photo by SusanLee Campbell Solar.

Photo by Susan Lee Campbell Solar.

Governor Death

George W. Bush was inaugurated governor of Texas on January 17, 1995, hours after a mentally retarded man named Mario Marquez from San Antonio was lethally injected. The previous governor Ann Richards during her last hours in office did nothing to stop the execution. Bush left office in Texas halfway through his second term on December 21, 2000, to prepare to occupy the White House. One hundred and fifty men and two women were executed by the state during his almost six-year term in office, a fact which earned him the nickname "Governor Death."

During Bush's last year in office Texas executed 40 people, nearly half of the 85 put to death across the US that year. That was more than in any one state since 1862; when 39 indigenous Americans were hung by the US military in a single day in Minnesota. Since the resumption of executions in the United States in 1977 after a Supreme Court-ordered lull, Texas was responsible for approximately one third (246 of 707 as of April of 2001) of the executions in the nation. Almost two-thirds of those were executed while George Bush occupied the governor's mansion in Austin, a two-and-a-half hour drive from the death chamber in downtown Huntsville. It was a drive he never made to witness a series of events that will, one could argue, ultimately characterize his tenure in the Lone Star State, and perhaps his public record for posterity. Neither had his predecessors.

In January of 2000, as Bush began his last year governing Texas and geared up his presidential campaign, 11 men were executed in 15 days in Huntsville, including a mentally ill man and a man whose crime was committed when he was seventeen. This "killing spree" made news all over the world as the Bush campaign lent spotlight to the issue of capital punishment. In contrast, Republican Governor of Illinois, George Ryan, declared a temporary halt on executions to study the capital punishment situation in his state where wrongful convictions were turning up 50% of the time.

The essential questions

Several questions engaged me as a native Texan, born and raised in Houston — which is, depending on your perspective, either the shining star or the belly of the beast of capital punishment in this era. About a third of the inmates on Texas death row come through Houston courts.

First, are there innocents on death row? And if so, how did they get there? And with both state courts and federal courts theoretically reviewing cases, why is it that people with extremely perplexing issues of innocence remain on death row for years, deprived of freedom to pursue normal lives. How is it that, once a person is found guilty, the appellate process works like a tightrope with no net? What happens to the families of innocents, or even people who are guilty, who are executed? How are Texas governors able to exempt themselves from the process of clemency?

Beyond that lie questions of morality and mercy regarding the execution of people who committed capital crimes before the age of 18, who are mentally retarded or mentally ill, who were under the influence of mind-altering chemicals at the time of the crime, and who almost always come from chaotic and/or abusive households. Could they have been diverted from killing in a society that provided more resources for mental health and sex offender treatment, more assistance to families in trouble, more investigators and refuge for severely abused children? Texas ranks last in the nation in spending per capita on most social services, despite the wealth in the state.

Questions of racism have to be evaluated in a state where there are almost four times as many blacks on death row as their percentage of the base population would predict.

And ultimately there is the question of what our state, or any other, gains by killing anyone, no matter how remorseless and violent they are. What does it serve to kill someone who has changed, who appears to be making a positive contribution in difficult circumstances?

Although Texas has led the nation in executions since 1976, our murder rate is also the highest, higher than similarly populated states without capital punishment such as New York.[1]

What should be done with those who have murdered others, in some cases viciously, yet pose no further threat after they are in confinement for awhile, who sincerely reform themselves, like Karla Fay Tucker? Do the injustices done to victims require perpetrator deaths, an eye for an eye?

Even if one believes in an-eye-for-an-eye justice, what conceivable ethic is served when the wrong person is executed or incarcerated for a crime?

What I found

Without extraordinary effort I came across a number of cases which, upon investigation, indicate that the system doesn't work.

I discovered convictions that raise very troubling questions, questions that cost me sleep and ripped away a certain naïve trust I carried from my personal friendships and blood relationships with attorneys of high integrity on both sides of the bar, prosecution and defense.

I listened to stories of grief and devastation from the families of men on death row, stories of men executed after legal proceedings that left too many questions about innocence for a person of conscience to be complacent or even comfortable with the death penalty. I realized these cases, each one of them, are of classic tragic magnitude. Like Josefa "Chipita" Rodriguez whose "*No soy culpable*" is said to linger in the wind along the Nueces River, the social echo of each wrong or even questionable execution haunts family, community, and civil society for generations.

I came to the conclusion that the innocents are on death row primarily because they lacked money to hire a topnotch defense attorney to scare off the prosecution if the case happened to be shaky, as it would logically be in wrongful convictions. As Sr. Helen Prejean says, quoting a luckless (and guilty) Florida death row inmate named John Arthur Spenkelenk: "them without the capital gets the punishment."[2] They usually did not come from "good" or socially prominent, white-skinned families — thus they were expendable.

Some, like Pablo Melendez, Jr., had competent trial attorneys, but they lacked adequate resources to fully investigate and were up against a prosecution working hand in glove with a police detective who may have concealed crucial information from the defense and possibly even from the prosecution. Many, such as Gary Graham, Ricky Jones, and David Stoker received excellent attorneys at the final stage of federal appeals, but too many doors had already slammed shut. Their expert assistance arrived, as former Texas Court of Criminal Appeals Judge Charles Baird put it, at the wrong end of the judicial process.[3]

Ft. Worth defense attorney Robert Ford estimates that 5 % of death row inmates are in fact innocent.[4] If he is correct, some 23 of the persons now on Texas death row have been wrongfully deprived of their liberty, convicted and sentenced to die; and about 12 of those executed since 1982 were murdered by the state. That also means if Texas stopped condemning people to die now and simply went about fatally poisoning the people already on death row at the rate (40 annually) of executions in the year 2000, an average of two innocent persons a year would be killed for the next 11 years. Is that a price we are willing to pay for public safety or to honor demands by an aggrieved public for justice for the victims of the 38 condemned murderers who are actually guilty?

University of Houston constitutional law professor David Dow thinks the figure is 1%, although Dow doesn't like the question because he thinks focusing on "actual innocence" is the wrong approach.[5] Doug Robinson, a Washington, D.C. attorney who has represented *pro bono* two Texas death row inmates he believes are innocent (one who is already free), thinks we might "reduce death row by half" if we adequately funded the investigation of all the cases now on the row.[6] Williamson County prosecutor John Bradley, on the other hand, says there are no innocents on death row, because the system works too efficiently to allow that.[7] Research conducted for this book contradicts Bradley and suggests that Dow's estimate, and even Ford's, may be overly conservative.

Who gets charged and prosecuted

Most Texans believe that capital punishment is reserved for only the most hideous crimes and the most unredeemable killers. In fact, only a small percentage of all Texas murders lead to capital murder charges, and there's not a lot of rhyme or reason to explain why certain ones are chosen.

Between 1982 and 1999, less than 3% of people who committed murder were punished with loss or threat of loss of their lives. Approximately 30,000 homicides and non-negligent homicides occurred in Texas in this 17 year period, yet just over 700 condemned killers had either been executed or sat on death row awaiting execution. Fewer than a hundred had left death row either by commutation or death or had simply been released.[8]

Some of the homicides didn't fit the definition of a capital crime as set forth in the 1973 legislative revision of the Texas criminal code. For instance, between 1982 and 1999 only about 20 % of the homicides for which a suspect was placed under arrest qualified as capital cases. To be a capital offense the crime had to include (in addition to murder) rape, robbery, burglary, car theft, larceny or a child victim. The other cases, which involved relatives or friends or acquaintances slaying each other due to conflict, didn't fit the definition of a capital crime.[9]

Of the approximately 5500 arrests that could have led to capital trials, around one in eight, less than 13%, of the offenders wound up on death row. In 1999 in Harris County, there were 237 murder convictions; only 15, slightly over 6%, were pursued as capital cases.[10]

The routine conviction rate in capital cases is around four out of five cases. In Harris County it's 75%, in Dallas County, where they try only the most winnable cases, it's 94%.[11] That implies that less than a thousand, or fewer than one in five cases which could be tried as capital cases, reach that stage. Many are pled to life or lesser sentences. Texas allows most of those who are arrested for capital murder to live. This happens before the cases come to court. Some murder suspects, in fact, are never even arrested, though evidence for their guilt abounds, as some of the stories in this book will show. Because they are willing to "sing" and implicate someone else, even someone who is innocent, to save their own skin, they escape prosecution.

David Dow, a native Texan and graduate of Rice University and Yale Law School who teaches constitutional law at the University of Houston, didn't start out philosophically opposed to the death penalty. When he got involved in some cases related to his teaching about federal law, he wound up on the side of the abolitionists because he became convinced the system is corrupt.

> What I mean by corrupt is — if it were possible to rank order the most horrific crimes from one to 100, with one being the most horrific and 100 being a kind of accidental homicide where there's recklessness (but no evil intent), in principle the ones getting the death penalty would be one through ten. In practice, that's not what happens at all — you just throw a dart at the list of the top 100 and that's how you decide .... Not that there's somebody throwing a dart but that the cases that are being singled out are for reasons that generally don't have very much to do with how high they rank on that list, they have to do with other things, like whether the prosecutor thinks they can get a death sentence, which [may be a function of] the race of the defendant, the race of the victim, the financial resources, the competence of the lawyer, all of those.[12]

The revised Texas death penalty statute was crafted by criminal justice attorneys (defense and prosecution) and legislators in 1973 after the old statute was swept away by the 1972 *Furman v. Georgia* Supreme Court decision which caused legislatures across the nation to rethink and rewrite their laws.

The new law was designed to overcome the reason for the 1972 decision which was the arbitrary application of capital punishment by prosecutors and random sentencing patterns by capital jurors. The 1973 statute defined a capital murder to be any murder of a peace officer or fireman, or a murder in the course of a kidnapping, robbery, burglary, arson, rape, obstruction or retaliation, or the murder of a penal institution employee while a prisoner was incarcerated, or a murder committed while escaping or trying to escape from prison, or while incarcerated for murder or serving life or 99 years for kidnapping, rape or aggravated robbery, or a murder of more than one person, or for pay, or a murder of a child under six years of age.

Not withstanding these definitions, district attorneys and their legal staff can and do decide which defendants they'll charge with capital murder. They can offer plea bargains — usually to a life sentence or sometimes less, including a walk — if they can get one co-defendant to provide necessary testimony against someone they have a better chance of prosecuting successfully. The *Dallas Morning News* reported that in 1993, one quarter of murderers walked away from the courthouse with probation or deferred adjudication. If they met the judge's conditions, there was not even a mention on their record.[13]

Also, prosecutors can choose to go to trial in a capital case not seeking the death penalty, leaving the jury with the choice of life or acquittal. Some prosecutors are believed to have pushed capital charges at a particular time for campaign purposes. Former Attorney General Jim Mattox told the *Houston Chronicle*, "Everyone operates in their own little system out there. And that creates an un-standardized process . . . (which) might not be such a problem if you could get a system at the top that brings about the proper kind of review, which doesn't happen in Texas."[14]

Geography

Geography is a primary factor in who is selected for a capital murder charge. By 1990, 90 % of all executions in the United States in the 20 years after the *Furman* v. *Georgia* decision occurred in the former Confederate states — a solid block of states with death penalty statutes and relatively large black populations.[15] Between 1976 and 1988, Texas, Florida and Louisiana alone accounted for 63 of the 101 executions that occurred.[16] Oklahoma and Texas, which lead respectively in per capita and sheer numbers of executions in the nation, have lower percentages of blacks statewide than the other Southern states. However, the cities with higher proportions of blacks, like Houston which is 20% black, send more of their defendants to death row; and disproportionate shares of them are black.

Counties fund the courts. Large, urban counties have more money than rural and small counties. They are able to maintain large, well funded, experienced prosecution departments who can afford to pursue capital charges and seek the death penalty frequently. Poorer rural counties may hesitate to take on the very expensive long-haul process of trial and post-trial appeals, estimated to cost the county and state around $2.3 million per case on average, unless the crime is particularly horrifying and politically explosive.

The personality and the philosophy of the chief prosecutor, the county district attorney, also play an important role. For instance, Harris County's recently-retired D.A., Johnny Holmes, a born-wealthy native of the city, was possessed with an admiration for the frontier justice personified by the "hanging" judge of West Texas, Roy Bean. Known as the "Texas Terminator,"[17] Holmes reportedly hung a sign entitled the "Silver

Needle Society" in the office which focused on death penalty cases, and threw champagne parties when a death row inmate sentenced in Houston was led to the gurney for lethal injection.

Holmes had led a petition drive at the University of Texas as a student against integration of athletics and dorms, but denied that his prosecutorial decisions were effected by racism.[18] Along with other prosecutors and some judges, during his 21-year elected tenure as D.A., he tenaciously fought reforms in the legislature which would reduce the use of the death penalty, such as life without parole, which the recently-retired Holmes predicted during the 2001 legislative session would end executions. Harris County contributed about a third of current Texas death row inmates as of 2001, meaning that if the county were a state, it would follow Texas in numbers condemned to die. Houston reporter Mike Tolson prefaced the lead story for a major series on the Texas death penalty in this way:

> To kill within the arbitrarily drawn boundaries that define Harris County is to risk entering the most productive death row pipeline in the Western world. A handful of U.S. cities can boast similar enthusiasm for capital punishment, but none the same bottom line: 61 executed inmates, 150 more waiting their turn.[19]

That same issue of the *Houston Chronicle* carried a separate report on the financial fuel that drives Harris County's relentless pursuit of capital cases from indictment through appeals. Their annual budget was almost always granted without quibbling by the County Commissioners. Under Holmes, the D.A. office for Harris County employed over 200 attorneys with obvious expertise in prosecuting capital cases. Holmes' reputation as a good administrator who ran a tight ship and his political popularity ensured the multimillion dollar budget that allowed his office to prosecute as many capital cases as they had the staff and stomach to fight.[20]

In poorer counties, no matter how popular the death penalty is, the high cost of pursuing a death penalty through trial and appeals is a deterrent. Galveston County, for example, rarely files a capital charge, and in West Texas, a case has to be pretty horrendous to draw D.A. attention. A former Lubbock County defense attorney noticed each D.A. liked to get one or two on his record, but wasn't keen on racking up more.[21] Just to go to trial on a capital case in Dallas County is estimated to cost the citizens over $250,000. The total cost to the state for each death penalty case, from start to finish, not counting the state's role in fighting the inmate on federal appeals, is around $2.3 million. Holding an inmate in maximum security at Terrell until his natural death would save citizens about $1.4 million.

Sr. Prejean's[22] point about poverty being a pre-requisite for residency on death row had been made years earlier by Don Reid. Reid was a native Texan and veteran newsman, the editor and publisher of the *Huntsville Item*, a man who watched 189 executions between his arrival in Huntsville in the late 1930s and the 18-year suspension of executions that began in 1964. In 1973 he wrote *Eyewitness*, a classic account of one man's journey from detached reporter to student of — and then dedicated opponent of — the system. His research into the files on condemned inmates revealed that "no white man had ever died in the chair for murdering a black, raping a black, or robbing a black with firearms."[23] This even though, murders of blacks by whites were common, and in those days rape and armed robbery could be punished by death. He came to this conclusion about the famous Texas electric chair used to kill inmates between 1924 and 1964:

> 'Old Sparky' was a social weapon, an instrument of discrimination against black males, Mexican-American males and poor white males. And the frightening thing was my belief that in my home state, a state I loved, a majority of the people wouldn't give a damn about the truth if I wrote it across the sky in letters of fire. Racial and social discrimination were as much a part of Texas as oil and cattle.[24]

Gender and the death penalty

In the late 1980s, criminal justice and law professors studied the revised Texas capital punishment system and noticed that female victims were more likely to earn an accused killer a cell on death row, especially if the female is white. Over a third of the executions since 1982 came from cases with white female victims, even though white females were less than 1% of murder victims in the state. Rapists were less likely than murderers to have their sentences commuted in pre-*Furman* days when rape was a capital offense in Texas, and of those, the rapists of white females were least likely to have their sentences commuted. Rapists of Mexican American females were the most likely to have their sentences commuted.[25]

Turning to perpetrators, it is neither coincidence nor that women are the gentler sex who rarely kill that explains the fact that only two women have been officially executed in the state since Chipita Rodriguez went to the gallows in an ox-drawn cart in South Texas in 1863.[26]

In *Eyewitness*, Don Reid explained that he, a mainstream journalist who accepted the death penalty as a fact of life that benefited him financially whenever he wrote articles about it, became a leader of the effort in the 1960s to abolish the practice. Reid explained that it was the absence of women in the death chamber that sparked his serious study of the tradition after ten years of reporting on the executions that took place within walking distance of his newspaper. A Houston journalist friend commented that women committed 25% of the murders in the state but were never executed, and few were even prosecuted for capital murder. Only three women received death sentences between 1924 when Texas centralized executions with the electric chair in Huntsville and 1972 when the Supreme Court temporarily emptied Texas death row.[27]

After several years of research spurred by this realization, Reid came to the conclusion that there was no way to eliminate the problems at the core of our system of capital punishment, and therefore, as a matter of principle and faith, he began to speak out against it.

A rough analysis of statistics supplied by the Texas Department of Public Safety by the author revealed that between 1982 and 1999, women of all ages and races committed about 9% of the approximately 30,000 murders and non-negligent homicides.[28]

Robberies constituted by far the largest category of murders between strangers, but murders between acquaintances or persons related by blood or marriage far outnumbered homicides by people unknown to the victims. Arguments were a frequent cause of murder, and wives seemed to murder husbands, boyfriends and common-law mates only a third less frequently than the reverse. Still, women killed less often and less in the categories that would send them to court on capital charges, but there were far fewer women on death row than their number of arrests would indicate, if all things were equal in the courts. Instead of the seven women now on death row, there should be at least 53. Instead of the two women executed since 1982, there should have been 22.

In April of 2001, over 450 men sat in cells on the Terrell men's unit in Livingston, Texas, northeast of Houston. By contrast, all the women on Texas death row in the Mountain View Unit could have fit comfortably into a small house. Women committed around 2700 murders in Texas in the last two decades. Possibly one fifth (540) met the qualifications for capital punishment; yet only rarely did prosecutors or juries feel they constituted such a danger to the community that their lives had to be taken.[29] Yet, if women were the victims, at least if they were white, the law would relentlessly pursue their killers. One might say that with reference to violent death, being female gave a woman or her corpse a certain advantage.

Race and capital murder charges

A report by the Government Accounting Office on racial bias in capital sentences included the observation that in 1993, for example, Texas had executed 17 men, 11 of whom were black, and the victims of 8 of those 11 had been white. The report inspired a provision in a 1994 Congressional House crime bill to allow "statistical evidence of racial bias in executions" to be used in defending minorities against capital charges. The provision was opposed by "national associations for attorneys general, district attorneys and law enforcement groups," including Texas Attorney General Dan Morales, who said the provision "would effectively end the death penalty,"[30] a deeply disturbing comment and conviction.

At the end of January 2001, 180 of the 439 men on Texas death row were black — about 41% in a state where the black population is less than 12%. Among women on death row, three of seven were black, for a similar percentage of 43%.[31] Of the 39 men and one woman executed in the state in 2000, 40% were black — exactly the same proportion as of blacks executed in the nation that year.[32] Between 1982 and 1999, of the 30,000 homicide arrests in the state, blacks were about a third. Hispanics constituted just under a third, and whites were arrested just slightly more frequently than blacks — despite the fact that whites were over 60% of the population. Blacks were arrested for murder at a rate almost three times their proportion (12%) of the citizenry. Whites were arrested at a rate about 40% lower than their proportion of the population. Beyond that, blacks were being condemned in even higher proportions (41% versus 33%) than the proportion of their arrests.[33] Hispanics constituted 22% of the Texas men's death row in 2001, a few percentage points less than their 25% proportion of the population, but much less than their arrests might lead one to expect.[34]

It is easier to gain a capital conviction against someone with a prior felony record. A report, released in the fall of 2000 by the Justice Policy Institute, revealed that "one of three young black men (29% of the black male population between 21 and 29) are in prison, jail, probation or parole in Texas on any given day," and that blacks "are incarcerated at a rate seven times greater than whites," a rate that is "nearly 63% higher than the national incarceration rate for blacks." In fact, blacks constituted 44% of the total prison and jail population of Texas, almost four times their representation in the total population.[35]

Racial profiling at the street level may initiate a domino effect — arrests and jail time, even if brief, affect employment possibilities and personal finances, and this then makes police, judges and juries more likely to believe a person is guilty the next time around. Furthermore, blacks receive lower proportions of probationary sentences (21% of the total caseload) and are under-represented in substance abuse programs (27%) compared to their proportion of the incarcerated population.[36]

Studies released in 2000 and 2001 by Building Blocks for Youth, backed by a coalition of groups including the American Bar Association Juvenile Justice Center and the National Council on Crime and Delinquency, reveal "negative race effects at one stage or another of the juvenile justice process" which result in over-representation of youth of color in detention. These studies made the astounding observation that 82% of cases filed in adult courts were for minority youth.[37]

The "Youth Crime/Adult Time"[38] study, released in October 2000 by Dr. Jolanta Juszkiewicz, studied juvenile felony cases prosecuted in adult courts in 18 large urban areas in the US, including Harris County. One of the findings of the study was that, compared to the number of felony arrests of African-American youth, blacks were sent in higher percentages than whites to adult courts and were more likely to be held in adult jails pretrial, although they were granted lower bail than whites. They were also less likely to be represented by lawyers hired privately than whites. Eleven percent of blacks had private attorneys versus 21% whites. White youth were twice as likely to see their "charges reduced to a misdemeanor."[39] African Americans (58%) and Latinos (46%) were more likely than whites (34%) to be sentenced to jail, and if sentenced for whatever offense, African-Americans got longer sentences than Latino or white juveniles.[40]

In Harris County 83% of juvenile cases filed in adult courts concerned minorities. "African American youth accounted for approximately one out of four felony arrests, but represented one out of two felony cases filed in criminal court." All youth in Harris County who were detained awaiting trial were held in adult jails. There, only 36% of African-American youth and 33% of whites had private attorneys, versus 75% of the hispanic youth. All youth with private attorneys had a better shot at escaping conviction or getting transferred back to juvenile court, and — presumably because more had private attorneys — hispanics were more likely to receive split sentences or probation.[41]

Marquart and Sorenson report that a person of any race who murders a white person is over five times more likely to wind up on death row in Texas than someone who kills a black.[42] And while almost one of every four state homicide victims are black males, only about one in 200 of those put to death in the same era were there solely because they had killed a black male.[43] In Texas, it hasn't happened that a white has been executed for killing a black since pre-Civil War days, when a white man killed a plantation owner's favorite slave and was hanged for stealing. In the United States through September of 1999, only 10 whites had been executed for killing blacks out of the 600 or so executed to that point since executions resumed in 1977.[44]

Former Court of Criminal Appeals judge, Morris Overstreet, commented during a panel on capital punishment at the University of Texas Law School, Hemann Sweat symposium in April 2001, "There are no African American District Attorneys in Texas. Since prosecutorial discretion (judgment about whether to press capital charges and go to trial) is so important in deciding who gets the death penalty, that African American perspective needs to be there." St. Mary's Law School professor, Jeff Pokorak, authored a study in 1999 showing that 98% of the District Attorneys in capital cases in the U.S. are white — only 1% black.

People of color are also under-represented in the legal profession. In May of 2001 the Texas Bar Association's membership was 11% people of color, whereas the population was 40% people of color. Only 3.6% of the Bar members were African-American, less than 6% Latino, barely over 1% Asian.[45]

Overstreet suggested that "prosecutors should have to present to a judge a public statement whenever they *don't* go for the death penalty when the facts show they could." This would make racial imbalances in prosecutorial discretion more transparent. He also pointed out "not enough is done about the exclusion of African American jurors."[46] Defense attorneys say the Court of Criminal Appeals winks at these problems.[47]

In the fall of 2000, the Texas Defender Service, a small non-profit group of attorneys who work on capital defense primarily at the appeals stage, released *A State of Denial: Texas Justice and the Death Penalty*.[48] The study included an analysis of homicides between 1995 and 1999 in Montgomery County, a suburban and rural area northeast of Houston — 85% white, historically a conservative area sharing the racial and political views of East Texas.

East Texas is dominated by members of the Baptist Church and other fundamentalist Christian religious expression. It was the Texas slave and plantation center prior to the civil war. Between 1995 and 1999, nearly a third of the homicides in Montgomery County were against people of color, but none of those led to death sentences. In over 40% of the crimes against people of color there were no arrests, compared to a 92% arrest rate when the victims were white. While all but 10% of the cases involving white murder victims went to trial, including three that led to death sentences, the murders of seven Latinos in separate incidents led to only one arrest. The daughter of one black man killed when his home was invaded said she was treated rudely by the district attorney's office, which didn't even acknowledge her loss, in contrast with the intensive media coverage and solicitous treatment received by relatives of a white couple killed in similar circumstances. Clearly some victims were valued more than others.[49]

One would like to believe Montgomery County is unusual, but it is widely acknowledged in Texas, and confirmed by studies, that the pattern is all too typical of the state, probably of the region and possibly of the nation. The *Wall Street Journal* reported in March of 2001 that of the 85 persons executed in the US in 2000, 40 were black while the percentage of blacks in the nation is less than 13%. Texas accounted for nearly half the total executions. 40% of those were black, neatly mirroring the national image, and the percentage of black males on Texas death row.[50] A recent study in North Carolina of 502 homicides from 1993 through 1997 showed a similar pattern of racial discrimination. Murderers who kill white people are 3 1/2 times more likely to get the death penalty than those who kill nonwhites," but the race of the killer doesn't seem to affect the verdicts much.[51]

To put this in national perspective, an analysis of the 707 executions in the United States until April 10, 2001, revealed that 83% of those capital cases involved white victims, although only 50% of the nation's homicide victims were white. Thirty-five percent of the executed persons were black males, almost three times their proportion in the population as a whole. A 1998 report for the American Bar Association by Professor David Baldus found that the race of the victim mattered more in the South and the race of the accused mattered more in the North in capital prosecution and conviction. A Philadelphia study of homicides indicated blacks there received the death penalty at a rate 38% higher than others accused.[52]

A Justice Department study of the federal death penalty released in September of 2000 showed "minorities account for 74% of the cases in which U.S. attorneys recommended the death penalty." There were 19 federal death row inmates that year; 13 of those were black; six (five blacks and one hispanic) were from Texas.[53]

Yale and Florida State University professor and NAACP assistant counsel George Kendall says, despite the 1972 *Furman* ruling which temporarily halted the death penalty on the suspicion that race played a role in its application, and in spite of subsequent attempts to write better laws "race is still a factor . . . . Since we can't remove race from the death penalty, we should get rid of it."[54]

Media distortion of violent crime

In April of 2001 a report published by Building Blocks for Youth analyzed media coverage of race, youth and crime after examining all major credible studies on the topic.[55] The report found a majority of the studies agreed there was an over-reporting of homicide in general, especially by people of color, and in specific, of juvenile homicides, and a corresponding underreporting of the murders committed by whites. A 1993 California study of local TV news revealed that "More than two-thirds of violence stories involved youth while more than half of all stories that included youth involved violence.". . . [56] "In news coverage, blacks are most often the perpetrators of violence against whites and other blacks, whereas in reality whites are six times more likely to be homicide victims at the hands of other whites.". . . [57] "Homicides of white victims resulted in more and longer articles than homicides of black victims.[58]

The report found that media stories about youth exaggerated the proportions of youth involved in violence. In addition, when youth were portrayed in media stories related to violence, youth of color were rarely allowed to speak for themselves, or even to have their lawyers speak for them. Thus youth of color remained de-personalized, abstract symbols upon which strangers could project their fears, as opposed to appearing in a context portraying them as individual human beings. A study of stories of violence on local TV news nationwide in 1995 and 1996 found blacks were portrayed as perpetrators 37% of the time, Latinos 32%, whites 27% and Asians 7%. The same study reported that "whites were 89% of the anchors, 78% of the reporters, 87% of the official sources, and 80% of the victims."[59]

Reporting of violent crime increased in the 1990s though violence, especially juvenile violence, was decreasing as drastically as the coverage was increasing. Since three quarters of the U.S. population say their opinions about crime are formed by the news, the result is a serious distortion in public understanding of the realities of how much violent crime exists, who perpetrates it and who is most likely to be the victim. "A 1998 poll found that nearly two-thirds of the public believes that juvenile crime is on the increase, even though there was a 56% decline in homicides by youth between 1993 and 1998."[60] One study included in the report analyzed *Time* and *Newsweek* cover stories over several decades, and noticed that between 1979 and 1982, "crime coverage in *Time* increased by 55%" though crime itself only increased 1%. Similarly, between 1990 and 1998 homicides dropped 33% while network news increased its homicide coverage by 473% — almost five times.[61]

Exaggerated coverage of crimes reporters considered unusual or particularly shocking, coupled with the general failure of reporters to provide background and context in their reporting about murders, helped to explain "why the public consistently overestimates the rate of crime" and tended to believe whites were more often victims of crime, particularly by people of color, than is actually the case.[62] An experiment with students exposed to mug shots of crime suspects showed that students rated black suspects as more often guilty, more deserving of punishment, more likely to commit future violence, and less likable than the white suspects, about whom they had been given precisely the same information. Surveys on racial stereotyping and crime found people with stereotypical views on race reacted differently to blacks and whites placed in a crime context: they assumed the blacks were guilty, but not the whites.[63] Since capital juries are drawn from the public, and are overwhelmingly non-black, the implications for their verdicts on capital cases are worrisome, to put it mildly.

System shot through with holes: legal defense of the poor

SMU human rights advocate and Southern history professor Rick Halperin says the death penalty represents "class war — war against the poor."[64]

Marquart and Ekland-Olson found a pattern of what they called "cultural exclusion" in those condemned to die. After conducting a study of interviews with death row inmates, they saw these common themes: the inmates were poor, poorly educated, from the social fringes, and had experienced "disrupted family life."[65] These factors, plus race, meant those eventually given the ultimate penalty were vulnerable socially, politically and legally. They could be arrested, prosecuted and sentenced to die without causing political repercussions because those more fortunate and powerful saw them as having little value as human beings.

The system of providing legal representation for the poor varies widely from region to region and county to county in Texas. Even so, across the state attorneys for the indigent are appointed by locally elected judges who control fees paid to the defense, and the funds available to them for crucial investigation, or for hiring experts. The political careers of these judges often rest on their providing employment for political allies, and in supporting politically powerful prosecutors in their mission of conviction. To ensure punishment of persons believed by the community to be guilty of shocking crimes — crimes that raise emotions capable of toppling judges perceived to be soft on crime — is often an elected judge's most effective campaign strategy.

A five-year study on indigent defense, commissioned by a committee of the Texas State Bar Association and supervised by Fort Worth judge Allan Butcher and sociologist Michael Moore of the University of Texas at Arlington was released in 2000. It reported that 79% of judges surveyed admitted their appointments were governed by political factors such as who had contributed to their campaigns. Half acknowledged they appointed attorneys who would move cases through pretty quickly.

Stephen Keng, a Central Texas defense attorney and former prosecutor, says, "I have had a District Judge (who shall remain unnamed) tell me that the reason he had appointed a certain attorney in a capital murder case was that he knew the attorney would do enough so that the conviction would not be reversed, yet not enough to have the defendant acquitted."[66] Attorneys with records of discipline by the state bar for various offenses, including failure to file for clients and brazen substance abuse, have unfortunately been commonly appointed in Texas capital cases.

Kerry Cook, freed after over twenty years on death row for a crime he didn't commit, says about some of his fellows there, "their only real crime was poverty . . . whenever you have a system so wholly tilted favoring one side, there will be profound injustices. And unless meaningful legislation is passed here regarding the appointment of competent counsel for those too poor to afford it — then behind the public's closed eyes and the silent sea of media faces on the six o-clock news regarding this subject, innocent people will continue to die."[67]

Dr. Michael Moore says, "The Texas system is a national embarrassment. We are the *third world* of the justice world."[68] His study done with judge Alan Butcher for the State Bar Of Texas, released in the fall of 2000,[69] showed that from misdemeanor cases through capital offenses, attorneys were selected often without reference to standards of competence (none existed in the state) and were underpaid relative to lawyers in private practice. To meet their overheads they were almost forced to run plea mills and what Kerry Cook calls "K-mart justice."

Stephen Bright, a Yale Law professor who also runs the Southern Center for Human Rights in Atlanta, says that in Texas system "you're better off to be rich and guilty than to be poor and innocent."[70] Federico Martinez Macias of El Paso found that to be true when his attorney did so little pre-trial investigation of his claims of innocence, he didn't even examine a neighbor who could have testified Macias wasn't the man she saw driving around the home of the victims before the crime. A volunteer commercial attorney from Washington, D.C., Doug Robinson, found the neighbor years later when he took on Macias' appeal.

Texas is only one of 11 states that leave paying for indigent defense up to the counties. Needless to say the resources vary widely, not to mention the inclination of judges regarding pay of attorneys and funds available for investigation and experts. Moore and Butcher were told one judge actually told the defense attorney which experts had to be used. All states in the nation were ordered by the U.S. Supreme Court in the decision on *Gideon v Wainwright* in 1963 to supply lawyers for those too poor to afford them; clearly Texas has not met its responsibility fully.

In 1990 a study by the National Law Journal of capital cases in Texas and five other Southern states showed "trial lawyers who represented death-row inmates have been disciplined, suspended or disbarred 3 to 46 times more often than peers in their states."[71]

Pam Perillo, who was removed from the Texas women's death row unit after the Fifth Circuit determined her trial was grossly unfair, was represented by a lead attorney with no experience in capital murder cases. His co-counsel had defended the main witness against her in a separate trial and coached that witness when she testified against Perillo. The witness, who had participated equally in the murder of two men who had befriended a trio of hitchhikers, went free in exchange for testimony against Perillo and a co-defendant. This is not an isolated case; it happens frequently not only in Texas but elsewhere. To get one conviction prosecutors may make very favorable deals with equally or even more guilty collaborators, or in some cases, the real perpetrators, whose motive is to frame someone else for their own misdeed.

In its examination of 131 case histories of persons executed during George W. Bush's tenure in Texas up to June of 2000, the *Chicago Tribune* found that in 40 of the cases, defense attorneys presented only one witness or no evidence at all during the sentencing phase. In 43 of the 131 cases, trial defense lawyers had already been or were later disbarred, suspended or otherwise sanctioned for misconduct; three of them were actually convicted of felonies. Two served jail time for contempt of court for mishandling criminal cases. Walter Prentice, who represented for their first appeals three men executed under George W. Bush, served jail time. So did Ron Mock, Gary Graham's lead trial attorney, who represented 19 men on trial for capital murder, 16 of whom were condemned, and 4 of whom were executed under George W. Bush by July of 2000.[72] There have been widely publicized cases of snoozing trial attorneys, which figured in the cases of three condemned men, one already executed. Several attorneys in the last decade in Texas were appointed to submit appeals for death row inmates over their own protests that they were not qualified and didn't know how to proceed.[73] Former Criminal Appeals Court judge Charles Baird called the situation regarding indigent defense a crisis in the summer of 2000 and said Texas wouldn't act to change it.

Frequently the compensation level of the appointed defense lawyers falls below the average overhead costs of an attorney, according to several studies. The trial attorney for Martinez Macias was paid less than $12 an hour for his defense. The Fifth Circuit court in reversing his conviction and sentence commented that the quality of his defense reflected that price. In contrast, famed Houston defender Percy Foreman defended over a thousand accused murderers. Only one was executed.[74] Foreman, like his protégé and partner Dick DeGuerin today, would not have been on the list of court appointed attorneys because there were too many paying customers standing in line seeking his top-quality personal investigation, meticulous jury selection and courtroom skills.

Dick DeGuerin estimated in 1992 that it would cost well over $150,000 to save the life of Anthony Graves at trial, a man who he believed to be innocent, who was backed by credible alibi witnesses, and who had no early record of violence.[75] Today that would likely be a very low-ball figure for him.[76] Even back in the 1970s, it took close to a million dollars of Fort Worth billionaire Cullen Davis' fortune to hire Houston top attorney Racehorse Haynes plus a legion of back-up attorneys and investigators. For big bucks, these attorneys were able to keep Davis off the row for two murders and two attempted murders — for which there were wounded but surviving eyewitnesses.[77]

Huntsville journalist Don Reid interviewed 189 men prior to their execution from the late 1930s to the mid 1960s. Only one was wealthy — a handsome young East Coast industrialist's heir who killed his fiancée in a moment of emotional reaction while they were driving across West Texas, and confessed the crime to Texas Rangers after passing two lie detector tests.[78] Today that man would not be eligible for the death penalty because there was no rape, abduction or robbery attached — unless he'd left with his fiancee's engagement ring, for example.

Even if the appointed defense lawyers were competent, they were usually not provided adequate financial resources by the county to begin to level the playing field against district attorneys with larger salaried staffs and adequate budgets for investigation and experts. Douglas Robinson, a litigator with a mammoth commercial firm in Washington, D.C., spent a "couple of thousand hours" of his and his staff's time investigating the case of former death row inmate Federico Macias Martinez, who was eventually exonerated and released. At a low-ball figure of $50 an hour, that would represent a million dollar budget. Macias' original trial defense investigator submitted a bill for the maximum allowed: 10 hours at $50 an hour. That's not a level playing field by any stretch of the imagination.

Death-qualified juries

Beyond the hurdle of having enough money to mount a defense against an often well-oiled and funded prosecution engine lies one even higher. To sit on a jury in a capital trial, a juror must state his or her belief in capital punishment and be willing to condemn someone to death. In addition most jurors are white, able-bodied, middle class. A person who might be part of any group that might have experienced oppression and thus might sympathize with the accused, is summarily let go.

Under Henry Wade's regime in Dallas County, women were also struck from juries, as they were believed to be inherently more sympathetic to the defense. For decades Wade's prosecutors taught most district attorneys in the state how to select juries. The *Dallas Morning News* analyzed the racial composition of juries at felony trials in the county from 1983 to 1984 and found that in 96% of cases involving black defendants, all-white juries decided their fate. Overall, black jurors comprised only 4% of jury members despite the fact that blacks were 18% of the population.[79] Unfortunately, things haven't changed much in the last 15 years. Dallas attorney Larry Mitchell reports, "blacks simply do not serve on juries in Dallas County except where there is a black victim. Even then, it's only one or two black jurors at most."[80]

Even in Travis County, reputedly the most liberal county in the state, this occurs. A jury of 2 hispanics and 10 whites heard the case in May of 2000 of a young white man, Paul Anders Saustrop, who had confronted, followed, shot and killed an unarmed black man (Eric Smith) who he caught breaking into his date's vehicle. Saustrup was acquitted, which came as no surprise to him. He had already made lunch plans with friends for after the jury's verdict.[81]

Stephen Keng, the former county attorney from Lee County says he once "walked in on selection of a jury panel where a sheriff and District Judge were 'handpicking' jurors, rejecting some as 'too old', 'too-liberal' or 'crazy'."[82]

Robert Ford, the defense attorney from Fort Worth who has tried and written appeals on a number of capital cases, says, "It's depressing because the chances of winning are minimal. . . . They've built the system so they get a death prone jury; federal law says you're entitled to a death prone jury . . . If jury pickin' was different, oh man it'd be great, there'd be a lot of people with life sentences, a real capital life in Texas, if juries knew there was no chance of them getting out."[83] This is important because juries are told they have to choose the death penalty if they think the person might be a future danger to society. If they could recommend a sentence of life without parole, death row would be almost empty.

Texas whites are more than twice as likely to favor capital punishment than blacks (75% versus 32%) and hispanics fall in between at 62%.[84] Juries reflect these preferences. The same circumstances which make defendants vulnerable to arrest (poverty and coming from the social fringes) are likely to prejudice juries against them because juries are influenced by prevailing social beliefs.

In every case this book examines where grievous injustice appears likely, the death row inmates are those who by circumstance of gender, skin color, or poverty were primed to fall into the deepest holes of our criminal justice system.

Chapter Two:
Innocence in the Lone Star State

Kerry, Sandra and baby Kerry Justice Cook. Kerry Cook was released from death row after 22 years when DNA evidence proved him innocent.

Photo by Susan Lee Campbell Solar.

After 13 years on death row, on March 1, 1989, a year after Morris' film *Thin Blue Line* was released, Randall Dale Adam's conviction and sentence were reversed by a decision of the Court of Criminal Appeals based on prosecutorial misconduct.

Photo by Susan Lee Campbell Solar.

What constitutes innocence?

During the year 2000 as major print media and television network reporters competed to challenge George W. Bush on his claim that no innocents had been put to death on his watch, one grim history after another was dug up and displayed. Somewhere in each story a disclaimer usually lay in wait. The *Fort Worth Star Telegram's* Austin correspondent phrased it in this way:

> Although . . . news organizations managed to cast a glimmer of doubt about some condemned inmates' guilt, or to find irregularities in legal procedures such as defense attorneys snoozing during trials in other cases, no solid evidence emerged that Texas had executed an innocent inmate.[1]

It is a claim recited repeatedly by the Houston-based victims rights group, Justice For All, in their media interviews and in legislative testimony. Therein lies the rub for foes of capital punishment, for people who believe innocent family members have been executed, and for current death row inmates claiming innocence, such as Anthony Graves, Michael Toney or Pablo Melendez, Jr. What actually constitutes proof of innocence in the current judicial context in Texas and federal courts?

In England a deathbed confession, which came after an execution and indicated the unfortunate victim of capital punishment had in fact been innocent, was taken as proof. Public uproar about such a case led to the abolition of capital punishment in England in 1964. Today, in the Texas Court of Criminal Appeals, or the Fifth Circuit Court of Appeals in New Orleans, or even in the U.S. Supreme Court as currently constituted, such an event wouldn't lift an eyebrow.

In the governor's office during Bush's last term, a written confession mailed to Bush was ignored when inmate Ochim Marino tried to cleanse his conscience — at the risk of his life — to free two young men wrongfully imprisoned for a rape and murder he had committed.

University of Houston constitutional law professor David Dow wrote after Gary Graham's execution that his case "illustrates two things: it's virtually impossible to prove that someone innocent was executed, and asking whether someone is innocent is the wrong question."[2] He argues eloquently that focusing on actual innocence "obscures the more urgent issue: the system of appointing lawyers for indigent capital defendants is corrupt, with the result that many . . . are inadequately represented."[3] Dow faults the Texas system in which elected judges, who cannot afford to be viewed as soft on crime, are in charge of such appointments. Judges often excuse attorneys who contribute to their campaign chests from mandatory, low pay, time consuming case work. Instead, they appoint colleagues who have been less generous for whatever reason, or are greener, or less competent, creating several obvious conflicts of interest.[4]

Arguably, a focus on innocence could leave intact a system in which money sets you free and lack of it sends you to the gurney. A focus on innocence alone also leaves issues of mental illness, retardation, child abuse, and addiction in the mire. Nonetheless, proof of the execution of an innocent person or persons may be the only thing that will move elected officials to oppose capital punishment. Certainly such proof, highly publicized, played a major role in the abolition of the death penalty in France and the United Kingdom in the last half century. It was the eye-opener that caused Illinois Governor Ryan to declare a moratorium on the executions. The studies he ordered showed a system so flawed that he commuted (on his last day in office) the sentences of everyone on death row in his state, and freed inmates whose trials had been fraught with error.

Of course, fraudulent claims of innocence from death row are legion. One North Texas defense attorney warned the author against including his client in this book if she wished to maintain credibility, as there were 17 DNA matches to the condemned man at the crime scene where two young women were murdered. The attorney said he regularly got calls from as far away as Tasmania from people who believed what he described as the fictional account on his client's webpage. Another death row inmate didn't expect a writer to have read the files at his defense attorney's office with enough attention to pick up the inconsistencies in his story.

Yale-trained psychiatrist Dorothy Otnow Lewis[5] came to believe during her work with violent offenders that some were victims of such hideous early abuse that they had developed multiple personalities, and truly believed they were innocent. It was their "alter" personality that had done the crime, which explains how some guilty people pass polygraph tests.

Still, it is not difficult to discover instances of the execution of innocent people in Texas.

Lynching, Texas style

Even a relatively brief investigation of claims of innocence of condemned Texans, past and present, turns up symptoms of a certain fatal fallibility in the Texas criminal justice system when it comes to capital cases. The case of Chipita Rodrigues was certainly not the only questionable one.

A useful compendium on Texas justice, *Lone Star Justice*,[6] relates the 1863 hanging by an angry mob in San Antonio of a white cowhand who had been acquitted by a district court judge of drunkenly firing his guns in the street, apparently causing no injuries. Between 1889 and 1942 it catalogs long lists of lynchings of men often merely accused and never tried in court. The blacks were mostly in East Texas, the whites mostly further west and listed as outlaws. In 1890, for example, 18 men, all black, were lynched for reasons as incomprehensible as accusations of "racial prejudice," gambling and larceny, though the majority were accused of rape or murder.[7]

Following the thread of apparent insufficient cause for execution, the next year two blacks were accused of being "troublesome" and hung; another "for making insulting remarks." In 1894 a black man dangled for writing "an amorous letter to a white woman." Nine blacks, including two women, one from Brenham, were hung in 1895 for accusations of "racial prejudice," presumably relating to Reconstruction activities. In 1897 a white minister, Reverend Captain Jones, swung for "elopement." Between 1901 and 1911 two black men were hung for "verbally insulting a white woman," and five were hung for "quarrelling over a profit-sharing arrangement." In 1906 a black was hung by a mob for marrying a white woman in Reeves County, and in 1908 an unfortunate case of mistaken identity led to the lynching of a black man for an unknown reason in Beaumont. Six members of a black family in Huntsville, including several females, were hung because a male family member allegedly threatened a white man in 1918; that same year a mob lynched a black man "after a disagreement with a white man."[8]

The year 1922 was a bad one for lynchings. Three blacks in Freestone County were tied together and burned in the city square on suspicion that they murdered a white teenage girl from a powerful family, but two white men from a rival family to the victim's were soon thereafter arrested for the crime. In the same county seven months later the uncle of a black man accused of attacking a sheriff was lynched in place of his nephew by frustrated vigilantes.[9]

Reform

In her biography of Jessie Daniel Ames, who fought against lynching in Texas and the South, Jacquelyn Dowd Hall writes that "in 26% of the 4,715 known lynchings committed between 1882 and 1946, the victim was accused only of some minor infraction or of no crime at all."[10]

Hall believed the phenomenon occurred because whites projected their own repressed sexuality and criminal instincts on blacks. She thought lynching was used to maintain white privilege and repress black revolt, and that it was motivated by the political egos of men willing to exploit violence to further their own careers as academics, journalists, law officials and governors. She also noted that lynchings rose when the price of cotton dropped.[11]

Ames, a white businesswoman from a prosperous Williamson County family, was widowed young with small children to support. But with energy to spare, she took it on herself to educate and organize against lynching, starting locally. One of her early Texas tactics was to personally investigate the circumstances surrounding the act. She was often able to show that local newspaper coverage was biased or patently false. Ames convinced the editor of the *Dallas Morning News* with her efforts.

Ames also supported Dan Moody, a courageous young Williamson County prosecutor who actually got convictions against two white Georgetown men for savagely beating a black salesman accused of having an affair with a white widow, thus ending the most violent phase of the Klan in that locale. Moody, running on an anti-Klan platform, later became attorney general and then governor with the support of the women Ames organized behind him. Once elected, however, his anti-Klan fervor diminished.

In 1929 Ames left Texas to direct the women's division of the national Interracial Cultural Commission. She initiated the Association of Southern Women to Prevent Lynching, which played a key role for the next ten years in ending the violence and summary justice of the era. A second phase of attempts to inject more justice and mercy into the Texas justice system was initiated three decades later by Don Reid, editor of the *Huntsville Item*.

It was not so much these cases of wrongful or at least dubious judgment that brought about reform in Texas capital punishment. People tired of spectacular and horrific cases: blacks soaked in oil and burned alive, mutilations, mass hangings in front of crowds of hundreds or even thousands of adults and children. Eventually public revulsion in the late teens and early 1920s of the twentieth century led the state to replace hanging with a less public kind of civil killing. Old Sparkey the nation's first electric chair was located in Huntsville in the heart of lynching territory, in plantation and logging territory, nestled in the verdant piney woods of East Texas, then and now the core of the Texas prison system.

Centralizing the location, designating the method, and delegating legal killing to state officials, however, didn't remove the component of injustice from the institution of capital punishment. Marquart and

Eklane-Olson in *The Rope, The Chair and the Needle*,[12] relate first person accounts by numerous black males in Harris County during the 1940s. Their stories claim innocence and document beatings and torture by law enforcement officials to extract false confessions. This tragic tale from Wilson Moore, # 310, black and from Harris County, vainly seeking relief from his impending fate, illustrates the continuation of the problem:

> I was arrested February 25, 1948 at my home by four officers from Harris County. On the way to Houston they drove out in the country and started beating me up. They kept beating and kicking me and wanted me to say I was guilty of the rape charge, but I would not admit something I was not guilty of. One of them grabbed my privates and started squeezing them, so then I told them that I would admit anything because I couldn't stand the pain any longer. They read me something off a sheet of paper to the effect that I had raped a white girl and tied her boyfriend up. They called the sheriff of Harris County and told him to meet us at South Main at the underpass. . . . I told (the sheriff) I was real glad to see him because they had been beating me up something awful. He said I wouldn't be glad to see him unless I told him what he wanted to hear . . . that I had raped a white girl and tied her boyfriend up, and I told him I had not. He then hit me in the mouth, and put me in his car and carried me out in the country again. It was then that they started beating me up and squeezing my privates again, so . . . I signed a piece of paper.[13]

Moore was executed in February, 1949. He was thirty years old. Lest we think his case singular, another black executed for rape in 1950 told a similar story of torture in the Houston jail until he confessed after 36 hours of sleep deprivation and beatings on May 30, 1948.[14] And much closer to the present, Cesar Fierro's confession to the murder of a cab-driver in 1979 was extracted under the illegal circumstances arranged by El Paso police who arrested and threatened to torture his parents across the Rio Grande in Juarez.[15] Ricky Jones' confession to the abduction and murder of a young woman in 1986 in Hurst, TX, occurred after he was told his girlfriend's baby would be taken from her and that she would get the death penalty too unless he confessed to a murder that substantial evidence indicates his sister's boyfriend committed. Jones was executed in August of 2000. Witnesses who said that the mentally limited Jones was involved only as a cover-up arranged by the perpetrator were not heard by any court.[16]

In the late 1980s, an Austin police officer coerced a terrified young Mexican American man named Christopher Ochoa into signing a confession that was manufactured by the detective, to rape and murder. The confession sent two innocent youths to prison for life and left the victim's family doubly traumatized by the false and sadistic details of the crime and later by the injustice done three more young men in the victim's name. Ochoa was released on the basis of DNA evidence after twelve years of imprisonment.[17]

Innocents freed in recent years

Fast forward to the last decade of the twentieth century.

Randall Dale Adams, Clarence Brandley, John Skelton, Muneer Deeb, Federico Martinez Macias, Ricardo Aldape Guerra, Andrew Lee Mitchell and Kerry Max Cook all left Texas death row during the last 11 years of the 20th century through judicial reversals of their sentences. The reversals were based on prosecutorial misconduct that had led to wrongful convictions for murder. Others, whose arguments for release were similarly credible, were executed. The nightmare that wrongful conviction for capital charges manifests for those who find themselves on death row, for their families and communities, cannot be overstated.

Details of these more recent instances of unjust conviction are instructive. Together they paint a picture of a system of justice that is clearly broken.

Freed by celluloid: Randall Dale Adams

Randall Dale Adams has achieved some degree of public fame through the artful 1988 documentary *Thin Blue Line*[18] and through his own book *Adams v. Texas*.[19] The movie, directed by Errol Morris, helped to set Adams free.

The ordeal began in October of 1976. Adams was a long-haired young white man headed for California with his brother when he unexpectedly landed a job as he was passing through Dallas. By late December he found himself being ordered at gunpoint, in a Dallas police station after hours of interrogation without food or drink, to sign a confession to fatally shooting a Dallas police officer. He refused to sign it, insisting he'd last seen the runaway teenager who accused him of killing the police officer several hours before the killing occurred. He maintained that he was asleep in the motel room he shared with his brother at the time of the crime.

That didn't stop local officials from proclaiming to the media that he had signed a confession, a fact he was unaware of because he was being held without access to media. He also passed two polygraphs and then was told he'd failed a third one. He had no attorney present until days later when his family hired a private attorney, who hired a partner and drove to East Texas to investigate Adams' teenaged accuser, David Harris.

Harris, an engaging boy who had a record indicating potential violence, came from Vidor in East Texas, a stronghold of the Klan. His record was ignored by the Vidor and Dallas police, who chose to believe the teenager's story, far fetched as it was. Harris claimed to have stolen a car in Vidor, then claimed to be passenger in that car. He claimed to have stolen a gun from his father, and that Adams shot the officer with that gun. Harris later helped officers locate the gun in a swamp in Vidor behind the home of one of his buddies.

Harris was too young to prosecute for capital murder — and the death of an officer called for somebody to pay the ultimate price. Adams was old enough to qualify. Adams had no record or history of violence and no motive. Harris, however, had bragged to a number of his peers within a few days after the crime that he had killed the "pig" in Dallas. Vidor police knew of these statements shortly after they occurred.

In the trial, when the defense brought forth as much of the incriminating evidence as the judge would allow against Harris, prosecutor, Douglas Mulder, who was the first assistant district attorney of Dallas County, successfully countered with paid, last-minute "eyewitnesses" whose credibility was highly suspect. He then withheld evidence that would have impeached the testimony of those witnesses. Mulder even lied to the defense about the availability of the witnesses when the defense sought to question them again.

The infamous "Dr. Death" (James Grigson) played heavily in Adams' death sentence. Grigson almost always testified for the prosecution in the sentencing phase of Texas capital trials and always reached the same conclusion, whether he interviewed the accused in person or simply reviewed a paper trail using "hypothetical" evidence. His recurring conclusion that the defendant constituted a "future danger" helped send well over one hundred men to Texas' death row.[20]

Grigson interviewed Adams by court order. During an interview that lasted less than 30 minutes, he asked the inmate to copy some geometric patterns, to interpret phrases like "a rolling stone gathers no moss" and "a bird in hand is worth two in the bush," and to answer a few questions about his background. Then, Adams says, the psychiatrist left and testified in trial against him for two and a half hours, beginning with an emphasis on his own degrees and expertise. Grigson diagnosed Adams with "sociopathic personality disorder . . . at the very extreme, worse or severe end of the scale." He said there was "no question in my mind that he is guilty. . . He will kill again."[21] He embellished on that notion, saying Adams was like Charles Manson and Adolph Hitler.

Recounting to the film makers his brief interview experience with Grigson preceding the expert's extended and harmful testimony, Adams shook his head and said, "The man's crazy."[22] Grigson was eventually censored in 1995 by the American Psychiatric Association, which apparently agreed with Adams. Unfortunately, Grigson's opinion was reinforced at trial by another psychiatrist, John Holbrook, who had worked within the Texas prison system and was frequently used by the Dallas district attorney's office. Holbrook agreed with prosecutor Mulder's assertion that sociopaths were people "who could work all day and creep all night," and said Adams showed no remorse for his alleged crime or any event in his life and, thus, clearly had no conscience.[23]

Judge Charles Baird, who was then a justice on the Texas Court of Criminal Appeals, critiqued Grigson's methods in a dissent to Fuller v. State (1992), citing passages from a 1990 article in *Vanity Fair*[24] that relayed Grigson's own accounts of attacking and discrediting the defense and manipulating the jury. Baird held the trial judge responsible under the Texas Rules of Criminal Evidence for determining the admissibility of an expert's testimony in each case.[25] That apparently put a damper on future use of Grigson by Texas prosecutors.

Dennis White, Adams' original attorney, was so troubled by the verdict he forswore the practice of criminal law and jury trials thereafter. Prosecutor Mulder left office not long afterward with a perfect win record to take on a lucrative defense practice and was never held accountable in any meaningful way for what White described in one of his closing arguments in the trial as an attempt to murder an innocent man. Adams' final attorney, Randy Shaffer of Houston, said on film that in Dallas County, prosecutors held that it was no great shakes to win conviction of the guilty, but it "took a really great prosecutor to convict the innocent.[26]

The case was upheld unanimously by the Texas Court of Criminal Appeals, but it was overturned in June 1980 by the U.S. Supreme Court in an 8:1 decision, with Justice Rehnquist dissenting. The reversal was based on a jury selection method condoned by Texas law that Adams' post-conviction attorney Mel Bruder argued "stacked the deck" against his client because it resulted in a "hanging jury." Anyone who had any personal qualms about the death penalty had automatically been excluded from the jury.[27] D.A. Henry Wade, who was notorious for his death penalty convictions, at first publicly proclaimed his intent to retry Adams. Then, about two weeks after the Supreme Court decision, he joined trial judge, Donald Metcalfe, and the Dallas County sheriff in writing the Chairman of the Board of Pardons and Paroles to request Adams' sentence be commuted to life. It was easier than going through another complex series of trials. Many cases overturned because of jury selection irregularities in the 1970s were recommended for commutation which was good for inmates who wanted to stay alive, but hard on those who wanted an opportunity to prove their innocence.

Governor Bill Clements signed the Proclamation of Commutation on July 11, 1980, despite the fact that Adams had not sought commutation and desperately wanted a second chance in the courts. Adams appealed the commutation to the Court of Criminal Appeals, which at first agreed with him in a May 1981 decision, but then reversed itself September 30 the same year on motion from the prosecution for a rehearing.

The Adams family's constant campaigning for the next five years for his freedom luckily coincided with the intention of filmmaker Errol Morris to make a film about Grigson. On March 1, 1989, a year after Morris' film *Thin Blue Line* was released, Adam's conviction and sentence were reversed by a decision of the Court of Criminal Appeals based on prosecutorial misconduct. The habeas judge offered that "on the basis of the evidence presented at the habeas corpus hearing . . . the court would have found applicant not guilty at a bench trial."[28]

In a taped phone interview with Morris, David Harris virtually admitted he'd killed the policeman, and plainly stated he'd blamed the crime on Adams because Adams hadn't offered him a place to sleep in the motel room he shared with his brother.

Blatant racism: Clarence Brandley

The Clarence Brandley case drew much notice in the late 1980s as advocates and eventually the Texas Court of Criminal Appeals decried the blatant racism implied in his arrest and conviction by an all-white jury after a first trial ended in a hung jury. Brandley was accused of the rape and murder of a white teen in 1980 at a school in Conroe. He was the black janitorial supervisor of four white janitors. The white janitors provided alibis for each other, although one initially told the investigator he'd seen another of his white co-workers with the victim before she disappeared. That witness later backed off. A Caucasian pubic hair had been found on the victim and blood inconsistent with Brandley's type was found on her shirt. The prosecution successfully resisted attempts to collect hair samples or blood from the white janitors.[29]

Thanks to the persistence of Brandley's family, two dogged local attorneys, the Houston NAACP, preacher-politician J. D. Boney, and the post-conviction work of attorney Mike DeGuerin, Brandley was freed in 1990 after coming within six days of execution. This in spite of the fact that crucial physical evidence (over half the trial exhibits) vanished from the office of the court stenographer the year after Brandley was convicted.

One of the white janitors had given a statement, which defense attorneys videotaped, saying he'd seen two other white janitors drag the girl into a bathroom. One of those two fingered the first man as the perpetrator, again on videotape, to the defense. The videotapes won Brandley a stay of execution and an investigation (in name only) by Attorney General Jim Mattox's office. The prosecution countered by announcing polygraphs favorable to their position and witnesses impeaching the credibility of the first janitor surfaced.

Brandley spent eight years on death row, receiving two stays, the first within 5 days of his death date, the second 13 days away. The court's decision which led to his freedom stated, "The color of Clarence Brandley's skin was a substantial factor which pervaded all aspects of the State's capital prosecution of him."[30] Eventually various locals, who had pieces of the truth, contacted Brandley's attorneys providing proof enough to convince an objective judge that justice had not been served — but only after they got several biased local judges removed from the case.

Mike DeGuerin said, "They could have gotten to the bottom of this long ago, but they've never been interested in anything that didn't point to Brandley."[31] Barry Scheck, on a tour promoting his book *Actual Innocence*,[32] pointed out that the racist factor in sentencing rape cases is still intact. Although only 10% of sexual assaults are inter-racial, over half the exonerations of the Innocence Project nationally involved black men accused of raping white women.

Freed but the catch is, no compensation: John Skelton

John Skelton, an Anglo from Ector County, was acquitted in December 1989 by the Texas Court of Criminal Appeals. His conviction for the dynamite murder of a former employee was overturned for lack of sufficient evidence. The U.S. Supreme Court upheld the acquittal and he was released in October of 1990. His appeals attorney filed a civil suit on his behalf challenging as unconstitutional the state law granting pardoned inmates, but not those acquitted, up to $50,000 in damages for pain, suffering and medical costs resulting from wrongful convictions. Under existing law, the acquittal removed his conviction, therefore he couldn't be pardoned, making him ineligible for the damage payment, which he needed to help regain his financial footing after seven years of wrongful imprisonment.[33]

No joke in Waco: Muneer Deeb

Muneer Deeb from McLennan County walked free in January of 1993 after a Fort Worth jury acquitted him on retrial for a charge of murder-for-hire related to the deaths of three teenagers at Lake Waco in 1982. Two 17-year-old females were raped and murdered. An 18-year-old male was stabbed to death. Deeb jump-started the miscarriage of justice when he got tired of the constant publicity on the unsolved crime and joked to a few not particularly good friends that he had killed the youth. Despite passing two lie detector tests — which are inadmissible in court but often deter prosecution — the young Saudi businessman was convicted and spent seven and a half years in prison, six of those on death row.

Deeb was accused of having taken out a life insurance policy, with himself as beneficiary, for a female employee who allegedly spurned his advances. It was held that he hired an assassin who bungled the job, killing the other teens when he mistook one of them for the employee who spurned Deeb. In fact, according to his attorney, Dick DeGuerin, Deeb had bought policies for all his employees as a form of worker's comp insurance. DeGuerin said he knew from the outset his client was innocent.

During his stay on death row, Deeb trained himself for a new career as a paralegal and was rewarded when DeGuerin offered him a job as clerk in his law firm upon his release. Deeb died in 1999 of liver cancer.

Good lawyering: Federico Martinez Macias

Federico Martinez Macias, a drifter and heroin addict from El Paso, was easy to convict for the machete murders of his sometime employers Robert and Naomi Haney in 1984. The case against him was constructed primarily with the testimony of co-defendant Pedro Levanos, who received immunity for testifying, and of a child who said she saw him washing blood from his hands. His court-appointed attorney, paid less than $12 an hour, didn't call any witnesses, although an important "alibi witness who directly disputed the state's evidence" was available.[34]

Martinez Macias came within two days of execution and spent nine years on the row. He was saved in 1993 by the 5th U.S. Circuit Court of Appeals and a federal district judge who ordered a review and investigation of the case that led to a reversal of his conviction.

Martinez Macias' surprising change of luck was based on the volunteer work of Douglas Robinson, an eminent civil attorney from a major Washington, D.C., law firm. Robinson got his client's case reversed within a year. He showed that the trial attorney failed to present alibi witnesses, and failed to discover an important witness who saw Levano, not Martinez-Macias, driving around the Haney home the day of the crime.

The trial attorney also failed to find others who would testify that the child witness wasn't even at the house the day she said she saw him washing his bloody hands.[35] His new trial attorney filed a motion to quash his indictment for re-trial, and a grand jury on July 1, 1994 found there was not sufficient evidence against him to warrant a new trial. Robinson says his firm spent millions on the case: "We treated it like a corporate takeover," and estimates half of any death row anywhere could be emptied by "good lawyering."[36]

Harassment and double jeopardy: Andrew Lee Mitchell

Andrew Lee Mitchell is an African American man from Smith County, a place known for aggressive and even perjured prosecution. This is the same county that wrongfully convicted A. B. Butler for rape. Butler, also of African American heritage, was released and pardoned by governor Bush in 2000 after serving many hard years, thanks to DNA tests which determined his innocence.

Mitchell was released 1993 after spending nearly 13 years on death row when his conviction was reversed. The reversal was based on the prosecutorial suppression of evidence showing Mitchell could not possibly have been at the scene of a fireworks stand robbery/murder in late 1979 for which he was convicted and sentenced.

Mitchell had been incriminated by his son, who was either guilty or an accomplice of the killer, an older man who made a deal with the state in exchange for fingering Mitchell. With wry humor, Mitchell recounts that he always told his son he'd die for him. He says the boy must have taken him literally. The son is now serving a long term in prison in another state and the two are reconciled. Mitchell's court-appointed attorney was a fraternity brother of the judge in the case, but had argued that the witnesses against his client were not credible and had been induced with plea bargains to incriminate Mitchell falsely. The older man, who had a long record, got immunity in exchange for his testimony.

The son recanted in 1984, just weeks before his father's scheduled execution. Tony Mitchell, who had been 17 at the time of the crime, said two deputies had taken him out into the countryside and beaten him until he agreed to incriminate his father, who was dealing drugs and fencing stolen goods at the time.[37]

A very light-skinned man, Andrew Mitchell recounts how the prosecution took pains to point out to the jury that though the accused looked white, he was black, counting on racism to secure a conviction and death sentence. It took seven minutes for the all-white jury in deep East Texas to convict him of capital murder, another four minutes to sentence him to death. Mitchell says they hardly had time to walk to the jury room and turn around to present their verdict. "I was in shock."[38]

On the row, Mitchell read a book that led him to an idealistic Austin defense attorney, David Botsford, who took his case to appeal pro bono. Botsford told an interviewer in 1997 that he'd devoted his life to defend citizens against "overzealous government," and that there was no question that "suppression of evidence and government misconduct" had occurred in Mitchell's case.[39] The original district attorney in the case, Hunter Brush, said ultimately that he believed Mitchell was innocent; that it was the son and his older companion who had committed the deed. However, the lead prosecutor David Dobbs was quoted in 1997 saying he still believed in Mitchell's guilt and that the victim "is still serving his sentence and it's a death sentence."[40]

Andrew Lee Mitchell was released on bail in 1993, and in 1995 sued the county for several hundred million dollars for wrongful conviction in a civil suit. A few days later one of his former prosecutors held a press conference re-opening investigation of him pursuant to re-trial on the original offense, i.e. double jeopardy. Mitchell eventually got $40,000 in reparations, a rare event in Texas, then had to spend most of it to defend himself once again from local officials who'd sent him to Huntsville in the first place.

In a terrible twist of a remarkable story, Mitchell was re-indicted in 1998 after a November 1997 opinion by a Court of Criminal Appeals judge, Steve Mansfield. Mansfield lied about his credentials during his campaign, was caught illegally scalping tickets to a sports event, and was defeated for a second term, but not before he re-wrote a statement of facts of Mitchell's case to justify his opinion. Mansfield's opinion held that re-trying Mitchell for the same crime twice did not violate the double jeopardy clause of the Texas Constitution.

This opinion contradicted an earlier opinion by the same court.[41] In his dissent, Judge Charles Baird, who was considered the liberal on the court, wrote that re-trial should be barred after reversal for prosecutorial misconduct as it was in at least five other states, and that the people of Texas deserve prosecutors who seek justice, not unjust convictions.

Terrified of being returned to death row, Mitchell pled to a lesser offense resulting in severe restrictions on his freedom. In his late fifties, Mitchell must wear an ankle monitor when he leaves home, to which he must return each night by seven. At home he cannot even go out into his own yard after the court-imposed curfew. Needless to say, travel outside the city of Tyler requires jumping through all sorts of hoops.

A twenty-two-year ordeal: Kerry Max Cook

Kerry Max Cook had the misfortune to be living for a few months in Smith County in his early twenties. He can testify that not only blacks get the short end of justice there. Cook was experimenting with homosexuality in 1977 after having worked at gay bars in Dallas where he found he preferred the values of gay men to the bubba mentality he'd encountered in small-town northeast Texas. He hitchhiked into Tyler with an older gay man who afforded him hospitality. The man lived in the apartment complex where a young woman, recovering from a disastrous affair with a married supervisor, had just arrived home from a suicide attempt. She and Cook had a brief dalliance. He left her room by the patio door, leaving a fingerprint. A few days later she was bludgeoned to death in her apartment.

A victim of media pre-judgement that portrayed him as a subhuman pervert and demented cannibal, Cook was convicted in 1978 of rape and murder. The fact that the victim's roommate told police after the crime she had seen the girl's married lover, who had short, silver hair, in the doorway of her room about the time of her death, didn't help. Cook was young and had long black hair. The roommate changed her description at trial and explained away the discrepancy saying maybe the light from the room made Cook's hair appear silver.

Cook's entire defense cost the county $500. His attorneys did no investigation and ignored his vows of innocence. The state used testimony from an "expert" who testified with no scientific basis that fingerprints could be aged to determine the time and date of deposit and that Cook's had been left at the time of the crime.[42]

The U.S. Supreme Court ordered Texas to review the case in 1988, just 11 days before Cook's scheduled execution. His conviction was overturned in 1991. He was tried again in 1992 and the trial ended in a hung jury. In 1993 a state district judge ruled that the prosecution had engaged in systematic misconduct, having suppressed key evidence which would have damaged their case. In 1994 Cook was retried and again condemned to death. In November of 1996 the Texas Court of Criminal Appeals reversed the conviction in a decision authored by Judge Steve Mansfield, the same judge who had twisted the law in Mitchell's case, but regarding Cook, wrote that "prosecutorial and police misconduct has tainted this entire matter from the outset."

At the beginning of a fourth trial in February of 1999, after having been out on bail for two years and facing a demonstrably hostile judge and a prosecutor who maintained the conviction was just, Cook understandably took a surprise offer to accept a reduced charge. His acceptance stipulated that the record show he did not admit guilt. A few weeks later it was learned that DNA tests conducted about the time of the reduced charge offer showed the victim's older, married ex-lover, the original suspect, was the donor of the semen found at the crime scene. Cook was released from jail without a pardon.

Cook's attorney Paul Nugent told the *Houston Chronicle* months later that he was preparing a petition for the Texas Board of Paroles requesting a pardon for his client.[43] Meanwhile, a Tyler grand jury was once again investigating the crime. At the end of 2001, Cook still had no pardon, thus was ineligible for the revised, more generous compensation allowances for those wrongfully convicted in Texas courts.

Cook is living in the Dallas area, getting on with what's left of his life after a nearly-fatal twenty-two year nightmare in which he endured brutality and repeated rapes at the hands of a cellmate, and the constant threat of execution. His relatively bright future, which includes an attractive peace activist wife, Sandra, and a child, Kerry Justice Cook, born to them in the fall of 2000, was the result of over a million dollars paid out for his defense. The unlikely saviors were two Wall Street financiers tapped by a tiny non-profit agency, Centurion Ministries, a New Jersey organization that fights wrongful capital convictions in courts across the nation. Cook recently responded to a French journalist who asked if he would content himself to focus on his own life and try to forget about the horror of his experience on death row:

> The answer to that is no. During my tenure on death row I had a front row seat in the charnel house of death row and I watched 141 men and woman go to their death — some, their only real crime was poverty, having been too poor to afford competent counsel. In the Texas criminal justice system, you get what you pay for. County District Judges appoint incompetent counsel so as to expedite the process, all to the accused's detriment. Whenever you have a judicial system so wholly tilted favoring one side and one side alone, there will be profound injustices. I watched justice die on death row — 141 times. I do not need to be a member of an abolition group to know that we have already executed an innocent person on Texas death row.[44]

Atlas shoulders injustice: Ricardo Aldape Guerra

A 19-year-old Mexican immigrant crossed the Rio Grande in a boxcar from his hometown in Monterrey. He got to Houston about the same time the economy there hit the oil bust skids and anti-immigrant sentiment rose. Ricardo Aldape Guerra was in a car with Roberto Carrasco Flores when Flores killed a Houston police officer conducting a traffic stop in July of 1982. Flores took the policeman's gun and soon thereafter was killed himself in a shootout with police. The officer's gun and the murder weapon were found on or near Flores' body. Aldape Guerra's fingerprints were notably absent from the weapon. A prosecutor admitted years later that the physical evidence "totally pointed towards Carrasco Flores" instead of the accused.

Eyewitnesses who originally said Roberto Carrasco Flores shot officer J.D. Harris were intimidated into changing their statements. Another juvenile at the scene who said she hadn't seen the shooting was told her child would be taken from her unless she cooperated. The D.A.'s office "coached the witnesses" so their testimony would be consistent.[45] The prosecutors repeatedly referred to Aldape Guerra's immigrant status and poverty during jury selection and the trial itself, a fact which his *pro bono* attorney, Scott Atlas, a civil attorney from the powerful Houston firm of Vinson and Elkins, pressed in his late-stage appeal in federal court.

The case had twice been affirmed by the state's Court of Criminal Appeals, but thanks to pro bono work of Scott Atlas and his team, Kenneth Hoyt, a federal judge for the Southern District of Texas, reversed the decision in 1995, ordering a new trial based on prosecutorial misconduct. Judge Hoyt barred the testimony of six of the eight witnesses used to convict Aldape Guerra, a decision upheld by the Fifth Circuit Court of Appeals in New Orleans. Eventually the prosecution folded after losing more skirmishes over re-trial in 1996 and early 1997.

Scott Atlas was recruited to help by the Mexican consulate in Houston. The consulate in turn had been pressured by extensive organizing by an immigrant rights group that demonstrated before the consulate and then brought the condemned man's parents from Monterrey to conduct a speaking tour. Guerra's case was assisted by the reporting of the Chicago-based *Tribuno del Pueblo* which published articles about his case over the years, and by a video by the *Tribuno*. "A corrido was written about his struggle and much pro-immigrant sentiment was generated due to this miscarriage of justice," writes Carlos G. Rodriguez of the *Tribuno* editorial board.[46]

Governor Ann Richards assured the Governor of the Mexican province of Nuevo Leon that Aldape Guerra would receive a stay of execution and a new investigation. The head of the Mexican Human Rights Commission had written Richards asking clemency for the condemned Mexican citizen, who was scheduled to die a few days after Governor Richards' reassuring words reached Mexico.

Atlas and his crew spent three million dollars of unbilled time over five years investigating and appealing the case. He was nominated for the Ator Legal Improvement Award presented by the University of Houston Law Center for his work in mainstreaming *pro bono* defense. This was small consolation for the tragic fact that his internationally famous client was killed in a car wreck four months after being released in April 1997, after fifteen years of wrongful imprisonment.

Perilously close to simple murder

Despite the media and public focus on George W. Bush's role in an assembly-line execution process during his tenure, he was not the first to draw criticism in that regard. His predecessor, Democratic Governor Ann Richards, was referred to as Bloody Annie during her term. Despite her reputation as a liberal, Richards proclaimed strong support for the death penalty and during her term 50 men were put to death, including at least four believed innocent in some quarters.

Consider the following macabre, bizarre, unnerving cases full of questions. What if only half, a third, or just one of these human beings executed by the state were completely innocent? What if only half were actually denied due process?

What these condemned men had in common was the lack of resources to hire a top-notch lawyer. They were, therefore, represented in a life-or-death matter by a privately-paid or more often, court-appointed lawyer with insufficient experience or talent or resources or curiosity or empathy to fully investigate and mount a defense for the suspect. They also had the bad luck to be dealing with unscrupulous police officers or prosecutors.

Edwin Callins: executed Feburary, 1994 despite sworn affidavit from former state judge saying someone else did the crime

Bruce Edwin Callins met his fate in the death chamber of the Walls Unit at Huntsville in February 1994, a day after the Supreme Court denied him relief despite an affidavit from a former state judge swearing that another man, his own client, was the killer. This inspired a fiery dissenting opinion by Justice Harry A. Blackmun, who wrote, "The execution of a person who can show that he is innocent comes perilously close to simple murder."[47]

Robert Nelson Drew: executed August, 1994 despite proof of innocence which came 71 days after court deadline

During the campaign between Richards and Bush for the symbolic political leadership of Texas, the case of Robert Nelson Drew popped up in the media. Drew was a 25-year old Vermont carpenter with no prior record when he hitched across the South in 1983. He caught a ride in the vehicle of a 17-year-old Alabama runaway headed west. Drew and an older man named Ernest Puralewski promised the Alabama teenager gas money. The body of the Alabama teen, Jeffrey Mays, was found with 13 stab wounds to the chest and neck. The body was found just inside Harris County, the capital for capital murder convictions in a state that leads the nation.

Drew was convicted and sentenced to death largely on the testimony of Puralewski, who was allowed to plead for a 60 year sentence in exchange for nailing Drew. Pralewski recanted 101 days after the trial, 71 days after then-existing state law allowed for the introduction of new evidence of innocence, saying, "I alone committed the murder of Jeffrey Mays. Robert Drew did not assist me in any way. Robert Drew is innocent."[48] Harris County D.A. John Holmes' response was that Drew lacked evidence he did not kill Mays and that if Vermonters didn't like the Texas law that limited claims of innocence to within 30 days of conviction they should commit their murders in Vermont.[49]

Drew's case drew national attention when his defense attorney objected to trial judge Charles Hearn's drawing of a "happy face" on his July 15, 1992 Execution Order for Drew. The *Houston Chronicle* reported that the "judge defended the signature, saying it expressed his Christian faith."[50]

Despite a 1994 decision of the Texas Court of Criminal Appeals on Gary Graham's case[51] to change the rules to allow new evidence of innocence to be presented to the trial judge after the 30-day period, Drew was executed at age 35 on August 2, 1994 during Richards' last few months in office. Vermont, a state with no death penalty, was outraged and swore off official visits to Texas. A state legislator threatened an economic boycott; citizens signed petitions and expressed outrage, to no avail. Drew in his final statement from the gurney, said, "Remember the death penalty is murder. They are taking the life of an innocent man."[52]

Jesse Dewayne Jacobs: Executed January, 1995 despite mental retardation and conflicting testimony in another court

When they sought and got a death sentence against him, prosecutors at the trial of Jesse Dewayne Jacobs said he alone had committed the crime which resulted in the 1986 death of a young Southeast Texas mother. Jacobs was a mechanic and drifter who'd been paroled for an earlier murder of a mentally retarded man in Illinois. He had confessed on video and in writing, saying he'd killed the woman at the request of her ex-husband who was dating Jesse Dewayne's sister. Later he changed his story twice, in the last version saying his sister shot the woman while he was outside the house; he just buried the body, but had tried to take the rap.

In another court room at the sister's trial in 1987, the prosecution used Jacobs as a witness, claiming that he didn't know she had a gun with her, and that the star witness against him had no credibility. They pressed a lesser charge against the sister, who had the motive for the deed (her lover was the woman's ex, and was allegedly being pressured for increased child support) but not the record of violence. She got ten years for involuntary manslaughter. After Jesse Dewayne's death, she claimed he'd falsely accused her, to try to beat the system, and caused her ten years of suffering for murdering a woman she'd never laid eyes on.

After the jury convicted him, Jacobs forbade his attorneys to put on witnesses for him during the sentencing phase of the trial and said if they had, he would have testified he "deliberately committed the crime and that I am and would be a continuing threat to society. I would rather die fast than slow in a cage." He claimed that he'd confessed to the crime to avoid a life sentence as an accomplice to his sister's crime.

According to a letter in the *New York Times* from Jacobs' lawyer Robert McDuff of Mississippi, after his client was executed at age 44 in early January of 1995 in the waning days of Ann Richards' term, the prosecutor later admitted the jury had made its decision to condemn Jesse on the basis of "false evidence and an erroneous presentation of the facts."[53] Nonetheless, the Texas Attorney General, Dan Morales, defended the execution on the grounds that collaborators in murders, even if they don't pull the trigger, are equally guilty. Jacobs said from the gurney: "I have committed a lot of sins in my life. Maybe I do deserve this. But I am not guilty of this crime." He added that he hoped he would be "the little snowball that starts to bury the death penalty."[54]

The Austin American Statesman editorialized that the case was an example of why the death penalty should be abolished. "If it is beyond the ability of the state, the appeals courts and even the nation's highest court to decide whether the prosecution and the juries were right the first time the second time, or neither, the state cannot fairly exact the ultimate penalty."[55]

Jerry Lee Hogue: executed, March 11, 1998 despite significant last hour evidence pointing to innocence

Jerry Lee Hogue's story was told by *Sixty Minutes*.[56] Accused of rape/arson/murder by woman and man who shared, along with him, a house with the female victim, Hogue was denied DNA tests. An arson investigator recognized similarities between the arson in Hogue's murder case and a later arson one of Hogue's former housemates and accusers was charged with the year Hogue was to be executed. The investigator called authorities to report the troubling discovery, thinking they would stop the execution. An acquaintance said the male, who accused Hogue of murder, had later bragged about getting away with murder. On the gurney Hogue spoke directly to the female accuser, Mindy Crawford, in the witness area, asking her why she chose sides with the "murderer" rather than with him. He said to her, "Mindy, you can stop this."[57] Presumably he paused to assess her response, then said, "O.K., I'm ready."[58] Hogue had been convicted of a rape in Colorado five years prior to the crime, a conviction which was later overturned, which undoubtedly made it easier to secure a conviction and death sentence.

David Spence: executed April, 1997 even though another person confessed to the crime

In Spence's case, both the police lieutenant who supervised the investigation and the homicide detective stated they had serious doubts about his guilt in the rape and murder charges in the Lake Waco crime for which Muneer Deeb was acquitted. The physical evidence against him was debatable. The prosecution reportedly suppressed evidence about another person confessing to the crime. A zealous narcotics cop used inmates who later recanted saying they'd received favors in exchange for witnessing against the drug-abusing sex offender. Spence was executed in April of 1997. From the gurney he directly addressed members of the victims' families: "I want you to understand I speak the truth when I say I didn't kill your kids. Honestly I have not killed anyone. I wish you could get the rage from your hearts and you could see the truth and get rid of the hatred."[59]

Is there a double jeopardy award for two wrongful death row convictions for the same crime?

James Lee Beathard: executed December, 1999 despite witness recantation that didn't meet the 30 day post trial limit for new evidence

James Lee Beathard, who was executed for the 1984 murder of a family of three, was convicted largely on the testimony of the son of the slain couple, Gene Hathorn, Jr., who had a violent past and guns, both of which Beathard lacked. Hathorn believed witnessing against his friend would save his own life, but if the prosecution had promised him that, he was betrayed. A year later Hathorn himself was condemned. He recanted his testimony against Beathard, who had accompanied him to the home unaware of Hathorn's plan, and remained outside hiding in the woods when he realized what was happening.

Because Hathorn's recantation, which constituted new evidence of innocence, was submitted more than 30 days after the trial, the Court of Criminal Appeals denied relief based on Texas law at the time. Three members of the Board of Pardons and Paroles voted to commute. The *New York Times* reported that when a reporter for a local paper asked Hathorn if Beathard had shot the victims, Hathorn had contemptuously replied that his co-defendant was "too much of a patsy to kill anyone."[60]

Hathorn had also confessed Beathard's innocence to fellow inmate Kerry Max Cook, a fact to which Cook alluded when testifying for a moratorium on executions before the Texas House State Affairs Committee in the spring of 2001. Just before being killed, Beathard wrote, "... as bad as it is to die in here, it's just a little worse to die without anyone saying, 'This is wrong.'"[61] Movingly, Beathard wrote in the notebook another inmate scheduled to die had passed around like a highschool annual for comments from other residents, " You're only one of a small handful who never let me down as a friend."

David Castillo: executed, September 1998, but a surgical error, not his crime, killed the victim

The conviction for which David Castillo was executed in September of 1998 seems as haphazard as the entire death penalty scheme. The 18-year-old high school dropout from Illinois purportedly stabbed Clarencio

Champion during a robbery of a liquor store in South Texas. Another man, with whom he lived and who was the main witness against him, was also a suspect and worked across the street from the liquor store. The wounds were not mortal until a clamp was left in Champion's stomach after surgery, which caused a fatal infection. The victim's widow sued the hospital and doctor for malpractice. Given $500 to investigate, the defense was denied a request for additional funds. Nor were they able to fund travel for several members of Castillo's family who wished to testify in the sentencing phase of the trial. Those who came were not guided in effective testimony, according to the father, who told the *New York Times* he believed he "must have done more harm than good because I didn't know what to say." [62]

Richard Wayne Jones: executed August 2000 despite low enough IQ to challenge his ability to be responsible for his actions

On August 22nd of 2000 Richard Wayne Jones died in the Walls death chamber for a 1986 Fort Worth abduction, murder and robbery there are strong reasons to believe his sister's boyfriend committed, but which he helped cover up by disposing of the body in exchange for the victim's checkbook and credit cards. Jones, who had an IQ of 75 and was devoted to his older sister who was involved in the murder, signed a confession to the crime. Police later admitted he was told if he didn't, his girlfriend would go to death row and would lose her baby.

His confession didn't fit the physical evidence, and witnesses to the abduction of the victim, including a mother and her teenaged daughter, disagreed on whether Jones resembled the man they saw. Jones had a small amount of blood on his pants and shoes but no blood on his shirt where the circumstances of the stabbing dictated he would mostly have been splattered. The sister's boyfriend had been seen by numerous witnesses with substantial blood on his arms and shirt while trying to sell the victim's credit cards and checks. One witness had even observed the boyfriend sell the credit cards and checks to Jones.

The trial judge refused to let the defense call witnesses to the sale. The boyfriend later told a cellmate in prison that Jones was the wrong man. European supporters raised over $100,000 for defense attorneys and investigators on Jones' case, to no avail.[63]

And one commutation: Henry Lee Lucas — out of state when Orange Socks was murdered, confessed to 225 other murders

While six of the seriously questionable executions listed above took place under the watch of George W. Bush, none drew statements of concern from him, his spokespeople or the Attorney General's office.

Bush did, however, ask the Board of Pardons and Paroles in 1998 to make sure of the guilt of Henry Lee Lucas, as he said he wanted no Texas executions where doubt of guilt remained. Or was he looking for a case that showed the condemned person flawed, and not the system?

Lucas, an unattractive man missing an eye and a few teeth, told Texas law enforcement agents that he had committed around 225 unsolved murders in several states. Corroborating evidence (at least demonstrating that Lucas knew the victims) was located for only three murders — of Lucas' mother, his fifteen-year-old female friend, and an older female acquaintance. In the early 1980s, when Lucas was under arrest as a suspect for the latter two crimes in North Texas, he embarked on his remarkable confession spree. Ultimately, Lucas was given all sorts of perks by Texas law enforcement agents to reward his confessions to multiple murders, including an unsolved killing of a woman in 1979 in Georgetown — known to police only as "orange socks" for the only apparel on her body when it was found.

During interrogation on the "orange socks" murder, Lucas was way off on the date of her death, the location, and the details of how she died, until the Williamson County sheriff helped supply information for his "confession." Several Florida witnesses, including two supervisors at Lucas' job site, swore at the trial that Lucas was in Florida at the time, but the jurors, after watching videos of Lucas bragging about a series of vicious killings, didn't believe the evidence to the contrary. They returned findings leading to Lucas' only death sentence.

Over the years more serious investigators who checked out Lucas' stories, such as *Dallas Times Herald* reporter Hugh Aynesworth the year before Lucas' 1984 "Orange Socks" conviction, found solid proof that Lucas was elsewhere when many of the crimes to which he had confessed were being perpetrated. Aynesworth and others persuaded Texas Attorney General Jim Mattox to formally investigate Lucas' whereabouts at the times of these unsolved murders.

Ultimately, two Texas Attorney Generals concluded that Lucas could not possibly have committed the vast majority of the murders he at one time alleged he committed, and that Lucas could have been wrongly convicted for the crime for which he was to be executed.

Jim Mattox said: "No rational jury could have found Henry Lucas guilty based on the standard of beyond reasonable doubt,"[64] and his successor Dan Morales told the *Houston Chronicle* a month before Lucas' commutation: "We became convinced that it was highly unlikely that he did that one."[65] Their statements helped his case enormously politically, which was the only game that counted by 1998. Even Lucas had struck out in the courts.

The *Dallas Morning News* congratulated the Governor for his display of "conscience" regarding the necessity to be sure condemned inmates were actually guilty, and with a gentle jab, opined that Lucas' guilt "like that of other death row inmates" was debatable.[66] Bush, in announcing the commutation to life of Lucas' sentence at the end of June, 1998, said he believed "there was enough doubt about this particular crime that the State of Texas should not impose its ultimate penalty."[67]

And so Texas' arguably most notorious serial killer, turned most prolific serial liar, escaped the gurney, only to die relatively peacefully less than three years later in his cell, presumably of heart troubles. He had been the best sewing machine operator in the old Ellis One Unit's death row garment factory.[68]

The barest shred of hope for innocents condemned

A review of the history of Texas capital punishment by scholars James Marquart, et al.[69] teaches us that public support for the irreversible punishment has dropped below 50% in this state during the last half century, corresponding with a dip in support nationally during the sixties. Enough unsettling particulars about probable innocents wrongly put to death could tip the balance against the practice as it did in England, given the right conditions, including more objective and investigative media coverage of crimes of violence, but mainly it seems, a leader with moral courage. France abolished the guillotine not by popular demand, for polls showed three quarters of the public still supported it, but by fiat when a new socialist leader was elected in the seventies.

Governor George Ryan of Illinois justified his announcement of a moratorium on executions in January 2000 by his concern about the potential execution of innocents. His state had released thirteen condemned men since resuming capital punishment in 1977, more than the 12 had been put to death in that period, and the *Chicago Tribune* and other media had raised the issue to a high level of public sensitivity. "I cannot support a system," Ryan said, "which in its administration, has proven so fraught with error and has come so close to the ultimate nightmare, the state's taking of innocent life."[70]

Ryan didn't base his action on polling data, which indicate that a majority of North Americans believe innocents have been killed by the state but still support the institution of capital punishment.

"I want to make sure we don't put innocent people to death, that's my concern," Governor Ryan explained recently. "The system right now is you can flip a coin to determine who's going to live and die."[71]

Perhaps, as Dennis Longmire remarked to a Discovery Channel TV crew on Odell Barnes, Jr.'s death day in March of 2000, "Now they've done it. They've executed an innocent person. This marks the beginning of the end of capital punishment in Texas."[72]

One could hope that no more people with credible claims of innocence will have to die in the pale blue room inside the red brick Walls Unit in downtown Huntsville to move the political will to stop state sponsored killing.

But a little further investigation into some of those claims leaves that hope hanging by the barest shred of imagination and will.

Chapter Three:
Appeals, The One Way Door

Photo by Susan Lee Campbell Solar

Photo by Susan Lee Campbell Solar.

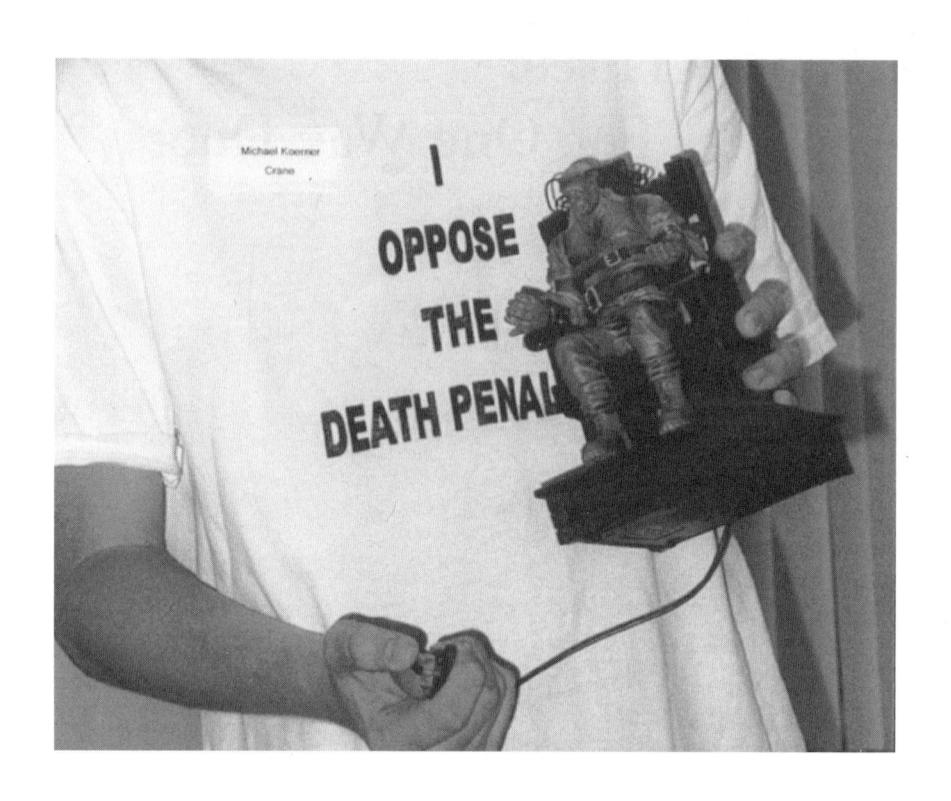

The one-way door

James E. Coleman, Jr., Duke University law professor, partner in a Washington, D.C. law firm, and chair of the American Bar Association's Section of Individual Rights and Responsibilities, who had handled three capital appeals himself, told a U.S. House of Representatives Subcommittee on Crime considering the Innocence Protection Act of 2000:

> In the last two decades, the ABA has extensively reviewed the administration of the death penalty in this country. In that review, the Association has found a legal process stood on its head. Inadequate, indeed, often grossly inadequate, resources are devoted to state court trials, appeals, and post-conviction review of capital cases.[1]

Coleman mentioned in his statement the recently-released study directed by Columbia University Law School Professor James S. Liebman,[2] which found 68% of capital cases nationwide had been reversed for serious trial attorney error, and on re-trial, 82% of the defendants were not re-sentenced to death, and 7% were found actually innocent. The study discovered a "reversible error in nearly 7 out of 10 capital cases in the 23 year period"[3] between 1973 and 1995. A.B.A. members had decided even before the Liebman study was released that the process surrounding the death penalty in this country was so flawed they passed a resolution in 1997 saying executions should be halted, at least until a serious study of the ever-more glaring problems had been completed.

The politics of fear: George Bush, Sr.

"Tough on Crime" was an easy ticket to office.

Events were unfolding during the eighties and nineties that seemed originally external to the courts but eventually influenced them through elections and legislative changes.

In 1981 a 17-year-old black, indigent Houston youth with a juvenile record and an addiction to cocaine named Gary Graham was charged with a murder he probably did not commit. At the time, Republicans constituted one fifth of the state's registered voters. Apart from the fact that wealthy Dallas businessman William Clements had been elected in 1978 and was the first Republican Governor of Texas since Reconstruction, the Texas GOP didn't have the steam to run candidates for statewide office. John Connally predicted that by the next decade Republicans would rule Texas. It took a bit longer than that, but by 1998 the Republicans had swept every statewide office and were within a few House seats of controlling the state legislature. The composition of the Texas courts made a dramatic swing to the right. That year the last Democrat was defeated and replaced with a Republican on the Court of Criminal Appeals (CCA), which had sole jurisdiction over death penalty appeals. By 1996, with the passage of the federal Anti-terrorism and Effective Death Penalty Act (AEDPA), for claims of innocence the CCA was the first, and probably for most the last, stop — a depressing thought for an accused, or for defense attorneys who examined the Court's record of decisions.

In 1988, when Gary Graham's case was submitted to the first layer of federal courts on appeal, former Texas Congressman George Bush (Sr.) was running for the White House. Top campaign strategist Lee Atwater and media man Roger Ailes had decided to take a crime issue discovered and raised by candidate Al Gore in the Democratic primary and run with it in the general election, because their pollsters told them the issue would sell.[4]

At issue was the weekend furlough program of the Massachussetts prison system over which Democratic front-running candidate Michael Dukakis nominally presided, a program which had allowed a black man incarcerated for ten years for murder to go AWOL in 1986. A year later in Maryland he held a young couple hostage, raped the woman more than once and stabbed and restrained her fiancé until the man escaped to secure help from police who arrested William Horton, Jr. in time to turn him into a major political weapon.

By June of 1988 Bush, Sr., the candidate, was referring to Willie Horton and the furlough program in his speech to the Texas Republican Convention and to Dukakis' opposition to the death penalty in contrast to his own support for it.[5] By August *Time Magazine* reported Bush strategist Roger Ailes saying: "The only question is whether we depict Willie Horton with a knife in his hand or without it."[6]

The sister of a man Horton allegedly killed in 1974[7] and the fiancé of the white woman Horton raped a year after escaping on his ill-famed furlough were sent out on speaking tours in Texas and elsewhere.[8] This became an early victim's rights call to arms in the service of the Republican party whose strategists had identified crime as a "wedge" issue.[9] Bush was quoted as calling Dukakis the "furlough king," adding "victims are given no furlough from the pain and suffering."[10] Bush even said Dukakis' response to criminals was "Go ahead: Have a nice weekend,"[11] ignoring the facts that the furlough program was begun by Dukakis' Republican predecessor, that it was remarkably glitch-free, and in fact a number of other states including Reagan's California had similar programs that worked.[12]

In Texas, 400,000 mailers with "Get out of jail free, courtesy of Dukakis" cards reached potential Republican voters. Nationally, campaign ads showing convicts, most of whom were black, passing through a revolving gate and spinning back at viewers which implied incorrectly that hundreds of "Hortons" had been unleashed on innocent victims under Dukakis' management.[13] The campaign doomed Dukakis' candidacy though he began the race in May with a 17 point lead. The ads "became the topic at every dinner table in 1988, just as Atwater hoped."[14] The Washington Bureau chief of the San Francisco Examiner wrote that a quarter of the voters had switched from Dukakis, originally seen as a moderate, to Bush, because of Atwater's "disciplined, ruthless and sustained series of attacks on Dukakis' record and character."[15] George W. Bush was assigned by the family to stick close to Atwater and be his father's liaison to them during the campaign. It is disputed how much of a role he played in raising funds for and enabling the more outrageous aspects of the Horton ad campaign, a campaign for which Atwater later apologized.[16]

The campaign set back the cause of rehabilitation for criminals at least a decade, as Horton was used as the symbol of a failed liberal illusion regarding errant reform. It didn't help that the Texas parole board released that same year the news that the average murderer in Texas prisons served only four and a half years before release, or that a crack-cocaine crime wave was then hitting the state hard. The fear of violent crime and bias against mercy engendered by the 1988 campaign, which played the race card blatantly while distorting the facts about the furlough program and demonizing criminals, was about to be exploited by Texas politicians of both major parties, magnified by some well-publicized Texas crimes.

Politicians took heed from Dukakis' defeat, including criminal court judges reviewing appeals. In the 1990 gubernatorial primary, former Governor and ex-Attorney General Mark White, who in earlier campaigns presented himself as a rational and moderate man, ran ads where he posed along a runway lined with blown-up photos of eight men executed during his earlier tenure. He then "faced the camera and intoned: 'These hardened criminals will never again murder, rape or do drugs. As Governor, I made sure they received the ultimate punishment – death!'"[17] Rick Halperin of Amnesty International and SMU compared White's ad to a Miss America pageant.[18] The campaign of candidate Jim Mattox, another ex-Attorney General, who had in earlier years expressed some ambivalence about the death penalty, also featured bragging about his role in executions. Ann Richards stepped up to the pro-capital punishment plate herself, under pressure from her Democratic rivals.

Politicians were also reacting to local indignation stirred up by nasty crimes committed by violent offenders who had been released on parole, such as Kenneth McDuff, who became the poster boy for capital punishment in the early nineties. As a young man from an affluent Central Texas family, McDuff had raped and killed a small town North Texas teenage girl after shooting her two teenaged male companions in a senseless, shocking murder. The *Furman* decision by the U.S. Supreme Court allowed his sentence to be commuted to life, along with everyone on death row, in the days when life sentences weren't really for life. McDuff's mother, a dozen years later in 1989, allegedly bribed the chairman of the Board of Pardons and Paroles to get him, now a middle-aged man, loose.

He got back to work strewing ravished corpses of more women around the state, and was tried and condemned again in 1993 for one of at least three rape-murders, for which he was put to death in 1998. John Bradley, a top prosecutor from tough-on-crime Williamson County and a former legal aide for the Texas Senate Criminal Jurisprudence Committee, responding to a question about whether the death penalty was about retribution or deterrence said, "McDuff answers this question . . . There are people that are evil and others will die, McDuff proved it."[19]

True, but more to the point would have been to replace the death penalty with sentences of life without parole. Texas prisons were, however, under court order from federal judge William Wayne Justice to reduce crowding. The parole board allowed many violent offenders to regain their freedom. In 1990, for instance, four out of five parole requests were granted.[20] Several other paroled offenders in addition to McDuff had substantial impact on public fears.

The heavily-publicized parole in the early nineties of sex offender Michael Blair of North Texas, who may or may not have abducted, raped and murdered a young Plano child named Ashley Estell in 1993, helped raise the public fear quotient. Molly Ivins believes he was the Willie Horton of the race between Bush and Richards in 1994. Richards' few openly gay and lesbian political appointments had upset the Christian right and Blair's re-arrest for child kidnapping and murder was political fodder against her in spite of her support for the death penalty.[21]

Fifty persons were executed under Richards' watch, including the mentally ill, the retarded and several likely innocents. One of George W. Bush's campaign planks when he ran against Richards was a "war on sex offenders." He promised to cut paroles drastically.[22] Richards had already cut them by 45%. After two years of Bush's leadership and the replacement by "tough-on crime" Republicans of several Court of Criminal Appeals judges, the rate of paroles granted was one in five; a year later it was about one in six.[23]

Victim advocacy or vengence?

A group which became a strong political force for tougher laws, longer sentences, fewer paroles and the frequent application of the death penalty arose in Houston in 1993, in part by commenting critically on the media play Gary Graham's case and his celebrity supporters were gathering at the time.

Justice for All came into being when an attempted rapist sued his intended victim and her husband for mental anguish. Notice of his eligibility for parole pushed his near-victim, Pam Lynchner, to act. She became an attractive and effective advocate for victim's rights and the first president Justice for All, which she founded along with Dianne Clements, the mother of a young boy who was shot to death by a neighborhood youth. After Lynchner was killed in a 1996 TWA crash, Clements inherited the leadership of the organization. Justice for All members are often quoted in the media throughout the state and nation, but especially in the Houston area, speaking for victims' rights.

Some are members of murder victim's families, and others are friends or allies, such as Dudley Sharp, a realtor who says he was moved by one particular family's plight and eventually became one of the chief spokespersons for the group. Sharp, in a February 2000 op ed piece in the *Fort Worth Star Telegram*, argued against the need for a Texas moratorium similar to that decreed by Illinois Governor Ryan. He said that racism and the execution of innocents didn't occur in the application of the death penalty except maybe in Illinois. He used national statistics instead of state figures to "prove" Texas was immune to racist application of the death penalty. He accused abolitionists of hypocrisy in their sympathy for criminals instead of the victims of violence. Like Governor Bush, Sharp said that appeals and executive clemency were adequate safety nets for the wrongly convicted.[24]

Justice for All wields far more political leverage than their numbers would warrant. It has accomplished much good by advocating funds to compensate crime victims, giving families of victims of violence a support system, and opposing mindless releases of violent offenders. However, it unerringly supports capital punishment, criticizes opponents of the institution, and opposes any hint of change or leniency in the criminal justice system. Asked by an AP reporter if she thought Texas prisons were too punitive, Clements responded: "Can you be too punitive when you're protecting innocent victims? The fact that Texas has a system run like a prison and not as a resort is something citizens should be proud of."[25]

Clements and Dudley insist the Texas judicial system is fair and effective. They deny the evidence for wrongful convictions or grounds for mercy. Clements, referring to a seven-state study by the Quixote Center which reported 16 innocents had been executed including four in Texas under Bush said, "They're trying to re-create fact based on fiction."[26]

Reacting to a memorial stamp with Karla Fay Tucker's smiling image produced by Danish artists protesting the death penalty, Clements observed: "Once again, the victims are discarded and forgotten. It is an insult to surviving family members, not to mention the sensibilities of caring individuals, who realize it is twisted and contemptuous to glorify a murder."[27] Shortly before his execution, Clements called Gary Graham the "poster boy for appeals," and said "the fact that he's had as many reviews as he's had just re-emphasizes his guilt."[28] Legislators discussing criminal justice reform bills in the 2001 session were often careful to ask how the legislation would affect victims, who they presumably thought had more of a voting constituency than offenders.

Sam Kinch, veteran Texas political journalist who covered both Bushes, father and son, for decades, believes the former Governor listened very carefully to the views of the victim's rights group.[29] The younger Bush had certainly witnessed the power of angry victims in his father's campaign against Dukakis, and observed the benefit of positioning oneself to appear pro-victim, a position he found useful after 9/11 to garner support for pre-emptive military campaigns. This paternal influence, along with the power of the judiciary and the district attorneys in the state, especially Houston's powerful John Holmes, doubtless helped strengthen Governor Bush's resolve to support prosecutors and ignore the arguments of the defense in every capital appeal. He made an exception only for Henry Lee Lucas, proven by the media to be somewhere else at the time of the crime. Such an execution would have been a serious tactical error for a candidate with higher ambitions.

Until the emergence in late 2000 of Murder Victims Families for Reconciliation, a group that opposes capital punishment and seeks reconciliation and restoration instead of retribution, Justice For All monopolized the media and dictated safety parameters for politicians, including elected judges, eager to appear tough on crime.

Fast track

At the time the death row inmates in this book were accused of committing their crimes, the fervor for capital punishment was at its peak in the state. By the mid-nineties, at both the state and federal levels, the appellate system for capital cases in Texas had been fast tracked and, some might say, taken hostage by hard-line politics. So not only would innocent death row inmates not recover their freedom, but most likely they would be executed within five or six years as their strictly limited appeals were exhausted before courts which almost never granted relief.

Hurricane Carter's co-defendant John Artis was a track star and Boy Scout with a college scholarship and bright future, which he lost when he was wrongly convicted and condemned with Carter of a triple murder in New Jersey. Artis, freed years ago after 15 years imprisonment, visited Austin in 2001 and commented on the pace of executions: "I'm scared to death of your state. You guys got a fast food thing going on here."[30]

Despite strong evidence in some cases for their innocence or at least serious grounds for doubt, condemned prisoners in Texas no longer languish for decades while their lawyers seek technical flaws to justify retrials. This was common between 1982, when Texas resumed executions after an 18-year de facto moratorium, and 1997, when the machinery of death got cranked up and rolling again. In the intervening years, state and federal courts litigated and seemingly resolved many disputed issues of the new capital statutes, so there were few appeals left hanging on the outcome of larger constitutional issues. Public attention was drawn to the tortuous and expensive decades inmates languished on death row. Texas Court of Criminal Appeals Presiding Judge Michael McCormick said in the eighties the court had a backlog of 6,000 cases of all kinds. In the nineties the court added four attorneys just to read through capital cases and prepare briefs on them for the court.[31]

The 1988 presidential contest between George Bush Sr. and Michael Dukakis demonstrated the perils of opposing capital punishment. The political advantage of being hard on crime energized local, state and national electoral campaigns, and influenced judicial appointments on the district and superior criminal courts. One opposition campaign researcher bragged that he could "come up with murder cases" and "really grotesque criminals" in a candidate's region.[32]

George W. Bush, in a campaign against Ann Richards for governor of Texas in 1994, charged her with coddling death row inmates by allowing them to languish in jail at taxpayer expense instead of rapidly sending them to their deaths. The campaign, masterminded by dirty-tricks specialist Karl Rove, featured an image of a policeman grabbing a youth by the neck. Another video drama sequence, designed to look real, showed a man pointing a gun at a woman in a parking lot followed by a policeman pulling a blanket over a corpse. The campaign ads manipulated statistics and said violent juvenile crime was exploding. They described young offenders as "thugs who walk into people's homes and blow their heads off."[33]

Richards, who liked to compete with the "good ole boys" in the machismo category, responded by promising legislation to short-circuit lengthy appeals, and by November the Houston Chronicle was criticizing both candidates for the unseemly spectacle of attempting to outgun each other in promising rapid elimination of death row inmates.

Within a week of taking office, Bush urged the legislature to enact laws to abbreviate the appeals process for death row inmates. Following his lead, the 1995 Texas Legislature set a strict timeline for filing direct and state habeas appeals. New laws required that the state habeas corpus appeal (a claim that a person is being held in violation his or her constitutional rights) had to be filed within 45 days from the time the direct and automatic appeal from the trial was filed. This leaves little time to develop evidence of innocence and almost eliminates the possibility of recourse if the attorney filing the direct appeal is incompetent, because it leaves the habeas corpus lawyer no time to evaluate the appeals lawyer's performance.[34]

Since then, a number of appeals have been rejected due to late filing by newly appointed and green appellate attorneys or incomprehensible rigidity on the part of the Court of Criminal Appeals, as in the case of Hank Skinner. Skinner's writ attorney's investigator quit before a deadline a few years ago. The new attorney submitted a timely request for extension, and then was notified of denial two hours before the deadline to present his appeal — on the other side of the state. This might not be a big deal in Delaware, but in Texas, it can take 10 hours or more to cross the state. The appeal arrived a day late and was rejected on that basis.[35]

Furthermore, if claims weren't raised at the state level, new federal restrictions stipulated that they were lost. They could not be raised at the federal level. And while the law required the appointment of "competent" counsel for post-conviction appeals, no standards which defined "competent" were set. The higher court has yet to set these standards and included some rather questionable attorneys, with records of disciplinary actions, for example, on their list of attorneys the court may appoint. The Court also determined a maximum pay of $25,000, including investigation, for the important work of the state habeas writ, once again guaranteeing advantage to the prosecution, and certainly to the wealthy.

Topnotch East Coast attorney Doug Robinson, who worked for free to get Fernando Macias Martinez off Texas' death row, estimates he and his assistants spent two thousand hours investigating his client's case.[36] Investigators' fees range from $35 an hour, on the low side, for court-appointed defense in Tarrant County, upwards to $75 an hour. The investigation alone of Macias' case would have cost at a minimum $75,000. The cost of time for an adequately paid attorney to research the particulars of any capital case and to find relevant case law could easily equal or exceed that amount.

Tough-on-crime judges

Justices on the courts of appeal at the state and regional level who really studied the law and factored in human rights issues and mercy were replaced during the late eighties and nineties. On the state level they lost elections to "tough on crime" opponents. Federal appointments went to activist judges who had vowed to speed up executions and stop the fairly common practice of reversing convictions because of constitutional violations — violations sure to occur given the shoddy quality of some appointed trial lawyers.

The terrorist factor: AEDPA (Anti-Terrorism and Effective Death Penalty Act)

The revulsion and fear spawned by the bombing of the federal courthouse in Oklahoma in 1995 added fuel to a fire for retributive or punitive justice that had been stoked for thirty-odd years and gave rise to further curtailment of appellate rights. In 1996, a year after Texas modified its capital appeals law, President Clinton moved on the national level to co-opt the Republican right by pushing for the 1996 Anti-Terrorism and Effective Death Penalty Act (AEDPA). Among other things, it limited the federal habeas corpus appeals process, the purpose of which is to ensure that a citizen's constitutional rights have not been violated.

High profile perpetrators like Willie Horton and Kenneth McDuff, combined with the overwhelming impact of the Oklahoma bombing, set the political stage for vote-getting judicial reforms that limited the time death row inmates were allowed for appeals and habeas review. This helped to seal the fate of Houston's Gary Graham, and well over a hundred other Texas death row inmates over the next dozen years. The politics of fear took the steam out of legislative reform efforts and abolition for at least a decade, and set the stage for future curtailing of constitutional rights under the Patriot Act as well as the huge round up of Arab Americans who where held for months in jail without ever being charged after 9/11.

Texas Court of (No) Criminal Appeals

Trial judges are elected at the local level and don't want to take the heat if a violent offender escapes punishment. One would hope that higher state and federal level appellate judges would catch major mistakes, such as the one a Houston-area judge made in the George McFarland case, when he ruled "the Constitution doesn't say the lawyer has to be awake." The Texas Court of Criminal Appeals judges, however, affirmed not only that conviction and sentence but two others (also from Houston) in which attorneys snoozed through their clients capital murder trials. Yale law professor Stephen Bright said these attorneys gave a new meaning to the term "dream team," in the case of indigent defendants facing the death penalty.[37]

The results of political pressure to be hard on crime, the ensuing changes in legislation, the significant changes in the philosophies of the judges elected or appointed by conservatives and their unwillingness to risk public outcry and electoral defeat, show up most convincingly, however, not in rulings on individual cases but in the percentages of cases reversed at the state and federal appeals levels. Before the changes, Texas was behind the national average of 68% in successful death row appeals. According to a major nine-year study headed by Columbia University School of Law professor James S. Liebman, which was released in June of 2000, between 1973 and 1995 approximately a third of Texas capital convictions were reversed.[38]

Within the last decade the chances of reversal took a nosedive. Between 1990 and 1995, according to an analysis of Texas Court of Criminal Appeals statistics[39] by this author, 33 cases were reversed out of 226 capital appeals (both direct and habeas corpus), a reversal rate of 14%. Most of those reversals occurred prior to 1994, after a peak year in 1993 when 19 out of 82 cases, or almost one in four, were reversed and sent back for new trials.

But in the period between 1995 and 2000, the percentage of successful capital appeals in the Texas high court plummeted and only 8 out of 278, or 3%, resulted in reversal of the original trial verdict. There were only six reversals of a sentence.[40] Some of that decline may have been due to resolution of legal issues surrounding the Texas and other capital statutes. For example, the 1988 Franklin decision released many cases held up on similar appeal. In 1989 the Penry decision by the U.S. Supreme Court clarified that juries must be given a vehicle to consider mitigating factors such as mental retardation at the sentencing phase. A number of sentences were then sent back to trial court for that purpose. By 1995 most appeals based on that issue had passed through reviewing courts. A former member of the court who declined to be quoted for attribution felt the dramatic decrease in reversals also reflected a "change in composition of the court. We simply had the courage to do what was right. If a reversal was required, at least five members would step forward to do the right thing, regardless of the consequences."[41] That no longer happens.

The political change on the court began in 1992 when Richards appointee Pete Benavides was defeated by Republican, Lawrence Meyers. It accelerated in 1994 when two judges, Charles Miller and Sam Houston Clinton, declined to run again and Charles Campbell was defeated by Steve Mansfield. Houston newspapers made a great deal of Campbell's vote — for technical, legal reasons — to reverse the conviction of the car jacking killer of Tracy Gee, a young woman from a prominent Houston family.

Mansfield had campaigned on a platform of denying appeals based on "technicalities" (which could be seen as application of the law evenhandedly, as in the Gee case), regardless of the circumstances. However, he lied about having Texas roots and extensive experience in criminal law. Although the deception was exposed prior to the election, he won anyway, but after an arrest and plea for scalping football tickets, declined to run again.

Sharon Keller came on the court also in 1994, and as of 2001 is chief justice of the highest state court for criminal matters. Of the eight cases between 1995 and June 2000 when the CCA voted to reverse a conviction or sentence, Keller voted to deny the appeal six times.[42] Keller, a Dallas native, has embarrassed the state in a different way than Mansfield, who was a judge and ticket scalper. She is nationally known for dismissing the appeal of Roy Criner accused of the rape and murderer of a Montgomery County teen after two DNA tests, which had not been available at the time of his trial, excluded him. The original trial judge recommended a new trial after seeing two DNA analyses by different labs which excluded Criner as a suspect. Even so, Keller and four others, a bare majority, endorsed the original prosecutor's arguments that the victim was promiscuous and that Criner had worn a condom, arguments that had no basis in either fact or even logic if one were familiar with the details of the case. On a nationally televised PBS program, *Frontline*, Keller defended her decision, but when asked how someone could prove their innocence, she replied "I don't know, I don't know."[43]

Former Judge Mansfield who had voted with Keller on the decision, changed his mind after watching *Frontline*, and told *Chicago Tribune* reporters he had made a mistake. Judge Tom Price, who had dissented from the ruling to deny Criner's appeal, said the decision made the court "a national laughingstock."[44] Former CCA judge Charles Baird says Keller is the "poster child for the need for intelligence and integrity in the court."[45]

The President of the Texas Criminal Defense Lawyers Association wrote:

> The Court of Criminal Appeals ignored evidence exonerating Mr. Criner, created new theories never offered at Mr. Criner's trial for the sole purpose of keeping an innocent man in prison, and trashed the victim's reputation. Mr. Criner eventually was released only because the district attorney, sheriff and trial judge all sought his pardon. . . . Because the Court of Criminal Appeals failed in its duty, Mr. Criner remained in prison a full two years after the evidence clearly showed his innocence. That isn't an isolated case — the Court of Criminal Appeals works injustice on a regular basis.[46]

The Criner case is not the only one in which the Texas high court has ignored trial judges or prosecutors when they recommended a defendant be given a new trial. Cesar Fierro's former prosecutor said he wouldn't have pursued the case had he known the circumstances of the confession, and that the CCA's decision in denying him a new trial "flies in the teeth of the Constitution."[47] Keller's 1996 majority opinion that Cesar Fierro did not suffer harm sufficient to justify a new trial despite the fact that an El Paso policeman perjured himself at the trial has received a lot of criticism. The policeman lied about Fierro's confession being extracted when the suspect knew his parents were being held and tortured by Juarez police.

The CCA turned its back on a Houston trial judge's proposal that Calvin Burdine should have a new trial after an evidentiary hearing regarding his sleeping lawyer. The CCA also rejected West Texas district Judge Brock Jones's recommendation that Ernest Willis — who was involuntarily drugged by the prosecution during his trial for the death of two women who died in a fire to which he was linked by circumstantial evidence — should have a second chance at defending himself. One of Willis' trial attorneys was later sentenced for cocaine possession and surrendered his law license — to which the court responded that his co-counsel alone could have effectively represented Willis. Willis' hotshot pro bono New York attorney from the giant Latham and Watkins firm, James Blank, said "We'll do whatever we have to do to prove his innocence and that he didn't get a fair trial."[48]

Amazingly, the Texas CCA has six times granted inmates new trials based on "fundamental violations of their rights," then changed its mind, leading to the execution of the unfortunate applicants.[49] Certainly for inmates, their family, friends and loved ones, this is nothing short of torture.

Former Judge Morris Overstreet, who left the court in 1998 to run unsuccessfully for state Attorney General, dissented from an opinion denying an appeal because a lawyer was late in filing it, saying the decision "bordered on barbarism" because it punished the inmate for his lawyer's mistake.[50] Yale Law professor and Southern Center for Human Rights director Stephen Bright wrote in 1999 that "by denying competent lawyers and suspending due process, the Texas Court of Criminal Appeals runs the fastest assembly line to the death chamber in the country. A person may be condemned to die in Texas in a process that has all the integrity of a professional wrestling match."[51] Tarrant County appeals attorney Robert Ford says arguing his clients' cases before the Court of Criminal Appeals came to resemble speaking to the deaf, dumb and blind.[52]

Texas Appeals Court appointment of writ attorneys

Between 1995 and 1999, the Court of Criminal Appeals appointed attorneys from a list generated by the Court itself to write the crucially important final state appeal, the writ of habeas corpus.

Unfortunately, the quality of lawyers on the list has varied wildly. Some have had serious disciplinary sanctions, and others are new to habeas law and totally unprepared to handle such an important task. In the case of Ricky Kerr, who had claims of innocence that later attorneys found very credible, his appointed writ attorney, who had only three years of criminal law experience, didn't raise any claims about Kerr's particular case, and simply challenged the revised Texas death penalty statute. Kerr requested a new lawyer, which the CCA denied, over the dissent of Judge Morris Overstreet, who wrote that the court made a " 'farce and a travesty' of Kerr's rights and that if Kerr were executed, the court would 'have blood on its hands.' "[53]

Former CCA Judge Charles Baird, who helped to set up the Court appointment system, said under-funding reduced the number of competent attorneys willing to undertake capital appeals. Attorneys understood they would wind up footing the bill themselves for most of the work and refused the work. Baird says Texas puts its resources at the wrong end of the process anyway, since much of the damage is irreversible once a conviction and sentence are accomplished.[54]

Federal Appellate Courts

On the federal level, the picture is not much rosier for an inmate or his or her attorneys.

The passage of the Anti-terrorism and Effective Death Penalty Act (AEDPA) in 1996, designed to curb "abuses" (multiple appeals) by death row inmates and their lawyers, confused the process for appellate attorneys and their clients. Federal courts were directed to defer to state courts on habeas corpus (wrongful conviction) appeals. The AEDPA mandated that new claims of innocence could not be raised at federal levels if evidence for that innocence *could have* been discovered and raised at the earlier, state level. Therefore, callused or inexperienced and underfunded, appointed lower-level attorneys could essentially kill their clients by neglect and incompetence in the first weeks of work on the case.

The hastily-written legislation left different regional federal courts to create their own interpretations of its meaning. This has resulted in geographic variations between, for example, the Fifth Circuit, whose judges come from Texas, Mississippi and Louisiana where support for capital punishment is high and the appointed judges are conservative; and the Ninth Circuit court in the northwestern part of the nation where such support is lower and judges sometimes interpret the AEDPA in a fashion more favorable to the inmate.

AEDPA also set a one-year limit for starting the federal habeas process, after an inmate has lost his or her case in the state courts. The resulting time often does not allow for adequate investigation by the new federal level lawyer. Seasoned civil rights lawyer James Harrington writes:

"Federal habeas corpus doctrine has developed into an incredibly complex and arcane body of law, with all branches of government working together to create an almost impenetrable labyrinth of barriers to effective habeas corpus relief; resulting in the dominance of procedural and technical legal barriers over concerns for constitutional rights or actual innocence."[55]

Texas Defender Service attorneys explained the gravest problem with the revised federal habeas law. After 1996, the federal courts were no longer authorized to examine whether or not a defendant had received a fair trial. "Instead, the federal court must focus its attention on the state court's decision denying relief. The question is no longer, 'Did this defendant get a fair trial?' but 'Did the state court, in denying relief, act *unreasonably*?' which imposed a 'psychological barrier' on the reviewing federal judges, who were forced to declare peers' decisions 'unreasonable' rather than simply mistaken."[56]

The federal courts are also now required to accept the state court findings of fact. The Texas Defender Service analysis of over a hundred cases of capital appeals showed that the state trial court nearly always adopted wholesale the prosecutor's suggested findings of fact, not the defendant's or even a mix of the two. Because the Fifth Circuit has approved this procedure, it is almost impossible to prove a lower court's findings unreasonable, since their findings are taken as fact.

In Texas capital appeals the conclusion is so nearly forgone that the Fifth Circuit will speed up its decision on a case if there is a pending execution date to accommodate the executioner's schedule, which is unusual for circuit courts.[57]

Occasionally a Federal decision has nudged the state to lighten up. For instance, in 1997 the Supreme Court found Texas law forbidding judges from explaining to jurors that a life sentence meant a minimum of 35 years without parole conflicted with a 1994 ruling of the high court. Justice Stevens, who frequently sides with Justices Breyer, Souter and Ginsburg on death penalty, said the practice "tips the scales to favor the death penalty." In 1999 the Texas legislature changed Texas law to allow judges to inform jurors that life sentences meant 40 years before a person was eligible for parole.

While it seems the Fifth Circuit shows more mercy than the Texas high criminal court, its decisions are erratic and unpredictable. And beyond the Fifth Circuit, it's a rare case that the U.S. Supreme Court agrees to hear, and when it does, even rarer that the hard line majority budges.

The end effect is that once a person is accused and convicted in the state courts of a capital crime a gate to their freedom and often their life slams shut. It is a one way door.

Well they brought me out some big old pants and told me to put them on. So I did. So when they searched me with the scanner my belt went off, so the lady say, "No. You have to strip." I took off the belt and dropped the pant, left me standing there with nothing but my panties and my top. Then she did my back and my bra-hook went off. She told me I had to take it off. I said, "No problem. You can't do nothin to me no worse than you're planning to do to me. You want me to get buck naked, I will."

> Elnora Graham, on how she was treated the day her son was executed.

Chapter Four:
Gary Graham (Shaka Sankofa)

Elnora Graham, mother who raised Gary

Photo by Susan Lee Campbell Solar.

Appeals and the question of doubt

The case of Gary Graham or as he preferred to be known, Shaka Sankofa, has been heavily covered over the years, especially toward the end in June 2000 as his execution date neared and passed.[1] Graham's zig-zag pilgrimage through state and federal courts helped define and highlight the problems of proving innocence after the fact of conviction. Graham's external characteristics also perfectly fit the "most likely" profile to land on death row, starting with the fact that he lived in Houston. He was also young, and most significantly, black and indigent.

Sankofa's bitter struggle all the way to the gurney where he was strapped down, battered and defiant, on June 22 of 2000, garnered vast publicity nationally and internationally. His case illustrated a common dilemma for the condemned. If the initial attorneys ignore evidence available at the time of the original trial, such as the several eyewitnesses who said from the outset that Graham did not even resemble the murderer, the law makes it almost impossible to get that evidence examined in court after conviction. In Graham's case, as in the majority of capital cases, there is no DNA evidence to settle the matter. Tough luck for the death row resident — the lackadaisical efforts of his attorneys could be the major factor in his forbidding fate. It could be called murder by counsel — or by judicial appointment, if a judge knowingly appoints an inexperienced or otherwise incompetent trial lawyer to a capital case.

Perhaps the problem could have been caught in the early stages of appeals, but the volunteer attorney handling it had no resources to conduct the thorough investigation the defense had never done. By the time attorneys with sufficient know-how and resources arrived on the scene, the inmate was almost in the execution chamber. State and federal courts had toughened up, and during his second round of appeals, laws changed which foreclosed avenues previously open to prove innocence.

Graham allegedly killed Bobby Lambert, a 53-year-old white man from Arizona, outside a northeast Houston grocery store one spring night in 1981. Graham was 17, had dropped out of school at 13, was addicted to crack cocaine and right after Lambert's death embarked on a ten-day string of brutal robberies in which he shot three people who wound up in the hospital. He finished off the spree with the abduction, robbery and rape of a middle-aged female cab driver, who tricked him into coming home with her, where he fell asleep long enough for her to grab his gun and hold him until the police came.

A product of a mentally ill birth mother and an alcoholic father who'd separated soon after his birth, Graham had numerous caregivers during his youth and had spent time in juvenile detention facilities. Following his arrest for capital murder, he was appointed a young black defense attorney three years out of law school. Ron Mock was known around the Harris County courthouse for barely resisting the prosecution efforts to convict clients. He eventually gained fame among inmates of death row for helping to swell their ranks by at least a dozen with his lackluster defense efforts. While Mock had some strong points, putting up a fight for a man he decided at the outset was guilty not only of the crime at hand, but others as well, was not one of them. Mock has since been disqualified to represent capital defendants because he failed the test Harris County imposed in 1995 to improve such representation. Mock used to brag about flunking criminal law courses in law school.

Judges, to stay in office, had best watch their backs; and angering a local politically powerful D.A. by derailing capital convictions through appointing and funding an aggressive and competent defense would not be a wise strategy in some situations. Mock fit perfectly the needs of the prosecution and the judiciary at the time, and so Graham was convicted and condemned in 48 hours of courtroom time in October of 1981. Mock's co-counsel, Chester Thornton, also a young attorney recently out of law school at the time, told a reporter 18 years later that the trial was lost at the jury selection stage. The prosecution succeeded, he said, in picking jury members (all white) they knew would go with them on the verdict.[2]

David R. Dow, a professor of constitutional and death penalty law at the University of Houston, summed up Graham's problem at trial in an article in the *Christian Science Monitor*.[3] His lawyers failed to force the prosecution "to prove beyond a reasonable doubt that the defendant committed the crime." Of the 19 years afterward he said, "Except for cases where DNA evidence is available, it is virtually never possible to prove someone didn't commit a crime."[4]

Richard Burr finds new evidence

Richard Burr was a public defender who moved from Florida to New York to direct the NAACP's Death Penalty Project in the eighties. The NAACP saw the death penalty as the ultimate form of applied racial prejudice. In that role in 1989 he criticized a proposal to limit federal capital appeals recommended by a committee set up by Supreme Court Justice William Rehnquist to alleviate the roadblocks to executions.

The committee, which included North Texas federal judge Barefoot Sanders, recommended the changes apply only to states which agreed to fund attorneys for state appeals of capital sentences. It was a carrot-and-stick approach to the problem of providing fair representation to defendants for their appeals while at the same time satisfying prosecutors and victim families who wanted swift retribution.

Burr said the proposal failed to recognize the "widespread problem of inadequate legal representation for murder defendants at the trial level."[5] Supreme Court Justice Thurgood Marshall, the first African-American appointed to that court, made a similar point four years earlier at a judicial conference in Pennsylvania, saying because of the problems in indigent defense, appeals were not necessarily a remedy.[6] The phenomenon of "murder by counsel" was indeed the root problem of the man who was to become Burr's most famous client, Gary Graham. In fact, Graham's direct appeal to the highest state court had been turned down a year before Justice Marshall stated the point in Pennsylvania. Inadequate trial defense for indigents was linked to another core problem in the Texas system of capital punishment, which Burr outlined when interviewed in December of 1992, when he was still based in New York: "There is an unholy and inappropriate partnership between judges and prosecutors."[7]

When Burr, working with the NAACP Legal Defense and Education Fund, first got involved in Gary Graham's case in 1992 and began to investigate it in depth, it was the first time such an investigation had been conducted — despite the intervening eleven years of court procedures.

The intervening volunteer appellate attorney from 1988 to 1993 had no funds to investigate. Even so, he had pursued the inmate's appeals through initial state and federal habeas corpus proceedings in 1988, a Fifth Circuit affirmation, and a stay of execution pending Supreme Court decisions which remanded the case back to the Fifth Circuit. There a panel vacated the death sentence in 1990. That ruling was reversed by January of 1992 by the full bench of the New Orleans-based court, which affirmed the 1988 lower federal court's denial of *habeas* relief, which was in turn affirmed by the Supreme Court in January of 1993. If reading about these procedures was dizzying, imagine being the lawyer responsible for the life of a defendant, or that defendant locked up on death row for 11 years wondering if the facts of the case would ever make it into a courtroom.

By 1994, Burr was working for the Houston branch of the Texas Resource Center, which administered federal funds for indigent capital defense at the appellate stage. They were joined in 1996 by Mandy Welch, also with TRC. That year Burr and Welch formed their own firm and were joined on the Graham case by Jack Zimmermann. They conducted a serious investigation of the case for the first time and turned up witnesses who had a much longer time to observe the killer than the key witness against Graham. These other witnesses had never believed the 5'10" Graham was the short man with the thin face they had watched before he shot Bobby Lambert. The defense team also discovered Lambert had been in an unusually dangerous position at the time of his death. He was about to turn state's witness in a federal case in Oklahoma against a former drug importing partner he was afraid of. The attorneys in that case believed his death had been a drug hit. In Lambert's van on a nearby street, police found weapons, several drivers' licenses in different names and some marijuana.

Furthermore, Lambert was killed by someone who lurked in full view of store attendants for a half hour or more and then killed him in front of witnesses in a parking lot of a busy grocery store, rather than waiting until he got into his van. Six thousand dollars in his wallet was untouched. It had all the hallmarks of an out-of-state hit and object lesson to any one else inclined to turn state's witness, not of a local random robbery. There was certainly enough new evidence to convince Burr that Graham's consistent claim of innocence might hold water, despite the demonstrated violence of Graham's crime spree that followed Lambert's death.

Unfortunately, back in October 1981 when Graham was on trial, his lead attorney Ron Mock thought because of Graham's crime spree that he was guilty of Lambert's murder. In his judgment it was not worth ruffling feathers in the Harris County courts or police department with a serious investigation or vigorous defense.[8] Even if Mock had intended a serious investigation, he would have been strapped for funds as the court allowed him only $500 for that purpose. The jury never even heard from the Houston police department's firearms expert who determined Graham's gun left six tracks on bullets instead of the eight tracks on the bullet that killed Lambert — indicating that Graham's gun could not have been the weapon.

Certainly Mock did not introduce jurors to the troubling questions that the case produces if one carefully studies it. He could have cast doubt on eyewitness Bernadine Skillern's identification of Graham after she first remarked on the differences between his features and the killer's in a suggestive photo line-up where Graham was the only clean-shaven man with a short Afro hairstyle. He could have countered her trial testimony with that of the other witness who'd worked at the store and for various reasons had watched the shooter before the crime. Their names and statements disputing her identification of Graham were available in the police offense report. And surely the circumstances of the victim might have given pause for reflection. But Mock did none of these things. His defense inspired signs at demonstrations in later years that read "Mock made a mockery of justice."

As Burr and Welch were submitting Graham's new appeal based on the evidence of innocence their investigation had uncovered, several momentous events occurred in Washington, D.C.

Supreme Court refuses to hear new evidence claims

In late January of 1993, former Supreme Court Justice Thurgood Marshall, a man who had thrown his weight into opposition to capital punishment during his 24 years on the court, passed away. The next day, the Supreme Court in *Herrera* v. *Collins* ruled, by a 6-3 vote in an opinion authored by William Rehnquist, that condemned prisoners at the end of their appeals process could not be saved by new evidence presented to the federal courts. Rehnquist, Sandra Day O'Connor, Antonin Scalia, Anthony Kennedy, and Clarence Thomas proclaimed that the presumption of innocence granted North Americans by the Constitution "disappears" when a person is convicted at the conclusion of a trial. Justice Harry Blackmun dissented, saying allowing the execution of a person with a case for innocence "comes perilously close to simple murder." John Paul Stevens and David Souter declined to join the majority but didn't sign on to that portion of Blackmun's statement.

The evidence for innocence in the *Herrera* case was not strong, and the justices did not totally slam the door on last-minute claims, as several justices added that more persuasive new evidence could open the door to a federal hearing.[9] Herrera was condemned for killing one South Texas police officer. He admitted killing another officer, but claimed his dead brother actually had killed the officer for whose murder he was about to be executed.

Overall, however, the decision was a chilling one for defendants and attorneys who harbored hope for relief in the federal courts on claims of innocence. Later in the year a closer decision (5-4) dashed hopes of inmates that the high court would once again throw out the Texas death penalty law, as it had done along with most other states in 1972 in the *Furman* v. *Georgia* decision. This time the appeal had been on the basis of a provision limiting jury consideration of certain mitigating evidence such as youth or turbulent family history. The broad issues were mostly resolved now regarding the Texas death penalty; the defenders were constrained to sift through the narrower causes for appeal. "They done greased that death machine" was the comment of one doomed inmate, Ruben Cantu.[10]

In Houston a few months after the *Herrera* decision, on April 27, 1993, Graham's attorneys were up against TCCA judges who said that since none of the other witnesses they'd found had seen the actual shooting, their testimony was of no value. However, the new witnesses had seen the same man in the white coat Skillern first described, both minutes before and immediately after the shooting, running away. An hour before that hearing, the Harris County D.A's office had finally released their file on Graham to the defense, and it contained within the police offense report two more witnesses helpful to Graham. Armed with this revelation, Graham's defense used their last tool to hold the dike against Graham's impending execution date of April 29, 1993. They made a direct appeal to Governor Ann Richards for a stay, the only action a Texas Governor can take on behalf of a condemned person without direction from the Board of Pardons and Paroles.

Richards was no softy on crime; she had told reporters to their surprise early on in her term that she liked the death penalty. Richards didn't know Graham's attorneys and only granted two reprieves during her term, but Burr believes she saw the problems with Graham's conviction and granted him, on April 28, a month's stay. It was a politically surprising move, for a *Parade* Magazine poll showed 87% support in the nation for executions.[11] A new execution date was scheduled for June 2. An insider who spoke off the record says it was Richards' constituency, which let her know she'd pay a price for denying the appeal, that motivated her action, not her attention to the legal particulars.

That 30-day stay from Governor Richards helped Graham survive another seven years. Immediately his attorneys filed a writ of certiorari with the U.S. Supreme Court, which turned it down by late May. The trial court set a new execution date of August 17, 1993. Graham's attorneys filed a civil lawsuit to stay the execution that was turned down at the local level but appealed. A civil judge for the Third Court of Appeals in Austin granted an extension of Richards' one-time stay in June of 1993, based on the civil suit that requested a chance to raise the new evidence in a clemency hearing set for August 10. The Harris County District Attorney appealed this stay to the Texas Court of Criminal Appeals, but it granted its own stay. By this point the case had attracted several famous entertainment and political personalities to Graham's cause, including Danny Glover, Susan Sarandon and Jesse Jackson. Steve Hall, a publicist and former aide to Democratic Attorney General and several-time gubernatorial candidate Jim Mattox, had been hired in the spring by the Texas Resource Center to bring media and political attention to Graham's innocence claims. Hall stayed on as an able administrator for the Center, where he continued to assist with the case.

Dick Burr moved to Houston in 1994 to help what he describes as a small, overburdened group of qualified capital defenders. He continued to fight for Gary Graham's life through the rest of the appeals process as the case bounced back and forth between federal and state courts like a ping pong ball over the next six years. On April 20 of 1994 the Texas Court of Criminal Appeals, in response to Graham's appeal, lifted the stay of execution granted him the previous summer by the civil court and more importantly, overruled state law limiting the presentation of new evidence for innocence to thirty days post-conviction.[12]

In 1995 the Texas legislature heeded new Governor George W. Bush's call for streamlining the state appellate process for capital cases and passed legislation doubletracking state and federal habeas appeals, a change that promised to shave at least two years off of most appeals. The house bill was introduced by Southwest Texas Democratic representative, Pete Gallego.

Graham had an appeal pending before the Fifth Circuit in New Orleans based on incompetent representation at the trial stage. It had to be decided before he could return to state courts with his new evidence. In 1996 the Fifth Circuit judges gave their answer. They said Graham had merit in his claims to innocence and ineffective trial counsel, but he hadn't yet exhausted his remedies at the state level for an evidentiary hearing. The court believed an opportunity had become newly available. The next two years saw Graham and his attorneys exhausting the last state possibilities, to no avail.

In 1998 they returned to the Fifth Circuit which said it couldn't hear the case they'd determined had merit in 1996 because the court now believed the federal Anti-terrorism and Effective Death Penalty Act (AEDPA) should apply retroactively to Graham. It barred successive petitions claiming that his trial attorneys were ineffective. He was out of luck.

The defense was pushed to the wall and went back to the Supreme Court with a petition for writ of certiorari challenging the retroactive application of the AEDPA to Graham. In May of 2000 the Supreme Court denied the petition.

Now Graham's defenders were down to the last step. They prepared a clemency petition for the Board of Pardons and Paroles. The defense's offering included videotapes of the new witnesses and affidavits of several jurors who said they wouldn't have voted to convict had they known about the conflicting eyewitnesses who didn't appear in court. Five members of the Board voted to commute Graham's sentence and three to grant a 120-day reprieve, a very high number of votes for the defendant compared to other appeals.

According to former Texas Court of Criminal Appeals Judge Charles Baird, clemency is supposed to be a gift, an act of grace, of leniency or mercy reserved for the executive to grant at will.[13] Scholars tell us that in the early years of the centralized Texas death penalty, clemency was often granted because citizens in a region drew up petitions arguing to spare the life of the condemned. Sometimes a prominent community leader, an older woman, for example, wrote on behalf of a poor person she knew or who had worked for her, saying that the crime had been an aberration in an otherwise harmless life.[14]

The day before Graham's execution, George Bush told a national association of Hispanic reporters that he would review the Graham case in the same way he reviewed all 134 others that had come across his desk in the previous five and a half years. He would ask his famous two questions: "Innocence or guilt, and whether the person has had full access to the courts of law."[15] The Sunday after Graham's death, which provoked much less tumult in Huntsville than predicted, Bush was quoted on his conclusion: "Over the last 19 years, Mr. Graham's case has been reviewed more than 20 times by state and federal courts. After considering all the facts, I am confident justice is being done."[16]

The Texas Defender Service emphasizes in their review of Graham's case that in all those years and reviews by various courts, Graham never got an evidentiary hearing in which judges listened to the newly discovered witnesses in a setting where they could be cross-examined. Striking evidence that Graham did not commit the crime for which he was executed was never heard in court — not in 19 years, not in one of the 20 reviews George W. Bush used to bolster his confidence that justice had been done.

The *Chicago Tribune* summarized the problems in Graham's case a few days before his execution. There was no DNA evidence to help him. The newly discovered witnesses from the scene, "who were certain that Graham wasn't the killer," had never been heard by a jury or any court. This despite the "hundreds and thousands of hours" Graham's highly respected and experienced final defense team put in on the case trying to secure a hearing. His trial lawyer actually "served jail time" for mishandling criminal cases, and according to a Northwestern University law professor, Larry Marshall, "set new levels of incompetence during trial," losing a case with so little evidence it "is off the charts." The article stressed "the disparity between the legal work at trial and that at appeal" which was of the highest quality.[17]

Kafka-esque scenarios such as this give cold feet to many who, in principle, support the ultimate penalty.

GQ's James Ellroy is a writer who came to Texas to check out the Graham case. The child of a murder victim himself, Ellroy was in favor of the death penalty when he arrived. But Ellroy left Texas convinced by Mock's co-counsel Chester Thornton's honesty about the shabbiness of Graham's trial defense and the ambiguities he found in Graham's case, that Graham should be spared, and the death penalty itself abolished, because "if we continue like this, innocent people will fry."[18] His article "Grave Doubt" appeared in GQ's June/2000 issue. It was just one of hundreds of articles that month covering the latest aspects of Graham's case — his pronouncements from death row, vows of Graham supporters to block his execution, public statements by officials determined to carry it out, the hue and cry of worried Huntsville residents facing the prospect of warring hordes of Klansmen and Graham supporters. Black nationalists promised to bear arms. Graham promised to go down fighting.

Jonathan Alter, writing in *Newsweek* the week after Graham's execution, explained how the case had turned him into a "moratorium man" despite his hard stance on crime. Alter reviewed the facts: of the eight eyewitnesses, only one identified Graham; two contradicted her but weren't used at trial; the appeals courts refused to review the case because "the higher courts . . . tend to trust the original jurors — unless the original jurors have new doubts. Then their views don't matter. Three of the original jurors in the Graham case said that if they had heard all the witnesses originally, they would have voted to acquit." Alter concludes:

> The "full and fair" access to the courts that Bush brags about is now a mirage. In *Herrera* v. *Collins* (1993) the Supreme Court made it much tougher to bring a constitutional claim of innocence. And the 1996 Anti-Terrorism and Effective Death Penalty Act — pushed by the Clinton administration — sharply curtailed federal review of state cases. Despite numerous appeals, the facts of the Graham case were never formally revisited...That left a claim of "ineffective counsel," which is like buying a lottery ticket. The Supreme Court has only twice in two centuries granted relief on those grounds. Lower courts also routinely reject such claims...(applying) what is jokingly called the "mirror test" — if it fogs up because of the lawyer's breathing, he's "effective."[19]

Dick Burr says the experience of losing the battle was "heartbreaking."[20] He adds, however, that he doesn't believe his client's life was a failure. In fact he admires Graham for what he achieved in the daunting circumstances of death row. Burr thinks his client had probably raised his IQ 30 points during that time, becoming an articulate and galvanizing world figure from the confines of his cell in deep East Texas, and forging himself into a dedicated warrior for justice. Others, including Ellroy, saw Graham as a brutal thug based on his actions during those ten days in 1981, whether or not they believed in his innocence for the murder of Bobby Lambert. Graham's stepmother Elnora says simply and sadly, "1981 was a bad year for Gary."[21]

The year 2000 was perhaps worse for the Graham family. Besides facing his own pending execution, Graham faced the arrest of his son Gary Hawkins, who was charged with capital murder in Houston a few months before Graham lost his own last battle.

A mother's lament

In a long interview with Elnora Graham on the day after Christmas, 2000 she drew this portrait of the family of a man condemned to die.[22]

The minutes tick away

We went down there the 21st of June. . . . They told me to pop my trunk. I informed them that I didn't have no drugs or weapons, or nothing. I told them I had dirty clothes, including dirty underwear. Did they want me to take out my clothes? "No." They would take them out, so they pulled them out, dropped my dirty clothes and under things on the ground. They told me they would deny me the right to visit Gary because I had a poster of Gary, *Stop the Execution of Shaka Sankofa*, in my trunk. They told me they had the right to deny my visit, but they were going to let us go on in.

Locked up

And when we went in, they locked the doors with me and her between them. I said to Dietra, "Do you have a ticket or something? They have gone and locked us up." She said, "No Grandma, I don't have one." So I wonder what is the problem. In about 3 to 5 minutes the Warden came and the prison guard. . . . He said, "I know you all going through a lot, and I know you all doing a lots of things. We don't know which way this thing is going, so what do you want to do with the remains?" [They were praying for a stay of execution.] He said, "Dietra, your dad left everything, all his property, to you." Dietra said, "Don't talk to me. Talk to my grandmother." He said, "We can't go anywhere until one of ya'll answer me." We let him repeat his question the third time. He said he was going to leave us to make up our mind and he would come back. I never been locked up before, I feel scared, I said, "Let Ross have it." So he said, "OK."

Locked out

As we approach in there, my baby daughter was already in there, and [other family members]... My other daughter said she has to go down to the Warden's office. They have one of my grandbabies that Gary don't know. I say, "Don't go down there.". . . She said she don't know what he want with her down there. She go anyway. . . . She come back crying. I said, "You went to the warden's office." She said, "Yes." I said, "You can't go back down there where your brother is cause he can't see us. You can't go down there if you go to the Warden's office. . . .We can comfort each other, but who's going to comfort him. He's the one on the other side."

He [Gary] said, "Mama, tomorrow I'm going to go over there [to the unit where executions take place] but when I make it back [depending on the stay of execution] I'm going to write a book." He said somebody wanted that book and they was going to give him some money and he wanted to tell me how to use that money for his kids. So I said, "OK." He said, "Dietra, go out to Mama's car and look at Moma's trunk to get some money [to take some pictures]." Then I left out to smoke a cigarette. I asked the people at the window, "If I go out to get some money so I can take a picture, can I come back in?" They said, "Yeah." When I got ready to come back in they said, "No."

So I stayed [locked]out there so long that he [Gary] thought I did go. So his daughter, she came out and told me, "Daddy said we could come back in." And I said, "Dietra, they told me we can't come back in." We went back and they said, "Visiting hours is over."

TV

So they said you all have four hours to visit tomorrow. So both of us was trapped on the other side. We came on home. We went to my daughter's house. She went to look at TV to see if we got a stay. We see a white van and all these police cars and a helicopter. It says Gary Graham is being transported. They don't move anyone until they getting ready to kill him. But Gary got moved on the 21st instead of the 22nd.

Strip

When we got there [the next day] they denied my oldest access, said she wasn't on the visiting list. She said, "That's my brother, you're going to kill him, let me see him." They denied her the right. Then they turned to me and told me I could not visit. I said, "Why can't I visit. I was just in there yesterday. Why can't I go in?" They said, "You are not dressed appropriate." I said, "Come on, give me some pants, give me anything and let me see my child because ya'll are maybe going to kill him in a few hours." They denied me. I had on some shorts. It was hot and I knew after I got to see him, I was going to be out there protesting. It was June and it was hot. The shorts come down to my knees, about as far as a skirt would come. They denied me. Jesse Jackson come in and said, "You must be Mrs. Graham because you are awfully upset." I said, "I am." He said, "What seems to be the problem?" "They are denying me the right to be with my child." He said, "Don't worry. You're going." He went to talk to somebody. Well they brought me out some big old pants and told me to put them on. So I did. So when they searched me with the scanner my belt went off, so the lady say, "No. You have to strip." I took off the belt and dropped the pant, left me standing there with nothing but my panties and my top. Then she did my back and my bra-hook went off. She told me I had to take it off. I said, "No problem. You can't do nothin to me no worse than you're planning to do to me. You want me to get buck naked, I will."

There was a quarter in my pocket. She made me throw it away. Like I have money to throw away. My daughter had just paid $14 for a hat because it was so hot out there. They made her throw that away. It was real, real ugly down there on the 21st as well as the 22nd.

The last time I seen my baby alive

He [the guard] said, "You gonna have a visit like you've never had before. There ain't no one round there but him, so don't you be scared." I said, "I am not scared of my baby, what are you talking about?" Then when we get there we looked at his [Gary's] left side. He was holding it. Brenda and Dietra, they went. They was crying when they left. Jackson went. He [Gary] was standing there, in a dirty, dingy old jumper, a bunch of stuff thrown on the floor, very nasty looking back there. He said, "Mama, how come you left me yesterday? They brought me over here." I said, "Yeah, I seen it on TV." He said, "What you didn't see on TV — eight of them took me down to Captain somebody's office and they broke me up pretty good." "Feel," he said, "They broke my rib." I said, "Did they carry you to the doctor?" He said, "No." I said, "Soon as we get this stay [of execution], they'll have to carry you to the doctor before they take you to back." I said, "Just stand and be strong baby, because we all need you." He said, "When I got over here about five more roughed me up." A tear rolled down his face. He saw the family out there. I said, "Don't worry. We going to win. You gotta be strong, cause we fighting like hell outside."

They said, "Visiting hour is over." Reverend Jackson said, "Then we'll pray." And they said, "Visiting hours is over, you have to leave." Our own Reverend came in and began to pray. They broke into the prayer and told us to leave.

They told me to come out one side and take off the [prison issue] pants. I did and a gang of policemen came out of this room and said, "What do we have her for?" I said, "You don't have me for nothin' I'm just trying to get off your property." They went to laughing, and they laughed, and that was the end.

In a final indignity, three months after Graham's execution, Elnora Graham lost her longtime job as cook in a Houston elementary school due to the publicity she received in the final months of her stepson's life. Although she finally got another job in the system, the unsalaried months when she couldn't pay the mortgage threatened her with the loss of her modest home. The hordes of journalists had long since left, and death penalty abolitionists had their hands full on other fronts. Elnora Graham faced her tribulations in private, shored up only by family and friends. She had another trial to face.

In spring of 2001 Gary's son, Gary Hawkins was convicted and sentenced to life despite a determined defense by a topnotch local volunteer attorney convinced of his client's innocence. During his trial Elnora Graham stood sentry outside the courtroom, waiting to be called as a witness, her handsome, mahogany features chiseled in sorrow.

Chapter Five:
No Clemency, No Mercy

Drawing by John Paul Penry who has an IQ of between 53 and 60 and the mind of a 7 year old child.

Penry was receiving a resentencing hearing when the U.S. Supreme Court ruled in *Atkins* v. *Virginia* that it was no longer constitutional to sentence offenders with mental retardation to death. The judge declined a motion to stop the hearing and the jury again sentenced Penry to death. Most knowledgeable observers believe the death sentence will not stand inPenry's case.

Penry has been icarcerated 24 years for the brutal rape and murder of Pamela Moseley Carpenter in October 1979.

Photo by Susan Lee Campbell Solar.

Napoleon Beazley's written statement, distributed by Texas authorities after his execution on May 28, 2002, for a crime he committed as a minor:[1]

> *The act I committed to put me here was not just heinous, it was senseless. But the person that committed that act is no longer here — I am. . . .*
>
> *I'm not only saddened, but disappointed that a system that is supposed to protect and uphold what is just and right can be so much like me when I made the same shameful mistake.*
>
> *If someone tried to dispose of everyone here for participating in this killing, I'd scream a resounding, "No." I'd tell them to give them all the gift that they would not give me ... and that's to give them all a second chance.*
>
> *I'm sorry that I am here. I'm sorry that you're all here. I'm sorry that John Luttig died. And I'm sorry that it was something in me that caused all of this to happen to begin with.*
>
> *Tonight we tell the world that there are no second chances in the eyes of justice. Tonight, we tell our children that in some instances, in some cases, killing is right.*
>
> *This conflict hurts us all, there are no SIDES. The people who support this proceeding think this is justice. The people that think that I should live think that is justice. As difficult as it may seem, this is a clash of ideals, with both parties committed to what they feel is right. But who's wrong if in the end we're all victims?*
>
> *In my heart, I have to believe that there is a peaceful compromise to our ideals. I don't mind if there are none for me, as long as there are for those who are yet to come. There are a lot of men like me on death row — good men — who fell to the same misguided emotions, but may not have recovered as I have.*
>
> *Give those men a chance to do what's right. Give them a chance to undo their wrongs. A lot of them want to fix the mess they started, but don't know how. The problem is not in that people aren't willing to help them find out, but in the system telling them it won't matter anyway. No one wins tonight. No one gets closure. No one walks away victorious.*

Building a firewall

Charles Baird, now a visiting judge who served for eight years on the highest criminal court in the state, the Court of Criminal Appeals, believes the justification Governor Bush used to reject clemency appeals for commutation to life or pardon was incorrect.

As governor, George W. Bush frequently repeated his criteria for execution — is the person innocent or guilty, and has the person had full access to the courts of law. While these criteria present a surface logic, in fact, they display according to Baird an "essential misunderstanding of the relationship between the judicial and executive branches of government."[2] From this misunderstanding of tripartite government, came the killing spree that earned George W. Bush the name *Governor Death*.

Baird says the Bush questions are the territory of the courts, not the Governor.

> Clemency is an act of grace from the government and should encompass the particular circumstances of the defendant, both at the time of the commission of the crime and their years in confinement; the rehabilitation of the defendant, if any; religious conversion; the wishes of the victim's survivors; and any other extenuating circumstances that would lead one to conclude the defendant was no longer worthy of execution.[3]

It is clear that evidence for actual innocence is, in some conservative appellate courts, such as the Texas Court of Criminal Appeals and the federal Fifth Circuit Court in New Orleans, often irrelevant or highly unlikely to ever be aired. A case can pass through the courts a dozen times and never have the basic facts brought to light, due to the complex workings of the many layers of the law and a shift to the right in judicial elections and appointments. Thus, wisely, the institution of clemency is purposefully outside the courts, in the hands of the chief executive.

If clemency worked as it should it would correct the excesses of overly zealous or even corrupt prosecutors, inept attorneys and appellate courts that almost never grant relief, all of which exist in abundance in Texas today.

Issues which have merited clemency in the past — beyond the last-ditch effort to establish wrongful conviction or actual innocence that slipped through the courts unheard — include rehabilitation and mitigating circumstances. A governor who has an informed vision of the purpose and use of clemency, who studied the flaws rampant in the systems that lead to state-supported execution, like Governor Ryan of Illinois, would be able to summon the executive power of clemency for appropriate use.

Governor Bush of Texas got more mileage out of being tough on crime. His record in Texas was not incompatible with his fast-tracking of American jurisprudence after 9/11. This was not a Governor, or President, who had much interest in the rights of the accused at home or abroad. The local saying that trying to explain due process to George W. Bush is like trying to explain a sundial to a bat, is not unfounded.

On the other hand, the peculiarities of Texas history have combined to protect modern Texas governors from the taint of scandal that followed governors in the 1930s, who allegedly took money in return for pardons. If the Board recommends relief for the inmate, the Governor has discretion to grant the recommended commutation or pardon. If the Board declines to make such recommendation, the Governor is empowered only to grant a thirty-day reprieve from execution.

The Board of Partons and Parole began in 1937 with three members, one of whom was appointed by the Governor. It was expanded to six members, all appointed by the Governor but confirmed by the Senate, in 1983. Seven years later it was expanded again, to 18 members chosen by the Governor, all of whom received fulltime salaries of $80,000 a year, operated from their homes, and served staggered six-year terms. The Texas Board of Pardons and Paroles has recently been reorganized, reduced in size, and they have regional offices, which may lead to more thoughtful and active consideration of clemency petitions in death penalty cases.

That said, the Board has been infamous for its high rejection rate of parole requests, and its abdication of mercy in capital cases. Governor, Ann Richards granted no commutations, and only two thirty-day stays, one to Gary Graham who was executed seven years after that stay. The other was to Johnny Frank Garrett, who at 17 raped and killed an elderly nun in the Texas Panhandle. The Pope appealed for mercy for him, because of the sexual and physical abuse Garrett suffered as a child, which caused multiple personality syndrome as well as other mental damage. The Richards Board voted at a rare hearing, 17/0 with one abstention, to deny his appeal. Beginning in 2000, Bush's last year as Texas Governor, the Board was all his, since Richards' last pick left at the end of 1999.

After two major campaigns (his father's presidential race and his own race against Richards) that were organized around "tough on crime" stances, it is no surprise that George W. Bush picked conservative, pro-prosecutor members for his Board of Pardons and Paroles. This board meets rarely, and while attorneys send many boxes of materials in support of each appeal for clemency, board members are under no obligation to read or even glance at these details of life or death. Members regularly fax in rubber-stamp "nixes" on death row appeals.

Karla Faye Tucker's attorneys were among the first to challenge the fairness of the Texas clemency system in the state and federal courts. They found in 1997 that, in essence, all of the Texas death sentence commutations since the reinstatement of the death penalty in 1973 had occurred for reasons of "judicial expediency."[4] In those cases, prosecutors themselves requested commutations in order to avoid retrials on guilt/innocence and punishment following reversals by appellate courts. One of Tucker's attorneys, Walter Long, now states that, since 1973, there has not been a single instance of clemency granted in Texas solely because a death row inmate requested it.[5]

This was not always the case. In 1964, Huntsville newsman Don Reid, who had witnessed at close quarters the electrocution of 179 men, was able to save a black man on the day of his scheduled date with the electric chair by making a phone call to the chairman of the three-person Board of Pardons and Paroles. He related the story he'd just heard from the condemned man who said the killing was self-defense. The Board investigated his claim and commuted the sentence by mid-afternoon. The man was eventually released and lived a productive life elsewhere in Texas, writing Reid annually on the anniversary of his near-fatal date.[6] Others were saved because the Governor or Board members were touched by letters from family or prominent citizens or petitions from the inmate's region, which vouched for his normally good behavior. This no longer occurs.

The firewall

Thousands of citizens of this state and of other states and nations, the Pope, members of European Parliaments, the governments of Mexico and Canada, even Madeleine Albright, have written in vain to Texas Governors Richards and Bush and to their Boards of Pardons and Paroles. They have begged for mercy for the mentally ill, for retarded inmates, for juveniles, for women, for possible innocents, to no avail.

In fact, since 1990 there has been only one commutation, Henry Lee Lucas, a thoroughly erratic human being who exchanged confessions for food and was in another state when the crime for which he was to be executed was committed.

Alas, in other cases where innocence was likely, but where there was only minor media focus, men have gone to the gurney with no relief —

men such as Troy Farris, Bruce Edwin Callins, Irineo Montoya and James Beathard. Others, such as Randall Adams, Federico Martinez Macias and Kerry Max Cook were saved only by extraordinary efforts from out of state, contradicting Bush's oft-repeated claim that the Texas justice system works.

So why, in the last decade of the 20th century, is there no executive clemency in Texas? The word itself implies mercy. The institution of clemency was intended to balance error or impropriety in the judicial branch of government.

Instead, the Board of Pardons and Paroles is an effective firewall constructed by the executive branch to protect itself from the responsibility of making life and death decisions. Officials can rant "tough on crime" rhetoric during campaigns, ride the politics of fear to office, and then pass off responsibility for state sponsored killing to a puppet board, which rarely meets.

And so, the skids are greased by George W. Bush's fast-track legislation and by AEDPA (Anti-Terrorism and Effective Death Penalty Act) for the Texas death machine to roll at a rate unprecedented since the Great Depression. Local trial judges set the execution dates once appeals have been exhausted at the state and federal levels. Governors have no technical responsibility for the increased numbers of human beings escorted to the gurney in downtown Huntsville for the lethal injection. Or do they? How much state sanctioned murder can be justified by the politics of fear? And where might it lead a nation?

The human faces of no mercy

The execution of those with mental illness or "the insane" is clearly prohibited by international law. Virtually every country in the world prohibits the execution of people with mental illness.

The UN Safeguards Guaranteeing Protection of the Rights of those Facing the Death Penalty, adopted by the UN Economic and Social Council resolution of May 25, 1984, states: "...nor shall the death sentence be carried out...on persons who have become insane."

In 1997, the UN Special Rapporteur on Extrajudicial, Summary or Arbitrary Executions stated that governments that continue to use the death penalty "with respect to minors and the mentally ill are particularly called upon to bring their domestic legislation into conformity with international legal standards."

In April 2000, the UN Commission on Human Rights urged all states that maintain the death penalty "not to impose it on a person suffering from any form of mental disorder; not to execute any such person."

U.S. constitutional law is in line with some of these international safeguards. The execution of the insane — someone who does not understand the reason for, or the reality of, his or her punishment — violates the U.S. Constitution (*Ford v Wainwright*, 1986)."[7]

Joe Cannon: childhood schizophrenia, abuse, brain damage

On September 30, 1977, Joe Cannon shot San Antonio attorney Anne Carabin Walsh as she pled for mercy.

Cannon, a 17-year-old parolee, whom Walsh's brother Dan Carabin had helped get released, and whom she'd taken into her home because he had no family to speak of, shot her six times, leaving her eight children motherless.

The family learned later that Joe Cannon suffered from brain damage and atrocious childhood abuse, had been diagnosed with childhood schizophrenia at age 5, and was removed from public school during the first grade. At age 10 and 15 psychiatrists recommended he be placed in a mental hospital. The victim's family contends the state did a lousy job of investigating Cannon's problems, which included drug abuse, and the potential for danger in releasing him.

The victim's whole family wanted Cannon's execution, which occurred in April, 1998, after a ten-minute delay blamed on a collapsed vein. Pope John Paul II sent an appeal to Bush. The foreign affairs committee of the Italian Parliament asked for an end to the death penalty. Cannon expressed regret and said he wanted people to know he had repented. Cannon was 37 when he was killed after twenty years on the row.

In the ten years preceding Cannon's execution the only countries to execute persons whose crimes were committed when they were minors were Iran, Iraq, Nigeria, Pakistan, Saudi Arabia, Yemen and the United States. Cannon was both mentally ill and a minor when he committed the crime.

Johnny Frank Garrett: chronic extreme sexual abuse, multiple personality disorder

Johnny Frank Garrett was eventually diagnosed as a multiple personality by Yale-trained psychiatrist and violence specialist Dorothy Otnow Lewis. In 1982 he, like Cannon, was just old enough to be "death-worthy." He was seventeen when he raped and stabbed to death an elderly nun in her room in the Amarillo convent where she'd spent most of her life. The good sisters of St. Francis found the thought of an intruder who would rape and murder one of their own impossible to believe. When Sister Catherine's blood-stained, nude body was discovered in her room after she didn't appear for morning services, they sent her off to the morgue without calling the police, assuming a heart attack had overcome her in the night. It was only later in the day, when one of the nuns spotted the broken window and slit screen in a hall, that foul play was considered.

Garrett, like Cannon, had recently been released from a facility for juvenile delinquents. The night of the crime he had spent time at the home of his grandmother and mother. Based on interviews and psychiatric analysis, Dorothy Otnow Lewis postulated that a multiple personality had taken over, triggered by a psychosis re-stimulated by whatever happened during that visit. She traced the psychotic break back to early years of unspeakable physical, emotional and sexual abuse at the hands of the grandmother (who may have had multiple personalities herself) and to a lesser extent the grandfather, who sexually abused Garrett. There was also a long history of sexual abuse by stepfathers and adults to whom Garrett was prostituted as a child.

Otnow Lewis believed this chronic abuse provoked disassociation in the form of multiple personalities, so that when Garrett denied raping and killing the nun, he was sincere. He couldn't literally remember it because other personalities (alters) had taken over. One of his alters had appeared during childhood when he was being repeatedly raped, to "take my pain" because he was tough, he could stand it. The name of this split-off self was Aaron Shockman.

Otnow Lewis interviewed and videotaped Garrett for a final time in January 1992, a month before he was executed. The video tapes were presented to the Board of Pardons and Paroles as evidence of Garrett's split personality. This extraordinary in-person hearing of a board that never convenes was engineered by Governor Richards, to take the onus off her to respond to clemency pleas from the Pope and many organizations in the U.S. and Europe. The Board ignored all mitigating evidence of horrific abuse presented by relatives and social workers, as well as Garrett's taped interview. It took them 45 minutes to vote 17/0 with one abstention to deny clemency, hardly even time to glance at the material. Otnow Lewis was stunned by the process.

Garrett believed his Aunt Barbara, who lived within him as one of his "alters" or alternate personalities, would save him from execution by taking the poison herself. In fact, on the gurney, the personality which presented itself acted like the tough alter Aaron Shockman, who after sending love to Garrett's mother, told the guards and wardens they could "kiss my ass."

Otnow Lewis reported (and documented on videotape) that Garrett's personalities not only spoke with different accents and degrees of sophistication, each had different facial features and handwriting.

The psychiatrist finally understood why Garrett had picked an elderly nun on that particular night as his victim. When puzzling over the case after his death, she picked up the fat notebook of mitigating evidence prepared for the clemency hearing, which she herself had not had time to read. An affidavit from a cousin Garrett's age, who had also been dumped by her mother at the grandparents' door snapped the last pieces of the puzzle in place. Garrett had only mentioned through his alter Shockman that he had suffered "too much love" from the older couple, blaming a stepfather for a terrible burn on his backside from being held on a white-hot gas heater as a young child. The cousin mentioned that incident in her statement. She said his screams as his grandmother held him there had been the worst she'd ever heard, and went on to detail a dizzying range of abuse by the grandparents best left unrepeated. The cousin found this abuse all the more unforgivable since both her mother and Garrett's had sent them toward it knowing full well what it was like from their own experience of it when they were children.[8]

Dennis Dowthitt: severe mental problems

Dennis Dowthitt was 55 on March 7, 2001, when he finally, on the gurney, admitted his guilt and remorse to the family of two slain girls from Montgomery County. He murdered Gracie Purnhagen, a 16-year-old who was dating his son, and her nine-year-old sister Tiffany. The oldest he raped with a bottle and slit her throat. He strangled the younger girl.

From the beginning Dennis Dowthitt had blamed his teenage son Delton, who at first admitted killing both girls, but later recanted, saying his father had intimidated him into taking credit for both, when he'd only strangled Tiffany Purnhagen.

The jury was denied critical information: the son had earlier raped another teen, and he told a number of people that he killed both girls. His testimony against his father in a plea bargain arrangement netted him a sentence of 45 years in the pen. Dowthitt was condemned to die in 1992.

An Amnesty International report on the case alleged that the elder Dowthitt:

> . . . suffered from mental illness since he was a teenager. His original trial lawyers did not investigate this issue, or the abuse he

suffered as a child, to present in mitigation. One of several mental health experts who have assessed Dowthitt since his conviction, concluded that his profile was 'consistent with paranoid and schizophrenic features'. A second expert has stated that the tapes of Dennis Dowthitt's interrogation showed his 'severe mental problems'. She also said that he 'functions quite peacefully and successfully within the prison environment', undermining the jury's finding of his likely future dangerousness, a prerequisite for the death sentence in Texas. Dennis Dowthitt is reported to have been a model prisoner for the nine years he has been on death row. His only disciplinary write-up was for having hung a sheet in front of the toilet in his cell on 11 November 1997.[9]

Jerry Lee Griffin: "something told me"

A Houston man, whose case received little public attention at all, but who may also have been a multiple personality and had for sure been a mental patient before he committed murder, was executed in November 1992. Jeffery Lee Griffin in March of 1979 killed the 19-year-old night manager of a north Houston convenience store and a seven-year-old errand boy with a deer hunting knife because he said once he entered the store, "something told (me) to do it." Griffin was black, 24 at the time, with an education of seventh grade or less. Unfortunately for understanding what motivated Griffin, no Dorothy Otnow Lewis appeared to help unravel the threads that led him to the gurney.

James Edward Smith: serious doubts about mental competency

Another Houston death row inmate, James Edward Smith, who'd killed an insurance executive during a robbery in 1983, waived his appeals. His mother carried the case to the US Supreme Court, where in June of 1990 four justices felt there were "serious doubts about Smith's mental competency to make such a decision." But though the four votes were enough to order a review of the case by the highest court in the land, they couldn't stop his death date. Justice William J. Brennan, Jr. wrote: "For the first time in recent memory, a man will be executed after the court has decided to hear his claim."

Jasdeep Singh Basra: increasing despondency

In a more recent Houston case, an Indian of college age, Jasdeep Singh Basra, confessed after failing a polygraph test that he had beaten his parents to death with a baseball bat, then set the bedroom on fire. A relative mentioned that the parents had discussed sending their son to a psychological counselor because of increasing despondency and inability to work or attend college. Singh was indicted by a grand jury for capital murder. Too bad for him his parents hadn't migrated to Norway, or even New York, instead of Texas.[10]

Jermarr Arnold: insane in Colorado, insane in California, but sane enough for trial and execution in Texas

Jermarr Arnold volunteered for Texas death row from a California prison in 1988. He wrote the Nueces County D.A.'s office saying he had information about the identity of a man known as Troy Alexander, seen in the vicinity of a jewelry store where "Cricket" Sanchez was killed in 1983. She had been killed by a shot which entered the top of her head. He asked to be extradited to Texas to lead detectives to the murder weapon, confessed he was Alexander, and at trial blew off his attorney's advice and told jurors if acquitted he would kill again.

There was no physical evidence to tie him to the crime and the murder weapon didn't manifest after all. The top assistant prosecutor in the county refused to prosecute him and resigned later, believing that Arnold was trying to get the state to kill him.

Arnold had a bizarre past. He'd been an outstanding and well-rounded student in high school who won a journalism scholarship to college. The summer before he would have enrolled at the University of Kansas his grandmother died. He flipped out and raped two women at knifepoint. A psychiatrist said the rapes resulted from a psychotic schizophrenic episode; and adjudged him insane, therefore not guilty; and sent him to the maximum-security ward of the state mental hospital in Colorado.

However, the security was flawed. During a transfer between wards, Arnold escaped and, according to him, wound up first in Corpus Christi where he killed Cricket Sanchez, then in Los Angeles, where he robbed two banks, sans disguise. Sentenced to three years in California, he engaged in self-mutilation, set himself on fire and attacked other inmates.

He was transferred to the Medical Facility in Vacaville for psychiatric evaluation, where he slashed an inmate's throat and privates and cut off his eyelids, an attack for which Arnold was acquitted by reason of insanity.[11]

That's when Arnold applied for extradition to Texas, the hot spot state for death penalties. A Corpus Christi jury obliged with a death verdict. Once on Texas death row, Arnold stabbed Maurice Andrews in the head with a sharpened bolt.

When asked directly by *Dallas Morning News* veteran crime reporters Dan Malone and Howard Swindle if he'd killed Ms. Sanchez, Arnold pondered a moment before replying, "I really don't know ... In the past, I've had episodes where I thought I was somewhere else and I was someone else that seemed very real to me."[12]

The criminal investigator assigned to his case, an experienced woman whose fiancé was slain by a man sent to death row for the crime, a woman who favors capital punishment, believes Arnold is clearly insane and should not be where he is.

She described to the *Dallas Morning News* reporters what happened when she told Arnold she'd located some members of his family, after he'd maintained he had none. She says his face changed instantly and remarkably, he uttered a "guttural" sound, and she perceived a strange smell. The hairs stood up on the back of her neck, and she found herself wanting to leave real fast.[13] Later she said it beat her how a person can be insane in Colorado, insane in California, but sane enough for trial and execution in Texas.

Don't look to the Texas Legislature for help, or the Governor

In the spring of 2001, advocates of the mentally retarded inmates of Texas death row were feeling mildly optimistic that a bill to ban the execution of those with recorded intelligence quotients under 70 would pass. A similar measure had come quite close in the previous session in 1999, and if not for the opposition of George W. Bush probably would have become law. When Lois Robison asked why a provision to ban the execution of people who are mentally ill couldn't be included in the same bill, she was told it would kill the bill.[14]

There's always been a peculiar attitude in Texas toward mental illness, a stigma that perhaps explains the abysmally-low funding levels for services to the mentally ill. Texas ranked 42 in the Union in per-resident expenditures for mental health care in 1999 according to the vice president of the National Mental Health Association.[15] Larry Robison preferred a premature death by poison to the shame of going through an appeal for clemency based on declaring himself mentally incompetent. Even an inmate with a low IQ, like Oliver Cruz, expressed his dismay at the characterization intended to save his life; but for people like Robison, of high, if damaged, intelligence, the label added insult to a life already steeped in humiliation. Others like Johnny Paul Penry wouldn't know what an IQ is.

Chapter Six:
Larry Robison

Lois Robison, Mother of Larry

> "*Last in funding for mental illness, first in executing the mentally ill.*"[1]
>
> Lois Robison

Threnody

Lois Robison is mom and apple pie, a third grade teacher who's retired now, plump, curly white hair surrounding a pretty, and a pleasant be-spectacled face. Her story is enough to drive any parent mad: years of having her son turned out of mental hospitals and treatment programs that couldn't keep him because he wasn't violent.

The details of the story read like classic Greek tragedy. The inherent flaw in her son was biochemical, an inherited disease, paranoid schizophrenia, that no one in his immediate family knew ran in the dead father's lineage until after the son lost control over the voices. Listening to her recount it, two days after the state of Texas had led her son Larry Robison to the gurney and activated the mechanical process that released lethal chemicals into his body still in its prime, was like being in the audience of a Sophocles play, listening to the lament following the inescapable tragic climax of the drama. The word "threnody"[2] comes to mind.

Larry was born in Abilene, in Northwest Texas, on August 12, 1957, and moved to Kansas when he was seven with his natural mother Lois and adoptive father Ken and their blended family of eight children. His biological father, an alcoholic, was dead of a brain tumor by the time the boy was two. Lois left her ancestral family home in Huntsville, where decades later she would wait for the state to kill her son, to attend college at Abilene Christian. A minister at the church Lois and Ken both attended in Abilene knew both of them were single parents and suggested they might hit it off. Lois took the initiative by sitting beside Ken one morning and says the rest is history. She adds with a big smile that he's the best thing that ever happened to her.

Larry was a model child and student until he was twelve: loving, smart (straight A's), tested out in the top 2% in intelligence, was on the swim team, played percussion in the band and was a Boy Scout. A nasty fall resulting in a concussion when he was a toddler didn't seem to have hurt him. Much later, after Larry was convicted, Ken and Lois learned that he had been sexually abused from the age of five by an older child who had himself been abused by an adult. When he was twelve, his half brother was kidnapped by the birth mother. Larry's grades dropped and he started acting out in class, playing hooky. Lois and Ken tried to get help from Family and Child Services in Kansas City, where Ken was teaching Spanish at the time; but the staff there missed the problem and thought Larry was normal. Psychologists interviewing Robison on death row, after the Supreme Court ordered evaluation for mental competency for execution just days short of a scheduled death date, concluded that Robison's high intelligence had enabled him to hide his mental illness and delude examiners, which was not unusual.

After Larry tried to run away when he was 15, the worried parents took him to the psychiatric department at the University of Kansas Medical Center, where the diagnosis was "adolescent adjustment reaction." Testing and diagnosis were incomplete, though he saw a psychologist for a year. The disease was developing; it is typical for paranoid schizophrenia in males that it becomes evident in the years between 15 and 25. When he was 16, Larry and his younger brother Steve were beaten up on a playground just a few blocks from home. The neighborhood had turned violent. There were racial tensions and a lot of drugs available. The perpetrators went to trial and were convicted. There were threats on the Robison boy's lives. Ken Robison resigned his job the night of the attack and the family moved to a small town just south of Fort Worth, Texas, a safer haven they thought, though Ken took a large pay cut as a result.

Larry, meanwhile, was self-medicating as is frequently the case with the mentally ill. He admitted to abuse of alcohol, pot, and eventually speed and hallucinogens, as well as anything else he could get his hands on, sometimes financed by petty theft. He dropped out of high school his senior year and joined the Air Force, thinking it would keep him out of trouble. He tested very high and went into jet engine mechanics. A year later he called from Amsterdam to say he had been honorably discharged, though he'd been caught stealing gas for his vehicle. His mother believes the Air Force knew he had severe mental problems and discharged him to avoid paying for long-term treatment. Looking back, she also says his age at the time was about right for the inherited disease to manifest in a blatant manner.

During his Air Force service he experienced his first psychotic break. He heard voices and believed he could move objects with his mind, that he had special powers. But when he returned to his parents' home in Burleson, twenty miles from Fort Worth, they at first believed they had "the old Larry back."[3] When he built a plywood pyramid and insisted on sleeping under it, they thought he was just experimenting. It was the dawn of the "New Age" culture, and such ideas permeated a certain age and lifestyle group.

Trying to get help for a mentally ill son

Within a few weeks Larry moved to Fort Worth and got a construction job. He lived in apartments, usually with roommates, and made occasional visits to his family, who were clueless as to how sick he was. Occasionally he would call and say, "You've got to come,"[4] and then not remember why they arrived. He married an exotic snake dancer, whom his mother believes was also mentally ill. Once his landlady called and told Lois her daughter-in-law was violent and might hurt Larry. Then he called saying the same thing. Ken and Lois drove over to get him. While Larry was collecting his things, the woman appeared with a male friend and tried to get him to stay. There was a lot of yelling and Lois called the police, who told her son to make up his mind, to go one way or the other. Larry stayed. Lois says she was "terrified they'd kill him. It was days before we knew he was alive. I nearly lost my mind. Then he called to say his roommates had stolen his car, that the woman was doing him wrong."[5] Another time he called and told her to come get him; she took the police with her that time. When they arrived Larry's head was bandaged. He said she'd run him down with a car.

They divorced. He was depressed and delusional. In November of 1978 he again called his parents to come get him saying people in the drugstore were following him and knew his thoughts. When they got home he and his brother went out to play football with friends. After a few minutes Larry returned and said he had to go back to his apartment. Later Larry's brother told their parents Larry had "forgotten" how to play football. While they were talking Larry called again, said he was flying out of his body, that the CIA and Air Force were after him. Lois called the emergency room of the hospital and said they would be bringing him in. His roommate at the time told her he was relieved. He said the Halloween punch had been spiked with LSD but Larry was the only one who'd had a psychotic reaction to it. On the way to the emergency room, Larry confessed he'd killed someone but he hadn't meant to, using the power from his head to explode a man's car.

The emergency room doctor came out fast and told the family Larry had the worst case of schizophrenia he'd ever seen, that Larry needed long term care because he was very ill. The Doctor asked for insurance. Larry had turned 22 shortly before the incident, and was no longer on his parents' insurance. The cost to hospitalize him in a private residential treatment program was around $200 a day. With a large family, Ken's teacher's salary and Lois in school, there was no way they could do it. The state didn't have the political will to adequately fund mental health services, though the per capita income was high relative to other states which did much more for the mentally ill. This was still Bubba land, where most people wouldn't let it be known they were seeing a psychologist, much less a psychiatrist, and if someone went off to a mental hospital they were stigmatized for life.

The Robisons drove Larry to the John Peter Smith County Hospital with his brother on one side of him and a buddy on the other in the car.

They were kept waiting seven hours once they got to the hospital. All the while, Larry kept repeating he had to get out of there, people were trying to hurt him. When they finally got in to the examining room, Lois kept asking the doctor if they could help her son. The doctor said he wanted overt symptoms. She said, "That's easy. He's talking about Charles Manson."[6]

Three days later the hospital put Larry in an open ward from which he called a friend who brought him drugs. Lois learned about it during Larry's first trial when staff at the hospital testified they thought his mother had brought drugs to her son. The parents asked the staff a lot of questions, like "How should we react when he says he hears voices?"[7] but the doctors wouldn't tell them anything, citing the privacy act. After three weeks the hospital called to tell Lois they were going to discharge Larry and under no circumstances should they take him back home with them, as he was too dangerous.

She asked what should they do with him? The reply: Put him on the streets, we do it all the time. Lois replied, "He has no job, no car, no money, no home. We can't do that."[8] They sent him home on thorazine and haldol, which had "terrible side effects. He walked like a zombie."[9]

Frantic, she called a place downtown where she'd heard people were admitted in similar conditions. They said they couldn't take him unless he was violent. Lois asked if he could get in the Veterans Hospital in Waco. It turned out he could be admitted there but the family would have to take him to the hospital. They talked Larry into voluntarily signing in. Two weeks later there was a collect call. Larry had run away. He said he'd been treated badly and he'd kill himself if he had to go back. Lois spoke to a woman near Larry at the payphone and asked her to watch where he went. She said it took longer to get the hospital to agree to go pick him up than it had taken to talk him into voluntarily returning if they did.

A few weeks later, they got another call, saying they were going to discharge her son and he'd be returning home on a bus that morning at 11. "Is he well?" she asked. "No, and if he doesn't get treatment, he'll get worse. We can't keep him over 30 days if he isn't violent." She asked the doctor, "What am I supposed to do?"[10] The answer: he could be an outpatient at MHMR. Another Catch 22 sequence followed. It would be three weeks before they could get him in for an intake interview. Then they got another call from the discharging physician, explaining his hospital had forgotten to get Larry to sign for release of his records, and only MHMR could put him back on the medication he needed.

The hospital had sent him home with two weeks worth of medication. By the time the necessary records arrived for MHMR to prescribe meds, Larry had been off them for a month, was paranoid, and thought someone was trying to poison him. By the time his date with an examining MHMR physician rolled around, Larry had disappeared, borrowed his sister's car, drove it into a ditch, appropriated a rental truck, was chased down in Weatherford and arrested for felony theft. His parents left him in jail there for six months, while Lois talked to his attorney and begged another doctor to commit Larry to the treatment "everyone says he needs."[11] She got the same answer: unless he was violent, they couldn't help him. She says among all those she consulted no one ever told her Larry should take psychiatric medication every day.

Determined, she called every agency in a very thick directory of social service agencies in North Texas. On the last page, she found a man at VOA (Volunteers of America) in Burleson who would listen to her. VOA had a facility that was a halfway house for probationers. Larry lived there a year. But the VOA didn't understand Larry's problem either. Larry got a construction job, moved out, met a girl, got her pregnant, visited his family on holidays. He was not taking any medication. On Mother's Day that year, she thought "a miracle had happened and he was better."[12] But she was wrong. He soon had one of his episodes and was jailed briefly. Although he hadn't used drugs in several months, the delusions and paranoia had a life of their own.

On release, Larry, who was just short of 26 years old, decided he'd go to Kansas because his girlfriend and baby were there with her family, where she'd gone because Larry's psychotic thinking was scaring her. He was unable to find work in Kansas but the couple decided to reconcile. The woman gave notice at her job and Larry returned to Texas in August of 1982 with his sister Vicky, who'd driven up to get him. He was thinking he could get construction work again. He had a letter from a friend offering him a place to stay in Lake Worth. His sister dropped him off at the friend's house. He visited her on Friday the ninth, they learned later, with an intent to kill her. He'd bought a gun earlier and had it with him, but struggled with the impulse. He said he was going to his parents' home and she called them later to see if he'd arrived safely. He hadn't come. Apparently if he had, they would have been history; but again he'd averted the murderous voices. His mother called him that night, invited him to come home on his birthday on the 12th and asked what he'd like for his gift. He told her he didn't need anything.

On August 11, Lois helped one of her daughters buy supplies to begin her first teaching job. Lois and Ken had been getting counseling for months from a graduate student at the Bright Divinity Center at TCU for their concerns over Larry's situation. The young counselor had been advising her to stop being a mother hen, that her son was over 21 and she needn't worry about him so much. She met Ken outside the counseling center that afternoon at the appointed time and told him what she'd heard on the radio — that a "Larry Keith Robinson had been extradited from Wichita, Kansas," but she was puzzled because she thought Larry was in Texas. Ken stumbled and nearly fell flat on his face, saying "Oh no, no, no . . . I don't want to tell you."[13]

He had heard people discussing at the office the news about a terrible multiple murder at Lake Worth and that someone had been arrested for it in Kansas, but no one had caught the name. He hadn't put it together. She told the counselor what she'd heard; he turned white. They called home and their daughter Vicky answered the phone. She said, "Where have you been? We've been trying to find you all day long! The reporters are calling."[14]

Lois said that the counselor couldn't wait to get them out of his office. "It hit the five o'clock news and our friends from church started pouring into our house. We had never kept Larry's mental illness a secret. They all knew how hard we'd tried to get help for him."[15] Vicky had recognized the house on the front page of the paper that morning as the place she'd dropped Larry off to stay when she brought him home from Kansas.

The next day, on Larry's 26th birthday, while Lois and Ken were being interviewed by three television stations, he called home from jail in Kansas, and the first words out of his mouth, according to Lois, who says it's all she can remember now of that conversation, were "Mom, I'm so sorry, I'm so sorry."[16] His birthday card was lying on a table in the room where the interviews were taking place. After the third interview, she fell apart, telling Ken she couldn't do it anymore.

Larry's first and only recorded episode of violence, toward humans at least, was newsworthy indeed. That day in Lake Worth just northwest of Cowtown, on August 10, 1982, he sexually mutilated, decapitated, ferociously stabbed and shot, and perhaps cannibalized his 31-year-old roommate Ricky Lee Bryant, whom the media and trial witnesses described as his homosexual lover. His mother said he was just a friend whose amorous overtures the night before had seriously disturbed Larry, perhaps harkening back to the childhood sexual abuse from an older boy. He then "fingerpainted"[17] with the victim's blood on the walls.

Next door he killed a woman in her thirties, her mother and her young daughter, then shot her boyfriend when he arrived. Afterwards he sat over the corpses a couple of hours, waiting for them to come back to life and thank him, as he'd been told that they would by the voices which directed the slaughter, for saving their souls.

When that didn't happen, he cleaned himself up, took some of the victims' jewelry, wallets, and a car, bought more ammunition, and drove to Kansas. He was apprehended in the middle of the night in the parking lot of a church in Kansas City, where he'd pulled over to sleep. He'd been spotted by a policewoman, who called his license plate in and found there was an APB out on it. He told someone later he was trying to find the psychiatrist who'd treated him in his teens, hoping the man could explain to him why his acts hadn't produced the expected result. He readily confessed to the crime, and in fact had one of the murder weapons with him, the gun he'd bought a few days earlier to prepare for his mission of killing people to save their souls. His goal was 2,000 deaths.

Larry told police in Kansas that two weeks earlier he had bought a machete in Wichita, Kansas and lured a dog into a garage, where he killed it and drank its blood. Later he related his struggle with the voices telling him to kill his hosts and friends in Wichita before he left there. Later they told him to kill his sister and parents, his common-law wife and their daughter. He said the voices had been telling him to kill since that first psychotic episode in the Air Force. He had resisted them for four years. Even in 1999, when interviewed by teams evaluating his mental competency, Larry Robison believed that, though what he had done was legally wrong, he had saved the souls of his victims and it was all okay in the big picture.

A mother's nightmare: powerless but guilty nonetheless

After the terrible crime in Fort Worth, Larry Robison finally qualified for long term care. What he got was confinement in prison, first in Tarrant County, where the crime was committed, then post-trial, on death row, in the Ellis Unit outside Huntsville, until a deadly mix of chemicals ended his life at age 42 on January 21, 2000.

But before Larry Robison became Number 99 on George W. Bush's execution list, and Number 203 in the state since the resumption of executions in 1982 (the same year he dispatched five persons on his soul-saving mission) there were two trials and many tribulations, as well as many appeals on his behalf. Ken Robison speaks in his quiet way, telling the reporter two days after his adopted son's death-by-poisoning that Larry spent the year after arrest on the psychiatric floor of the Tarrant County jail. The family brought him lots of books and smuggled in pieces of kids' crayons for him to draw with. Larry wrote the judge that he wanted a speedy trial, as the Constitution guarantees. He was in a solid steel cell with a closed porthole, no radio, no television. A week after he was jailed, one of the houses in which the murders occurred burned down. Larry heard about it and smiled, saying he believed he had done it. He slit his arm twice with a razor given him for shaving. He was rushed to the hospital and given transfusions and plastic surgery. They gave him medication and he saved it all up, took it at once. They pumped his stomach and saved him again. The state is very protective of its turf.

The first court-appointed trial attorneys told the Robisons they thought the best they could get for Larry was life, since most people thought he should be killed for what he'd done. Lois says it was clear the attorney who relayed that information shared that opinion. They kept telling Lois not to let the jurors know when she testified that Larry had spent any time in jail or on probation. She knew they would already have that information, and she wasn't in the habit of lying, so it put her in a terrible position because the defense was telling her if she let that information slip she was putting her own son on death row. The prosecutor, Tarrant County assistant District Attorney Larry Moore, said Lois was lying about her battle to find help for her son; that she always "got him off " that way, and urged the jury not to "let her get away with it."[18] The tension was terrible, and shortly before the jury found Larry guilty of capital murder, after a day of cross-examination in that vein, she collapsed outside the courtroom. "They couldn't get a pulse."[19] She felt that it would be her fault if Larry were condemned because she'd testified badly. She spent the next four days in the hospital and was sedated when both the guilty and the death verdicts came in. Ken had to tell her.

After another week of bed rest at home, anger began to swell up in her. "Larry had begged us for help; we had begged everyone. People don't know you can't get help; that we kill the mentally ill. I vowed I'd get on T.V. and in the *Reader's Digest*" to tell Larry's story, the terrible futile search for help before he exploded in a day of carnage that left five people dead.

A 1998 article in the journal *Psychological Services* reports that "clinical studies suggest that 6 to 15 percent of persons in city and county jails and 10 to 15 percent of persons in state prisons have severe mental illness."[20] E. Fuller Torrey, M.D., a schizophrenia expert and former special assistant to the Director of the National Institute of Mental Health, indicates that it was not until the mid-eighties that researchers on the illness began to get adequate funds to discover structural evidence of damage inside the brain linked to the disease, evidence showing an actual shrinking of the brain or change in size of ventricles, for example, or altered electrical patterns.[21]

An Amnesty International report on Larry Robison's case points out that to establish legal insanity the defense had to prove that at the time of the murders, Robison's mental illness "deprived him of the knowledge that his actions were wrong and of the ability to conform his conduct to the requirements of the law."[22] But Robison 's illness was such that at times over the years after arrest he was lucid and appeared sane and at others entirely delusional. How could one establish in a fluctuating field from the past, exactly what his mental condition had been on the day in question? And there was an even heavier burden on the defense in the sentencing phase, because Texas law prohibits telling a jury the result of declaring a defendant not guilty by reason of insanity.

If the jurors were free to assume, for instance, that he could be out, free to butcher and mutilate again, there's no way they'd declare him not guilty. The average juror would feel protection of society from an established multiple murderer far outweighed the protection of the constitutional rights of the accused. Even though a federal court ruled in *Lyles* v. *U.S.* in 1957 that jurors have the right to such knowledge, the principle has not been raised to the level of a constitutional right by the Supreme Court. Texas doesn't honor it; and Larry Robison was sentenced to death, no matter what the jury believed about his mental condition at the time of the offense.

After he arrived on death row on September 9, 1983, Larry wrote the judge asking to stop all appeals and to set his death date.

Seventeen years of anguish, then more of the same

Instead, an appellate attorney from Fort Worth whom the Robisons believe is excellent, Allan Butcher, found a reason for reversal that, within months of sentencing, convinced the sitting judges of the Court of Criminal Appeals. A juror had been seated who had said in advance he didn't believe in the insanity defense. Five years after the first trial, Larry was retried.

This time, the defense had something besides Lois's testimony to offer the jury to bolster his claim of mental illness. An aunt on Larry's father's side had been trying to find Lois since she'd seen her on the Oprah show talking about Larry's case. She told the Robisons that Larry's paternal uncle and a grandfather had both been mentally ill. One had tried to shoot his wife. A cousin had three mentally ill children. Because the stigma around mental illness is so harsh, the rest of the family hadn't wanted her to make it known. It was a family secret.

Larry's new court-appointed attorneys, Sherry Hill and David Bays, did better than the first trial team, but they made mistakes. It was Hill's first capital case. The male attorney mis-advised them on one count. He said they didn't need Larry's medical records, what they needed was a witness; but in court, the judge wouldn't allow the witness to testify without the medical records. The D.A. argued the killings were strictly caused by Robison's drug abuse. The second jury never heard of the genetic trend to madness in the family. The battle lines stayed essentially the same from 1982 until January of 2000 when Larry waived all appeals and surrendered to a death he saw as freedom from death row. The prosecution blamed a drug addict for the crime. The family blamed the untreated mental illness.

Once again, the Robison family sat outside a courtroom not knowing what was going on inside, because they were to be used as witnesses in the trial and couldn't be inside except during their own testimony. Once again, Larry was condemned to death, despite medical and genetic evidence, probably because that evidence never reached the jury. Once again Allan Butcher took up his cause and believed he had even better chances of reversal from the second sentence because his client was so obviously insane.

One of Larry's sisters, Carol, was diagnosed with a form of schizophrenia about a year after that second trial. Lois raced to the attorney, hoping this would be grounds for a new trial. But she was informed that since the "new evidence" came in more than 30 days after the sentence was passed, it was therefore irrelevant. And as for the direct appeal itself (which can only be based on errors in the conduct of the convicting trial), the Court of Criminal Appeals by the time that second appeal reached it had begun to change, reflecting the political tenor of the time. "Tough on crime" candidates for judicial as well as other offices were bumping off even well-seated incumbents, if they could accuse them of "coddling criminals" convicted of violence, especially if drugs were involved. The Court rejected the direct appeal.

In 1999, a woman whose background is in the ministry and law, Melodee Smith, a Florida attorney who worked as a trial lawyer and as an appellate lawyer on clemency issues in capital cases, took up the Robison case, without pay, bringing with her outside resources, and a passion for Larry's cause. She had met Lois and Ken though Journey of Hope, a group of victim and offender family members who work together to heal themselves and society in the context of the restorative justice movement.

In August, despite intense national and international public and media attention on Robison's plight as his date with the needle neared, the Texas Board of Pardons and Paroles voted 17-0 to deny his clemency appeal. When the Supreme Court stayed his execution just hours before the deed was to be done so there could be a mental competency hearing, his parents were arriving at a restaurant in Huntsville where his allies had gathered. As they walked up, they heard an outcry inside and Melodee came racing out to tell them, cell phone to ear, that a reprieve had been granted. They had already managed the last visit with him, and expected to leave the restaurant to gather at a church for a memorial service. Instead, they held a celebration there. In retrospect, Lois says in the long run the stay was cruel to Larry, who had to prepare twice for his unnatural death.

Melodee returned to Florida but called Lois a few days later on Saturday from the road when she heard the trial court had just set the hearing to establish the parameters for the competency hearing for 9:30 that Monday morning. She said she had to return or Larry was a dead duck, with only the somewhat disinterested court-appointed attorney to plead his cause. Lois said, "You can't drive back – you've just spent 15 hours driving away from here. We'll fly you down."[23] She called a friend with a travel agency who went in on the weekend and found a flight for Smith Sunday night. Monday morning Smith had just gotten out of the shower, hair dripping wet, when she got a call saying the time had been moved up to 9 A.M. They raced down to the court, arriving just minutes before the hearing. There she went "toenail to toenail" with the prosecutor, assistant D.A. Greg Pipes. He wanted to set the hearing a week away, too soon to allow for any meaningful mental evaluation, and to have a mere "paper hearing" with no witnesses, without Larry present, no new examination of her client, just some doctors somewhere reading his records. The prosecution told her, "That's the way it's done in Texas." She replied, "Maybe you need to learn the way it should be done, the way it's done everywhere else."[24] She demanded the doctors actually examine Larry. She got the extension she needed. The family got to choose three doctors, the prosecution two, the judge one for the hearing that fall.

One of those on the defense side who volunteered his expertise was Anthony G. Hempel, from the state mental hospital in Terrell, who was infuriated by the state's treatment of the mentally ill inmate patients he was seeing at his hospital. Some were arriving almost dead from the heat in non-air-conditioned vans during the summer, for example, when patients on psychotropic drugs can't take such temperature extremes. Mentally ill, overweight and diabetic, Emile Duhamel died on Texas death row in the heat wave of the summer of 1998.

In a report on Larry Robison, which indicated that he had reviewed the paper trail on Robison, conducted an 8-hour interview with him, interviewed Lois Robison for four hours and attorney Robert Hagar for two, Dr. Hempel wrote that Robison "still experiences auditory and visual hallucinations. It is my belief that Mr. Robison was sincere in his delusional beliefs and that his bizarre statements are his way of comprehending and making sense out of his psychotic symptoms. At times he could mention the hearing of voices."[25] He says Robison described his struggle with the commanding voices persuading him to kill, but believes "his killings were so he could 'save their souls from damnation.' 'They are now protected souls.' 'I wasn't going to get any peace until I killed those people.' "[26]

Hempel's diagnosis, unsurprisingly, was "chronic paranoid schizophrenia" and he asserted his opinion that Robison "was experiencing severe psychotic symptoms immediately before and during the crimes he committed." Hempel cited from an article he'd co-authored in the *Journal of the American Academy of Psychiatry and the Law*[27] the fact that 40% of "mass murderers...exhibit psychotic symptoms at the time of their mass murder." He cited the "brutal overkill as evidenced by the multiple gunshot wounds to the victims and an extreme number of stabbings to the victims' dead bodies" to back up his claim that psychosis ruled Robison's actions.

The Robisons spent $15,000 on Larry's clemency appeal. Ken Robison is still teaching, at age 70, as a result. The Robisons didn't know there hasn't been a single grant of clemency at an inmate's request since 1973, or they could have saved their money and their false hopes.

Larry was executed on a cold, damp January Friday evening, a night he'd chosen because it was a full moon, a choice offered in exchange for his dropping all his appeals, a deal which his court-appointed attorney Hagar had negotiated with the prosecution. It was a deal his *pro bono* attorney and dedicated advocate Melodee Smith fought futilely and which his mother hated. Interviewed the weekend after Larry's execution, Smith said that his execution hurt like hell because he was a mentally ill man literally dying to get off death row. He made them promise we wouldn't do anything more besides ask for mercy. But he didn't want to be called incompetent. He was ashamed, embarrassed at being thought mentally ill. He'd say, "Melody, we have to surrender to the Divine Will." She'd say: "Do that, but not to the State. It's the State that's killing you." Robison would say "bizarre things, like he didn't have to eat; he could get nutrients like a plant from air and light."[28]

Smith says the death row battles are "not so much about being successful as about being faithful." It's the kind of interpretation you'd expect from an attorney who also wears a minister's robe, but it's also probably the perspective needed to sustain such a fight on such a tilted playing field. Smith felt that employees from the Governor's Office and the Board of Pardons and Paroles were empathetic with Robison's cause. The family was told by someone with an inside track that there wasn't a dry eye among the staffers who had to deal with his case on the night he was executed.

Smith came at times to live with the Robisons in their home in Burleson, gathering papers, making copies, visiting Larry with the family. After Larry's execution was stayed by the Supreme Court justices in August, she arranged for the parents to tour Europe in October, where they spoke to audiences and visited with officials in seven nations, to tremendous acclaim. The European Parliament, the European Union, the governments of those nations and the Pope all requested clemency and commutation from Governor Bush and the Texas Board of Pardons and Paroles. To no avail.

The competency hearing in the fall, with both sides presenting opinions as to Larry's ability to know that his actions were wrong, and that he was going to be executed as a result, ended badly. Unsurprisingly it resulted in a judge's decision that the inmate knew his actions were wrong and why he was to be killed by the State. Bizarre as it might seem to a layperson, it didn't matter in the eyes of Texas law whether or not Larry was mentally ill. The state was not concerned with the fact that Larry had lucid moments. It didn't matter if he could, or couldn't, control the voices and impulses that drove him to murder one day, and the next day to odd, but harmless, delusions. The several prior diagnoses as well as the more current ones of paranoid schizophrenia meant nothing. All the court had to find was that Larry knew killing people was bad and that he'd get the death penalty because of it. It's difficult to imagine a more ignorant interpretation of mental illness than that employed by the courts in Texas.

Larry's time was up.

Robison told his family and other allies he didn't want to die, but if he had to die he was ready and he'd rather go out on the full moon. The full moon date had been suggested to him by one of the strange people death row inmates sometimes attract. A woman, a founder of a nonprofit group, who had participated in a Journey of Hope tour including the Robisons had begun writing their son. Eventually she got his confidence and was a witness at his execution, which she described to Lois's horror at the memorial service for her son as "beautiful" because of the way Larry had "hopped up onto the gurney" and departed passively.[29]

The same woman had been one of the last persons who'd spoken to the condemned man before his death. She had used those last moments to convey to him messages of pain and hatred from the victims' families, information which observers said caused him to fall to the floor wailing, saying he deserved to be killed because he could never wash the blood from his hands. The woman had told Robison a full moon was the best time for his soul to pass to the other side. She had researched and found a map of the stars that would be dominant that night and gotten the map to him, so he could navigate his soul's passage from earth.

No matter if or how he navigated the stars that night, the Governor's decision not to grant a reprieve was conveyed to the defense at 5:30 P.M. A half hour later, Texas executioners pulled the levers that sent poison flowing through tubes into the veins of the mentally ill first-born son of Lois Robison. He never got the medical care he needed. His mother said

— weeping, two days after he was led to the gurney — that in her last visit with him, a few hours before his death, Larry "poured his love for them out of his eyes"[30] as only he could do. He thanked her for giving birth to him, told her he loved her, that she was not to worry, that he'd see her again. Lois says that last week Larry mentioned he believed he was going to be "beamed up to the mother ship."[31]

The State had certified him mentally competent to stand trial and later to be executed, this former mental hospital patient with a progressively deteriorating condition who'd been certified mentally ill in the four years before he attacked five individuals with deadly intent. Texas ranked close to last in per capita funding for mental health services, but as his mother pointed out, headed the list in killing the mentally ill.

Over the years, Lois Robison spotted other children who were headed for disaster, eight year olds in her third grade classroom where she used imagination and gathered resources way beyond the pale to inspire her students to learn. One angry young boy she calls "My little Bobby" was out of control. She began to investigate, and found out what she didn't want to know and his family didn't want to tell: he'd been raped at age four, at least once, and for how long thereafter she doesn't know, by an older boy. Although she tried to get him counseling help, it didn't happen, in part because the family opposed it, in part because the resources just weren't there in the school, with one overburdened psychologist for 600 children. Eventually, Bobby wound up with a life sentence in a Texas prison, for a stabbing death in which he was implicated by accompanying the wrong person at the wrong time. She says this state has got it all wrong. We put our resources at the punitive end, not at the preventive end. She chokes up again, describing her failure to get Bobby the help he needed, any more than she'd been able to find it for her own son.

And this drives Lois Robison nearly mad with grief. Like the educator and nurturer her life has proven her to be, however, she has transformed that rage and grief into leadership. She and Ken direct the Texas chapter of CURE (Citizens United for Reform of Errants), a prisoner advocacy group. They advocate for all Texas prison inmates to be tried and treated in ways consonant with the highest ideals of democracy, human rights and dignity. She and Ken speak and travel throughout the state and anywhere in the world they're invited and can afford to go, telling Larry's story.

Chapter Seven: Anthony Graves (Part 1) Crime and Conviction

Arthur Curry and Demetria Williams, brother and sister of Anthony Graves listening to attorneys explain court proceedings.

Having to live your life as a family member of someone on death row is like being there yourself. Every pain they feel, you feel. In the case of an innocent man serving time, not only does it destroy the life of the accused, it also wipes out the hopes and dreams of a whole family and in the end, everyone loses — no justice, no victory.
                                                    Arthur Curry

Yolanda Mathis, Anthony's only non-family alibi witness was intimidated into silence by a terrifying prosecutorial trick that involved telling the judge, on the day she was to testify, that she was a suspect for the crime of killing six people.

Gravemarker for four-year-old Jason Davis, one of six people killed. August 18, 1992, a shocking and heinous crime.

Photos on this and preceding by Susan Lee Campbell Solar.

The heinous crime

By dawn on Tuesday, August 18, 1992, residents of Burleson County and bordering Washington County in Central Texas, about an hour and a half east of Austin, knew that a horrifying crime had occurred in the middle of the night in Somerville, a town 17 miles north of Brenham, and about that far south of Caldwell. Four small children, ranging in age from four to nine were killed. A popular teenaged female athlete at Somerville High School and her hardworking, talented and well-liked mother who was grandmother of the children, had also been slain. It happened at the grandmother's home between SH 36 and the Santa Fe railroad tracks, in the small town's eastside black neighborhood. The home was set ablaze. Jewel Fisher, the black police chief, spotted the fire while he was cruising in response to a call concerning a prowler nearby.

The fire department was on the scene by 2:20 A.M. The fire was quickly subdued and six bodies were carried out to the lawn and declared dead by the Justice of the Peace within the hour. A nephew of the grandmother, Michael Davis from Houston, who'd been living with the family, entered the home before the bodies were removed and was escorted out by the sheriff, who oddly noted he was "overly upset."[1] The Texas Rangers were called by 4 A.M. because blood had been spotted on the clothing of two of the partially burned girls. The bodies, which had been picked up by a Brenham funeral home, were soon on their way to Travis County, where medical examiner Robert Bayardo determined the cause of death. By mid-morning a DPS Crime Scene Team was heading east from Austin to Burleson County and the ruins of Bobbie Joyce Davis's three-bedroom brick home.

Calls poured in to local law enforcement from terrified residents all hours of the day and night until arrests were made. The community was appalled and overwhelmed, especially those who had to deal directly with the crime scene. When the coroner's report was complete a few days later, it detailed the violence suffered by the victims – a total of 61 stab wounds on the six, plus five bullets pumped into the teenager and a hammer used on the grandmother.

Three Rangers (Ray Coffman, the lead investigator, Jim Miller and George Turner) spent the next four days interviewing Davis family members and friends, and possible suspects. They questioned two people who had reason to have grudges against the Davis family. Neither of those panned out, but on Saturday the 22nd, they got a break. Robert Earl Carter, the biological but absentee father of the youngest murdered child, 4-year-old Jason, showed up at the funeral service in Somerville with bandages on his hand, ears, and face. He and his wife told mourners that he'd been burned in a grass fire or lawnmower accident.

By 5 P.M. the Rangers arrived at his house in Brenham. He was out front talking to a neighbor and greeted them with the comment that he had expected them, given his burns. After Coffman read him his Miranda rights, Carter went in to tell his wife, Theresa "Cookie" Carter. She drove him to the DPS office in Brenham where he had agreed to be questioned by the Rangers. They advised her not to wait and told her they would bring him home. It never happened.

Ten hours later in the Houston DPS office, after failing a polygraph test administered by a Sgt. Hilton Kennedy, Carter had signed a "confession" that he'd driven another man, a cousin of his wife's, over to the house. He maintained that he remained outside in the car while the man went in to "find a woman."[2] This other person was the killer, Carter the innocent bystander. The wife's cousin's name was Anthony Graves; and he lived in Brenham. Because of the number of victims, the Rangers were convinced that at least two people were involved in the slayings. Carter's story gave them another person.

By that Sunday afternoon, Anthony Graves was in custody; within hours he was in Houston taking a polygraph himself, which he says he requested. The operator told him he failed, though his first defense attorney, Dick DeGuerin, was never able to secure a copy. Graves has not seen a minute of freedom since.

That night, Anthony Graves was moved to a jail in Milam County. Meanwhile, at the Burleson County jail in Caldwell, jailers were making special preparations. They were moving inmates around and when they were done, the two men accused of the Somerville crime were put in cells across from each other. The woman who arraigned them both at the Burleson County jail said the huskier of the two (Graves) "made her flesh crawl" because he showed no remorse, only concern about the amount of his bail.[3]

It was mid-day Monday before Graves got a look at the person who was accusing him of the horrific crime.

The investigation, the suspects, the grand juries

Anthony Charles Graves, number 999127, a resident of death row in the Terrell Unit since 1994, was the second death row inmate I interviewed in October 2000. Sitting behind the glass as I was ushered past a gaggle of Mexican television reporters in front of serial killer Angel Maturino Resendiz, Anthony looked solid and relatively healthy. You couldn't miss the gold tooth centering his smile. But Graves had reason to be depressed.

On May 31, 2000, the man who'd implicated Graves in the Davis family tragedy had recanted, for the 23rd time, on the gurney into a mike dangling above his head while witnesses waited for lethal drugs to flow into his veins thus ending one phase of a grim saga. The man, Robert Earl Carter, said twice in his final statement, "Anthony Graves had nothing to do with it. I lied on him in court."4

It was a claim Carter had made before, first to the grand jury (when he also said he was innocent, a bit hard to swallow, given the circumstances) on August 26, 1992;[5] and most importantly, again, repeatedly in the 48 hours preceding his capital murder trial in Angleton, Brazoria County, in October 1994, in the presence of Burleson and Washington County D.A. Charles J. Sebesta, Jr.[6]

Carter's claim that Graves was innocent was not revealed before trial to Graves' defense team, which law requires, given that it is of an exculpatory nature. In fact, District Attorney Charles Sebesta, on May 18, 2000 actually denied it occurred during a formal deposition.[7] However, in several interviews taped by this author within the next several months, Sebesta acknowledged it had happened.[8] He says it escaped his memory in May, given the large volume of cases he's prosecuted, including seven capital cases. Carter said in the May deposition that the assembled men were unified in their response to his statement regarding Graves' innocence: "You said you didn't want to hear that coming out of me."[9]

According to Carter and Sebesta, they wrangled for hours, including on the night before Graves' trial, which would have fallen apart without Carter's accusations. Carter was given a lie detector test, which he was told he failed. There is no record of the test, according to the D.A. But here's the interesting part: the questions put to Carter by the polygraph operator, according to Sebesta in an interview[10] and again when he cross-examined Carter in the May deposition, did not concern Graves' role in the crime, but that of Carter's wife Theresa, or Cookie.[11] She had been indicted along with Graves and Carter in September of 1992. For lack of evidence or an accuser, she was released after several months in jail in Bastrop County and never brought to trial, despite the fact that she had a small burn, which she attributed to a curling iron at the time she was arrested. Graves had no burns of any kind. There was no DNA evidence collected at the crime scene, nor were the murder weapons ever found. There was no bloody clothing or any physical evidence whatsoever, although in September of 1994 Carter led officials to several spots near a family compound in Clay, a half-hour's drive east of Somerville, where he said he'd disposed of the hammer, gun and knife used in the crime.

Sebesta claims that Carter "broke down in sobs"[12] when told he'd failed the polygraph on Cookie's role. Sebesta claims the original agreement between Carter and himself was eventually modified to include a proviso that if Carter testified against Graves, he would not be further questioned about Cookie. Also, anything Carter said in that testimony could not be used against him if his case were reversed by a higher court, and retried. In the Graves trial, the story Carter told (which was now his sixth official version of what transpired at the Davis home that night) left Graves the perpetrator of five of the six murders, supposedly motivated by his mother's loss of a supervisory position to Bobbie Davis.[13] Carter admitted only to killing Nicole. Had the prosecution or jury in Carter's own trial bought this version, he would not have been eligible for death row. A single murder of a person who is neither a police officer nor a prison guard, who is over six years of age when there is no associated rape, burglary, robbery, or murder for hire is not a capital offense.

Carter said he told those gathered on the state's side in Angleton during the Graves trial that Graves was innocent. These included his attorneys, Charles Sebesta and Bill Torrey,[14] the Texas Ranger and the prosecution's investigator E.K. Murray. Carter said he also told his older brother Hezekiah and at some point his "second mother," a teacher who'd been close to him most of his life. He also told a post conviction attorney, Mary Hennessy, who confirmed the claim. Graves' mother and her housemate and co-worker Bertha Mieth[15] said Hezekiah Carter came outside the courtroom at a recess during Carter's testimony and told them he had no idea why his brother was doing that, as Robert had told him earlier he wasn't going to lie on Anthony any more.[16]

Some time before 1997 Robert Carter also revealed his perjury regarding Graves to a longtime resident of death row, Kerry Max Cook, who was eventually proved innocent and released. While he was working as a trustee laborer repairing plumbing in Carter's cellblock, he said Carter acknowledged Graves' innocence, and said that before he would let Graves die, he'd recant his story. Cook implored him not to wait, warning him that getting off Texas death row based on innocence was not an easy task, as Cook knew only too well. For Cook it took 23 years, the intervention of Centurion Ministries, and the generosity of Wall Street bankers who believed his story and then funded a million-dollar legal battle to set him free. After the fact, DNA proved Cook was telling the truth when he denied his involvement in the battering death of a young woman who'd had intercourse with her killer shortly before she was murdered in Tyler in the seventies. Cook convinced Geraldo Rivera to include Graves when Geraldo was filming Cook for a special on the death penalty on MSNBC.[17]

Cook is white, and he was freed before 1998, when the Texas Court of Criminal Appeals fell to Republican judges, the majority of whom have an agenda that has resulted in an almost non-existent reversal rate (3%)

for capital cases on appeal. Graves is black, and from Brenham. His family has no money. They have good standing in the local black community and the churches they attend, but that didn't help much. One of Graves' friends, a white businessman named Roy Allen Rueter,[18] was so sure Anthony was innocent, he handed Graves' mother a check for $10,000 to hire famed Houston criminal defense lawyer Dick DeGuerin. That money paid for the high-dollar attorney's investigation and courtroom work in a habeas appeal aimed at setting Graves free on bond. Then the money was gone and so was DeGuerin's expertise.

Rueter says he had no idea how much it would cost to get Anthony out of trouble.[19] DeGuerin,[20] whose first words about the Graves case are that he believes Anthony is innocent, says his initial analysis of the case after personally investigating it was that the prosecution had no evidence against Graves and his conversation with Rueter was based on what he knew at the time. However, in the habeas hearing the state suddenly had evidence DeGuerin wasn't aware of, witnesses — Burleson County Sheriff's employees and a friend of the sheriff's — who swore they had overheard Graves admit to the crime in conversations with Carter in the Caldwell jail. DeGuerin felt sure it was false testimony. According to Rueter and Doris Curry,[21] who sat outside the courtroom because she was a potential witness, people emerging from the courtroom after DeGuerin cross-examined them were flushed and in the case of the young jailer, Shawn Eldridge, close to tears as they warned the next witnesses that Graves' attorney was fierce. However, DeGuerin had warned Graves that it was election year. Judge Jack Placke would probably deny bond for anyone with any previous conviction in such a horrendous crime. Bond was denied.

Graves had encountered Sebesta before

A fine amateur league third baseman, Anthony had the talent to be a pro, according to Rueter, who managed the slow pitch softball team Graves played for, which was sponsored by Rueter's father's multi-million dollar machining business. But in August 1992 Anthony was out of work and not playing ball. Rueter had laid him off earlier due to a downturn in the sales of oilfield equipment. The softball team had folded in 1991 when new owners declined to support it, and Graves left for a temporary job on the Dell assembly line in Austin. Rueters says he believes Graves may have had a learning disability in math. He was great with the machines, but a machinist also has to know the numbers, and Graves' pride kept him from asking white co-workers for help when he got in above his head. When the Dell job ended, Graves came back to Brenham, looking for work, collecting unemployment. He spent the time with his three young sons by different mothers (all were still his good friends), his girlfriend Yolanda and her family, his own younger brothers and sisters, his aunt, and his mother, Doris Curry. He had sleeping space on the living room floor of the apartment rented by his mother for his youngest siblings, Arthur and Dietrich Curry.

Graves had been caught in 1986 in a Brenham Against Drugs (B.A.D.) bust for selling $50 of pot to a professional narc, a charge which was split into two felony indictments. He says he turned himself in when he heard what was going down. Graves talked about how he became aware the charge was for cocaine distribution not pot — "Hold on! I don't even know nothing 'bout no coke; the only thing I've ever done is marijuana. They start talking about plea bargain for fifteen years. I start cryin'. 'I can't do no 15 years for this!'"[22]

Sebesta told him if he agreed to a cocaine charge, he would give him ten years.[23] Graves got an attorney, who was later disbarred, and who pled out to two charges for the incident — one for selling marijuana and the other for selling an unspecified illegal substance. Anthony got ten years probation with four months "shock probation" in prison in Sugarland, where his family could visit and bring his oldest son Terrell, who'd been diagnosed with sickle cell anemia as a toddler.[24]

Demetria Williams,[25] Graves' sister, was an Austin resident with a stellar academic and steady employment record studying for a graduate nursing degree at U.T. She says her boyfriend (later husband) got caught up in that early bust because he was dating her, despite the fact that "everybody knows how straight-laced my boyfriend and his family"[26] were (and are; his dad was well-known and respected in Brenham, her boyfriend was college-bound). They arrested him at his family's home on a drug charge. "Of course he didn't know anything so they yelled at him and threatened him . . . they ended up letting him go the next day without any charges being filed . . . he was never harassed again. He's not easily intimidated."[27]

Graves said he learned much later how bad a deal he got. For a first offense and for the amount of pot he'd sold, he should have drawn no more than two years probation and a fine. However, according to Graves and his family and Rueter, Sebesta (who retired at the end of 2001 after 25 years in office in Washington and Burleson County) had a reputation for differential sentencing. If you were black, an outsider, or somehow otherwise vulnerable, you were out of luck in his territory.

Rueter says, "There are a lot of guys who got railroaded or rushed to justice to take pleas that other guys with more money and resources would get preferential treatment on . . . I knew a (white) guy who got busted with a whole field of weed up around William Penn, in the north part of Washington County. Granted he'd never really had any (prior legal) troubles, and he got off with probation and the same day they sentenced this black guy to a couple of years for stealing a battery out of a truck. This was '78 or '80 . . . I'll never forget that. . . . It was a glaring thing about how the system works. . . ."[28]

Cross currents swirl through two capital murder trials

Explaining the motives for the savage Davis killings, Sebesta says he believes Carter was just "weak,"[29] caught between two women, and that Graves was really the instigator and the bad actor in the plot. Sebesta maintains this despite Carter's many recorded and written recantations following losing his state appeals in 1997, which is when Carter contacted Graves through another inmate and told him he was ready to tell the truth. Carter then contacted Graves' consulting appellate attorney, Roy Greenwood, and told him the same thing. Sebesta says if he "believed, for a moment, that Graves was innocent" he could not have participated in his prosecution.[30] He admits he has never met or spoken to Graves except in court or in the Grand Jury hearing. Sebesta offers as gospel the story (which Carter later recanted) that Graves' mother Doris Curry had been passed over for a promotion at the State School. The promotion had then gone to Bobbie Davis because of her liaison with a male supervisor at the school. This event which happened four years earlier, Sebesta claims, was Graves' motive for wanting to kill four children and two women, one of whom was Bobbie Davis. Lisa Davis testified, in Carter's trial, and colleagues of the two women testified at Graves' trial, that the women were friends. They said Curry did not compete for the job Davis got, and that Curry brought Davis pecans every fall because she knew how much the Somerville woman enjoyed them.[31]

Graves had never been charged before with violence, nor had anyone in his immediate family. His mother raised five children with little help from the father, who according to Rueter, was a gambler and numbers runner, had never been around much, and was shot to death in a Houston bar when Anthony was a young adolescent. Anthony, the oldest son and child, took care of the younger children, cooking, scolding, keeping them out of trouble and tidy, while their mother worked several jobs to get the family out of the projects as soon as possible.

Anthony's sister Demetria Williams says he was known for his love of children. During the period he worked for Dell and lived with her in Austin, he came straight from work to care for her baby until her husband got home so she could attend school. He moved out into his own apartment because he didn't agree with her husband's use of physical punishment to discipline children. Graves never used it on his own children and couldn't stand to witness the practice on his young nephew.

Apart from being black in Brenham, his father's absence and the resultant financial afflictions, the pot bust and encounter with Sebesta, and a DUI which included recovery of some pot from his vehicle (a probation violation), Graves' luck hadn't been too bad. He was well-known for athletic prowess, and he'd been very popular with the women, according to Williams and Rueter, who says, grinning "Women loved Anthony!"[32] But on Sunday, August. 23, 1992, it began to look like Anthony's luck was running out.

The night of the murders, Anthony Graves and his girlfriend Yolanda Mathis,[33] his brother Arthur and his sister Dietrich[34] *all* say they were spending a normal night at home in his mother's apartment. They got fast food and videos for the night. Their mother's co-worker, Bertha Mieth,[35] as a favor to Doris Curry,[36] called to check on the family at 12:30 a.m. She spoke to Anthony, Arthur and Dietrich.

These events were confirmed at the time by numerous alibi witnesses, including Arthur Curry's older (white) girl friend. Dick DeGuerin says she was prepared to brave racial prejudice to testify that, while she and Curry were on the phone most of the night, she'd heard Anthony in the background kidding Arthur about a song he'd sung to her which he'd just written for her. The witnesses had been rounded up by DeGuerin, who like his mentor Percy Foreman does his own investigation. This information, however, was not shared with Graves' later defense attorneys, until a former judge from Houston, Jay Burnett, entered the case at the request of Austin attorney and veteran capital appellate defender Roy Greenwood, who replaced habeas attorney Patrick McCann, when he was called by the national guard to go to Bosnia. This was a turning point for Anthony's case.

None of the earlier attorneys had requested documentation of Graves' alibi. Greenwood, who'd been on the case for years as a consultant hired by European allies, discovered DeGuerin still had the alibi notes. Burnett got the files, which clearly establish the alibi Graves maintained all along should have been used to prove his innocence. Three additional very specific witnesses who confirmed Anthony's story were not used at the trial, including both Dietrich and the woman working at the Jack in the Box who recalled who was in the car, their exact order and what part of it was for Anthony.

Anthony Graves and the others at the apartment learned of the tragedy when his mother called to tell them early Tuesday morning, August 18. Anthony didn't know the family, so he didn't drive to Somerville with his mother and sister to pay respects to the surviving Davis family members. A few days, later he called his cousin Cookie to see how Robert Carter was doing, given the loss of his son. He also needed a ride to Austin in order to get his repossessed 1984 Nissan out of hock. He was going to combine his unemployment check with help from his mother to get his vehicle back. Cookie told him she and Robert had to go to Houston and couldn't do it.

In May of 2000, 13 days before he died from lethal injection, in an 85-page official deposition, Robert Earl Carter explained, under direct and cross-examination, how he alone had killed the Davis family. Two days later, he said that he drove with his wife to Houston where they traded in two cars, including the vehicle he'd driven that night. Present at the deposition were: his final appellate attorneys Bill and Emily Whitehurst, Graves' appellate attorneys Greenwood and Burnett, Sebesta, an assistant Attorney General named Tommy Skaggs, Ranger Coffman and another attorney formerly from Burleson County.

Back on the afternoon of August 22, 1992, when the Rangers took Carter in for questioning, he had a ready explanation for his burns. It was a story that differed somewhat from earlier stories to medical personnel who'd treated his wounds, and from what he'd said to people at the memorial including Lisa Davis, the bereaved daughter of Bobbie, sister of Nicole, and mother of his child Jason. He said he'd set a grassfire the morning after the murders to kill some weeds near the edge of his house. The Rangers found a three-foot long, six-inch wide strip of burned grass next to the house. To them, it wasn't a convincing explanation for Carter's extensive burns. By 9 P.M. the Rangers and Carter were at a stalemate and someone suggested a drive to Houston for a lie detector test. The Rangers, minus Pearson, accompanied the suspect. By 11 P.M. Carter was informed he'd failed.

What happened next depends on whom one believes. One could believe the version of a condemned man who over the course of eight years gave at least seven different versions of the story of what happened in the wee hours of August 18. Carter claimed in the Grand Jury that he was told by the Rangers that he wouldn't make it back to the Caldwell jail unless he told them who else was with him at the Davis home that night. Given the three weapons that autopsies had revealed were used in the slayings, the Rangers had concluded there must have been two if not three or more killers involved. One could believe the Rangers.

However, consider these facts. Carter was athletic, a member of the statewide basketball championship team in high school. Rick Carroll, his supervisor for three years at the state school for mentally impaired in Brenham, said he was in very good shape. Bobbie Davis knew him as the longtime lover of her daughter Lisa and the father of her grandson, as well as a co-worker, with no prior history of violence, and had no reason to fear him. Four of the children were under ten and well under a hundred pounds, asleep in the middle of the night as was the athletic teenager Nicole when he arrived on a school night after midnight. The victims were unarmed. It seems possible the Rangers may have operated from an erroneous assumption.

Further, Roy Allen Rueter's independent investigation, using his Somerville employees to ask around about the murders before Anthony's trial, revealed some talk of the involvement of a local man described as a loudmouthed scrapper, who had lived in California and split town just after the crime. None of these descriptions fit Graves. Another of Rueter's employees, whose brother had fathered a child by Carter's wife Cookie, reported seeing her driving south out of Somerville toward Brenham in the early morning of August 18. He had been driving to Somerville on a food run from a campsite on the nearby lake. She was apparently seeing a man in Caldwell, who admitted the affair to the Rangers, so she could have been just coincidentally passing through Somerville on her way home down highway 36. She maintains to date that she and Robert were home all night and he burned himself due to a grass fire the next day. Within a week or so of the crime, the Rangers interviewed a man who admitted being her lover at the time. Marital discord was certainly in evidence, and Carter said in his May 18 deposition that his wife suspected he was still seeing Lisa Davis.

The Burleson County grapevine offers a variety of scenarios having to do with drugs, car deals, love affairs, parental issues and several varieties of public corruption, which explain why Carter made up so many different stories about who helped him kill so many people. Nonetheless, in his May 2000 deposition, Carter denied anyone else's involvement and gave a very specific, convincing, and horrifying account of bumping off the victims, one by one, mostly in their beds asleep, to settle the tension with Lisa over his romantic and marital allegiances, and over her filing a paternity suit. He denied that there was anger between them, saying they'd always gotten along very well.

In his second accounting of his behavior during the hours the crime occurred, and his first officially recorded statement to the Rangers at 3 A.M. in Houston the Sunday after the funeral, Carter said his wife's cousin (Anthony Graves) had called him early Tuesday around 12:45 A.M. He said Anthony had asked if he could come over to Carter's house and that they had gone out, driving around from town to town, after midnight. Carter stated that Graves wanted Carter to get him a woman. Carter said he had suggested Nicole, with the caveat that she was only 16 and that Graves was undeterred and had entered the Davis house alone. Carter reported that within "a second or two" he heard a shout and, alarmed, went to the door, calling "Kenneth, let's go!" (In the grand jury, Carter corrected the name Kenneth to Anthony.) Carter then said he entered, saw Bobbie Davis sprawled on the couch, heard shooting and screams in the bedrooms, started down the hall, saw blood everywhere, ran back out to get fresh air and recover from shock while Graves went to a storage shed for gasoline and returned to set the house afire. He said Anthony rushed out, knocking him (Carter) down face first into the flames, explaining the burns. He said they then returned to Carter's car and drove off, Graves throwing the gas can out the window as they drove. Carter said he dropped off Graves at the apartment Graves shared with a girlfriend. In fact, it had been several years since Graves had had his own apartment with a girlfriend. Then Carter said he returned to his home for the remaining hours before he woke Cookie for her early morning shift at the state school.[37]

Needless to say, the Rangers didn't buy this preposterous story of barely-compromised innocence. For example, they quickly learned Bobbie Davis kept no gasoline and had no lawnmower. However, they did buy his incrimination of Graves with almost no investigation, while they quickly dropped suspects with seemingly greater motives. For starters, neither Frankie Lee Bell, the accused in an aggravated assault case for which Bobbie Davis was to serve as a juror on the 18th nor the father of Lisa Davis's other child, whose name, interestingly, was Kenneth Porter, were ever called. Bell was never questioned about whether he had any knowledge concerning the Somerville murder. The Ranger report on the interview with Kenneth Porter showed it focused solely on whether he owned the Geo Tracker that Carter said Graves was driving the day Carter was arrested. Graves' mother and sister describe Porter's odd behavior the day after the deaths and wonder if he had something to do with what happened.[38]

Graves was arrested Sunday afternoon August 23 as he returned to his mother's apartment in Brenham. He was driving his own car. He couldn't imagine why he was being arrested; and when they informed him at the Brenham police station that someone named Robert had accused him of participation in the multiple murders, he couldn't place the man. He says he asked for a polygraph that night and was taken to Houston for the test at 8 P.M. by the same operator who'd tested Carter the night before, Hilton Kennedy. Graves believes the polygraph turned out to be ". . . another ploy to manipulate me and get me to confess to something I didn't do."[39] He says he was instructed to face the wall with his back to the machine and its operator, and could hear the operator "tearing up the results once the paper came off the machine . . . and throwing it in a box"[40] behind him. Because Anthony didn't know anything of polygraph process, he thought perhaps that was standard procedure. "When my attorney (DeGuerin) asked for the results of the test, they could never produce them. . . . Since then, no one has ever mention(ed) this mock polygraph. . . . As a matter of fact, they didn't remember what part of the polygraph I was supposed to have failed."[41]

Sebesta in a recent interview couldn't remember whether Graves had taken one, in fact thought he hadn't, and said had he taken one and passed, of course everything would have been different. Sebesta is very sure that Theresa Carter refused to take one, and remembers Carter's two tests clearly.[42] Hilton Kennedy refused to discuss the results of his test without a court order.

Graves was told he'd failed the lie detector test and was questioned again by the Rangers; and there his freedom ended, though he has maintained his innocence from day one. He writes, "I knew that they were trying to scare me; because if a polygraph is suppose[d] to work, and I'm telling you the truth, then how could I have failed? Right then, I knew that they were not interested in the truth!"[43] It was only the next day, when he arrived at the Caldwell jail, which at the time was literally a converted dog pound, that he recognized the man he barely knew as his cousin's husband Robert. Anthony had never had more than the most superficial conversations about sports with Carter, a man with whom friends said Graves wouldn't be caught dead hanging out.

Rueter says the Brenham party crowd, which included Graves, were careful to exclude people like Carter, who worked in law enforcement as a prison guard and was seen as a "pretentious Christian boy."[44] Add allegations from several sources that Carter was involved with drugs, and you have a man presenting conflicting facets of behavior and values.

Graves went to the grand jury two days after his arrest, on August 25, 1992, without an attorney, believing his innocence would be obvious. "I voluntarily spoke to that jury, without the assistance of an attorney, because I thought they were seeking the truth, not trying to build a case!"[45] He told the jurors in Burleson County the same story he repeats today, corroborated by interviews with his family and Mathis: how he spent the day and evening of the 17th and the early morning of the 18th surrounded by friends and family including his girlfriend Yolanda Mathis. His testimony to the grand jury was buttressed by her testimony that he'd been with her the entire night. He was asked if he ever carried a weapon, to which he responded in the negative, then specifically to a series of questions that followed, "Did I own a gun? No! A knife? No! . . . in my mind I was still saying no to owning any weapons, because I've never carried a weapon on me, or own any."[46]

Carter went to the grand jury on August 26 with an attorney appointed just for that day. She says she had little to say to him except to advise him his testimony could be self-incriminating, and not to testify. Carter's story to the grand jury was completely different from his statement to the Rangers a few days before. It refuted his confession, said he'd fabricated the whole story including implicating Graves. Carter said he'd been at home the whole night. He said he'd made up the story because the Rangers wouldn't accept his denial, and "told me they would cut me a deal, that I can walk if I give up a name and give up a story. And that's what I did."[47] Carter also told the Grand Jury that the Rangers "told me they were going to get me on the way back home. If I didn't come up with a name or a story that they was going to do something bad to me on the way home since I was a baby killer . . . they was telling me because of my burns, that they can give me the lethal injection."[48] Carter acknowledged to the Grand Jury that he hadn't gone to the funeral home to see his son's body until Friday night, and pled the fifth when Sebesta asked if it were true that Carter rarely visited his son. Sebesta appeared to try to get Carter to re-incriminate Graves by insinuating that Graves had testified against Carter in his Grand Jury appearance the preceding day. Grand Jurors made much in their questions to Carter of his economic folly in buying two new cars after receiving the paternity suit notice.

In later depositions, Carter admitted lying to the Grand Jury about when he'd acquired two new cars in exchange for used ones, giving a trade-in date for one a week before the murders. He said he'd lied to them about how he knew the details of where the bodies were because he'd overheard his wife's end of a phone conversation about the crime. He'd also lied about his .22 pistol being stolen six months earlier from his car, and had lied to the Rangers about conversations and meetings with Graves prior to the killings regarding Doris Curry's job. But he apparently had told the truth, consistent with his final deposition, to the Grand Jury about his distant relationship with Graves and about Graves' innocence, despite leading questions from the D.A.[49]

Between August 26 and September 2, jailhouse (snitch) testimony began to come in. While the informants claimed they'd heard the conversations on the 25th or 26th, they didn't note them in their log book or report them to Texas Ranger Ray Coffman until the first and second of the month. There were no tape recordings of these conversations.

All the "snitches" were connected to Sheriff Ron Urbanovsky of Burleson County either by employment or personal relationship. It is interesting to note that Urbanovsky was beginning to come under attack by

Charles Sebesta. About a year later, after several dozen indictments and grand jury ordeals over such things as an employee taking home a partly eaten ham, Urbanovsky resigned, raising questions which will have to remain speculation, for Ron Urbanovsky isn't talking.

On September 9, the grand jury of the 335th Judicial District, whose foreman was William Broaddus, a man close to Charles Sebesta in the First Baptist Church of Caldwell and a prominent businessman in the town, indicted Graves for capital murder along with Robert and Theresa (Cookie) Carter. At Graves' trial the D.A. in his opening statement told the jury that the Grand Jury had indicted the defendant for *all* the Davis murders. Because there are no minutes from the grand juries during the whole of Charles Sebesta's quarter of a century tenure, there is no record of what the jurors heard or saw to convince them to indict Graves.

They knew of the brutal horror of the crime, and of Ranger Coffman's notes of his investigation prior to the 9th, which included an identification of Graves from photo and live line-ups by a woman clerk at the Somerville Stop and Go. She said he'd been one of two men who had come in the night of the crime around 10:30 P.M. and again shortly after midnight at which time he bought gasoline in a can and a large Dr. Pepper. They had interviews and affidavits from the people mentioned above regarding the alleged overheard conversations.

Graves says he learned afterward why officials went out of their way the night of his polygraph test to take him to the Milam County jail rather than to the Burleson County jail in Caldwell. They were moving the inmates around so he and Carter could be opposite each other. Graves believes this was to set up the circumstances to make allegations of overheard incriminating conversations between them believable. Graves says the noise level in there was such that he would have had to shout to make Carter understand what he was saying. Anthony has always wondered if anyone seriously believes a man charged with the capital murder of six victims would shout out a confession in a jail housing a dozen or so other inmates and in the presence of an intercom that worked at least intermittently.[50] Steve Jennings, the former jailer, a man who took his job seriously and followed the law scrupulously, says it's perfectly possible to have overheard conversations between inmates in there, but he wasn't working the shift prior to Graves' arrival. He said he never heard about such arrangements being made for any reason. Jennings did, however, instigate charges against Ron Urbanovsky, the Sheriff at the time, for requesting procedures that violated the law and prisoners' civil rights. Urbanovsky would order Jennings to withhold phone calls from an inmate, or mail privileges, or keep prisoners from contacting media during the time that interrogations were being conducted.[51]

Ranger Coffman reported on September 21 that he had no evidence against Theresa Carter, so "her indictment apparently stemmed from (her) testimony [before the Grand Jury],"[52] which was never recorded.[53] The state dismissed the case against Theresa Carter a year or two after the two men were sentenced to death, for lack of evidence, and because, according to Sebesta, they were afraid her attorneys would invoke her constitutional right to a speedy trial, foreclosing the possibility of later trying her if new evidence emerged.[54]

Interestingly, the grand jury that indicted both Graves and Carter was operating without authority because its term had expired. This fact was uncovered by a Burleson County cattleman, Richard Surovik,[55] whose mistrust of Charles Sebesta goes back decades. Surovik also discovered the Sebesta had not been bonded for most of the 25 years he held office. He also found Sebesta was operating a second grand jury over which he had no constitutional authority, in the 335th Judicial District, presided over by his former law partner and fellow member of the Masons and First Baptist Church of Caldwell, Harold R. Towslee.[56]

Dick DeGuerin says, based on numerous reports from defense attorneys, defendants, and certainly in the Graves trial, that Towslee was afraid of Sebesta and almost always ruled with the D.A.[57] Interestingly, a few months before Graves' trial in June of 1994 a new grand jury, from the 21st District, presided over by Caldwell fundamentalist minister Donald Laird, was asked to re-indict Graves. The two members of the grand jury who were reached couldn't remember hearing any testimony; apparently they were asked to re-indict because the first indictment had some technical problem they couldn't quite recall.[58]

Trial by jury

In April of 1993 Anthony Graves was waiting to hear from the Attorney General regarding his request for an investigation into his case. Carter's first private attorney, Frank Rush, a black attorney-minister from Houston, asked the judge to introduce into the record a note he'd received via Cookie Carter purportedly from the mother of a young Caldwell jail trustee named John Brymer. The note said Brymer was willing to testify he'd been given food and drink by Texas Rangers to lie about hearing incriminating conversations between Graves and Carter. It said that another inmate, named only Chubby in the note, had been told if he'd lie on Graves and Carter they would "drop the charges against him and would let him go home."[59] Rush asked the judge to subpoena Brymer and his mother and Theresa Carter for a hearing on the issue of coercion or bribes for false testimony. However, Brymer's aunt, contacted in early

2001, said his mother had died five years before her son was in the Caldwell jail and no stepmother existed, so the letter was generated by someone other than the deceased mother!

At a pre-trial hearing, on June 3 of 1993, Sebesta told the Judge and Rush that there were at least seven witnesses who had overheard such conversations, but only two related to Carter. He said, "We're not even sure because of certain legal precedent that we're going to call those witnesses in this case."[60] He suggested that if they did decide to use those two, the time for a hearing would be the final pre-trial engagement.

Rush complained to the judge that for the second time he had wasted his time traveling for a hearing on a specific issue, which had not happened. Three different Brazos County former D.A.'s, one a senior state district judge, who at various times have defended clients against Sebesta, said that was the district attorney's favorite tactic against out-of-county defense attorneys. Run them over frequently for hearings to run up their client's bill and draw out the process until the client is broke and buckles to a plea, even when the evidence against him or her is minimal or nonexistent.[61]

Eleven days later, Rush finally got a hearing on the issue of suppressing tainted potential testimony, to examine two jail inmates who claimed to have overheard somewhat incriminating statements: John Bullard, a forger on anti-depressants and Greg "Scotty" Burns, in for attempted murder, who said a sheriff's deputy (and the D.A.) had approached him about what he'd overheard *after* he was sentenced to 20 years.

Carter's defense also brought in Graves' mother Doris Curry, who said Burns had told her on her weekly visit that Charles Sebesta had offered him *before* he went to trial on September 3, 1992, a "lighter sentence" in exchange for lying against Graves in the grand jury.[62] Burns and Sebesta denied any such discussion between them and pointed out Burns had gotten the maximum sentence; but Rush seemed highly cynical, particularly since Burns at one point said: "I said what they asked me to say." Pressed on that point by Rush, Burns denied that the prosecution had planted words in his mouth.[63]

All this was for naught, because Carter's family had run out of money to keep Rush on the case and by mid-July he withdrew. Within a few weeks Judge Placke appointed two Austin attorneys for Carter: Dain Whitworth for the trial and Walter Prentice for his direct appeal. Whitworth quickly agreed to a trial date and venue in nearby Bastrop County. Rush had been wrangling with the judge over the venue, as Rush wanted a big city like Houston or Dallas with a large black population to draw on for the jury. Whitworth was a former executive director of the Texas Criminal Defense Lawyers Association, but had helped write the

1973 death penalty bill for the legislature because he believed "we needed it at the time."[64]

Whitworth says he kept trying to get Carter to come up with a credible story for his defense, but every time his client tried and they tested him with a polygraph, he failed. Finally, just before his trial date, Carter had one that got Whitworth excited and hopeful. It included Jamaican drug dealers from Houston. But the polygraph results came back the same: no go.

In February of 1994 Robert Earl Carter was sentenced to die by Bastrop County jurors. Whitworth, having gotten no help from Carter, winged it. He tried to convince the jury that Anthony Graves was the sole perpetrator. Whitworth failed to explain away Carter's many conflicting and patently false statements and, most importantly, his extensive and serious burns, not to mention the fact that he'd been served a few days prior to the murders with paternity papers by Lisa Davis, which seemed a plausible motive, though to many, so incommensurate with his reaction as to be incredible. Charles Sebesta argued that Carter had paid Graves to kill Jason (evidence being Graves' forking over $558 in cash to get his aging Nissan out of hock in Austin two days after the murders). This produced a capital charge, murder for hire, for Carter as well as Graves. Graves had explained to the grand jury with Sebesta present that the money came from his unemployment check and his mother. It was a claim he could back with documentation.

To grease the wheels for the jury to deliver a death sentence, in his closing remarks Sebesta told the jury that if they opted for life imprisonment instead of death for Carter, he could be out in a few years. The minimum term for parole eligibility from a life sentence was at least 30 years. This deliberate misstatement of the facts should have guaranteed Carter a re-sentencing hearing, according to his later federal appeals attorney, William Whitehurst. But this was Texas, and the turf of the conservative Fifth Circuit federal appeals court, and the hearing didn't fly. Needless to say, the original jury delivered the goods the D.A. sought, and Carter was hauled off to spend the next five and a half years awaiting the lethal needle.[65]

Bonanza for Sebesta

If Carter's case was a slam-dunk for the prosecution, Anthony Graves' was just the opposite, despite DeGuerin's departure, until the summer of 1994, when Robert Carter and Roy Allen Rueter, the latter unintentionally, supplied the missing links — an eyewitness and a weapon.

Carter's first post-conviction attorney, Austin's Walter Prentice, who'd been appointed to the case by 21st District Judge Jack Placke prior to Carter's trial, asked the Burleson County D.A.'s office if there was any way they could mitigate Carter's sentence. Sebesta badly needed more evidence against Graves. At that point he had Carter's initial admission, recanted to the Grand Jury and shot full of holes by the Rangers' investigation. He had the various statements by "jailhouse witnesses." He also had a legally shaky identification by Mildred Bracewell, the clerk from the Stop and Go (which her husband did not corroborate) of Graves as one of the two men who supposedly bought gasoline in a container at 10:30 p.m. and again around midnight. Graves had solid, multiple alibi witnesses for both those times.

Sebesta says he told Carter's attorney, "We're certainly interested [in mitigation]... but we're not doing anything until we hear what he's got to say."[66] Eventually the prosecution and the defense worked out a deal. Sebesta explains that he told Prentice,"... if his case gets reversed on appeals, if he wishes to testify, we'll allow him to come back if he chooses and plead to life." Sebesta says they wanted the inmate to testify as well about the involvement of his wife Theresa (Cookie) Carter, but it's unclear whether Carter ever agreed to that.[67]

In late June 1994 at one of Graves' pre-trial hearings, Rueter bumped into Graves in the Brenham courthouse:

> I went up and tried to shake his hand. I hadn't really talked to him in a year or so. They came over and wanted to talk to me and asked me all these questions... who I was and if Anthony ever had a knife. I said, 'He never carried a knife.' They said, 'To the best of your knowledge, did he ever own a knife?' I said, 'I gave him a knife one time, it's a switchblade, it's a piece of shit ... wouldn't even hardly stay together. I've got one just like it in my office.' It was stupid, I wasn't thinking, but I didn't have anything to hide. So he went and got it and I had it rubber banded up so it would stay together and the officer said, 'You're right, this thing comes open in your pocket.'[68]

Rueter says he told the investigator, E. K. Murray, and Sebesta's assistant prosecutor Bill Torrey, that the knife was too flimsy to ever hold up through even one, much less 61 stabs into skulls and bones; but in his estimation Torrey, though friendly, had political ambitions and was "scared shitless" of the D.A.[69]

That knife, in the prosecution's hands, became a deadly weapon against Graves. Sebesta called it "a nail in the coffin," supplied in part by

Rueter, but definitively by Robert Bayardo, the Travis County medical examiner who had autopsied the Davis family victims. Bayardo, according to Sebesta, "looked at it and said, 'Yeah, that's the knife, that's the knife.'"[70] Rueter was told by Sebesta's investigator in mid-August that Dr. Bayardo, who was described to the shaken Rueter as an "impeccable expert," had said absolutely that that knife, or its twin, was the murder weapon in at least two of the deaths.[71]

Background on the "impeccable expert"

Bayardo is the same man whose medical opinion on the timing of injuries sent Austin's 11-year-old Lacresha Murray to jail for several years in the late nineties for the death of a child in day care at her grandparents' home. A forensic expert hired later said the child had received grievous blows (consistent with injuries from a car accident) hours before arriving at the Murray residence, and in fact had a series of older injuries, and was severely undernourished — facts which suggested severe chronic child abuse by her primary caregivers, not the occasional babysitter. Eventually after three years of relentless publicity and investigation resulting in a storm of public protest, Lacresha Murray was released, to the embarrassment of longtime Travis County District Attorney Ronnie Earle.

It turned out that Bayardo had had slides in his possession since the toddler's death in 1996 that proved a crucial timing factor that would exonerate Murray; yet any mention of those slides was absent from his autopsy report.[72] According to Barbara Taft, who quit her job to fight for Murray's freedom, the political context for the Murray case was significant. Travis County D.A., Ronnie Earle, was facing his first serious political challenge in 20 years from a Republican. Earle seized on the case for media attention, announcing Murray's name and guilt as soon as she was charged, unusual for a case in which a minor is involved. He called the tragedy an instance of the "hideous malady" of "child killing child" sweeping the country.[73] Judge John Dietz, who was Earle's former campaign manager, appointed an inexperienced public defender for young Murray, and allocated only $300 for experts for her defense.[74] Bayardo's role in this tarnished situation is even more troublesome, viewed from the perspective of his importance in the case against Anthony Graves.

Besides the stunning news of Bayardo's conclusion about the flimsy knife as the murder weapon, Rueter says the prosecution also,
. . . gave me a copy of a letter Anthony had sent [his ex] Betty saying, "I want you to go to the storage shed and I want you to find the souvenir" (knife), so I'm like, "Why would he be doin' that," and they said, "You

know why he's doing it." Well, I'm all messed up . . . and they convinced me that he was guilty . . . That's the first time I ever met that f———n' Sebesta. He was in there and he's like "You know we know that you don't have exactly a sterling reputation." I'm going, "Shit, I've got my family and I've got my job, you know." I found out later he wanted her to find that knife [to give to his attorneys to test], so he could prove to those people it wasn't the murder weapon . . . if anybody knew anything about that knife . . . It was very cheaply made . . . one strike anywhere and the thing would've broke into a thousand pieces.[75]

The prosecution also told Rueter that Graves had threatened and assaulted Carter in the Caldwell jail, which Carter again denied in his May 18 deposition. All of this completely unhinged Rueter. He writes:

> Once they had my knife and convinced me by the tests of Bayardo that it more than likely was the murder weapon, I fell really hard and just quit caring about much of anything except staying high . . . and I firmly believe that Sebesta's office preyed on that conditioning. I am not a victim here. . . . Anthony is the victim in all of this tragedy.[76]

Rueter was also involved in a civil suit, and he knew his job at the firm his father had previously sold was going to disappear. After almost two years of being drug and alcohol free, he had fallen off the wagon in early 1994, and was using by March.[77] Besides Murray's not-so-subtle threat to him about the prosecution's knowledge of his illegal drug use, Rueter says a man introduced to him as a narcotics agent would "happen to drop by" as he and the investigator drank together at a local watering hole on several occasions, only increasing Rueter's paranoia. He not only agreed to witness for the state that he had given Graves a knife identical to the one now in the possession of the state; he even secretly taped one of his employees who was known to be close to Anthony, while grilling him over whether he knew anything regarding Graves' participation in the crime. He didn't.[78]

When the prosecution asked Rueter if he'd ever known his friend to be violent, he told them about a workplace fight and gave them a name of a witness, an employee named Thomas Genzer who had come up from Houston with the Rueters when they moved the company. Rueter expresses regret now about any collaboration with the prosecution.

When asked for details of the fight in an interview in 2000, Rueter recalled that it started over donuts on a Saturday, between Graves and a white employee. The other man had "bitch-slapped" Graves and used the "N" word. A bigger man, he had Graves down on the ground. Graves asked him to let him up; the man agreed, saying, "But that's the end of it." According to reports, Graves then sucker-punched the guy, breaking his nose, and in his fury was going for a paring knife in his lunchbox when fellow employees restrained him. Rueter chewed Graves out subsequently, lecturing him on the folly of reacting to racism so thoughtlessly when he had chosen to stay in an area where it was rampant. Rueter suspended both employees for a few days.[79]

None of the context of the incident was brought out in the trial by the defense.

The D.A. bluffs

On August 31 at a pre-trial hearing, Sebesta told the judge and Graves' lawyers that Carter would be a state witness only if he passed a polygraph test regarding his proposed testimony against Graves, once he completed his statement to the investigators. Sebesta now admits that test "possibly fell through the cracks" until the night before Carter testified against Graves in Angleton. He says they were rushed to begin jury selection on September19.[80] Carter's attorney, Walter Prentice, acknowledges the test never happened, at least not as promised, and that this fact is important.[81] Attorneys who hadn't dealt with Sebesta before, and who didn't know his reputation for bluffing, might have taken him at his word and assumed that Carter's story had passed the promised polygraph test. That would make him a more daunting witness, and perhaps discourage their cynicism and their challenges to his story; furthermore, it would be a discouraging "reality," sapping their hope for an effective defense of their client.

Ranger Coffman traveled to Huntsville in September (the statement was taken on the 7th, according to trial testimony) and to the Caldwell jail in early October to visit Carter, taking still another statement of what happened that night. Not counting the various versions only Dain Whitworth heard, Carter told six different stories about what happened on August 18, 1992, from his first questioning by the Rangers in Brenham through his pre-execution deposition. In only half of them did Graves play a role — the original "confession" where Carter said Graves killed them all while he waited unawares in the car; the second version to Ranger Coffman prior to Graves' trial where he said he killed only Nicole and Graves and a third person named "Red" killed the others; and the version from Graves' trial, where he blamed Graves for five of the deaths and only admitted to killing the teen.

Graves says he was "elated" at the news Carter would testify, believing that there was no way he "could look in my face and lie on me."

Graves said he was moved to Brenham the month before the trial, which he found out later was because Carter was brought back to Caldwell "to manipulate that man and get him to commit perjury against me!"[82]

Court appointed legal counsel face D.A. tricks

After Dick DeGuerin bailed out as a result of the conflict with Rueter over his pay, Graves went to trial. It began on October 21, 1994 after a month of jury selection. Small-town attorneys Lydia Clay Jackson and Calvin Garvie told prospective jurors and still maintain that their client was absolutely innocent. Graves' sister Demetria Williams says Sebesta stayed back as long as DeGuerin was on the scene, but the minute he left the D.A. "flew in like a pigeon going after bread."[83]

The new court-appointed attorneys were up against an established district attorney who seemed to have checked any scruples he might have had at the courthouse door. He was buttressed by a judge whom DeGuerin felt was intimidated by the D.A.[84] He had also brought in for the capital cases a hard-charging, very competent Brazos County prosecutor, Bill Torrey, who now works in the state judicial ethics commission, who had been lured into Sebesta's fold with the promise that the D.A. would retire. Torrey intended to run for the position himself on the Republican ticket, according to Rueter.[85] The defense ran into roadblocks from the state. Lydia Clay Jackson says the D.A., in contrast to Harris County prosecutor practice in capital cases, for example, kept his files closed to the defense.[86] Sebesta denies this.[87] In the pre-trial record, Garvie complained to the judge for months about the prosecution not providing a witness list with adequate contact information,[88] while the judge mildly rebuked the D.A. and failed to follow through on the repeated requests.

For some reason Graves' youngest sister Dietrich Curry wasn't brought by the defense as an alibi witness to buttress the Arthur Curry and Yolanda Mathis report about Graves' whereabouts after midnight. Nor was Bertha Mieth, their mother's friend and co-worker. Dietrich says Sebesta had subpoenaed her over some outstanding traffic tickets and told her if she'd testify against her brother, the tickets would be dropped. She didn't take the deal.[89]

A number of observers believe Graves was hurt even before the trial started by his own defense team. Rueter and some family members believe the male defense attorney was incompetent and sold Anthony down the river.[90] Graves himself blames the D.A. alone and thinks the attorney, Calvin Garvie of Sealy, who'd asked to be appointed when he learned about the case from his secretary, Graves' sister Demetria, was new to the game and no match for Sebesta's tactics.[91] The record shows Garvie at times putting up a good fight and at other times ignoring leading questions and distorted evidence.

Since both defense attorneys were black, both prosecutors white, and 11 of the 12 jurors in Angleton were white, in an area notoriously conservative and with a high conviction record for blacks and a legacy of racism, one wonders if the trial wasn't tilted just by the race of the defendant and his attorneys. Tom McDonald, a senior state district judge and former D.A. familiar with the region, said going to trial in Brazoria County defended by a young female black attorney "who wears those hats" would have hurt Graves by itself.[92]

Garvie, who'd never tried a capital case but who was in charge of investigation, hired an investigator who turned up very little information, according to his more experienced co-counsel Lydia Clay-Jackson.[93] Neither the investigator nor Clay-Jackson, who handled that portion of the case, discovered the indictment against the witness John Robertson, as well as his prior assault charges, his son's legal troubles, and other factors that might have coerced him to be overly helpful to the state. The political dynamic surrounding the former Sheriff who was linked to all the "jailhouse confession" witnesses, and who was under siege from Sebesta himself, also made the testimony suspect. The defense didn't mention it. And while they did manage to request witness testimony from Carter's trial, they didn't seem to have read pre-trial documents related to Frank Rush's battle over the legality of jailhouse eavesdroppers.

Garvie never asked DeGuerin for his files, and had no specialized forensic expert on crucial weapon testimony as later attorneys were able to provide, and must not have dug very hard into Bayardo's reputation and expertise, as he made no effort to impeach his credibility at trial, which wouldn't have been difficult. One prosecutor said if he had a major case, he would hope to have someone other than Dr. Bayardo as the medical examiner.[94]

Then when the prosecution pulled a trick that should have gotten the case reversed, neither Garvie nor co-counsel Lydia Clay-Jackson, who'd tried and won several capital cases by then, responded in a way that would have blocked or mitigated the effect.

The trick was this. Yolanda Mathis was the only non-related alibi witness for Graves' whereabouts in the middle of the night on the 18th. She had withstood the intimidating ordeal of being transported by what she describes as three huge white Rangers to Caldwell for interrogation, where she was called "little girl" though she was in her early twenties, and was told if she lied she would be charged with being an accomplice.[95] Mathis had stuck to her guns and her story that she was with Anthony all night at his mother's apartment. She told the Grand Jury the same story, and was prepared, despite her mother's trepidation about ramifications to her life for opposing the white man's law in Brenham, to testify as Graves' chief alibi witness in Angleton.

As required by law, she was outside the courtroom ready to be called, when Sebesta asked the judge to excuse the jury and told the attorneys present that Mathis had become a suspect in the case and if she testified, it could be used against her. Garvie and Clay-Jackson were stunned, and went outside to inform Mathis what had just transpired, whereupon she began, according to Clay-Jackson, literally shaking in her shoes,[96] and fled the courthouse, leaving Graves' defense team with a huge hole in their case. It was a hole Sebesta enlarged in his closing arguments when he referred to her absence without any explanation to the jury of why she hadn't appeared.

This maneuver, according to a former Travis County prosecutor, might be unethical, but was not illegal, since perhaps the prosecution could have reasoned that if she said she was with him the whole night and he was at the crime scene, so was she. Garvie says there's no way anyone could have been prepared for that tactic. According to former criminal court judge, Jay Burnett, "Any attorney worth his salt would have said: 'Hold on a minute, Judge, I want a good faith hearing right now on that,'" and the judge would have been obligated to force the prosecution to show their evidence for suspecting Mathis.[97] Clay-Jackson said they never thought of responding in that way. Dick DeGuerin said if they'd tried it on him he would've tried to stop the trial until Mathis was represented by counsel.[98] It's hard to understand why Garvie and Clay-Jackson did nothing.

Mathis has never to this day been further investigated or charged. With Mathis eliminated with no explanation to the jury, the major remaining alibi witness for the hours after midnight was a family member, a category of witness traditionally discounted by juries. That witness, Graves' youngest brother Arthur, a stable working man and church choir director, says he now fears leaving his apartment and believes he should videotape his every move to shield himself from the kind of wrongful conviction Anthony suffered.[99]

Carter testified that he'd killed only Nicole and Graves had killed the rest, shocking Graves, who'd been told by his attorneys to show no emotion. Carter also told the court that Graves had choked and threatened him while they were in the Caldwell jail (which he said never happened in his May 2000 deposition). The paramedic who treated Carter's burns in the Caldwell jail and had signed an affidavit in 1992 saying that she had noticed choke marks on Carter's throat, was not brought in to testify. It appears, however, her affidavit was offered to the Grand Jury and to Carter's jurors at trial to explain away Carter's first recantation of Graves' guilt to the Grand Jury in 1992, the theory being Graves intimidated the smaller Carter with physical violence into perjuring himself to the Grand Jury.

Testimony of a co-defendant has to be corroborated to be sufficient for conviction, and in Graves' case there were two main sources of corroboration. The state brought in several of the witnesses to the purported "jailhouse confessions" of August 24th and 25th including one who wasn't in Ranger Coffman's report, John Bullard, a man in jail for forgery, who admitted under cross-examination he was on medication for depression and had been suicidal. There were three others from the group rounded up by former Sheriff Urbanovsky: his friend John Robertson, who was still under indictment by Sebesta; former sheriff's deputy Ronnie Beal, and young former jailer Shawn Eldridge.

The witnesses used gave different stories, all incriminating Graves. Bullard said Graves asked Carter after he returned from the Grand Jury if he'd "told them everything" to which Carter responded in the negative, and after Bullard warned them the intercom was on, they began using hand signals, testimony implying both men had something to hide. Robertson said when he entered the jail to bring a meal to a friend from church, jailer Wayne Meads, he saw Graves and Carter in their cells directly opposite each other and overheard conversation between them and other inmates.[100] He stuck close to this original affidavit when he testified:

> Someone asked Graves a question, and he said, 'We fucked up bigtime.' He told Carter they'd taken care of the evidence and there was no way it could be traced to them, (adding) 'they had to protect Cookie at all costs', and that [because Carter was burned] he might have to go down for all of them.[101]

In cross-examination Clay-Jackson tried valiantly to cast doubt on the witnesses' ability to identify who was talking. How could Robertson see the inmates through brick walls, for example. Crossing Shawn Eldridge, who said he heard Graves say: "Yeah, motherfucker, I did it. Keep your mouth shut,"[102] Clay-Jackson established that the jail inmates had either a loud fan or air conditioner and a television on almost all the time. The inmates were in another building separated by brick walls and steel doors with no line of sight. The jailer normally noted everything that happened in his log but didn't report that conversation in the journal until nine days later. The cell intercom worked intermittently in Graves'

161

and other cells. In Carter's trial earlier that year his defense attorney Dain Whitworth told the jury that other inmates in the jail at the time that he interviewed had overheard no such confessions.

Former deputy Beal testified he was visiting the jail at the same time as John Robertson and Police Dispatcher Stifflemire, and the threesome overheard Graves say, "Keep your damn mouth shut. I done the job for you. Make them make their own damn case!"[103] or something along those lines, and how "they had to protect Cookie because she could go down for life."[104] He said they called the sheriff and went for a tape recorder, but by the time they returned the conversation was over. Beal admitted, under Clay-Jackson's questioning, as did Eldridge, that he had received her letter asking them to contact her, and had ignored it.[105]

The defense also established that Beal had not met Graves nor heard him speak, and that he couldn't remember if he had noted the conversation on the log or his scratch pad. But Clay-Jackson didn't explore with Beal and Robertson how their versions of what they claimed to have heard simultaneously differed from each other and from other accounts.

Lydia Clay-Jackson was in charge of questioning the witnesses to the overheard conversations. In spite of the fact that jailhouse snitch testimony is notoriously suspect, she did little to discount the content of the statements. Her investigation was apparently limited to a physical inspection of the site.

Clay-Jackson says the original state case against Graves was based around a shaky identification of Graves by Mildred Bracewell, the clerk at the Somerville convenience store. She didn't testify, so was not cross-examined, perhaps because Carter's first attorney had fiercely attacked that same "evidence" due to the hypnosis component, and Graves' defense had in vain filed a motion to suppress it at the beginning of his trial.[106] Sebesta says it was questionable and the weakest part of their case by this point.[107] Nonetheless, statements by both Bracewells about seeing the two men, with the wife identifying Graves as one of them, were part of the jury exhibits at the trial.

The weapon

Roy Allen Rueter's presence in this case is bizarre and erratic. First he donates $10, 000 for Anthony's initial defense, then pulls out. Later, he is convinced or intimidated into collaboration with Sebesta's team, providing not only the knife but also testimony that he had given the knife to Anthony, which then cast Graves as a liar for telling the Grand Jury he'd never owned one. Then he gives the prosecution a character witness for the sentencing phase, a colleague of Graves named Thomas

Genzer who has to testify, against his will and better judgment, that Graves was violent. Rueter says Genzer has never forgiven him for placing him in that position.[108] Admittedly Reuter was often stoned out of his mind, which perhaps explains what at best can be seen as a long string of blunders if what he'd been doing was trying to help friend he knew to be wrongly accused of murder.

Rueter says nonetheless, that he had tried to contact Garvie, leaving messages about leads for him to follow, but Garvie never returned his calls or followed up the leads, and though he knew Rueter was going to be a state witness, didn't try to contact him until too late:

> . . . at the time he [Garvie] wanted to interview me, it wasn't five minutes before I was supposed to testify...and I just looked at him and shook my head and said, "No, I don't have anything to say to you". . . it was more contempt than anything . . . and the fact that I was extremely, extremely high . . . and I thought that Garvie, with any street sense he might have . . . would know that I was wired, and I was holdin', and I didn't want to go to jail.[109]

Since Graves had testified to the Grand Jury that he didn't own a knife, thinking that they meant a weapon knife, the prosecution characterized this as perjury and hammered on it in the trial to destroy Graves' credibility.

Roland Searcy, a Bryan defense attorney and former prosecutor, says setting up a perjury charge from a grand jury is a favorite Sebesta tactic when his evidence is weak.[110] Rueter says had he been able to talk with Garvie before the trial (an interesting comment since he also said he'd refused a pre-trial conversation), he could have told him what questions to ask on the stand to elicit information about the flimsiness of the knife.[111] But it didn't happen.

The knife testimony (from Dr. Bayardo, who simply said the knife or one like it *could* have been the murder weapon, and Ranger Coffman who backed him up); and the knife itself as an exhibit were cited as the top reasons for the jury's decision by jury foreman and two other male jurors contacted by this author six years after their verdict.[112] Sebesta, in an ABC interview in 2000, called the knife conclusive "physical evidence"[113] despite the fact that the actual knife used in the murders was never established.

Ray Coffman, the lieutenant in the Texas Rangers who'd played a supervisory role in the initial investigation, was presented as a knife expert. He testified that the tests which he and the medical examiner

Bayardo had conducted, by plunging Rueter's knife into wounds in the actual skulls of several of the children, constituted proof that the knife's twin, placed in Graves' hands by Carter's testimony, was the murder weapon used on all six victims. This was an amazing leap of mind, if not an outright sham. In the state writ filed on Graves' behalf several years later, attorney Pat McCann summarized the damaging testimony by Ranger Coffman:

> The State then somehow qualified Ray Coffman as some form of weapons expert, and he testified that in his *expert* opinion, the murder weapon *was* the *missing twin*. Coffman had no training in metallurgy, forensic analysis, medicine, pathology, weapons manufacture, or even knife fighting, but apparently that was not required to provide *expert* testimony at this trial. . . . Prior to this trial, the undersigned counsel had never seen a fact witness, particularly an investigator on a case, be qualified additionally as some form of nebulous *expert* during the trial.[114]

The D.A. attacked the integrity of the opposing defense expert witness on the knife, a San Antonio medical examiner named Bux, who tried to demonstrate that almost any knife could have made the wounds. Sebesta insinuated the expert's name (*Bucks*) implied he was a paid hack.

On other matters the defense brought in a co-worker of Doris Curry and Bobbie Davis, who rejected the prosecution's motive theory of Curry's jealousy over Davis' supervisory position and detailed evidence of friendly relations between the two. One wonders why the defense didn't call Rick Carroll, the supervisor of both women as well, who when interviewed recently readily discounted the idea of enmity between the women and said Curry had never applied for the supervisory position created for Davis.[115]

Graves' attorneys also attempted to cast suspicion on Kenneth Porter, the father of Lisa Davis's other child. Porter had appeared in Brenham around 3 A.M. on August 18 at the home of a neighbor of Carter's, John Isom, whose testimony may have appeared incredible to the jury in light of his conviction for dealing cocaine. In addition to Isom, a former girlfriend of Porter who was close to the Graves family testified that Porter was abusive and threatened "to set my face on fire."[116] Sebesta asked her source of income, why she'd quit her Walmart job, and how much she received from child support, questions that seemed primarily intended to humiliate and discredit the witness. The defense did not object.

At the end of five days in court, after eight and a half hours of deliberation, the twelve member jury in Angleton (whose lone black, the foreman Clarence Sasser, snoozed and snored throughout the trial, according to Rueter and the Graves family),[117] convicted Anthony Graves of capital murder on October 27. The jury foreman told an interviewer in 2000 that despite Carter's highly publicized recantation on the gurney as well as those preceding it, he was convinced that Graves, not Carter, had the "balls" to pull off the gruesome multiple murder, based on the way Graves looked, compared to Carter. He says the crime itself affected him, the photographs of the children especially.[118]

Forensic anthropologist Dr. Harrell Gill-King of the University of North Texas was hired in recent years by Graves' defense to re-analyze the evidence. Gill-King described the methods used by Bayardo and Pearson as unscientific at best, and as destructive of the original evidence. In an evidentiary hearing in 1998, he said no man's life should be hanging in the balance due to testimony regarding a knife which had never been found in association with the murder; and further, that Rueter's knife could not be the weapon used in the crime.[119]

In another two days of testimony in the sentencing phase of the trial, Graves' marijuana conviction was presented as though there were two separate offenses. The vague wording of the plea suggested one of the offenses was for something besides marijuana even though this was not the case. The workplace fight was used to present Graves as a violent, reactive person; and the DUI from early August 1992 was entered into the record over his attorney's objections. For the defense, the psychiatrist who said Graves fell into the least dangerous category for people convicted of killing had his methods impugned by the prosecution.

After three and a half hours of jury deliberation, Graves was sent to Ellis Unit's death row outside Huntsville as a child killer, a category that can draw dangerous attention. It has brought him spit, spiders, ground glass and worse in his food, as well as verbal abuse from guards, isolation from his loved ones, and since early 1999, solitary confinement with no work or crafts privileges, like all the four-and-a-half-hundred inmates of Texas death row.

Several jury members were weeping and angry as they expressed to the Graves family and to Garvie that the state hadn't so much proved the guilt of the accused as the defense had failed to establish his innocence. One woman juror, Mary Anderson, kept looking straight at Graves' family during the verdict phase, shaking her head as though saying, "This isn't right." She had to be nudged twice by the juror next to her to give her verdict of guilty, with tears in her eyes, according to Graves' cousin Felicia DeShawn Graves.[120]

The jurors, mainly women, interviewed by Clay-Jackson and Garvie immediately after the trial ended, told them that the knife issue didn't play a large role in his conviction; that it was all Carter.[121]

Graves called his sister and close friend Demetria the night he was convicted to tell her in disbelief: "They convicted me!" She says, "He was crying, I was crying. Anthony would give you the shirt off his back, everybody who knows him knows that." She says the sentence has torn the family apart, and that she often awakens in a cold sweat thinking of what Anthony is enduring in prison.[122] To think that he might be executed is beyond her ability to imagine. Graves said in a recent interview at the Terrell unit: "They haven't tried once to tell the truth... how much have we really changed in the South? That keeps going through my mind.... Is it all just political? The judge granted him [Sebesta] everything he wanted. I kept telling my attorneys, this man is not giving us a fair shake."[123] Lydia Clay-Jackson says she ordinarily has great respect for prosecutors, but Sebesta is the exception.[124]

Calvin Garvie wrote Graves on death row on December 6, 1992: "Well, man, I don't know where the case went wrong. It seems the jury believed Carter, not all of what he said, but enough. However, we both still believe in your innocence. Also they messed over us by threatening to charge Yolanda."[125]

Anthony Graves
(Part 2) Railroad Justice

Sebesta will not seek re-election
seventh full term in 2000 race

retire after 25 years, exploring options for future plans

time Burleson and gton County District y Charles Sebesta an d on Tuesday that he t seek re-election to a h, four-year term in

ta, who has served since 1975, said he is retiring pursue other interests. a said he will not seek r elective office, play an roll in the 2000 election rse a candidate. Tuesday statement, "it has been a time to

CHARLES SEBESTA

several options. and I not attended law ntered the legal ave prob-

Texas A&M working as a s dent assistant in the Sports formation Office, and I a worked for *The Bryan-Coll Station Eagle*. I think ther a good chance that I'll end spending some time as a pu relations consultant writer," he said in a prepa statement.

If he remains active in the gal profession, "it will be special prosecutor, hand cases when the elected pros tor has a conflict and n recuse himself," he said.

Sebesta was recently re nized by the State Bar of T as Prosecutor of the Year.

During his 24 years, Sel has prosecuted some high file cases, including the tal murder convictio ESTA, pag

Sebesta to receive top prosecutor award

District Attorney Charles Sebesta has been named Prosecutor of the Year by the State Bar of Texas.

The award will be presented today during the annual meeting of the Texas District and

opposed in a primary or ge eral election, is nearing comp tion of his sixth, four-year te as district attorney.

Sebesta became the distri first, full-time district attorn in 1975 and the first to hav

Judge Tom McDonald, whose own father was also a district judge and later a presiding judge on the Texas Court of Criminal Appeals, sums up in the most disinterested way the opinion of numerous defense attorneys and prosecutors who dealt with Sebesta for decades. "If you asked me, 'True or false, is there prosecutorial misconduct on the part of Charles Sebesta?', I'd have to give you a Capital-Blazing-T, not in this case only, or that case only, but over a period of 20 years."[55]

A look at the prosecutor and his methods

Charles Joseph Sebesta, Jr., whose Bohemian ancestors were brought into East Texas to grow cotton in the rough black land in the eastern part of Burleson County around the turn of the last century, worked hard to convince the writer that he's civilized and reasonable. He is white and an Aggie in a part of Texas where that gives you a boost, and a nominal Democrat dating back to the era when Republicans were rare in this state. He voted in the last Republican primary and was pleased when the U.S. Supreme Court reversed the Florida Supreme Court on counting votes and sent George W. Bush to the White House.

He grew up in Snook, a tiny town in Burleson County between Caldwell and College Station, the home of Texas A & M University. Snook was once named "Sebesta," for his ancestors. There are Sebestas all over East Texas. His branch of the family accumulated a lot of land and wealth, and the social entitlement that implies.[1]

A graduate of Baylor University Law School in Waco, Texas, not far to the northeast of his home turf, Sebesta was appointed to his first District Attorney position in his home county, Burleson, by Governor Dolph Briscoe in 1975. Until 1987 he was also D.A. in Lee County and until 1991 in Bastrop County until population growth (according to him) caused division of the judicial region.[2] He retired at age 60 from the D.A. offices in both Burleson and Washington Counties where he'd ruled for the last quarter century, a prosperous man with land and oil leases around the state. These holdings are supplemented by his D.A. retirement and military retirement as a bird colonel in the Army. The Brenham Eagle reported a retirement bash for him attended by 400 persons, including many officials of both counties.

A woman, whose final years of county service were marred by a spurious charge pushed through by the D.A., says media reports of the event left the impression that "he was the most loved man in the county; but he's the most hated!"[3] Another resident of Burleson County, a longtime elected official, says there's a reason Charles Sebesta used local funds to hire bodyguards in later years. The official, who long urged audits of the D.A.'s office for equity reasons, was hauled before grand juries many times over the years over petty matters, but says the grand juries always just laughed at the charges and threw them out.[4] There aren't many who had such good fortune.

Thomas Torlincasi, a North Texas businessman and squeaky-clean Aggie who did business in Burleson County to his peril was convicted by what he deems a "hanging jury"[5] in the Caldwell courthouse in February of 2001. The conviction was on one of three felony charges pursued by

Sebesta for a matter Torlincasi and his attorney David Mendoza say is a business conflict and civil case, at most. Mendoza, a former criminal court judge from Houston, also says it was an issue over which Sebesta actually lacked venue authority, since the charge pressed against him involved money pursuant to a contract sent from Hays County to Tarrant County to Torlincasi's office.

Torlincasi says local residents have told him the D.A. has abused his power for years and is soundly hated by those who've encountered his tactics, but who fear retaliation against themselves or their families and business associates if they fight back or speak out.[6] A number of local residents, including former elected officials, declined to be quoted for that reason. Famed defense attorney Dick DeGuerin says even local attorneys won't speak out against him though he's theoretically out of power, for fear of consequences.[7] In Torlincasi's case, he was indicted in 1999 for theft with no investigation that included asking Torlincasi's side of the story or examining his documents, and his attorney was called a liar in court by the D.A.. When Torlincasi attempted to defend himself to the first grand jury, his testimony was labeled perjurious (based on the evaluation of the plaintiff, who'd concealed evidence from the D.A.) and generated a second felony indictment from a new grand jury, which is a favorite Sebesta tactic.[8]

After filing a complaint against Sebesta related to the perjury charge, Torlincasi was hit with a third indictment, for tampering with government documents. Over the next year and a half his proposed biomass energy project, which he says would have brought jobs and income to the county and had local support in Somerville, was destroyed. His reputation and company were wrecked. His wife and business partner suffered two miscarriages, which her doctor attributed to the stress of the indictments.[9]

Sebesta offered him numerous deals, but they all amounted to Torlincasi admitting wrongdoing, which he wasn't about to do. Just before they originally went to trial in late 2000, Sebesta offered one deal in which Torlincasi would forswear the right to appeal the decision. The case appeared to be going Torlincasi's way the first time around, after his attorney demolished the state's key witness. Mysteriously two different jurors, two days in a row, called in sick, and the judge, who is reputedly on to the D.A.'s ways, was forced to declare a mistrial based on that circumstance, a very rare occurrence. Sebesta suggested another trial date, which would have eliminated the presiding judge because he would have had a conflict. The judge didn't buy it and volunteered to come out of retirement to hear the case a few months later.

Unfortunately for Torlincasi, even a sympathetic judge was unable to prevent the derailing of justice that occurred in the second trial. Sebesta, who was losing the case, point by point, to the defense, delivered a closing argument in stentorian, Southern preacher tones. He painted the defendant as a con man who'd deceived the local populace on many counts not previously argued, because they were irrelevant to the case against him, and he called Torlincasi a liar eleven times.[10] He then persuaded his co-prosecutor from Houston, James Leitner, to make a point relating to Torlincasi's grand jury testimony that had been disproved in the previous trial. The jury bought it, as did Leitner, at least at the time.

To add insult to injury, Torlincasi learned post-conviction that the D.A.'s office had convinced Leitner that Torlincasi's wife had divorced him (patently false), presumably to make the point that the defendant was such a scumbag he had no one but a few blood relatives standing by him.[11] An attorney from the region theorized that the jury pool had been handpicked by Sebesta.[12] At least one of his neighbors, a fellow Baptist, was in the jury, and the foreman's brother was from Snook.[13]

In 1995 in a Grimes County case in which Sebesta inserted himself as a special prosecutor when a request had actually been made for his assistant Bill Torrey's aid, a claim of tainted jury was raised by defense attorney Kenneth Keeling because Sebesta was kin to the Grand Jury Foreman. In Burleson County, according to a county resident with friends in the courthouse, one can pack the jury wheel so tight that the names won't shuffle as it turns. If one adds a handful of names one wants to the opening, they'll stay put after the presumed mixing of the wheel.[14]

Defense attorney, former prosecutor and county judge Stephen Keng of Lee County relates an early example of the way Sebesta criminalized conduct that was not a crime. Back in the mid-to-late seventies, at the beginning of his career, Keng represented a client from Burleson County who had a well-documented drinking problem, and who lay down along the railroad tracks atop his coat for a snooze. Awakened by a passing freight train, he stumbled off, leaving the coat with his I.D. behind. The train conductor feared he'd run over someone and tried to trace the coat's owner, which brought the drunk to the new D.A.'s attention. Sebesta brought out an old law from the 19th century, designed to deter train robbers from blockading the tracks, and indicted him for trying to stop a train.[15] Sebesta visited the jail and convinced the poor man that he would spend five years in the pen for his offense, until the young, court-appointed Keng confronted Sebesta. Keng told Sebesta he could set the trial date, but argued the D.A. would find it difficult to convince a jury his client had intended to block the train, given his history. The D.A. backed down, asking, "What charge would your client accept?" "Public intoxication," responded Keng, and so the matter was resolved.[16]

Keng comments, as did several other defense attorneys who've gone up against Sebesta over the years, "No telling how many poor people went to the penitentiary because they didn't know any better" or, as Robert Kuhn of Austin put it, "because some lawyer pled them guilty after he (Sebesta) told them a bunch of lies about what he had. . . . He was just notorious for that."[17] The state of Texas seems to lack a structure or mechanism to evaluate, discipline and penalize D.A.'s gone off the tracks. Keng and three former Brazos County D.A's interviewed about Sebesta say there used to be such a structure in the Texas State Bar, but it was underfunded and understaffed and eventually cut by the Sunset Commission.[18]

Brooks Kofer, a former assistant County Attorney and County Attorney in Brazos County for 17 years, in an era when the County Attorney was also a prosecutor on criminal matters says:

> When you went to Burleson County, you didn't go to the court, you went to Sebesta's barn, you might call it, and the way he ran things was a little unusual. . . . He was a dominating type prosecutor, using a loud voice in the courtroom as well as threats and more or less disregarding the elected judge who was presiding at the time. . . . Of course he had numerous little funny deals about wanting to get a case and he would fabricate some evidence for you, and you'd say, 'Well, that's not the way it is.' But the only way to straighten it out would be to go to trial. But if he gave you a deferred adjudication or offered it, you'd accept it because that was the best for your client.[19]

Robert Kuhn pulls no punches when describing his experience with Sebesta:

> I've been tryin' cases against Charles Sebesta for a long time off and on. He will lie, cheat and steal. . . . Charles just doesn't have any scruples, he just will do anything, but he's really bad about lying to you about what the evidence is, to try to get you to plead, because he'll tell you he 's got all this evidence and he's gonna be able to do this and do that and he really doesn't have anything. . . . I have never lost a case to him.[20]

Kuhn describes a recent case in which a client was falsely charged with criminal conspiracy regarding a used tractor he'd taken on inspection, then decided it was not worth fixing, not knowing it had been stolen. "Sebesta had the original thief who'd stole it, he just had him blatantly lie about all these things. We caught him and showed that he was lying. . . . Charles was bad, maybe still is, in trying to suborn perjury, to try to get people to lie, he would encourage witnesses to lie."[21]

> When told Sebesta had been named Prosecutor of the Year, Kuhn's response was: "You're not telling me the truth . . . Prosecutor of the Year! Good lord! What were they thinking. . . (laughs) . . . that is terrible! I've known Charles so long and he is so sorry . . . . He just would do anything, he just would lie to you, lie to everybody about stuff all the time."[22]

Pat Holloway, now of Austin but formerly from Giddings in Lee County when Sebesta's turf was larger, once was threatened in court with indictment for obstruction of justice by Sebesta.[23] Holloway was appointed as a pro bono lawyer to defend a thief but found a good legal precedent to free his client based on a search and seizure irregularity. He says Judge Placke warned him to drop his motion to quash the indictment or Sebesta would have him indicted, and Placke didn't want to have to worry about him coming back in his court as a defendant.[24] He says Placke offered a good deal for his client, who did not want to go to trial, as sweetener.[25]

Holloway also tells one version of a story told with different circumstances by different sources, of the D.A.'s inaction when faced with wrongdoing where bringing charges would harm his own financial or political interests:

> We caught a guy red-handed stealin' oil off one of our wells. . . . It's a violation of all kind of laws, federal and everything else. . . . I had the guy taped threatening me. I got the guy to confess on the telephone to having stolen oil out of my well, and when I told him who I was (I was masquerading as somebody else), he threatened to kill me if I prosecuted him, on the telephone, which is pretty serious, so I took it to Sebesta's office and got an investigator and we brought the guy in and we got the guy to confess again in front of the detective . . . so he was guilty of all kind of serious felonies and Sebesta never would prosecute him, never would *touch* him, let him go, and he'd been stealing for a long time. . . . I think he had some kind of a deal working with the guy.[26]

He minces no words either in describing the D.A.:

> He's a chicken shit, no good lyin' son of a bitch. He's really a bad guy.... he's done bad, bad things.[27]

Phyllis (not her real name because her son requested her identity be concealed) is a landowner and longtime resident of Burleson County. She spent $24,000 defending her son against baseless charges of sexual abuse against his two-year old son, filed (without investigation and finally dropped) by his alienated wife in Burleson County during and after a divorce and child custody battle in the summer and fall of 1993. The ploy was supported by Sebesta, who was friends with the wife's father, a law enforcement worker in the county. The ex-wife got custody of the boy and put him into mental institutions several times in ensuing years for no discernible reason, according to the grandmother. After winning custody, due to the pending charges that the father had abused the son, the mother's attorney turned around in court and said the woman still wished the father to have the boy alternate weekends and every Tuesday night, which certainly cast doubt on the validity of the charges.[28]

When it all started, Phyliss's son received notice at the end of one week that he was up for indictment before a grand jury the following Monday. He had his attorney call the D.A.'s office to ask if they could postpone the grand jury until he returned from a work-related conference so he could testify in his own behalf. The attorney was told it could be postponed to the end of the week. When the young man returned from his trip he learned he'd been indicted that Monday, in part because the grand jury was told by Charles Sebesta's secretary that the defendant's attorney hadn't allowed him to come, leading them to think he had something to hide.[29]

Defense attorney Eric Perkins, a former prosecutor who spent three years with the Nueces County Attorney's Office as Criminal Section Chief, represented South Texas clients charged a few years ago with criminal conspiracy for stealing their own show pig from a slaughterhouse in violation of competition rules. They ultimately pled guilty to aggravated perjury despite the fact that there was no basis to the original charges. It was Sebesta's now famous grand jury technique (which really is nothing more than a gestapo-like interrogation) which yielded enough confusing and apparently (but not actually) contradictory testimony that persuaded the accused to yield to his pressure.[30] Perkins adds: Tom (Torlincasi)'s case... is so similar that it defies explanation. Sebesta informed me after the Grand Jury fiasco that if he determined that I had played any part in the presentation of perjured testimony he would prosecute me as well. I had never encountered anything like it in my life. [31]

Annette Hanna was an uncompromising attorney in Brazos County who ruffled quite a few feathers. She ran afoul of someone with clout with Sebesta, apparently, and found herself in the midst of a sting operation that her attorney Steve Brittain argued was set up to destroy her reputation and law practice. She was indicted on a charge of baby buying, handcuffed, and carted off to the Caldwell jail where, according to her attorneys, Sebesta "falsely informed jail personnel" that her high bond had not been lowered, "knowing that Judge Placke had lowered it — in an attempt to prolong her imprisonment."[32] It had taken three grand juries to get an indictment against her; the first two refused, and the third was misled into thinking they were just re-indicting for some technical reasons and never heard the case against her.[33] Hanna had health problems and the night she was arrested was taken to an emergency room with stress-related high blood pressure and elevated blood sugar.[34]

Before it was over she'd hired three attorneys to represent her and spent a year or so with her reputation under a cloud, and her career suffered as a result. She was acquitted, and then sued Sebesta and the witnesses against her. She died young in 2000.[35] Brittain said she was just trying to give a child a good home, and never should have been charged, were it not for the political ambitions of Charles Sebesta. According to one Bryan attorney, Hanna had angered Sebesta's cousin, who held a position in Brazos County, and that was related to Hanna's ordeal.[36]

Travis Bryan III, formerly a Brazos County prosecutor, defended the employee named in one indictment. This young black woman who eventually got her indictment dismissed as part of the settlement with out-of-state owners, who paid $250,000 to get free of charges Bryan said were unfounded. Bryan said when he announced to the local media that his client's name had been cleared, Sebesta called him up and threatened to re-indict her to punish him for "crowing to the press" about the victory.[37] Bryan told him he didn't think that would be a good idea, as it was punishing his client for something he'd done, not her, and that the D.A. "better not do it."[38] Sebesta didn't.[39]

Sebesta was named Prosecutor of the Year in 1999 by the Texas Bar Association, which Stephen Keng says he finds "hilarious."[40] About the same time, the D.A. announced his plans to retire, a move that surprised many and unleashed a crowd of candidates for his office that had gone unchallenged for a quarter century. Keng represents a client who perhaps had something to do with Sebesta's retirement — an independent cattleman named Richard Surovik, whose family has run cattle in Burleson County for generations.

Surovik crossed the D.A. originally when Sebesta tried to indict his father who was on the County Board of Appraisers. Surovik said he believes Sebesta was out to punish the board for not buying computer equipment from one of his cronies.[41] The son immediately filed an incident report on Sebesta for seizing board records without following any protocol.[42] Surovik reported that Sebesta learned of the report just before the grand jury met to consider the charge against Surovik's father for tampering with records, and had to drop the charges, return the records and apologize to the chief appraiser and the elder Surovik.[43]

In 1998, Richard Surovik learned that Sebesta had persuaded a local legislator to submit a bill to the uncontested bills calendar to quietly eliminate the post of County Attorney for Burleson County.[44] Sebesta, according to Surovik, told the legislator there was no opposition when, in fact, no one knew anything about it, not even the County Attorney.[45] Surovik gathered documentation and effectively organized opposition to it.[46]

Not long after, Keng ran as a write-in candidate for County Judge, a position he planned to use to audit the D.A.'s office.[47] Just before the filing deadline, Surovik was hit with a felony charge from one of Sebesta's grand juries.[48] The charge involved a threat, on tape — a very poor quality tape that was presented to Keng's attorneys when they requested evidence of the charge.[49]

Surovik began to research the matter and found the grand jury's authority had expired before it indicted him (and at least 54 others accused of felonies).[50] The D.A. dismissed the expired jury as a trivial matter and had most of the accused re-indicted, including Surovik, who continued his research, discovering that the D.A. had never turned in annual reports (required by state law) accounting for funds taken in and disbursed.[51] Surovik and Keng filed public information requests for the records.[52]

Another prominent attorney from the region was also investigating the D.A. in 1999. Surovik and others speculate that Sebesta saw the handwriting on the wall and chose to end his electoral career to avoid a defeat, hoping instead, according to Surovik, for an appointment to an appellate regional judgeship.[53] Local observers also believe that 21st District Judge John ("Jack") Placke deliberately delayed his own retirement for years to block Sebesta's access to his post, only announcing it months after Sebesta publicly vowed to retire from political life.[54]

Judge McDonald, whose own father was also a district judge and later a presiding judge on the Texas Court of Criminal Appeals, sums up in the most disinterested way the opinion of numerous defense attorneys and prosecutors who dealt with Sebesta for decades. "If you asked me, 'True or false, is there prosecutorial misconduct on the part of Charles Sebesta?',

I'd have to give you a Capital-Blazing-T, not in this case only, or that case only, but over a period of 20 years."[55]

McDonald cites a case where Sebesta appeared as a witness in a civil case where a black man, Rudolph Himmet, was charged (with no basis) for theft of an expensive truck he had actually purchased from the local Ford dealer.[56] The D.A. admitted he was doing legal work on the side for the same Ford dealer.[57] They sang in the Baptist choir together.[58] McDonald told the local judge who'd asked him in, "This case is bigger than Dallas, with racial overtones and malicious prosecution."[59]

Eventually the accused was acquitted; but in the meantime, he had to sell some cattle at a low price to get bond money, and pay several thousand to a defense attorney, so he was unable to make a lease payment on some grazing land. He had to sell his cattle because he had nowhere to graze them, and thus some of the hard-earned property of a stable family man in an adjoining county was stripped away from him.

The accused filed a civil suit against the Ford dealer for malicious prosecution and amazingly, when it was tried in neighboring Lee County, rural, Germanic and conservative, the black man won a substantial settlement against Ford and the white dealer.[60]

The judge explains how Sebesta was able to garner so much power, for example to control the docket, seemingly unchecked by the local judges. Because their jurisdiction covered several counties, judges were dependent on the office of the D.A. to supply needed staff and services when they were away from their home office.[61] Additionally, in Sebesta's case, one of the judges (Howard "Bob" Towslee) was a former junior law partner to the D.A. He was also a member of Sebesta's church, the locally powerful First Baptist Church of Caldwell. [62]

When Sebesta's appointment to the judicial post was blocked for the second time in 1983 by politically powerful persons in the region who were appalled at his methods, Towslee got the position in the newly-created 335th Judicial District. The record seems to indicate that Sebesta made sure the toughest cases with the least evidence went to his court.

McDonald said it took him a while to figure out that Sebesta was routinely intimidating jailed persons under indictment and not represented by attorneys into plea bargaining, and then bringing them to court telling the judge they needed representation, as they were about to plead.[63] McDonald put a stop to it when he presided, saying the attorneys would be appointed first, and not just from Sebesta's list of green "wet-behind-the-ears" lawyers who'd been told by the D.A. that if they didn't do as he wanted, they'd be taken off the list.[64]

McDonald says he eventually quit accepting visiting judgeships in Sebesta's region, because he would be so upset over the D.A.'s disregard for constitutional rights and due process he'd be unable to sleep.[65] He says he can tell you stories about Sebesta that would curl straight hair and make curly hair straight.[66]

Although McDonald had nothing to do with it, Anthony Graves *is* such a story.

Train Wreck

Graves is on death row despite the fact that the main evidence against him came from a co-defendant who bargained in exchange for incriminating Graves, and then changed his mind before the Graves trial and told the D.A. and his own defense attorney, as well as others, that Graves had nothing to do with the crimes. This witness was further pressured by the state to keep his bargain — to testify against Graves to keep the focus off his wife.

Three years after Graves was convicted under Judge Towslee's jurisdiction, the co-defendant, Robert Carter, began to recant, and continued to do so in various official and unofficial forms, until he was executed on May 31, 2000. He said twice, on the gurney, that Graves was innocent; that he'd "lied on him in court."[67]

There was no physical evidence in the case, no weapons were ever found, and Graves had numerous alibi witnesses. All of Graves' defense attorneys, including the famed Dick DeGuerin and former criminal court judge Jay Burnett, state unequivocally their belief in his innocence. At least one of the co-defendant's appellate attorneys says her client told her also that Graves was innocent. Sebesta admits that the night before testifying in Graves' trial, the co-defendant was given a polygraph test that focused not on Graves' role in the murders, but on his wife's. The corroborating evidence offered at trial to the co-defendant's testimony was a series of statements by Burleson County law enforcement officials that they had overheard incriminating conversations between Graves and his co-defendant in an overcrowded jail where the inmates knew a two-way intercom was always on. A jail inmate who admitted he was on medication for depression and had attempted suicide gave mildly incriminating testimony.

Another leg of the case was supplied by a medical examiner whose testimony is considered suspect by longtime Travis county defense attorneys and prosecutors. He testified that a knife that was identical to one Graves had been given years before by a former employer was most probably the duplicate of one of the murder weapons. A forensic expert from the University of North Texas later demolished that testimony, saying the methods used to determine the match were not only not scientific, but actually destructive of the physical evidence (skulls with knife wounds).

Graves' only prior convictions were a 1987 bust when he sold $50 worth of pot to a narc, and a DWI in 1992. A talented athlete whose main problem seems to have been his use of marijuana, Graves has been jailed with the threat of execution hanging over him for a dozen years, unable physically to even touch his three sons to whom he was very close, much less supply financial support. Time is running out Anthony on the train wreck of railroad justice in Texas.

But Charles Sebesta, 1999 Prosecutor of the Year, says he's "comfortable" and "satisfied"[68] with Graves' conviction and sentence; just as he's proud to defend the residents of his county against "white collar criminals" like Tom Torlincasi, who endured financial ruin and prolonged legal battles to clear his name.[69]

Anthony Graves sent this photo of himelf
to the author in a letter in June, 2000.

Anthony Graves
(Part 3) Post-conviction Chances

Roy Greenwood and Jay Burnett, habaes attorneys for Graves.

Photo by Susan Lee Campbell Solar

Anthony's youngest son, Alex.

Arthur Curry, Doris Curry, Anthony's brother and Mother, along with niece and nephew, Showntina and C.J.

Photos by Susan Lee Campbell Solar

Post-conviction chances for justice: slim to none

For a person like Anthony Graves with post-conviction evidence of innocence, prosecutorial misconduct, and incompetence of early habeas as well as trial attorneys, what happens after he is condemned and sent to Texas death row? Why is he still sitting on death row four years after the main "evidence" against him was recanted? And more importantly, what are Graves' chances of escaping a premature date with death by deadly chemicals?

As in the case of Gary Graham, following the twists and turns of the various stages and sub-stages of the Graves appeal saga is not for the impatient or simple-minded.

First stop: petition for re-trial

More than anything this first round was like talking to a wall. Good case, wrong judge.

It began soon after Graves' sentencing, in January 1995, when court records report Calvin Garvie and Lydia Clay-Jackson traveled to Caldwell for a re-match presided over by Judge Towslee. The occasion for the hearing was a motion Garvie had filed requesting a new trial based on jury misconduct[1] and intimidation of the key witness for the defense, Yolanda Mathis.[2] Several jurors were questioned regarding the impact of Carter's testimony and his credibility in their minds as they weighed the verdict. One juror admitted he didn't totally buy Carter's story, but was convinced enough to convict.[3] The jury foreman denied that he had "taken a nap" during the trial.[4] A female juror acknowledged she was crying as the verdict was delivered.[5] A bailiff denied conveying to assistant D.A. Torrey the course of jury deliberations,[6] although Graves' family members and friends said they heard the prosecutors discussing at a certain point that the jury was split 8 to 4.[7]

Garvie established that his key alibi witness, Yolanda Mathis, was prepared to testify until she was warned she had become a suspect and could be indicted. Sebesta, in questioning her, changed his description of his trial warning to her, saying "our concern was more from a perjury standpoint than being an actual participant. And we simply, for the Court's edification, wanted Ms. Mathis warned. We're not subject to what counsel may have gone out and told Ms. Mathis. . . . They did not call Ms. Mathis in and let her tell the Court that she did not wish to . . ."[8] Sebesta attempted to convince the defense and Mathis that the defense had altered what he had said, but Garvie insisted correctly that the record would reveal that the D.A. had warned "that you were a suspect in the case and that you could possibly be indicted for the same capital murder charge as Anthony Graves"[9] Telling someone that their testimony could amount to perjury is quite different from telling them that they have become a suspect in the case and could probably be indicted in the future on that basis. Somehow this distinct shift by Sebesta, which certainly calls into question the integrity of his position, does not seem to have been raised by Graves' later appeals. The salient fact here is that Yolanda Mathis, the essential alibi witness for Anthony Graves, never testified on his behalf.

Judge Towslee and Garvie debated whether Garvie had met the legal filing requirements of thirty days from sentencing, and the judge indicated that whether he'd met them or not, he was inclined to deny the motion to re-try.[10] And indeed he did.

In Texas a death sentence is automatically appealed to the high criminal court, the Texas Court of Criminal Appeals, or TCCA. It is known as a direct appeal, and it concerns itself with the conduct of the main players in the trial, particularly the prosecutors and the judge. Garvie and Clay-Jackson passed the Anthony Graves case to Virgie Mouton of Houston, who did a very competent job according to former Criminal Court Judge Jay Burnett, who serves on Graves' second post-conviction defense team.[11]

Second stop: Texas Court of Criminal Appeals

Guilty until proven innocent. It's difficult to avoid a mind-numbing sense of futility here.

Mouton's brief raised issues of sufficiency of evidence regarding Carter's credibility, the knife testimony and the "jail-house confessions."[12] It was responded to[13] by Larry Urquhart, a Brenham attorney hired by Sebesta.

First, Urquhart established that the law requires a court review of the sufficiency of corroborating evidence to the accomplice's testimony in order to eliminate that testimony from consideration.[14] Then, Urquhart presented *as fact* a number of claims that were straight from the accomplice who was supposed to be eliminated, "facts" that had been contradicted by defense witnesses or else were not corroborated.[15] For example, he presented *as fact* that Carter and Graves were friendly although Graves' defense had brought forth witnesses to question that allegation made by Carter.[16] He presented *as fact* that Carter and Graves had several times discussed Graves' mother's friction with Bobbie Davis over the latter's promotion, even though co-workers had testified that the two women were friends.[17]

Urquhart's main argument was the weapon.[18] He presented Graves' denial to the Grand Jury that he owned a knife.[19] He presented Rueter's testimony that he'd given Graves one, Betty Deaver's memory of seeing the knife on Graves' chest of drawers, and Genzer's recollection of Graves' showing it to him at work shortly after Rueter gave it to him.[20] He presented tests by Bayardo and Coffman showing the knife in question "fit like a glove" into the wounds.[21] In fact no murder weapon was ever produced by anyone.[22] The brief leaned heavily on the testimony of witnesses who claimed they heard incriminating statements in the jail, arguing that all this together "tended to connect" Graves to the crime.[23] Thus he satisfied the standard set by a 1993 TCCA opinion, *Munoz* v. *State*, which ruled out convictions based solely on accomplice testimony.[24]

The TCCA opinion authored by Judge Charles Baird[25] agreed with the prosecution's brief except on one part, the testimony of jailer Eldridge.[26] There the court agreed with the defendant that the prosecution didn't well establish the physical basis for his testimony. Since Eldridge had not been questioned as to whether he could identify Graves' voice, and if so, "by what means," "the trial judge erred in not requiring the State to properly authenticate this evidence."[27] However, the crucial part of the ruling on that issue was that the error was "harmless" to Graves' case since in cross-examination Eldridge supplied that information and the defense raised no objection to the testimony of the other two jailhouse eavesdroppers, which corroborated Eldridge's recollections.[28]

Baird gave serious consideration to the prosecution's insinuation of a "kissing cousin" relationship between Graves and Cookie Carter (presumably lifted from the witness who wasn't used due to her lack of credibility and who had speculated about such a relationship to one of the Rangers).[29] This seemed to be an effort to find a motive for Graves' otherwise senseless participation in the murder of six people. As the prosecution and judge reasoned, Graves might have been currying favor with Cookie by agreeing to get rid of her rival and solve her and her husband's problem regarding the increased child support.[30]

It is important to understand that the facts presented to justices on the appeals court come from a summary written by the previous trial judge. These trial judges typically adopt the prosecutor's perspective as though the defense hadn't presented contradicting evidence.[31] It is not surprising, therefore, that the reviewing court would rule with the "state" or prosecution.

For example, regarding corroboration of Carter's claim that there was friction between Anthony's mother and Doris Curry over a job promotion, the best the state could do was present a co-worker who said there had been talk that there possibly existed some envy over Davis' promotion but wasn't sure.[32] The defense presented a witness testifying that the women were friends, as evidenced by the fact that Doris presented Bobbie with pecans every fall.[33] If a thorough investigation had occurred the supervisor of both women, Rick Carroll, would have said they were never in competition for the same job, and were, in fact friends.[34] No one representing Graves ever asked Carroll.[35]

Nonetheless, the opinion read by the appellate judges said the state had elicited evidence in support of the friction over the Anthony's mother's job theory, supplying a motive to Graves which otherwise didn't exist. The Munoz standard (which says the corroborating evidence to an accomplice testimony doesn't need by itself to prove guilt beyond a doubt but simply has to "tend to connect" the victim to the crime) is a very weak standard indeed in a matter of life or death.

Likewise, the knife testimony presented by the prosecution was accepted as valid enough to incriminate Graves. Then jailhouse witness statements that Graves was overheard discussing with Carter getting rid of the weapons became corroborative of Carter's testimony about getting rid of the weapons. The judge opined for the apparently unanimous appellate court that "the statements of both men are further reinforced by the fact that investigators never found the murder weapons."[36]

With regard to the death sentence, Mouton had argued Graves had no history of violent behavior. The psychiatrist said if Graves had committed the crime it was a case of situational violence, not likely to be repeated, and "the evidence showed that he is a caring, loving, family-oriented person and he professes his innocence regarding the instant crime."[37] The judge pointed out that in past rulings the court had held that particularly "heinous" circumstances in the commission of a crime could justify a finding of future dangerousness absent any prior history.[38] He restated the extreme violence of the crime, the fact that "some of the children were killed in their own beds."[39] He thought the workplace fight and the DUI arrest where marijuana was found in the vehicle showed "a propensity to solve disputes through violence, to attack people without warning, when they are unable to properly defend themselves."[40] He said, "Graves was prone to attempt to use a weapon during a conflict . . . to violate controlled substances laws and drive while under the influence of alcohol and marijuana in a condition which could put others at risk. Thus the . . . extraneous offense evidence could reasonably be viewed as making it more probable that appellant would commit criminal acts of violence that would constitute a continuing threat to society."[41] Thus the death penalty was warranted because Graves posed a future threat to society.

Next stop: Writ of Habeas Corpus

Evidence aside, the only route left is to show the client's constitutional rights have been violated — this in a state suffering from the Bush effect on American jurisprudence.

In Texas, until 1995, (and in most other states to this day) providing lawyers at the level of writs of habeas corpus was left to luck or to the families of the condemned. They would have to find funders or idealistic attorneys who believed the case of their loved one was worth sinking a lot of resources into. State writs became crucial to a death row inmate's chances when the AEDPA (Antiterrorism and Effective Death Penalty Act) was passed in 1996 limiting, among other things, federal habeas relief. A writ of habeas corpus is the petition to be heard by the highest courts of criminal appeal, at state and federal levels, based on some claim of wrongful conduct in the judicial process leading to conviction, therefore wrongful imprisonment.

Another fast track habeas reform bill, specific to Texas and promised by George W. Bush in his gubernatorial campaign against Ann Richards, limited a death row inmate to one habeas appeal in state courts. It also provided, for the first time, that the state would provide habeas attorneys for this final state appeal. The legislature mandated that the Court of Criminal Appeals would ensure that the lawyers were competent. The language of the act establishing the right to state-paid habeas attorneys was written by sponsor Pete Gallegos, a Democratic Representative, who said the inmates deserved one very well-represented run at a habeas proceeding. The legislature also provided funds to pay attorneys and for investigation and research. Unfortunately only half the funds ($2 million instead of $4 million) that the Court requested were supplied.

According to Judge Baird, a member of the Court of Criminal Appeals at the time and one of several judges chosen to oversee the appointment process, the Court was in no position to guarantee competent representation at the habeas level.[42] The judges were overburdened to begin with, and were not administrators.[43] Furthermore, an initial group of competent attorneys recruited by the justices quickly became unhappy when they learned of funding problems halfway through cases.[44] Some of the financial problems, according to Baird, were the responsibility of then-Governor George W. Bush, whose office was sitting on some of the money.[45]

In fact, though, the TCCA was responsible for appointing and administering the fees for habeas attorneys from September 1995 when the new statute (11.071) took effect until four years later when the appointment responsibility was shifted to district courts. It never set standards for appointments, resulting in some highly inappropriate appointments and dismal performances.

The initial list of attorneys willing to be appointed, who met the judges' subjective standards, included some who were barely out of law school and had no idea how to go about representing a death row inmate at that stage of appeal. Veteran capital defenders by 1997 were getting swamped with desperate last minute phone calls from appointed attorneys who were in over their heads as deadlines neared for their client writs.

A few inmates like Anthony Graves had some reserve for such a problem. European supporters had learned of his case and probable innocence a year after he arrived at Ellis Unit I outside Huntsville. By April of 1997, when his direct appeal was denied, they had raised enough money to hire a very experienced capital defender, Roy Greenwood, as a consultant to back up Graves' appointed attorney. Greenwood had started writing appeals for death row inmates thirty years back while he was still in law school, and he had also for a while been a briefing attorney at the TCCA. Over the years, admittedly when winning reversals on capital cases was less of a Sisyphean endeavor in Texas, Greenwood had gotten "seven or eight" men off death row.[46]

Even with advice from Greenwood, Houston attorney Patrick McCann, whose law license wasn't granted until May of 1995, a year after he graduated from law school, may have sealed his client's fate through inexperience, lack of nerve, and carelessness. McCann was appointed by the TCCA in October 1997 to be state habeas attorney for Graves.

Greenwood immediately sent McCann a June 1997 affidavit he had received from Carter claiming full responsibility for the crime and exonerating Graves, and stating that he had lied about Graves after telling the prosecutor's investigator and his attorney at Angleton that Graves was innocent.[47] The affidavit was backed up by a similar videotaped statement. But McCann didn't follow up on this strong indication of actual innocence of his client.[48] In January of 1998 Graves wrote McCann that he had heard through another inmate that "Carter wants to tell all" and that Graves' attorneys should get a deposition fast.[49] Carter felt he would be executed soon, and for religious reasons wanted to come clean, according to the inmate, whom Graves said was Carter's "Christian brother."[50]

Graves suggested McCann get Carter under oath, and he asked the attorney to go over Carter's testimony against Graves and ask all the questions Graves had been asking him without response since August 24, 1992. "Why he said such and such, and who told him to say such and such. And last but not least, see if he will tell who did this crime, because I would like to know myself."[51]

Clash of defense attorneys: Carter's vs. Graves'

So what happens to someone on death row when their attorney screws up?

In June of 1998 McCann went with a court reporter to Huntsville to take a fairly lengthy statement from Carter, who explicitly waived his right to have his attorney present. Carter added to his insistence on his sole responsibility for the crime and Graves' innocence, which he'd asserted in an affidavit a year earlier, and made several other key points. He said that at Angleton, Sebesta had conveyed through Walter Prentice the information that Sebesta "would be satisfied" with prosecuting Graves and Carter, and by implication, would leave Cookie alone.[52] Carter also said he believed that Prentice warned him about the possibility of perjuring himself in testifying against Graves.[53]

Although he was armed with the 1998 statement, an earlier video deposition of Carter and the 1997 affidavit, McCann ran into a major obstacle. He had taken the statement without notifying the prosecution or giving them a chance to cross-examine Carter, after numerous explicitly discouraging conversations going back months with Carter's attorney Bill Whitehurst.

Whitehurst is a grey-haired, imposing and, from the looks of his lush office a stone's throw from the Texas capitol, a successful personal injury and medical malpractice attorney. He was appointed by Federal District Judge Sam Sparks, despite Whitehurst's lack of experience in capital cases and zero experience in capital appeals. Whitehurst says he couldn't refuse the appointment without losing his standing on the list of qualified attorneys to take federal cases, although he did request a more experienced co-counsel, which the judge denied.[54]

After meeting the inmate, Whitehurst was determined to fight for commutation to life on technical grounds, the best he could hope for, given Carter's insistence that he was indeed the sole perpetrator of multiple murders. In 1998, Carter had not gone on the record, in any form that would be admissible in court, admitting his guilt in killing all the victims, an admission which could have been used to derail Whitehurst's battle for his life at the level of the Fifth Circuit and the Supreme Court. Whitehurst says McCann's requests came at a "very sensitive time" in Carter's federal writ process.[55]

Perhaps if Whitehurst had been around longer fighting for death row inmates, he would have realized the hopelessness of his fight for a client with no claims of innocence, despite the good technical grounds he believed he had for getting a reversal of his client's death sentence. His briefs argued prosecutorial misconduct during jury selection when the jurors were misled to believe a life sentence was undefined at the time when in fact it was firmly fixed at a minimum of 35 years before parole could even be considered. He cited an error by Judge Placke that essentially directed the jurors to reconsider their original verdict, which would have resulted in a life sentence for Carter.

Or perhaps Whitehurst, like Carter's other post-conviction attorneys, who had also been told by their client that Graves was uninvolved in the crime, was caught between a rock and a hard place. His professional ethical obligation to defend Carter prohibited him from allowing his client to come clean when he still had his own journey through the courts ahead of him. Whitehurst confides that, in his analysis, the case against Graves was never based on evidence but on an assumption that he believes was erroneous — that Carter couldn't have acted alone.[56]

Carter said in his 1998 statement that he had contacted his interim attorney Mary Hennessy (appointed when Prentice was suspended by the Bar in early 1995 to finish the direct appeal), as well as Garvie and Clay-Jackson, sometime after Graves' trial. Carter wanted to offer a recantation and the admission that he'd lied about Graves in court, and was trying to arrange for them to visit him together, but nothing ensued, "it didn't pan out."[57]

Whitehurst is a past president of the Texas State Bar Association and the Texas Trial Lawyers' Association, which might have been intimidating in itself to McCann, decades younger and with far less experience. Furthermore, Whitehurst was threatening McCann with a grievance if he did depose his client. Whitehurst now acknowledges it was probably McCann's idealism and zeal to save his client which caused McCann to commit what Whitehurst believes was an "outrageous" violation of the lawyer's code of ethics in "going behind our backs" to take Carter's deposition.[58] It made the deposition inadmissible in court. Greenwood says the reason it was inadmissible was that it was not a deposition (though it was called that), it was a statement. A deposition could have been admitted as evidence, a statement was not.[59]

Novice Writ

If too many habeas appeals are successful wouldn't that mean our judicial system routinely violates the Constitutional rights of American citizens?

These appeals are hard to win even for the experts. A novice doesn't have much chance at all. And McCann was a novice.

He delivered a brief in his client's behalf to the Court of Criminal Appeals that is, at the very least, controversial in legal circles. It devotes much energy to an international human rights argument that has zip chance in any U.S. court, much less in Texas. However, many critics of the Texas system might well agree with the argument:

> . . . the entire death penalty scheme in which he has become entrapped is unconstitutional from start to finish. He was tried under a system that mandates that he prove his worthiness to live. He is expected to file an application for habeas relief under a strict time limit which is not required of any prisoner who is convicted of any lesser crime. Our legislature has created a two-tier system of habeas relief which makes it far more difficult to gain relief for capital applicants than for non-capital applicants. He can expect no relief from the Governor, as that office and its arm in the Board of Pardon and Paroles have no real review system, and what rules they have established are so completely arbitrary that they violate both the due process and equal protection clauses of the Constitution.[60]

Despite the philosophical merits or lack thereof of McCann's petition, former criminal court judge Jay Burnett of Houston, who chairs the state bar's death penalty litigation committee, says of his predecessor's work: "I've seen worse, but I haven't seen much worse."[61] He cites the improper deposition of Carter, and says McCann failed to sufficiently investigate. For example, in his statement of facts he referred to the medical examiner Robert Bayardo, of Travis County, who had supplied the damning and highly debatable knife evidence, as "respected and experienced."[62] If he'd dug a little deeper, questioning Travis County attorneys on both sides of the bar, he might not have used the first adjective. More important, had McCann investigated enough to discover DeGuerin's three extra alibi witnesses, Burnett believes Graves' appeal would have been harder to dismiss, even by the current Court of Criminal Appeals.[63]

Still, McCann raised issues that should have cast doubt on the verdict against Graves:

> 1. Carter's perjurious testimony and the inducement of that perjury by the prosecution via a polygraph which Carter interpreted to mean he had to lie to protect his wife Cookie

> 2. Presentation of falsehoods by the prosecution

3. Jailhouse hearsay

4. Bogus expert testimony by the prosecution and the twisting of the testimony of the medical examiner and Roy Allen Rueter to make it seem that a knife once in Graves' possession was the actual murder weapon, which in fact was never recovered

5. The intimidation of Yolanda Mathis, which McCann argued was prosecutorial misconduct of an extent to ensure a reversal under several articles of the U.S. Constitution and several sections of Article I of the Texas Constitution.

McCann argued that the clemency system under the present structure of the Board of Pardons and Paroles violates the 14th, 5th, and 8th amendments to the U.S. Constitution. This, in part, is due to its racist application since the only two men to have been granted clemency in the state since 1982 were both white males (Randall Dale Adams and Henry Lee Lucas).

The Constitutional arguments were a waste of paper and time given the political and judicial climate in the state.

1998 evidentiary hearings

A primer: How to keep evidence from being heard.

There were two separate dates set for the 1998 hearing in Angleton before Judge Towslee on the issues raised in that first petition. The first was in mid-November, and Greenwood attended. Afterward, writing to Graves, who had been bench warranted to attend, McCann felt the defense had established four things:[64]

1. There had been an error by the trial attorneys on the motion for a new trial they had submitted in January 1995

2. Yolanda Mathis' testimony was "critical to the case

3. There would be grounds for claiming ineffective trial counsel on the Mathis issue

4. Sebesta made major mistakes in going after Graves.

Furthermore, at the hearing, the D.A. had acknowledged something that stunned the defense. In Angleton, prior to his testimony, Carter had told the prosecution that Theresa (Cookie) Carter "held the hammer"[65] at the crime scene and that Graves "didn't have anything to do with it".[66]

At the second hearing date on December 1, important testimony regarding the knife evidence was offered by an expert witness who heads the forensic laboratory at the University of North Texas. Carter's 1998 deposition and 1997 affidavit were offered as exhibits. But Carter was a no show. That was because Whitehurst had written the judge (copying the D.A. and McCann) a week earlier, informing them that Carter had agreed with his advice to take the Fifth if brought to the hearing. Coupled with the threat of a grievance suit if Carter was bench warranted, the letter had its intended effect. McCann backed off, which Greenwood and Burnett maintain is part of his failure to adequately defend his client. McCann's back-up plan had been to introduce the videotaped testimony without Carter, but under Texas law it was "hearsay" without Carter there to be cross-examined.

Greenwood had urged McCann to request a subpoena for Carter. If the judge had ruled Carter had Fifth Amendment privilege, which Greenwood thought he did not under Texas law since his direct appeal had been denied, then an exception to the "hearsay" law would have taken effect. Since Carter would have been unavailable to be cross-examined, the other documents would have been admissible. Greenwood further argued that for two years Carter had been writing him, waiving his Fifth Amendment rights repeatedly, a fact which Whitehurst might not have known.

Whitehurst says he was very clear in explaining to McCann earlier in the year that once Carter had no further avenue left for saving his own life, Whitehurst would collaborate with Graves' attorneys in arranging the deposition McCann was seeking.[67] Whitehurst says he had no doubt about the ethics of his position, though it was a "tough" situation. He had to defend his client foremost, even though Carter had told him from the outset that Graves was innocent.

Greenwood also later questioned Whitehurst's ethics in claiming in the letter to Judge Towslee that Carter would take the Fifth. Carter had written Greenwood in November of 1999 saying "the only reason I didn't attend that hearing" was because "my lawyer made it seem as if I didn't need to be presence (sic) but I know differently now."[68] Carter repeated his desire to help Anthony by testifying in some official capacity "while I'm still alive."[69]

Because he was not a criminal defense attorney, much less a capital habeas specialist, it is possible Whitehurst didn't understand the time pressure on Graves' defense to depose Carter in time to use him as evidence in the final state appeal. The prosecutors had withheld important information from the defense during the trial which effected Anthony's case including Carter's recantation prior to his testimony, and the charge that Carter had been pressured to lie by Sebesta through the use of the polygraph on his wife's role in the crime. Carter's deposition was essential, but it didn't happen.

Possibly discussion between Greenwood and Whitehurst could have cleared this up at the time, but Greenwood wasn't Graves' official attorney, just the consultant to McCann, who was also inexperienced. Possibly there was a misunderstanding between Carter and his attorney. Perhaps Carter later didn't want to admit to Graves or Greenwood he'd backed down. Maybe Whitehurst misunderstood the law surrounding his client's availability under the law or possibly stretched the truth (and thus committed an ethics violation himself) in his letter to the judge, as Greenwood argued to the CCA later. It is unclear, but the result is not.

Carter was not bench warranted by McCann after he received Whitehurst's letter and thus the Carter recantation presented in the form of the transcribed 1998 deposition and an earlier videotape were not admissible. The prosecution objected to them as "hearsay" and the judge sided with the state.

The recanted testimony of the witness against him never made it into court record.

First supplemental writ

Déjà vu: Good case, wrong judge.

This was a potentially fatal event for Graves, as the 1995 legislation limited the defense to one application to the state for habeas relief. The court could rule the defense had their chance, blew it, and thus waived the right to raise the issue again. McCann asked Judge Towslee at the hearing in December 1999, and followed up in writing with a motion, to allow him to submit a supplemental habeas corpus petition to include new information. Carter's admission that Cookie had been present at the scene of the crime had been suppressed.

Towslee denied the motion in January of 1999, after Sebesta had filed a reply to McCann's request citing expiration of deadlines for such filings and also completely misstating McCann's claim. The reply claimed that Graves' defense was arguing that "the prosecution had illegally withheld from the Applicant's trial attorneys the fact that Theresa Carter was considered by the State to be a suspect in this case," which they contended was "ludicrous" because she had been indicted as a co-defendant.[70] Of course, McCann had argued nothing of the sort.

In any case, the prosecution held the trump card. Judge Towslee was the gatekeeper. In February 1999, he filed his Findings of Fact and Conclusions[71] regarding the hearings a few months earlier, in whch he said Carter's recantations did not meet the standards for new evidence proving innocence because "his refusal to be tested by cross-examination calls their truthfulness into considerable doubt."[72]

Towslee went further, saying Graves' defense "still has not explained why the traditional vehicle for consideration of newly discovered evidence, the clemency petition, cannot serve its primary purpose here."[73] One wonders if Towslee was serious regarding clemency, given the history of its use in Texas following the 1976 re-instatement of capital punishment by the Supreme Court.

Regarding McCann's attempts to establish the existence of prosecutorial misconduct in the alleged intimidation of alibi witness Yolanda Mathis, the judge struck a note to be echoed later by the TCCA. He maintained the defense attorneys themselves "essentially frightened their own witness into refusing to testify."[74] He added his opinion that "the prosecutor's comments to the Court . . . were not the cause of her refusal to testify."[75] He said, moreover, "Mathis did testify at the motion for a new trial hearing for Applicant, specifically about her refusal to testify at his trial,"[76] presumably removing the allegation that the defense failed in their job to introduce her testimony.

McCann fired back in March of 1999. His brief in opposition to the judge's Findings of Facts and Conclusions found fault with the fact that the judge didn't acknowledge Yolanda Mathis' alibi testimony as part of the new innocence evidence.[77] It objected to the fact that the judge ignored the "complete rejection of the state's 'forensic evidence'"[78] by Dr. H. Gill-King of the University of North Texas. McCann said the judge couldn't attack Carter's veracity on recanting and then also claim he was credible in court. He pointed out the problems with the judge's recommendation that Graves seek clemency instead of relief from the courts, stating that clemency did not offer "adequate protection" and reminding the judge that a federal judge in Austin had recently "severely criticized"[79] the state clemency process. Attacking the judge's conclusion that Sebesta had shown adequate cause for his warnings to the defense regarding Mathis' testimony, McCann pointed out that if Mathis was indeed a suspect, how was it that there had been no indication of that in the two years prior to the trial? He also argued that if the judge found the defense team guilty of intimidating Mathis and not the prosecution, then once again he couldn't have it both ways and deny Graves' claim of ineffective representation regarding the Mathis incident.[80]

Amended petition

Perhaps we should just start over?

McCann avoided communication with Greenwood for the next few months. By March of 1999 they were back in touch. Greenwood was furious when he learned how things had gone awry. He felt certain, however, that an amended petition would be admitted by the Court of Criminal Appeals. He requested an affidavit from Calvin Garvie that his team had not been given the information about Carter's admission in Angleton regarding Cookie's presence at the scene of the crime.[81]

By June of 1999 Greenwood wrote Graves "your case is one of the best I've seen, and shows substantial problems that are glaring in the record with regard to your innocence, thus I can only hope your case is the exception, not the rule."[82]

In late July of 1999 McCann wrote Graves jubilantly that the appellate court had agreed to hear arguments in mid-September on two of the issues in the petition he'd submitted with Greenwood's help: the intimidation of Yolanda Mathis and the ineffectiveness of trial counsel in the January 1995 hearing.

By the end of August 1999, Greenwood was totally exasperated with McCann, who was Graves' official lawyer, for his lack of timeliness in filing and what Greenwood perceived as his failure "to understand the statute under which we're working, and/or the rules of the Court of Criminal Appeals, yet he will not accept any guidance from me."[83] But he also had good news — the Court of Criminal Appeals had set Graves' habeas corpus successor petition for oral argument, only the third time for such an event in a death row habeas appeal since the new statute governing capital appeals took effect in September of 1995. The Court had recognized Greenwood officially as co-counsel, so he would prepare the brief for the hearing.

After the hearing in September of 1999, Greenwood told Graves that he could predict how the court might rule based on the arguments of the "three or four who will try anything to deny you relief." He thought, however, the judges were surprisingly sympathetic because there was a "substantial showing of innocence" in the case. He warned Graves not to get his hopes up because "there is just too much conservatism going on."[84]

In February of 2000, the Court issued its opinion confirming Greenwood's fears — the majority of justices agreed that the *defense* had intimidated the witness for strategic reasons. They adopted Judge Towslee's reasoning that the defense attorneys were the ones who had told Mathis what the prosecution had said. Since they were court-appointed and had subpoenaed the witness, they were therefore acting as "agents of the state" when they passed on to her Sebesta's statement. Justice Cheryl Johnson wrote a stinging dissent to the opinion, stating that if the attorneys had so acted on the basis of a strategic decision, that alone should guarantee reversal based on a claim of incompetent counsel.[85]

Carter had contacted Greenwood by November of 1999, offering again to testify on behalf of Graves, and to undergo cross-examination by Sebesta to make it official. Greenwood needed time to figure out how that could be done within the narrowing confines of the new state law. By the spring, he'd figured it out in consultation with Dain Whitehurst, who had the responsibility of defending his own client and keeping him from further self-incrimination while he was still on the appeals train. But Carter's train was nearing the death chamber. Carter had an execution date set for late April. On February 3, 2000 the state court ruled against Graves on the Mathis issue. Anthony's train was beginning to catch up.

On February 16 the Court denied Graves' subsequent writ which dealt with suppression of evidence with reference to Carter's admission to the prosecution, prior to his Angleton testimony, that Cookie was at the crime scene. Whitehurst filed a motion to vacate the death order with Placke's court, which the judge allowed, and filed a motion for stay of execution with the Supreme Court.

Doubtless discouraged by Whitehurst's grievance against him, McCann withdrew from the case by November of 1999, and Greenwood was appointed to replace him the next month. Greenwood was working on a motion for rehearing on the first writ, which was due in March, and agreed with Whitehurst to file with the federal district court in Austin, requesting that court to authorize a deposition to preserve Carter's testimony on Graves' behalf for use in future federal appeals. The agreement with Carter's attorney was that when the execution date was imminent, with no escape hatch, Carter could be deposed.

Carter's death date was moved back five weeks to May 31. The federal court in Austin set a hearing for late March to rule on granting the deposition Greenwood requested. Greenwood's motion for rehearing was one of the longest he'd ever filed in 30 years of practice, due to "so many errors, both factual and legal, and improper utilization of appellate rules throughout the February 3 opinion from the state high court. By the third week of March, Sebesta and the Attorney General's office had agreed to a voluntary deposition of Carter. Sebesta demanded that Greenwood file a subsequent *habeas* petition with the trial court based on newly discovered evidence even though they'd already raised it in the first petition.

Greenwood thought Sebesta wanted the ball back in Towslee's court, where he could pressure the judge to rule that Carter's recantation testimony was not credible.[86] He reasoned that since Towslee would have to rule before the deposition, no federal judge would accept a ruling of lack of credibility prior to the testimony being offered.[87] Since they were filing it anyway at the D.A.'s insistence, Greenwood and Burnett threw in something extra – a claim of incompetent habeas counsel.[88]

By April 5th the Court of Criminal Appeals had denied McCann's motion for rehearing (the first subsequent application for writ), to Greenwood's disappointment, ruling the trial attorneys had "procedurally defaulted" the issue of Mathis' testimony, when they "failed to perfect the issue."[89] Shortly thereafter, Greenwood filed motions with the federal courts to be appointed as Graves' lead counsel with former judge Burnett as co-counsel, a weighty addition whom Greenwood described as being "very inventive and very aggressive."[90] Burnett as a state district judge had been the first judge to offer death row inmate Calvin Burdine relief on the basis that his attorney slept through portions of his trial.

By May 16th Greenwood discovered that Sebesta had reneged on his part of the bargain. Sebesta and the Attorney General had agreed they would expedite the processing of this third habeas petition through the state trial court and on to the Court of Criminal Appeals for immediate review. However, when Greenwood called the Brazoria County Clerk, he found the petition had been checked out by Sebesta in early April and not returned. It could not, therefore, be transmitted to the higher court. Judge Towslee had no knowledge of the petition. Greenwood petitioned the court for an informal mandamus order to get the transcript into their hands.

On May 18th Carter was finally formally deposed in the Terrell Unit in Livingston. Two days later Greenwood reported on the event to Graves, saying Carter was great and convinced everyone there who was neutral (the D.A. and Ranger being the exceptions) and that all the big media sources (NBC, CBS, *60 Minutes*, *Newsweek*) were begging to interview his client. Ironically, it was Sebesta who had garnered the attention by mentioning the deposition when being interviewed about Carter's impending execution.

Greenwood was busy taking media interviews, negotiating for a federal filing deadline, and seeking copies of the two videotaped depositions he and McCann had taken from Carter in 1997 and 1998 (which the media wanted). He was also pursuing an affidavit from Carter's "Christian brother" Alvin Kelly regarding Carter's admissions to him extending back several years.

Dan Rather's evening news program mentioned the case on May 30, the eve of Carter's execution. A CBS news crew was on its way to interview Carter in his last days when they got word from TDCJ's public information officials that the inmate wasn't feeling well and so had cancelled the interview. This news was received with some suspicion, given the reports around the same time of other journalists being falsely informed. TDCJ, for example, had said that Gary Graham's media dance card was all filled up when in fact all supplicants were turned away by the TDCJ public information office.[91]

After Carter's last words on the gurney, Molly Ivins wrote a blistering column about the case. This irked Charles Sebesta, who told the author a journalist couldn't possibly understand the case unless s/he had been there as he had and followed the case step by step as it developed.[92] NBC had negotiated an exclusive agreement with Greenwood from the time of their interview with Graves until early September, when Geraldo Rivera's show on the death penalty aired. Graves passed a quiet summer, broken only by visits from his new friend and advocate Nickie Greer from Dallas and his faithful family.

In early September Rivera's special aired, featuring Kerry Cook and Graves among others. Not long before that Rivera had made a surprise stop at Doris Curry's home, pledging to her and other members of Graves' family who were present that he would not rest until Anthony was free. Needless to say, that boosted their hopes.

An October 2000 decision by the Court of Criminal Appeals, to hear oral arguments on their amended second subsequent state writ of habeas corpus, astounded Greenwood and Burnett. The hearing on the issue of incompetent habeas representation was a first for Texas. It's an issue Burnett says is bringing the case a lot of attention around the state and outside Texas. Though the courts had been required to provide habeas counsel since 1995 for death row inmates, there had been no consequence or appeal for incompetent performance, a situation Burnett describes as "a right without a remedy."[93] Though Burnett says he and Greenwood "like to fell over" when the hearing was ordered by the court, he was concerned that it was just for the appearance of fairness, given the virtually nonexistent reversal record of the court, and that they would continue to affirm the conviction and sentence in the case.[94] "They'll have to find some narrow, narrow exception in the federal law and ask for a hearing, and if we're denied, then we're in bad trouble,"[95] Burnett said.

The federal prospects were only slightly better, given the political composition of the Fifth Circuit Court of Appeals in New Orleans. However, slight grounds for optimism were offered by a December 2000 decision in the Fifth Circuit reversing the conviction of capital defendant Max Soffar for irregularities surrounding his confession, suppression by the prosecution of exculpatory evidence, and incompetent trial counsel.

The brief submitted by Greenwood and Burnett for Graves in December 2000 mentioned the new finding of exculpatory evidence possessed by the D.A and not shared with the defense as required by law.

For the most part, however, the lawyers stuck to the primary issue of the hearing and detailed how Patrick McCann, on numerous occasions, admitted to Greenwood he was incompetent to perform the task of a habeas attorney.[96]

The attorneys also argued in the brief that the effect of recent decisions by the U.S. Supreme Court governing the issues that can be raised in federal habeas proceedings, as well as the intent of the Texas Legislature in 1995 and 1999, and the Congress in its abbreviation of federal appeals, was to speed up the appellate process by requiring states to ensure competent counsel at all levels of capital case proceedings. Since McCann's faulty performance caused Graves to lose a major issue, ineffective performance of trial counsel should allow them to back up the train and start all over with a new habeas proceeding.

Greenwood presented oral arguments on the brief March 28, 2001 in Austin, with Burnett and Graves' family and attorneys from the Texas Defender Service and the Attorney General's office attending. The new Washington and Burleson County D.A., Rene Moeller, had contracted out the response to the Tarrant County D.A.'s chief appellate prosecuting attorney Chuck Mallin.

Suspense over Court's ruling on third habeas petition

Closing the flood gate.

At the end of 2001, there was still no ruling from the court. A number of cases with similar habeas issues were hanging, too, and several death row inmates who were headed for the gurney had been granted extra time because of the unresolved issue. The results of a favorable decision for Graves would have meant the re-hearing of a number of Texas capital cases where incompetent habeas counsel at the state level was raised and denied merit. A bad sign came when a new execution date was posted late in the year for Michael Moore, one of those reprieved by Graves' pending appeal. An ally visiting Graves who didn't understand the significance noticed Graves appeared disturbed when she mentioned Moore's date.

On the first day in January of 2002, media began calling Roy Greenwood in the morning for comments on the six-person majority ruling of the high court dismissing his client's claim as an "abuse of the writ." Greenwood wrote Graves immediately, prior to seeing the decisions, which included three separate dissents. The clock had begun ticking on the less than three-month deadline for submitting the first federal brief to the regional court in Galveston. Jay Burnett would have to write the appeal of the recent decision to the U.S. Supreme Court if the two men decided it was worth a run after reviewing the decision and dissents.

The majority opinion, authored by Justice Cochran, argued that since there was no constitutional right to a habeas attorney, there could be no constitutional claim that that attorney was ineffective. The state legislature's "act of grace" in providing counsel for the writ should not be distorted into a constitutional right. Furthermore, the justice interpreted the court's range of review extremely narrowly, limiting "cognizable" cases, i.e., those that they would consider, to those addressing jurisdictional, constitutional or fundamental rights, all assumptions challenged by Justice Price, who wrote the strongest dissent to the majority mind.

Justices Price, Johnson and Holcomb all agreed the court should follow the legislative intent, which was to provide "competent" counsel, meaning effective in practice, not just bar-qualified. Price specifically took the court to task for not acknowledging that in appointing an attorney barely out of law school for Graves' all-important appeal, they had not met their responsibilities. Price argued the court should set the boundaries of the cases it should consider in such a way as to ensure fairness. The dissenters also challenged the fear expressed in the majority document that granting Graves' appeal would open a "floodgate" of endless appeals, each alleging the previous habeas attorney had been inadequate.

The majority opinion presented a disturbingly one-sided review of the "facts" of the case, leaving one to wonder almost why Carter, who was described as Graves' "accomplice," had even been convicted. Cochran wrote that Graves' "motive was anger at the female homeowner for receiving a job promotion he thought his mother should have received. The five children just happened to be in the house at the time." The Justice totally ignored the evidence from Carter's trial, which she clearly had not read, and from Carter's May 18, 2000 deposition, which certainly should have attracted the attention of the high court, since he attributed the motive for the murders to the paternity suit and assumed complete responsibility for all the victims, exonerating Graves.[97]

Possibilities for relief at federal level

If he were your son?

Greenwood and Burnett argued in their last brief that in cases where actual innocence is raised, federal bars against consideration of issues already rejected by state courts may be bypassed. However, in a late 2000 interview Burnett seemed skeptical of obtaining Graves' freedom absent

DNA evidence. He was tenuously hopeful, however, that the lawyers could save his life to spend it in prison, a circumstance neither Graves nor his family would find acceptable, given that he rejected a plea to a life sentence years before, based on his (and his family's) insistence that he is innocent.

Doris Curry said Patrick McCann came to her side in Angleton after the evidentiary hearing in 1998 before the trial court. McCann asked Graves' mother how she maintained her calm determination. She told him she placed the Lord first, and let Him take care of the rest. McCann said he wished more of us could follow her example.[98]

Mrs. Curry needed all her calm faith. Moments before, Judge Towslee, standing next to her in the cafeteria line, had agreed with Sebesta that he didn't understand why Graves' defense was even there bothering to present new evidence — of Carter's recantation, expert testimony that demolished the knife "evidence," and allowing Yolanda Mathis to finally have her say.[99] Imagine the impact this would have on the mother of a person on death row who is innocent.

Graves' cousin Felicia says her cousin may be too fond of women, "but he's not a murderer."[100] Roy Allen Rueter agrees, upset after all these years about the fate of his friend and the role he unwittingly played in his conviction: "Anthony used to be like a mentor for my son when he was going through some real tough adolescent times. Anthony Graves is no murderer."[101]

Charles Sebesta says repeatedly that he's "satisfied" with the case against Graves:

> I'll tell you this, in the Graves matter, I'm comfortable knowing what I know about it. That doesn't mean I'm right, that's why we have the system that we have, why we have the appellate courts to look at these things . . . in my view, and having worked the length of time that I've worked in the case, I'm satisfied that Graves was present that night, I'm satisfied that Graves was the one that used the knife at that scene, and I don't have any problems with it.
>
> I'm leaving, I'm totally leaving the political arena. I've been in this courthouse 30 years, and I've enjoyed it. But I'm ready to do something else, and I will tell you the last thing in the world that I would want on my conscience is to have any question in my mind that Anthony Graves was not present that night, was not a party to that crime. I can tell you, it doesn't mean anything, but I can tell you, that I'm satisfied.[102]

Three jurors (all male), who convicted and agreed to the three statements that sent Graves to death row, said in interviews in early 2001 that despite Carter's highly-publicized recantation, and other evidence shared by the interviewer that might cast doubt on the witnesses regarding the jailhouse confessions — the methods of the knife "experts" for the state, the integrity of the chief prosecutor, etc. — they still believe Graves was guilty.[103] They based their reluctance to change their minds primarily on the knife testimony in conjunction with Carter's trial statements and original statement to the Rangers, buttressed by what the D.A. presented as Graves' self-perjuring testimony in the Grand Jury (where no records were kept) that he never had owned a knife.[104] Several of those male jurors said they handled the knife or were knife users, and were sure it could have inflicted the damage, statements that leave Roy Allen Rueter shaking his head in disbelief.[105]

The lone black juror, Clarence Sasser, the jury foreman, said that "the act" itself, and especially the photographs of the victims, before and after the grisly murders, had really affected him. He added that he thought Carter didn't have the "balls to plan and execute" the action, but Graves' "demeanor" in the courtroom convinced him otherwise. [106]

Rick Carroll, who was the former supervisor for both Carters, Bobbie and Lisa Davis and later two of Bobbie's sons, agrees with the juror on Carter's lack of capacity for such a scheme "unless he was really stoned."[107] Carter told his final attorney Bill Whitehurst that he was not on drugs when he committed the crime and that he did it solely because of the child support issue.[108] Carroll volunteered his low opinion of Theresa "Cookie" Carter, her bad temper (he says she was a "spitfire"), her unrequited hostility toward Bobbie Davis, and her startling physical change when he saw her a few years after the tragedy and nearly didn't recognize her.[109] He said she looked like she was heavily drugged, and, remarked that her current job as a stocker on the graveyard shift at the local Walmart, seemed to him like the behavior of someone hiding out.[110]

Whether the efforts of the defense lawyers, Doris Curry and her children, advocates like Nickie Greer and Geraldo Rivera, reforms in the Texas legislature, or a miraculous ruling by the U.S. Supreme Court, or a federal district judge, or the Fifth Circuit justices will make it possible for Doris Curry to hug her son before she dies, or Terrell, Torrance and Alex to know their father's touch again, or for Anthony Graves to swing a baseball bat, share pleasure with a woman, get training to be a criminal investigator as he says he'd like to do, or pick up a steak sandwich at a Jack in the Box, remains to be seen.

Charles Sebesta predicted at the end of 2000 as he cleaned out his Caldwell courthouse office to end his quarter century residency there, that the answers for Graves would most likely play themselves out by the end of 2002.[111] Sebesta ended his official involvement with the case when he closed the door on that phase of his career.

No matter what or when the final outcome, Graves probably has a lot of pancake and peanut butter sandwiches to face in solitary confinement, like all the other inmates on death row, and many more days of battling despair over Charles Sebesta and his brand of justice. On one of those dark days he vows from death row to file attempted murder charges against a D.A. he describes as having "lied, manipulated and . . . done everything under the sun to murder me . . . because the truth stared him in the face, and he turned his head, because I was just a young black man who he could use for political aspirations."[112] He also writes that he feels abandoned by his family, not because they don't believe in him, "but because they have been naïve about the system the same way I was when this first happen(ed) to me. They think because I'm innocent that everything will be alright. . . . that's not how it works. So yeah . . . I've felt abandoned for a long time, and I've also felt and still feel alone . . . one would think that with all the people out there trying to help me, how could I feel alone . . . No one gets up in mornings . . . facing this death sentence but me!"[113]

On a brighter day, he writes on rainbow margin notepaper, "But I have faith in my God and I know that the truth has its own legs and will stand by itself, even in the midst of a storm, which unfortunately I find myself in the middle of these past few years. But the funny thing is, through all of this injustice my life has taken on a purpose that I never really had before. I would rather take a needle in my arm fighting for the truth than compromise to an unjust situation for the sake of temporary freedom."[114]

Roy Allen Rueter says his son Michael has never gotten over what happened to Graves, and that for himself, "I felt ashamed, because I let my addiction get in front of just sayin' 'no, fuck you' because I was scared . . . because I'd told them at the beginning . . . 'Yeah, I'll testify that he's innocent.'"[115] He says Anthony's situation was part of his descent back into drugs he'd sworn off for several years prior to 1994. Clean again for years now, he's offered to fall on the sword, admit he was coked up when he testified at trial and when he was being manipulated by the prosecution.[116]

For Demetria Williams in Austin, rage over her brother and closest friend Anthony's situation ruined her marriage, her home, her sleep, her peace of mind. Their mother, Doris, has lost her life savings, and the companionship and assistance of her oldest son in managing her flock.[117] Graves' youngest sister Dietrich lost her emotional stability when the police took her oldest brother away. For them, for Arthur, Anthony's musically-talented and religious younger brother, for Anthony's three personable teenage sons, for Nickie Greer, the Dallas pediatric emergency room nurse who found Graves through a Canadian web site she chanced on while looking for a hip-hop performer named Dr. Death, and who then took on his cause and a close relationship with him and his family, for his European and U.S. allies — hope, whether based in faith or naïvete about Texas justice, has been all they've had.

In the summer of 2001, Graves' sister Demi stepped into the leadership role in the struggle and began to acquire new allies. They included a Somerville resident and neighbor of the Davis family, Bonnie Caraway. Her son was falsely accused in the late nineties of capital murder and spent a year awaiting trial in Harris County before the holes in one of his accusers' stories became apparent and he was set free. She has become an ally to several innocents on death row, including Graves and Michael Toney.

Based on the record in Texas in the last decade, as Graves told Geraldo Rivera in a segment of a special MSNBC show in September 2000 on the death penalty, grounds for that hope are "slim to none." But, as Kerry Max Cook could testify, cuddling his newborn son Kerry Justice Cook in a North Dallas suburb, or off-Broadway at the opening of a play which includes his story, or in Los Angeles working on a movie script, or testifying before the Texas Legislature for a moratorium on executions, or in France speaking to an international gathering focused on the U.S. death penalty, miracles sometimes happen.

Addendum: Imagine a basket of snakes[118]

A brief Summary of the progress of Anthony Graves' court battle for life since January, 2002.

The basket is woven together from threads of law, personality and politics and held together with the hard work of death penalty attorneys, Roy Greenwood and Jay Burnett, and the patience of a man, Anthony Graves, an innocent person who has been on death row for twelve years. The snakes are seven issues raised in as many habeas proceedings. The issues are specific ways in which Anthony's Constitutional rights have been violated. They all hinge on the issue of innocence, which if true, means his Constitutional rights have absolutely been violated.

The legal distance the Graves case has progressed since January 2002 is no less complex than the journey before then.

The Texas Court of Criminal Appeals denied a motion for rehearing in a second habeas petition (raising the issue of ineffective assistance of habeas counsel) and the case was published as Ex parte Graves, 70 S.W. 3d 103. End of story. The argument that the original habeas counsel, McCann, functioned below court standards for effectiveness was pitched out by the Texas Court of Criminal appeals. Since the Clinton administration passed the Anti-Terrorism and Effective Death Penalty Act in 1996, it has been difficult for attorneys to prove habeas violations for capital cases. The AEDPA reads like a step by step set of directions the courts can follow to deny habeas appeals. According to Greenwood it will take the US Supreme Court thirty years to define the parts of the AEDPA that relate to the Death Penalty, which Clinton initiated to get tough-on-crime points before election to his second term.

Next a Federal habeas petition was filed in US District Court in Galveston on May 24, 2002, after the federal case was reinstated following a previous abatement pending the state court of criminal appeals action."[119] It is against the rules of the Texas Court of Criminal Appeals for them to hear a case that is also being heard in a federal court. Thus the federal proceedings were put on hold until the state cases were decided. This made the deadlines for filing incredibly complex as federal and state habeas appeals used up each other's time for filing deadlines.

After the Texas attorney general's office filed its answer, and Greenwood filed his reply on August 13, 2002, the United States District Court in Galveston ruled three weeks later, on September 6, 2002, that even though the case presented 'monumental concerns' of federal habeas corpus issues, and that there was 'not insubstantial evidence of innocence' shown, that the court would deny habeas relief, basically finding procedural default with all of the seven issues presented.[120]

What the District Court in Galveston did by finding "procedural default with all the seven issues presented" was bump the case upstairs, to the US Fifth Circuit Court of Appeals in New Orleans.[121] Greenwood says the District Court in Galveston didn't want to deal with it.[122] So it maintained that because earlier habeas proceedings were flawed, they didn't have to deal with the merits of any of the seven issues Greenwood raised.[123]

This decision, made in three weeks, was probably a record for district court rulings in federal capital habeas matters (or even noncapital habeas matters) by any US District Court in the history of Texas. The average, for all capital cases since 1995, probably approximates 8-12 months.[124]

Notice of appeal of this decision was filed.

Anthony's brief was filed in the court of appeals in December, 2002. The State filed its brief in February, 2003. In an extraordinary action by the US Fifth Circuit Court of Appeals, the court ordered the matter set for oral argument, effectively finding that the District Court committed error in not granting a certificate of appealability to all of our issues, with the court ordering oral argument on April 8, 2003. That argument was presented in New Orleans, and we are now waiting ruling of the court.[125]

At the end of the 2003 legislative session, made famous by the Killer D's in absentia,[126] four bills met a quiet death as a result of efforts by Republican member of the Texas House of Representatives, Terry Keel, past D.A. and Sherrif of Travis County, who was primarily responsible for blocking all habeas corpus reform.[127]

Justices in New Orleans waited while the Texas Legislature considered four separate bills dealing with capital murder habeas corpus reform. One of these, Senate Bill 1224, known as the "Graves Bill," was passed by the Texas Senate in late March/early April.

It would have specifically overruled the 2002 Court of Criminal Appeals decision in Graves, and permitted retroactive habeas corpus challenges to legitimate claims of ineffective assistance of counsel under article 11.071. However, because of numerous major issues pending before Legislature, this bill was not passed by the eventual conference committee that sought to work out differences on May 30, 2003, thus the legislative session terminated without any reforms.[128]

Politics makes law a moving weave, a basket of snakes that forms, unravels and re-organizes itself.

After oral argument on April 8, 2003, the three-judge panel of the Fifth Circuit ruled on August 13, denying the Burnett and Greenwood request for relief on six issues, none of those rulings being *directly* on the *merits*, but for technical reasons. The panel, however, found that there was a error under *Brady v. Maryland*, where the State possibly suppressed evidence from the trial lawyers, i.e., statements made by Carter to District Attorney Sebesta during trial that Anthony "didn't do it." The Court of Appeals remanded that issue for hearing in the District Court.

Burnet and Greenwood filed a Motion For Rehearing *En Banc* to the entire 18 Judge Court of Appeals, and on November 15, 2003, the *En Banc* court summarily granted review of another issue, another *Brady* claim, remanding that matter for a hearing also. They rejected further review of the remaining issues. So, at that point, *two* issues were remanded for evidentiary hearings in the District Court and five issues had been denied review.

For the issues denied, they attempted to get the Court of Appeals to stay the proceedings in the Fifth Circuit so they would not have to seek immediate Certiorari review in the United States Supreme Court on those issues. The stay request was denied, so the certiorari petition was filed in January, 2004. In the meantime, the District Court originally set the evidentiary hearing for April 29, 2004.

A couple of weeks prior to the hearing date, the District Court entered an order refusing to bring Anthony back for the evidentiary hearing, in clear violation of federal law. Burnett and Greenwood objected to that ruling, and also submitted updated payment vouchers for attorney's fees for the previous eight months of work in preparation of the hearing. Shortly before the evidentiary hearing, the District Court entered three *bizarre* rulings: he canceled the April 29 hearing, transferred the entire matter to the U.S. Magistrate for any further hearings, and denied all of their requests for funding over the last months. None of these rulings were explained. So, Graves' attorneys had to start all over again in their preparation for the hearing.

The U.S. Supreme Court denied certiorari on May 17, 2004, thus making the hearing *critically* important. On June 10, the Magistrate conducted a preliminary hearing with regard to the District Court's denial of attorney funding and other scheduling and discovery issues. The Magistrate granted all of Greenwood and Burnett's discovery requests, including their request for his review of the entire district attorneys file in this case, to determine if there were further *Brady* violations. This was very unusual. The Court further scheduled a preliminary evidentiary hearing on some issues, including funding issues, for September 10, and a hearing on the merits of their claims on September 28.[129]

As this book goes to print, original copies of several of the author's audio interviews and letters, which have become critical pieces of evidence are locked in a safety deposit box — a tape on which, for instance, D.A. Charles Sebesta admitted he knew Carter had recanted before the Graves trial. We know he didn't bring it up when he was prosecuting Graves, which amounts to suppression of evidence, which if accepted by the court, could bring Anthony home.

Everything that goes on behind closed doors to determine whether or not the courts hear the issue remains the close-up and hair-raising concern of those few people privy to it. From a distance it looks like the old formula — young black man framed v. white D.A. and company covering their tracks.

And the question remains — does throwing millions of dollars and the vast expertise of death penalty attorneys at the system for decades change that formula much at all? If you believe in a civil society rooted in justice, you have to think it will.

Chapter Eight: Remedies

Photo by Susan Lee Campbell Solar

Living in the killing state

After spending 15 months of my life, averaging 80 or so hours a week immersed in investigation, reading, thinking, and talking with others from inside and outside death row, inside and outside Texas and the U.S. about capital punishment in this state, I have come to believe that I cannot ignore the issue. I am a citizen of the state and thus responsible for my state's actions as much as any other citizen.

But I have also been a victim of a violent crime perpetrated by a stranger, and I do not wish the perpetrator to be free to traumatize others by invading their homes and their bodies as he invaded my home while I slept, and my body after I futilely resisted. Nor do I, or any defense attorney or political activist, wish others more violent than my intruder to be free to torture and maim, or to mindlessly blast away others lives as they act out their own abuse and learned disrespect for the sanctity of life or their mental illness. I would like to believe that the chance of my home or life, or that of my daughters or anyone else I love or those I have never met, being invaded by a person or persons bent on harm, is as remote as my chances of winning the grand prize in the lottery. I would like to live in a community where the evening news does not regularly feature shocking stories of local violence, because it never happens.

It is equally important to me to be able to trust the criminal justice system in my state. I want to sleep soundly knowing that detectives and prosecutors pursue and arrest the truly guilty, that the guilty receive a fair trial with adequate resources at their command, that jurors think with compassion and wisdom not only about victims and their survivors but about the defendants and their families. I want to know that the people who will be entrusted with the future care of the defendants, no matter what their sentences, will treat them with humane regard. I need to know that judges who review the cases that come before them think only of the fair and wise application of the law, and not of their job security or political ambitions. I insist that prisons be transformed truly to reform errants, to send them out healed and ready to contribute to society. It is not enough to warehouse them and school them in the ways of brutality, dehumanization, and further destruction to themselves and others upon their eventual release, as happened to the young men who murdered James Byrd, Jr. so viciously.

But humans are many and varied in our backgrounds, in our values, in our states of mental health, in our addictions. Those entrusted with law enforcement responsibilities and those we elect as district attorneys and judges are as flawed, perhaps in different ways, as the defendants with whose cases they deal. If we need structures to deal with the excesses of criminals, ranging from fines to life imprisonment, surely we need structures to deal with bad cops, crooked or abusive detectives or district attorneys and their assistants, judges with rubber stamps that say Affirmed or Case Dismissed not because they are applying the law evenhandedly and thoughtfully, but because they believe their jobs and political futures depend on it.

Those structures, those remedies are surely within our realm of possibility, given the political will to reflect on them and vote the mechanisms and the money to put them into place. A well-staffed, sufficiently funded and politically protected agency to investigate prosecutorial misconduct and other due process violations by officials would be a good place to start. Several eminent legal scholars, David Dow and Stephen Bright for example, believe that replacing elected judges with appointed ones is essential to eliminate the political aspect of court decisions. That solution, however, raises other questions: who will appoint them, and for how long, and won't that also reflect political values, and how can we get around that dilemma?

A well-funded centrally-coordinated resource base of qualified investigators and attorneys specializing in capital cases to assist the indigent is on the wish list of many critics of systemic problems in the Texas capital punishment system. It would need to be protected with constitutional guarantees from transitory political winds, such as that which blew through the nation and the state in 1995, resulting in the de-funding of the Texas Resource Center. As a non-attorney, I can't help wondering, if we determine we are going to keep the death penalty, should there not be some sort of screening mechanism on capital cases before they ever get before a jury? If there are conflicting witnesses or none, if the case rests on a single eyewitness or several with reasons to lie, or the word of a co-defendant alone who was capable of doing the crime without assistance, or a confession given under questionable circumstances, or circumstantial evidence; if the defendant is mentally impaired and so unable to participate in his or her own defense, if any one of those conditions occur, the case should be flagged for further investigation and resources — before the defendant starts down a slippery slope, before a jury is selected for its willingness to impose the ultimate penalty.

Taking a critical look at what went wrong systematically and in particular cases

Eden Harrington, director of the Center for Public Interest Law at the University of Texas, came from Florida to major in philosophy at Rice University. She got her law degree at Columbia, and after practicing public assistance law a few years in California and in Kerrville with Texas Rural Legal Aid, was asked to direct the ACLU's Fifth Circuit Death Penalty Project in 1988. By the end of the year she had joined two other lawyers paid by the Southern Prisoners Defense Center (now the Southern Center for Human Rights) who were doing similar work, to teach a capital punishment clinic at the UT Law School, which in turn provided them an office. By the end of the year, they had applied for newly available federal funds and garnered a million dollars to hire staff for the Texas Resource Commission (TRC), which preceded the current Texas Defender Service (TDS).

The TRC was one of 13 such centers across the nation funded by the administrative office of the U.S. Justice Department. The Texas center, befittingly, was the largest. Directed by Robert McGlassen, the TRC created a body in Texas of highly-trained and effective capital defenders who now practice criminal law and teach in the state's law schools. For seven years they recruited, trained, assisted and monitored attorneys for Texas death row inmates until 1995 when a Republican-controlled Congress cut the funds for all such centers in the US. Harrington describes the changes since 1988, when the TRC moved out of the law school into their own offices and began hiring additional staff. She said they "spent an inordinate amount of time just trying to figure out who had lawyers," putting their "thumb in the dike," trying to get stays of execution while they sought out and trained willing and competent attorneys.[1]

Harrington says:

> ... many, many things are wrong with the system now that I can see but it has advanced so enormously ... that the nature of the problem is different; the focus now is more on who gets appointed and how and do they get paid enough to do a reasonable job and do they have the resources they need.... It is a different but not necessarily all that much better world.[2]

Harrington says that in the current legislative reforms, some major pieces are missing.

> It has long been perfectly obvious, that one of the problems with the way capital cases work now is that in the rare cases where the courts actually issue rulings chastising the prosecution or the police or whatever and finding problems, that's it, the end of the story.[3]

She wants a true follow-up, on a statewide level:

> ... along with the DNA law that raced through the legislature this year, what would have been in some ways an equally progressive proposal would have been to appoint a commission that looks into how cases go wrong — cases like Ricardo Guerra, Clarence Brandley... There isn't anybody who does that, unless the [D.A.'s] offices handle it themselves internally... from a public policy and just practical standpoint, that would be very useful. Politically I think it would be extremely difficult, and that's what drives the train. Prosecutorial misconduct hasn't been what's ringing the public's bell in the last year. It's been this problem of innocence. Even in the Illinois cases, the question of how did all these innocent people get on death row, you have to read pretty far to figure out what happened to all those prosecutors or the terrible defense attorneys. With the defense attorneys it is a little easier because you can do a search to find out if they've been reprimanded or suspended or disbarred. But we ourselves pursued cases where we alleged all kinds of terrible conduct by defense attorneys and prosecutors at times, where we felt like we had the facts to back it up, and we didn't file any kind of complaint. It was viewed as hopeless, not an effective enforcement mechanism.[4]

Besides the problem of a lack of oversight structure for prosecutors, and consequent impunity:

> Judges get off Scott-free too. There is a mechanism for judicial oversight, but the conduct has to be truly egregious. There are surely judges who've made serious errors whose cases have been overturned who aren't in fact sanctioned or trained or anything in response. We may want to have a [hands-off] approach to judges, I can see the reasons for that in theory, but there's no such reasons for prosecutors.[5]

Harrington suggests a "blue ribbon" commission funded by the legislature to examine not just systemic problems but also particular cases in detail, to determine how to prevent similar problems from recurring. She says that while the last year or so it has been relatively common to cite:

> ... inexperienced defense attorneys or sleeping attorneys, and I'm delighted by the attention, but it's not even-handed enough. It's become fairly uncontroversial to talk about whether

judges who are elected will have an effect on things or campaign contributions. Ten years ago [these things] weren't talked about openly. But there's not a lot of discussion about prosecutors or police officers bending the rules; and so if you were really going to try to attack this problem at all points at the same time, there would be a commission or several commissions to look into the potential players in this system and how they might presumably inadvertently or advertently be participating in justice gone awry, and one of the big players is the prosecution side.[6]

Harrington believes the emphasis on innocence serves a purpose, in pointing to systemic problems that permeate the justice system:

> If these things are going on in cases where people are innocent, then it's insane not to think they're going on in other cases too... if the problems there exist, they affect some portion of the cases. There were people whose convictions were overturned, meaning the courts obviously concurred with our arguments, and the people may well have been re-sentenced and for all I know, even executed, that happened too, but we should *still* be concerned about what went wrong at the first trial, instead of being happy that somehow the problems were eventually caught through the "fine workings of the system," which just isn't comfort enough.
>
> That's the fallacy of this — "all right, now we have a DNA bill and nobody innocent will ever get executed . . .when it's a minority of people who will ever have DNA-testable evidence. Nobody has any idea what the actual percentage is, but I know from looking at it, that a lot don't. When we were at the resource center we had a lot of funding including for physical testing, but the thorniest cases didn't have physical evidence. The ones that are the riskiest rely on snitch testimony or eyewitnesses or things of that nature and DNA just doesn't help and it's not ever going to.
>
> If I was the King of the Legislature, there wouldn't just be a DNA bill, there would be an Innocence Commission, an investigatory commission for these cases. . . . I do think we're on a pendulum and the amount of attention being generated on these cases and these issues is enormous, compared to what it has been

in the past, so I can only think that these are steps.... Nobody ever thought that this was a short fight.[7]

The Texas Defenders' Service in its publication *A State of Denial: Texas Justice and the Death Penalty* lists 27 suggestions to reform the current system of capital punishment in Texas, including the prohibition of psychiatric testimony regarding future danger until or unless validation studies prove the validity of such testimony, and a commission to investigate official misconduct.[8] The Texas Civil Rights Project report on the death penalty also lists numerous steps that could be taken to ensure justice, including adequate compensation for the wrongly convicted (up to $3,000 a month), which would be levied on their prosecutors. Many other studies, investigative reports and editorials have been written on the subject over the last several years. These provide directions for a multitude of actions that could be taken in addition to those reforms passed by the 2001 legislature to ensure that the quality of justice in this state reaches a level of excellence in keeping with the state's preferred and deserved image in many fields.

Studying alternatives to "Eye-for-an-Eye" justice

But beyond justice, lies mercy. And for mercy to take root in this state, there must be an underlying belief on the part of significant portions of the public and officialdom that there are alternatives to the brutal system of confinement and extermination that now characterize our handling of perpetrators of violence among us.

In March of 2001, Carol Byers of Murder Victims' Families for Reconciliation left for Norway as part of a delegation focused on the death penalty in the United States. Byars wrote on her return that what she found in Norway was:

> ... a country that takes care of its own... the police do not carry guns. It was hard for a Texan, like myself, to conceive of this way of life. Yet, their violent crime is very low. Their mentally ill are treated and general healthcare is provided... they have few homeless by comparison. This was a world that was totally alien to me. I love my country, but the problems affecting the U.S. [seem] overwhelming. While I have been in the Human Rights struggle for some time, I had no real comparison to base my understanding of what a peaceful society is like. Coming home, I wanted to weep for America, and especially for Texas. I wanted to weep for what we could and should be.[9]

Byars contrasted Norway with Texas, where "the exorbitant amount of money spent on executions takes away from victims' funds, crime prevention, help for the mentally impaired, and education."[10]

A Norwegian psychiatrist named Sissel Egeland who works with violent offenders in rehabilitation offered to take a Texas death row inmate named Michael Moore who she believed to be borderline psychotic and who was scheduled for destruction in March of 2001, and offer him the treatment he would have received in her country had he committed his crime there: one on one care with a therapist in a nurturing, peaceful environment until he calmed down enough to begin to consider his future and to work together with specialists on constructing an individually tailored education and psychological treatment program that would mold him into a constructive member of society. It was a concept that is difficult to grasp as a reality, when one comes from Texas and a knowledge of what the reality is here for violent offenders, even for nonviolent offenders.[11]

Scotland and New Zealand reportedly have great success with rehabilitation for their criminals. Perhaps some sort of exchange program could be set up, with delegations of Texas lawmakers from both major parties, mayors, wardens, newspaper editors, television commentators and civic and religious leaders touring other nations with advanced programs to learn about the range of possibilities.

Human rights advocate and Southern historian Rick Halpern of Southern Methodist University, put into words his view of the consequences of choosing to continue with the death penalty:

No issue gets to the heart of who we are more than this. It's a very simple issue, and the choices are crystal clear. You either believe that every individual regardless of who they are retains rights and dignity as people (even if they have taken the life of others) or you believe people can be exterminated for a variety of reasons. It is not an exaggeration to say that the death penalty is that first step.[12]

Chapter Nine:
Reconciliation, Not Retribution

Carol Byers (center) of Murder Victim's Families for Reconciliation.

Photo by Susan Lee Campbell Solar.

Healing alternatives to violence

Violent crimes rip the souls and devastate the lives of everyone they touch. Do we strike out in retribution, creating endless cycles of retaliation or do we reach out to everyone the violence has eviscerated and heal the wounds? Just as surely as the victims' family members weep into the small hours of the morning, so too do family members on the offender side of the crime. Do we work to heal imbalances in our society from which crime manifests or do we become perpetrators of more hate and violence?

In Texas, groups like *Justice for All*, a support group for family members of crime victims, maintain families achieve closure and peace only after the criminal has been executed. Afraid for their own safety, and wrapped in the fury of grief and revenge, a fury codified and sanctioned by the state, they demand that killers be killed — an eye for an eye. Governor George W. Bush used the pain and outrage these victims endured to justify his stand for capital punishment in the same way he used the grief of September 11 families to justify his invasions of Afghanistan and Iraq.

It is impossible to have too much empathy for the surviving family members of murder victims. Lives are shattered; grief-stained hours and dreams extend into drastic, frightening and empty futures for families who have their loved ones ripped away by violent crime. The same is true of the family members of murderers. For the families of death row inmates who are innocent, for mothers and fathers and sisters and brothers whose loved ones have been unjustly executed, there is the added trauma of public humiliation and stigma that lasts generations.

It's a sad business.

And, what happens when this eye-for-an-eye logic degenerates to absurdity, when the victims strike out, not at actual perpetrators, but at random, as happens usually in war, and as much as half the time when the state executes human beings at the end of the profoundly flawed system that has evolved in the United States? Even if one could assume the right person would be executed for every murder, another death often lightens no one's burden of grief. Many family members discover retaliatory problem solving does not bring peace or healing. Instead it paralyzes them in knots of anxiety and despair, the pain of which becomes impossible to bear. When that happens, some reach for another solution, one that is based on reconciliation. They go into prisons, meet offenders and work to alleviate social and economic problems that breed violent crimes.

Prison ministries, like Dove Prison Ministries, founded by Edwin Smith to serve death row inmates at the Terrell Unit in Livingston, Texas, help inmates cope with next to unbearable conditions. They help prepare inmates for the spiritual journey to death, but they also find pen pals and help prisoners communicate with abolitionists and organizations who help raise needed funds for the dozens of court procedures on which inmates' lives depend. When victim family members join various aspects of this work, reconciliation can begin.

Delving into case histories of individuals on death row, one inevitably feels a deep empathy for victims' relatives, on both sides of crime. Their stories range from cold fury to wrenching grief and loss that no act of justice can heal, to statements of astounding forgiveness, even love for the perpetrator. It is easy to understand the fury and desolation; what's harder for most of us is to imagine how one could arrive at a place of peace with the perpetrator of the most unforgivable damage imaginable. But some in our midst have done that, and their stories merit telling.

Victim Offender Mediation Services (VOMS)

Thomas Ann Hines was first the product of an abusive home, then an abusive husband. She left the marriage with her only child, a son who was the delight of her heart. A good kid, a good student, he went away to college. His freshman year, he took a study break in a video arcade between classes at Austin Community College. A young man asked him for a ride and then shot him from the side with a handgun. They found him slumped over the wheel of his automobile. The seventeen-year-old killer fled, but was apprehended not long afterwards and eventually sentenced to life, meaning 40 years before the possibility of parole.

Hines was consumed by grief and bitterness. She spoke constantly of hatred, pain, and the senselessness of her son's murder. Friends tired of it. She now believes she was stuck in the anger stage of grief because she didn't know how to move forward. She never thought in positive terms about the future, only about the irredeemable past. She began volunteering in prisons in 1994, thinking it might lessen her pain. Over the next four years, she spoke to men behind bars about how they could change their lives, make different choices, no matter what they had done.

During a talk at the maximum security prison in Huntsville in which she had intended to give offenders a piece of her mind, she realized she was looking at a "sea of broken humanity."[1] She was overwhelmed. "I looked at them, and all of a sudden, I became a mother again." After the presentation an inmate asked her why she had come. She told him, "If my son was sitting in this room, I'd want someone to reach out a hand and lift him up."[2]

In 1998, thirteen years after the crime, she was led through the *Victim Offender Mediation Services (VOMS)*, part of the Texas Department of

Victims Services, to the idea of meeting Charles, her son's killer. She agreed to have the meeting video taped.[3]

She prepared for the meeting for three years thinking at first she just wanted information about the last moments of her son's life. The killer was equally anxious about the meeting, afraid she would scream at him. When she got to the room where they would meet and saw the small table, she almost bolted, saying he would be too close; she didn't want to touch him. But it was too late to change the table; the video cameras and mikes were all in place, so she toughed it out, telling the staff of the VOMS that she'd already done the hardest thing a mother could do, bury her child and walk away.

The result is an astonishing videotaped encounter between a bereaved, tiny, middle-aged, white mother and a much larger, younger black man, who'd killed her beloved son. The turning point came when she asked him what books were read to him as a child. When he said none, her heart began to open. At the point where he put his head down on the table and began to sob, she could no longer brook the gap between them, and reached out to him. The meeting changed them both in ways no one could have foreseen, and brought her peace she had not imagined possible. Charles, for his part, no longer accumulates mountains of disciplinary write-ups for fighting and starting riots. These days, along with Thomas Ann, he speaks to groups about his transformation, though still serving a life sentence.

From violence to healing

In June, 2000 Carol Byers, the president of the first state chapter *of Murder Victims' Families for Reconciliation (MVFR)*, signed the first statement by a victims' group calling for a moratorium on executions. The first state branch of this national group was, fittingly, the Texas chapter, based in Houston, the capital of death row sentences in a state which leads the union and most of the world in state-sponsored killings.

Byars was the headliner in the press conference that formally announced the formation of *MVFR -Texas*, whose mission statement says they are committed to promoting healing through reconciliation rather than continuing the cycle of violence through retribution and vengeance.

Reporters issued a barrage of leading questions based on the opinion that the high rate of executions and capital sentences here reflect the public will, and that the *MVFR* position and a moratorium on executions would extend pain for victims' families and thwart the public will. Byars said she felt for the parents of murder victims and all their relatives, and that their pain was understandable, but from her own experience believed the position of *Justice for All* encouraged the continuance of destructive pain.

"In my case I had children I wanted to raise in a positive atmosphere and show them there was a better way than revenge and retribution — that was Jimmy's legacy. My husband was worth more than teaching his children to hate. I'm doing what I'm doing to honor him."[4] Later Byars added, "We are a healing organization; we don't promise revenge or retaliation. We believe you can't heal while you hold on to revenge and hatred. You can't do anything positive with all that negativity."[5]

Byars has undergone a 22-year journey of pain and has emerged into healing and activism. She returned to her trailer home later that afternoon on the far northeastern outskirts of Houston to find her youngest daughter, born soon after the fatal attack on Carol's husband, exclaiming with friends over the TV coverage they'd witnessed of the event. But Byars had no time to discuss it. She was expected at work at the café next door, where she worked as a waitress, hoping to eventually earn enough to replace or repair her dysfunctional vehicle.

The formation of the Houston MVFR group was an effort inspired by Byars' participation in the *Journey of Hope* in Texas and Louisiana in 1998 where she met Ron Carlson, another Houstonian. Carlson's elder sister, Deborah Ray Thornton was killed with a pick-ax by Karla Faye Tucker and her boyfriend Danny Garrett. Carlson came to not only forgive Tucker, but to become a close friend and advocate for commutation of her sentence, and was present on her side of the witness divide at the Walls Unit in Huntsville at her execution in February of 1998.

Byars was 21 and nine months pregnant with her second daughter when the husband she refers to as the love of her life was shot in the stomach by a neighbor. A few years ago, she lost most of her material possessions when a friend who was her employer slowly slid into financial disaster and her wages were first cut by half, then half of that, then nothing. Byars lost her apartment, but salvaged her clothes and took them to her eldest daughter's home. There a pet ferret ate at least one of each of her 100 pair of shoes, and the grandchildren got loose in the closet with a chocolate syrup extruder and there went the rest of her worldly goods. She says she thought, "OK, God, I don't need shoes. I don't need clothes. I don't need a home. What is it that you want?"[6]

About that time, a Florida-based organizer against the death penalty who was setting up the *Journey of Hope* tour, called and asked what her schedule was for the next few months. Byars told him she was free, and spent two months in what she describes as an incredible experience. She met Sunny Jacobs, who spent seventeen years in prison including five years on Florida's death row for a murder she never committed. Sunny's common-law husband Jesse Tafero was executed for the same murder, two years *before* an old childhood friend, film maker Mickie Dickoff, uncovered and presented publicly the evidence of innocence that set Sunny free.

New voices for compassion and reconciliation are loose in Texas, the most merciless state in the United States.

The James Byrd Jr. Foundation for Racial Healing

The family of James Byrd, Jr., arguably the most famous Texas murder victim since John F. Kennedy, Jr., found a non-violent path to heal the raw pain caused by the senseless murder of their family member, a black man dragged to death behind a truck driven by white racists. The Byrd family created a foundation for racial healing in the name of their murdered loved one. In the small town of Jasper, they have reached out to the families of the perpetrators with compassion and a spirit of reconciliation, understanding with wisdom that can only come from the deepest essence of our humanity. Their efforts for healing and reform have gained wide support.

Within three years of Byrd's murder, the State of Texas passed and Governor Perry signed into law the *James Byrd Jr. Hate Crimes Act*, which "strengthens penalties for crimes motivated by the victim's race, religion, color, sex, disability, sexual preference, age or national origin. It replaces previous hate crimes law that did not list specific categories of people who would be protected. In previous years, then-Gov. George W. Bush refused to support such legislation."[7]

Ross Byrd has become an outspoken opponent of capital punishment, joining abolitionists in vigil to protest the execution of his father's murderer. While he initially favored the death penalty for the men who killed his father, he experienced a change of heart. "When I heard King had exhausted his appeals, I began thinking, 'How can this help me or solve my pain?' and I realized that it couldn't."[8]

The Restorative Justice Movement

The restorative justice movement searches for alternatives to the punitive and retribution models that are the basis of prison life and capital punishment. The community that gathers together in this movement includes not only victims' families, but also abolition activists, defenders, the families of perpetrators, and death row inmates themselves.

Jim Marcus, director of the Texas Defender Service, said that losing the case of Kenneth Ransom was devastating for him, although he said attorneys who take on capital defense cases have to be able to withstand such losses, given the odds against them. The families and friends of Odell Barnes, Jr., Pablo Melendez, Jr., Anthony Graves, David Stoker, Gary Graham, Kenneth Foster, Randall Dale Adams, and Kerry Max Cook are also victims of a system that has declared their loved one dispensable, despite serious reason for doubt about their guilt. That has to affect one's self-esteem, one's worldview, one's sense of trust and hope in a benevolent universe. David Stoker's mother had a heart attack and died shortly after she learned her son's execution date had been set.

The families of those who admitted their guilt, like Larry Robison and Karla Fay Tucker, were traumatized for years by the fate hanging over their loved one. Is it disrespectful to the families of their victims to feel empathy for the families of murderers?

One of the daughters of James Byrd, Jr. demonstrated her answer to that question when she reached, after John "Bill" King was condemned by a jury, to comfort the aged and grieving father of the man who tortured and dragged her father, in the most hideous way, to death. It was a powerful gesture of mercy.

The *Journey of Hope* keeps a webpage devoted to stories of reconciliation. Carol Byers writes:

> It is past time for being silent about the death penalty. In Texas, we're executing record numbers each year. Things have gotten so bad because people have all been silent and let things get bad. We are told many times that we are not supposed to forgive — that when people do horrible things to us we should do something just as bad in retribution. Those of us who know better — those of us who know the power of forgiveness — need to speak up. Every chance we get, we need to challenge the mentality that compassion is a weakness. Compassion is the toughest thing of all, but it's the only thing that works to restore peace in our lives.[9]

Chapter Ten: Pablo Melendez, Jr.

"Here I am a victim's mother, begging the state not to kill the man that stands convicted of killing my only son, but he is not the killer. . . . Pablo Melendez has made plenty of mistakes but one of them isn't killing my son."[1]
Gracie Jett, mother of Michael Sanders, murdered September 1, 1994

Pablo Melendez family photograph.

Police composite drawing of person who shot Michael Sanders and Tommy Seagraves, composed on the basis of Seagraves's description while he was in the hospital recovering from gunshot wounds, shows murderer with facial hair and oval face. A probation photo which happened to be taken of Pablo Melendez days before the murder show him with no facial hair and a differently shaped face. At the time of the crime, Pablo Melendez was unable to grow a beard, and looked like the picture below.

Pablo Melendez, 6/29/94.

Mother of victim says wrong guy on death row

Gracie Jett doesn't fit the profile of the typical ally of a man on death row. She is not European, to start with, or a minister, or enamored of a death row inmate, or a member of a human rights organization, or an activist of any kind. In fact, Gracie Jett is the mother of a murder victim, whose accused killer is spending what may be the last days of his youth on Texas death row staring at an imminent execution. His appeals are well into the federal cycle, a journey from which few return alive.

It is a story of youthful neglect and abuse, addiction, gang culture on the street and in prison, drugs, thugs and deception. Cronyism, old boy networks and political ambition run through the story as well. The mother of the victim is convinced the person on death row for killing her son didn't do it. Her plain spoken voice seems a spot of sanity.

Gracie Jett didn't set out to challenge one of Fort Worth's leading prosecutors, a man named Mike Parrish who has worked for the Tarrant County District Attorney since he left Texas Tech Law School two decades ago. She was minding her own business when she got a call from her ex-husband in the middle of the night, the kind of call every parent dreads. "Mike's been murdered,"[2] he told her. Her only natural son had just been killed near his childhood home in North Texas.

Gracie Jett is a native Texan who raised her family in a neighborhood on the north side of Fort Worth, which she says was safe and wholesome at the time. But Sansom Park was riddled with crime and drugs by September 1, 1994. That was when her son Michael Wayne Sanders was shot in the back. He died on the floorboard of his new Chevy truck in the parking lot of the Toro Car Wash on Long Street at 31st, just before midnight. His new friend and companion of several weeks (or months, or years, depending on who's telling the story), Tommy Seagraves, was shot in the neck and seriously wounded just before Sanders was killed by unknown assailants. The police said it was a random robbery.

Sanders' mother had a second shock after that first call. She was told doctors had debated whether to take Tommy Seagraves into surgery because he had so much cocaine in his system they were afraid he'd die on the operating table.[3] Her daughter Mickie Ross took her four children out of school, and with her husband and Gracie's husband David Jett, drove to Fort Worth to attend the funeral and try to find out what had happened to Michael.

The investigation: contradictions abound

Tommy Seagraves lived, and within 10 days had recuperated to the point that he was able to describe the shooter. The crime report based on an interview in the hospital says the perpetrator was a young Hispanic male with a mustache, goatee, medium complexion, long sideburns, a ponytail, and a tattoo on his right shoulder.[4] The composite drawing shows a man with those characteristics, plus heavy eyebrows, wearing a gimme cap backwards.

There were two other witnesses. Susie Carrillo, a woman who lived down the street from the car wash, heard the shooting and saw a man, shorter than herself at 5' 5". She said he had a ponytail and goatee, wore a white tank top and dark jams. She saw him run from the scene down 31st Street. A young male living in the same block as Carrillo, Pvt. Maldonado, testified he saw a stocky Hispanic man wearing a white muscle shirt and long jams stumbling and running down the street after the shots.

Here's the story Gracie Jett got about what happened at that parking lot just before midnight, 11:20 p.m., September 1, 1994:

> My son's pickup was parked where the passenger side was up against the drive-up payphone, so when they drove up there and stopped, they were sittin' there waitin' on a phone call or fixin' to use the phone. . . . Whoever shot him walked up and shot Tommy [Seagraves] in the neck first. My son [Mike Sanders] panicked and started begging, "Please don't shoot me, don't shoot any more, just take the money and let me take my friend to the hospital!" He [the killer] made my son walk over to him and hand the money to him, about 58 bucks, according to the police, and my son had turned around and walked back to the truck and they shot him four times in the back and he collapsed onto his floorboard.[5]

Michael Sanders, just a few weeks past his 29th birthday, was a college graduate with a business degree from Texas Tech, a person "who took care of himself,"[6] Gracie Jett says. He prided himself on his appearance, was a young man whose lifelong friends told Gracie Jett he was the first to suggest leaving a party when it turned to hard drug consumption. He had a clean record. Recently he'd fallen on hard times. A year earlier he'd liquidated the equipment for his elevator company, and had been doing sheet rock work for a contractor, which was disappointing to him because he'd gone to college in order to be able to earn a white collar living. The driver's license, which enabled police to identify Michael Sanders, showed a clean-shaven young man with short dark hair, a receding hairline and a radiant smile.

But Michael Sanders had a problem, a taste for cocaine which he'd hidden from his family and old friends. His sister Mickie Ross[7] says it started when he was prescribed painkillers for a workplace injury. He got hooked, combined pills with alcohol, and once almost didn't wake up. When he did, he went to a treatment center. There were reports from friends and girlfriends that Sanders and Seagraves had taken things from the workplace of one of Seagraves' cousins who'd made threats against them.

David Jett, Gracie's husband and Michael's stepfather, thinks Seagraves was a snitch, and whatever happened that night had something to do with drugs.[8] He thinks Michael did not initiate the problem.[9] There were a number of things that didn't make sense, as the grieving mother attempted to find out what really happened that night.

> They had never mentioned to me one thing — whether there was any fingerprints or not. . . . There was some bullets, supposedly bullet casings they got at the crime scene, bullets out of my son that was not ever mentioned to me. It was never mentioned in the trial, whether there was fingerprints or whether there wasn't. They said they never found a murder weapon. . . .[10]

The prosecution's detective didn't allow Gracie Jett to see the coroner's photos, but she went to the coroner's office and demanded to see them and they had to allow her to look. She had to pay for the photo she wanted of her son on his back on the table showing "he had the hell beaten out of him."[11] His nose was broken, his face was skinned above the eye. The report said his eye was swollen. But the police say there was no fight. There was a full bottle of Coors Lite beer leaning against her son's left leg which was bent on the floor in front of the driver's seat where he'd pitched forward, with his right lower leg outside the truck. His torso and head were over on Seagraves' knee. Michael Sanders' jeans were covered with mud but there was none on the bottom of his boots.

Gracie Jett doesn't know how or when Michael Sanders got beat up, and Tommy Seagraves wasn't talking to her. She says the law spirited Seagraves away to East Texas as soon as he got out of the hospital. She tracked him down out in an East Texas town where his uncle owned a bar.

> I asked him, just please, tell me the truth. If the shoe was on the other foot, and he was dead and Mike alive, I'd do my best to

get Mike to tell his mom the whole truth. I said, "I don't care what y'all have done. It's too late for that, but at least I deserve the truth. Will you please come tell me." "Oh yeah," he replied, "I'll be over this weekend at my grandma's house. You can meet me over there." But he never showed up. I called his grandma back and she said, "Gracie, I hope and pray he does, but I certainly don't think he will.[12]

In order to understand what led her son into the fatal encounter, she began trying to find out more about Tommy Seagraves.

I found out he'd just gotten out of prison . . . with an eight-year probation . . . so I kept asking Detective Tefft, the detective who was working the case, "You know, what's the deal, why isn't he in jail?" He was at the scene of a murder, and he had cocaine in him and that should have broke his probation right there, and three times she [Detective Tefft] got in my face and told me I did not understand how grave Mr. Seagraves' injuries were, and I said, "Obviously not as serious as my son's because he's six feet under and Tommy's still out here walking around."[13]

Jett and her family posted flyers around the neighborhood with the composite picture of the man who ran from the scene and a contact number. Her daughter Mickey, who was closest in age to Michael Sanders, knew some of his friends. She asked around and came up with some information which Jett called in to Detective Tefft.

When Detective Tefft learned how Gracie Jett had come across the information, Tefft retorted, "I'll tell you one damn thing, if your daughters don't stay out of my investigation, I'll have them thrown in jail."[14]

Jett had the impression the police had written her son off as just another druggie. The investigation she and her family members conducted raised more questions than they answered. Months later, police reported back to Gracie Jett that they had a suspect, Pablo Melendez. They might have picked his name out of a hat, for all the sense it made.

A probation I.D. photo of Melndez was taken a week before Michael Sanders was murdered. It shows Pablo with a hairless face and short hair. The composite, however, of a man with long hair and a goatee, drawn on the basis of the hospital interview with Tommy Seagraves was a dead ringer for another member of the gang Pablo Melendez belonged to, Roel Gonzales, who was placed near the scene of the crime that night by several witnesses.

Key witnesses for defense never interviewed, suspects overlooked

One wonders, looking through the records of this case, how so much investigative material could possibly have been set aside by the prosecution and the police. Was there another agenda, a climate in which fear of gangs and drugs made it "acceptable" to slap a capital murder charge on any gang member just to get him off the street? Gracie Jett and her family wanted more than that. They wanted the truth.

Gracie Jett's ex-husband Gary Sanders [Michael's father], found another witness a few days after the crime, who placed more people at the scene of the crime. Gary Sanders had been walking the neighborhood, looking for clues. A man named Jeffery Jackson told Sanders he'd heard hollering as he was closing up his barbecue place, and had driven with his girlfriend over to the car wash parking lot. There he'd seen several young Hispanic men going through the pockets of someone quite alive, on the driver's side of a white truck by the payphone. They saw a woman sitting in a dark truck parked heading the wrong way on 31st Street. Jeffery Jackson asked if anyone needed help and was told everything was under control. He left because he had a sense something wasn't right and that he was in danger. Gary Sanders passed on the information to Gracie Jett, who then called and got the same story from Jackson.[15]

As revealed several years later in conjunction with a hearing about a motion for a new trial, Detective Tefft got a call September 14 from Bobby Davis Jr., whose father had made the threatening call to Michael Sanders' girlfriend a few days before Sanders was murdered. He provided information about drugs, debts and people that could have opened another route of investigation. There had been rumors that a drug deal gone bad was the motivation behind the killing.[16] The Sanders family who had been snooping around got the distinct impression that they were in danger.[17] The leads were ignored by police and Gracie Jett returned to Utah.

It was the next spring before she heard from the D.A.'s office in Fort Worth. They had a suspect in her son's death, a young Mexican American drop-out who was a member of the La Loma (The Hill) gang. His name was Pablo Melendez, Jr., an 18-year-old who'd been in and out of juvenile detention since age 12. He'd recently spent the better part of a year in jail for two separate gang related shootings.

A tip from a member of his own gang, Johnny Ayala, who was in a Tarrant County jail on an attempted murder charge, had betrayed him. Ayala, who was facing at least 12 years in the pen, was allowed to plea bargain in exchange for his testimony against Melendez. Ayala was brother-in-law to the La Loma gang leader, Robert Gonzalez, Jr. (brother of Roel Gonzalez who looked like the composite drawing) and lived in the same house.

Gracie Jett, her husband David and their oldest daughter, Mickey Ross, were asked to meet with prosecutor Mike Parrish and Detective Tefft, which they did in the summer of 1995. Michael Sanders' youngest sister blamed Tommy Seagraves for her brother's death and when the prosecutor mentioned his name, she said sarcastically, "Poor Tommy." Gracie Jett says Mike Parrish cursed her and shouted and "got in her face."[18] It seems Seagraves was valued in the D.A.'s office. Mickey Ross, however, said she'd known Seagraves since she was a teen. He used to hang around a neighborhood arcade, and he'd always been bad news, a druggie. Rumor had it that two men had come in the 50/50 Club the Saturday before Michael Sanders was killed looking for Tommy Seagraves.[19]

Mickey Ross, went back to the scene of the crime in late February of 2001 and spoke with one of the neighbors whose testimony was used at the trial, Susie Carrillo. She showed Carrillo a photograph of Pablo and asked her if that was the man with the ponytail she saw running away from the truck by the phone at the Toro Car Wash that night. Carillo thought not and insisted the guy was shorter than herself.[20]

Ross asked why Carrillo had identified Pablo as the man she saw that night when she was on the witness stand. Carrillo responded that, at the time of the trial, she was emotionally distraught because her son had been killed in prison. She told Mickie that Ross Tarrant County prosecutors nearly drove her crazy pressuring her to testify against Melendez. She says she kept insisting she wanted to see him first in a line-up to be sure it was the same man. Her demands were ignored. Shown a photo of Roel Gonzalez by Mickey Ross, Carillo said she couldn't tell unless she saw a profile shot of him.[21]

Susie Carrillo repeated to Mickey Ross the story she'd told the detectives shortly after the murder. She was the first one on the scene, with her son, after hearing the shots and then Tommy Seagraves' cries for help. She says Seagraves told her he was the one using the phone, not Sanders. She also said a dark truck with several occupants drinking beer pulled up while she was there and opened the door of the truck on Sanders' side but fled when they heard police approaching,

Defense investigator Larry Hickman thinks Carrillo isn't "wrapped too tight," which may be why no one relied on her testimony. Or maybe she was afraid of becoming involved.[22]

Trial and error

At home in Utah during the winter of 1995-96, Gracie Jett prepared to return to Texas for the trial. She was filled with dread at the thought of how she'd react in the presence of her son's accused murderer. She had expected to feel hatred and strong feelings toward Melendez since the day the prosecution had called her and reported they'd arrested her son's killer and told her his name. She was thinking the first day of the trial would be one of the hardest days of her life.

The trial, prefaced by jury selection in February, began March 4. When the trial started and the accused walked through the door, Gracie Jett says, "I felt nothing." Then as the family listened to the witnesses and saw the composite drawing the second day which bore no resemblance to the accused, and as the trial progressed, Gracie Jett and her family began to realize that "two and two just didn't add up."[23]

According to Jett, the prosecutor, Mike Parrish, went in with a full house. "There was a young judge on his first capital case, who was buddies with the D.A. The D.A. knew how to pick juries and how to pick witnesses."[24] Many of the state's witnesses were related by blood or marriage to Roel Gonzalez, and reportedly in the same gang. Pablo Melendez was the only gang member not related by blood to the other members. They were all in trouble with the law.

Against the juggernaut of the Tarrant County D.A.'s office, which boasts of a conviction rate of 90%, and employs more than 350 people,[25] Pablo Melendez had two trial attorneys and an investigator on a limited budget. The investigator says Melendez' trial attorneys were "topnotch, high-dollar" attorneys but "the thing of it is, if you go to trial in Tarrant County, 99% of the time, and it makes no difference what you're on trial for, they're going to convict you. The Tarrant County jury's mentality the day that trial started — the jury had Pablo Melendez guilty. If you're in court, you're guilty."[26]

Familial testimony on behalf of killer look-alike

Family members of Roel Gonzales, the man who looked like the composite drawing, testified in various ways at various court proceedings portraying Pablo as the killer. In spite of contradictions in significant parts of their testimonies and obvious conflicts of interest, the fact that the murder weapon was never found, and a bewildering array of he-saids and she-saids, the charge against Melendez stuck. On Friday morning, after four days' testimony in the guilt-innocence phase, the jury verdict came in. Melendez was guilty.

New witness at the sentencing phase

By Tuesday, they were back in court for the sentencing phase, but there was a surprise in store for the victim's family and for the judge and jurors. After both sides had closed their presentation of evidence, and the jury had been told to take a break before the closing arguments, the defense asked to re-open for a "*surrebuttal*" witness.

According to Gracie Jett:

> They subpoenaed a boy in jail there in Tarrant County, brought him up from jail in his orange jumpsuit. His name was Roel Gonzalez. The minute Roel walked through those doors I started shaking. I felt instant hate, like that whole building had fell on me. I grabbed my husband's arm and said, "He killed Mike." It was my mother instinct. Pablo's attorneys put him on the stand and asked him a few questions, then one of them walked up and put the picture (composite) up beside Roel, and it was just like Olan Mills took the picture himself, it matched so perfect . . . the hairdo, the goatee, tattoos, none of it Pablo had had when arrested . . . Tommy gave the right description; it just didn't fit Pablo.[27]

The defense attorneys got Roel Gonzalez to roll up his shirtsleeve and show the jury the tattoo on his right upper arm. It hadn't been recorded on the police record a few months earlier, when the witness went through intake before he was imprisoned for assault with bodily injury.[28] This move was prompted by Melendez, who knew the tattoo Tommy Seagraves had described to the jury was the one on Roel's shoulder. He'd worked on it some years before after a tattoo artist had done a bad job. Melendez didn't have a tattoo on his right upper arm.

Melendez' tattoos at intake upon his arrest for capital murder in April 1995 were described as being on his left forearm and wrist, right eye and fingers, upper back, and left upper arm. Parrish got the records officer to admit there was limited space on the computer form to describe tattoos. This planted doubt in the jury's mind. According to a jail tattoo artist who was put on the stand by the defense, there was nothing on Pablo's right upper arm until the winter of 1996 when the artist added the name of his new wife Carmina. Melendez' face, as always, was virtually hairless.

In his closing argument prosecutor, Mike Parrish, discounted the defense suggestion that Roel may have been the culprit. He said Melendez had confessed. Parrish also told this author that Melendez had confessed to his mother and sisters,[29] a fact they adamantly denied, maintaining consistently that he told them what he told Detective Tefft upon arrest.[30] He said the same thing to Gracie Jett in a letter years later. What Melendez said was that he was too muddled by paint-sniffing and alcohol consumption to remember. The gang told him he'd done it.[31]

Ironically, Mike Parrish told the jury Melendez' face was the "face of a killer. A cold-blooded, calculated, capital murderer." And regarding future dangerousness, Parrish misled the jurors, implying that if they didn't give the defendant the death penalty they would likely have him "in your block, in your neighborhood... six days from today, if he could move in, would you want him in your neighborhood?"[32] In fact, the minimum sentence a capital murder convict would serve would be 40 years before parole was a possibility. He also tried to muddy the water about Roel Gonzalez' resistance to Parrish's efforts to get him to say Melendez was guilty, telling the jury that Gonzalez didn't understand English very well.[33]

Towards the end of the trial Gracie Jett and Mickey Ross walked outside at a break and saw the defense's private investigator, Larry Hickman, standing outside taking a smoke break. She walked up and said she needed to talk to him. He put his hands up as though in self defense, "Now Mrs. Jett, we're just doing our job, don't take it personally."[34] Hickman says he had deliberately positioned himself far away from her to avoid any confrontation, and when she asked to speak to him, said he wasn't sure that was appropriate. He said what she said next bowled him over — "This kid did not kill my son. Y'all have proved that in court."[35]

After the jury returned the death sentence on Pablo Melendez, Jett and her daughter went over to the attorney's office to talk to the defense team. Jett says the two attorneys, James Teel and Warren St. John,[36] told her that at first they were just court-appointed, doing their job to defend Pablo, but the more they dug, the more they were convinced that boy was not her son's killer. Their meeting lasted four hours, as the mother and daughter told the defense "all that was going on."[37] They told about their suspicions about Seagraves' role and why he was sequestered instead of jailed after breaking probation. Why hadn't the state presented the evidence on Michael Sanders' body indicating a fight had occurred? There was at least one witness the defense attorneys never learned about, though Gracie Jett had presented information about him to the detectives and to the D.A.

Detective Tefft and prosecutor, Mike Parrish, both filed affidavits in 1998 disputing Jett's claim, and Parrish says regarding Tommy Seagraves' probation not being revoked: "I didn't have a goddamn thing to do with that."[38]

Gracie Jett wasn't done with Mike Parrish when the trial was done. In May she flew to Fort Worth again to testify in a hearing for a motion for a new trial based on the exclusion of testimony by Jeffrey Jackson, whom the defense believed could have muddied the water for the prosecution's case.

Jackson was the witness Jett had told the defense about, an African-American man who owned Jackson's Barbecue near the Toro Car Wash. He'd heard hollering and actually drove by the car wash to see what was wrong. He saw several Hispanic men going through the pockets of someone standing by the open door of a white truck. He saw a woman in another truck.

Jett says she phoned this information to Detective Tefft and to Mike Parrish within a few weeks of her son's murder, and presumed they had followed up, but there was no hint of Jackson's information in the trial. Defense investigator Larry Hickman and the defense attorneys themselves attempted in vain numerous times to contact Jackson before the trial, because the barbecue was located so close to the crime scene they thought perhaps someone from there might have seen something.

After Gracie Jett told them about Jackson's statements to her and her ex-husband, Hickman and Teel went straight over and found him. Jackson confirmed he'd seen several men and a dark truck next to Mike's truck around 10:30 P.M., and said he'd be happy to sign a statement. But when they returned a day or two later with an affidavit for him to sign, he refused. Hickman says Jackson explained: " 'You guys have got to understand I've got to make a living here.' Teel and I both feel somebody got to him . . . It was like someone took an eraser to his memory," Hickman says. "Jackson lost his memory and he lost it in a hurry."[39]

When subpoenaed for the May 1996 hearing on a motion for a new trial based on the evidence of this new and important witness about whom the defense believes the prosecution deliberately withheld information, Jackson ignored the court order. Jett and writ attorney Jack Strickland have a copy of a "While You Were Out" note from prosecutor Mary Galus' desk with the notation: "Jackson Barbecue – explained offer."[40] Jett thinks Jackson, an older man, may have feared the neighborhood-based gang. She also speculates the D.A.'s office told him not to testify and that he'd pay no consequences for ignoring the subpoena. "Right in there somewhere is where I think Mike Parrish saw he'd screwed up," Jett says. "He saw we weren't going to leave it alone, and we had an eyewitness that he had to stop. He had to shut [out] Mr. Jackson from coming."[41]

Mike Parrish stutters and responds, "Say that again" when asked about the note in his assistant Mary Galus' handwriting.[42] He says he knows nothing of it, that he was in court on another case when the hearing took place.[43] It was handled by an attorney from the appellate division.[44] True, Parrish wasn't at the hearing, which means as the state brief argued at appeal that he was not able to be cross-examined.[45] He later submitted an affidavit saying he never heard about Jackson from Gracie Jett, though he did remember hearing about a dark truck from another source.[46]

Parrish was incensed by her interference, according to Jett:

> I came back up here, and it was in the spring. I was outside working in my yard and my phone rang. I wasn't expecting anybody to call me, especially not Mike Parrish, so I ran in and got the phone and Parrish asked me what was I doing, going and talking to Pablo's attorneys.
>
> I said, "I can do whatever I want to."
>
> He said, "Just what the hell did you think you were doing?"
>
> I said, "Well, you know and I know, you just convicted the wrong boy."
>
> He says, "Well, just who do you think killed Mike?"
>
> And I said, "You know who did it as well as I do, it was Roel Gonzalez."
>
> And he said, "Well, I hope you know Roel will never serve a day in jail over killing Mike."
>
> And I said, "And whose damn fault is that?"
>
> I hung up the phone and it hit me after I hung up, "He just told you that Roel killed Mike!" and I couldn't prove it, I didn't tape it or nothing 'cause I wasn't expecting it.[47]

Jett says nailing Pablo was a win/win deal for the Tarrant County D.A.'s office and the gang members who turned him in. Gang members even got a $1,000 reward.

> The cops got Pablo off the streets, who was in trouble a lot, and the assistant D.A. got us off his back, and got a death penalty. I'm trying to give him the benefit of the doubt, but the minute they put Roel on the stand and could see the composite, Parrish had to know who the real killer was. He's been an assistant D.A. for years. He's been in it so long he really don't care about getting the person. He just wants to put someone on death row.[48]

Jett says the media made a lot of the fact that Melendez would be the youngest resident on death row if convicted. She says,

> They ate that up, it was in the *Star-Telegram* every day during the trial. The state of Texas got a long way on that one too: "Oh boy, look at us, we can put an 18-year-old on death row." In mine and my husband's opinion, the prosecutor railroaded him onto . . . death row . . . and he approached Tommy with a deal, either you say this boy did it or you're goin' back to prison yourself.[49]

Gracie Jett eventually began corresponding with Pablo Melendez after Michael Toney, another death row inmate with claims of innocence who was prosecuted by Mike Parrish a few years later, tracked her down and began writing her. Jett's daughter Mickey and son-in-law Melvin Ross began visiting both young men on death row early in 2001.

Youth spinning out of control

As she continued to try to understand what had happened to her own son, Gracie Jett found a world of young people who were clearly out of control. Why did Melendez, by age 12, gravitate to the habitual lies and criminal conquests of gang life?

It was obvious from the trial and from talking to the family that Pablo Melendez, born in Fort Worth in November of 1975, had a rough childhood. His sister Gloria Torres says his father unjustly claimed Pablo wasn't his child.[50] By the time Pablo was of school age, his older sisters were always working at Café Julia, a restaurant their mother owned for 20 years. Pablo was alone a lot of the time. The mother had left her first husband and six children in Sula Victoria, Mexico, to come to North Texas to work. She sent for the children after she had moved in with Pablo Melendez, Sr., a construction worker from Laredo who was a decade or so older than she. When Pablo Jr. was four or five his 21-year-old half-brother was killed in a club in an argument. The killers who beat him to death served little or no time for it.

A sister, during the sentencing phase of the trial said Pablo's father hated him. He believed gossip that the boy wasn't his, never wanted to spend time with him, picked on him constantly, never praised him, pushed and hit him in the head, and picked him up by one arm and drop kicked him across the room when he was three or four. The mother, who was also beaten by the father, was afraid of him and wouldn't stand up to him when her daughters reported the mistreatment. After Pablo's older sisters got married in their late teens and left home, Pablo was lonely and hard-headed, according to his mother. He didn't like school, and got into a fight with a middle school principal over school attendance.

The prosecution's exhibits in the trial record reveal Melendez was in special education and bilingual classes. He was suspected of having Attention Deficit Disorder. He went to Mexico for several months during fifth grade, was reading and doing math below level, and had to repeat the grade. In 1987 at age 11, he was arrested for an incident involving his younger half-sister. He was living at the time with his father and stepmother.

Melendez says the incident never occurred, that his stepmother reported it to the police to get rid of him. He says his mother, who speaks little English, had to hire an attorney to get him back because the stepmother and father told the police no one in his natural family wanted Pablo. He writes that he had no idea what he was being accused of until a jailer inquired for him after he'd been held several days. He said he didn't understand the word used to describe the charge. Two psychologists who tested him at that time reported he was "isolated and puzzled." The prosecutor stressed this early conviction twice in the punishment phase of the murder trial, and Melendez believes it was key in getting the death sentence for him.

From the prosecution, jurors also learned Melendez had a history of juvenile arrests for window breaking, carrying a knife to school, punching a younger boy and then stealing his motorized toy. He had also admitted to using pot, crack, coke, acid and alcohol and sniffing paint since age 12 — and to being a gang member.

He had spent time in a residential inhalant treatment program on the Texas border. After five months in the program, the teen had begun to show progress. Then his brother-in-law was killed in a workplace fight and the trip back home for the funeral proved disastrous for his addiction treatment. On learning shortly after the funeral that his mother wanted him to stay in treatment another six months as the counselors were recommending, he ran away, fought with Laredo cops and then got kicked out of the program after threatening another client and staff members with a pipe.

By the fall of 1991, Fort Worth therapists had terminated him from an out-patient treatment program at the Gainesville State School. He had relapsed on crack, failed to report and had run away from home. In the spring of 1992, he was back in the Gainesville State School, where an achievement test showed him at second grade reading level and just below fifth grade level in math. A counselor wrote that he had a learning disability, but tried hard and needed lots of one-on-one. He was selected for the Challenge Program championed by Governor Ann Richards, which emphasized a tightly structured routine like boot camp, plus therapy and education. In three months he had graduated successfully and was sent home.

On return to Fort Worth, he dropped out of court-ordered school and twelve-step meetings and began hanging out with other boys who liked to drink and sniff paint. Roel Gonzalez, the younger brother of Robert Gonzalez, Jr., the leader of La Loma, was one of his friends.

In September of 1993 Melendez was involved in two walk-by shootings. Trial records conflicted. One account said neither of the shots Melendez fired connected. In fact one was purposefully shot into the ground, but at another place in the record Mike Parrish says one hit the target's foot. Melendez went to county jail. In June of 1994, at that facility, Melendez injured another inmate from a rival gang so that his face required 22 stitches. The weapon was a sharpened piece of soap.

The negative part of this history, especially the early incident with the younger sister and the jail assault, were used at the punishment phase of the trial by the prosecutors to convince jurors Pablo would be a future danger to society.

Mike Parrish said prosecutors can "waive" seeking the death penalty in a capital case —

> for a variety of reasons – 17 years old, he's got no priors, or he does have a prior but . . . [not] a significant violent prior. . . . He may have a strong drug or alcohol problem that sets him up for a diminished capacity defense. . . . there are tons of reasons not to seek the death penalty. We reserve that for people with the violent past, criminal history, not a young person. . . . ."[51]

When asked if Melendez's serious problems with alcohol and paint sniffing didn't eliminate him, Parrish responded, "Not on that night."[52]

> When asked how he would know that, given that the suspect wasn't arrested for months afterward, Parrish said, "He was partying with his friends, his friends say drinking."[53]

When reminded that the "friends" who testified as to Melendez behavior that night included a gang member (Roel Gonzalez) who matched the composite, and that rest of the witnesses were Roel's relatives or their wives, Mike Parrish, dismissed the significance of the composite.

He said that in his experience "they're not that good" and that he could "find you a hundred out there on the doorstep who look exactly like that."[54]

Pre-murder photo shows Melendez is wrong guy

A probation photo of Pablo Melendez taken right before the murder, incredibly, was not introduced to the jury by the defense until after Melendez was convicted, during the punishment phase of the capital murder trial for the fatal shooting of Mike Sanders.

Pablo's attorney, James Teel said, "When I was cross examining Seagraves, that was my big point . . . to develop doubt, and to develop this other defendant as the real perpetrator. I had it [the composite] sitting right underneath Tommy Seagraves so the jury could see that, and then our last witness was the defendant [Roel] and he was sitting up there in the witness stand with that composite underneath him, and that was the guy!"[55]

Teel blames the testimony of Pablo's former pals in the gang for the jury verdict. Warren St. John says there's been so much water under the bridge since they defended Melendez, he can't remember when they found the probation photo, how much they said about it in trial or why they waited until the sentencing phase to bring in Roel Gonzalez. But he says he and Teel were "more than diligent"[56] about investigating the case, but they found themselves shut out by the police detectives and no one would talk on the streets. For Teel and St. John, the main issue is that the prosecution hid from them the information about the eyewitness from Jackson Barbecue.[57]

Little direct discussion of the probation photo of Melendez appears in the trial record. Neither Melendez' family nor Mickey Ross remembers hearing it or seeing the photo. Pablo believes the defense blew it up to at least an 8 X 10, but is not sure when it was used in court. Why didn't the defense capitalize, for example in the closing arguments of the guilt-innocence phase, on the obvious problem for the prosecution in the dissonance between the composite and its resemblance to Roel and the lack of similarity to Melendez as photographed by the law a week before the shooting?

There was a courtroom skirmish over Seagraves' competency in the hospital when he gave the description, where the D.A. led the detective in his questioning to say she "felt" Seagraves wasn't ready to fully remember what happened at that time. However, a physician's report the same day noted the patient was alert and responsive and gave appropriate answers to the doctor. Teel walked up beside Roel when he was being questioned and placed the composite just below him on a ledge. But the key evidence for the defense, the Melendez probation photograph, was almost ignored except for placing it, in its original small size, in the jury exhibits for the defense, *after* Melendez was convicted.

Perhaps for the jurors the information came too late in the trial. At that point, having rendered a guilty verdict, they may not have wanted to realize they'd made the wrong decision. They had been exposed to reams of material and hours of testimony about incidents in which Melendez fought with police and drug treatment staff, shot at persons, escaped from juvenile facilities, etc. They may have been more concerned with protecting the public from the accused than about wrongful conviction. In Texas, without the possibility of a "life without parole" sentence, jurors take seriously their mandate to protect the public from future harm.

Addiction problems or intimidation?

Pablo Melendez admits he was a member of the La Loma gang and was probably at the crime scene, but thinks he was passed out in the back of a truck from sniffing carburetor fuel. At any rate, he has no recollection of the crime itself. This is what he wrote Gracie Jett recently, what he told his sister, and what he confessed to Detective Tefft shortly after he was arrested in April 1995, after Johnny Ayala snitched on him from jail.

Gloria Torres, Melendez' oldest sister, says he showed up at her house the day after the murder, asking for some liquor. She asked, "What's wrong with you?" He told her he was scared because Roel had told him he'd killed someone the night before. Pablo said he didn't think he'd killed anyone, but couldn't remember. She said, "Why? Why you don't remember?" He replied, "You know how I get when I sniff the paint and all that." Torres says in her experience, he turns into a vegetable when high, is very passive.[58]

However at trial, staff from the *La Familia* inhalant abuse treatment program testified paint-sniffing tended to make abusers very aggressive. Pablo told her he woke up that morning in a bed in Robert Gonzalez' house. Pablo didn't remember anything about the night before. In the kitchen he had seen Roel and others reading a newspaper about a murder, but hadn't paid much attention. Melendez told her then, and the author in 2001[59], that he'd gone to Roel's house later that day and Roel asked him if anyone had followed him. Roel seemed very jumpy, looking out the window from behind the curtains.

After that Melendez showed up for his probation meetings for several months, but disappeared by mid-October. He hid out for awhile, even fled to Mexico, but his mother brought him back and tried to persuade him to turn himself in. He spoke with her Pentecostal pastor about it five or six times and was urged to "take care of business"[60] whether he'd done it or not. In the end, Melendez was arrested in mid-April, 1995, after the fugitive section of the Fort Worth Police Department got a tip-off he'd be at a certain house at a certain time.

In the midst of all this, he'd gotten a young woman pregnant, a ninth grade dropout about his age, and was living with her, helping her care for young children at home and prepare for the birth of their child.

Once Melendez was in custody, he at first denied any involvement in the crime. Detective Tefft, however, employed womanly wiles on him. He was allowed to sit in her office without manacles, leg irons fastened, across the desk from her. After the male detective left, Tefft came from behind her desk, sat down next to the suspect, and put her arm around his shoulders. He burst into sobs and blurted out his confession, such as it was.

Jett says Detective Tefft told her, "His exact words to me were: 'I don't know if I did it or not because I was so stoned.'"[61] His April 13, 1995 confession was in English, which he could not read or write. He spoke and understood it at some level, although most of his friends and family were Spanish-speakers. He learned to read and write in English on death row. He still can't read or write Spanish, although it is his primary language. Pablo's confession said he had been drinking beer all that day and sniffing paint.

> Jr. [Robert Gonzalez] had given me a gun, a .25, I remember being on the porch outside of the house down from the car wash, [the house of Robert Gonzales, or Jr.]. I remember having the gun in one hand and money in the other hand and Johnny took it away. He started calling me names and said, "What you do?" I heard sirens and then Johnny took me inside and told me to take off my clothes. He gave me some shorts. He told me to go to sleep. I woke up the next day and later Johnny showed me the newspaper about a 29 year old man dying at the car wash. Jr. looked at me and shook his head. I asked Johnny what happened when we were on the way to the store and he said to forget about it. . . . About a month later, I seen a poster about the shooting and a reward. I don't know what happened to the gun . . .[62]

Gloria Torres says her brother Pablo was presented in court as a bad person, a thief, but his main problem was getting high. She says she finds it difficult to believe the state's presentation of him, as with ample opportunity, he'd never stolen anything from his family, or from her wealthy employer for whom he'd worked for a while, and had never raised his voice to them.[63] More importantly from the standpoint of evidence, she said when she saw the composite drawing, it became clear the killer was not Pablo; he'd never been able to grow a beard or goatee.[64]

The defense attorneys themselves never talked to the family, just sent investigator Larry Hickman to ask questions about Pablo's childhood.

The issue of the beard never came up, although Hickman says they knew Pablo couldn't grow one because "he was just a kid. He didn't have the hormones yet to grow a beard."[65] The family also has a photograph of Pablo sleeping which his wife's sister took of him not long before he was arrested, and months after the murder. The stocky young man was lying on his left side, showing a right shoulder bare of tattoos.

Jett says that Melendez is scared of the gang. "He says, 'Gracie, you don't understand, they are dangerous.'. . . He wants out, yes, but is scared to come out."[66]

In his first letter to her, on July 16, 2000, written after learning that Jett and her daughter Mickey wanted to visit him, he tells her he couldn't tell the truth during the trial or even now, because he loves his family, including his "X-wife" very much. They mean more to him "than my life" and Roel and his gang know "where they stay" and his mom, to whom he is "very close" lives alone, and "He is out there and I am in here! I just hope you understand... I hope you do write back?"[67]

Melendez also wrote in that first letter that he'd learned to read and write English on death row by reading the Bible, and it took him a long time to write such a letter because of looking up so many words in the dictionary.

In the next letter he tells her:

> If I was to get this case overturn[ed] and the state would tell me if you give us the truth and a statement in [sic] what happen that night we will let you go today! Gracie do you think I would do that??? You better believe I would!!! I can't do it while I am in here! Me being out there with my family is a whole different story![68]

Gloria Torres is not worried for herself, her sisters or their mom. She'd like to see Pablo's story told, hoping publicity can save her brother, because the defense attorneys failed. Mickey Ross now lives in Conroe, not far from the Terrell Unit in Livingston where death row inmates are housed. She and her husband Melvin have visited Melendez and are in communication with his sisters. The Rosses along with Gracie Jett and her husband in Utah do what they can do to help Pablo Melendez get the justice they feel he was denied by the Tarrant County District Attorney's office and the court.

Motion for retrial denied, appeal denied

The first thing Gracie Jett and family did was to testify about Jeffrey Jackson's statements to them in 1996. It did no good. For one thing, the judge decided before the hearing began to accept the prosecution's position that he had no jurisdiction to accept their motion for a new trial. Prosecution said the motion was filed more than 30 days post sentencing, even though the original motion was filed within the 30-day deadline. The law has since been changed to eliminate the 30-day rule which only Texas and a handful of other death penalty states used at the time, small consolation to Pablo Melendez, whose attorneys were not allowed to present information as fundamental as who was present at the crime scene.

Another reason presented by the judge for rejecting the motion was that Jeffrey Jackson's affidavit from May of 1996 misidentified the victim's truck as blue and the extra truck as white. It also said the time was around 9:30 or 10 P.M. — too early to coincide with the shots heard by neighbors and their calls to the police, and several hours earlier than what he'd told investigator Larry Hickman on March 26. Since neither Hickman nor Gracie Jett had taped or gotten signed statements from Jackson, their testimony was legally only "hearsay," worthless. Jackson has since died, although presumably the girlfriend, who was with him that night according to his original statements, is still available as a witness.

Gracie Jett called the attorney for Melendez' direct appeal, Allan K. Butcher, who was appointed the day Melendez was sentenced, and offered to help any way she could. He never called her back.[69] As to Butcher's argument that his client deserved a new trial to hear the testimony of Jeffrey Jackson, the prosecution's responding brief, which was adopted word for word, point for point by Judge Wisch in October of 1998, argued that Jackson's testimony was not relevant or material.[70]

Throughout the brief, the prosecution rested its case on the testimony of eyewitness and surviving victim Tommy Seagraves, despite his obvious perjury in several instances and the fact that he was a parole violator.[71] The Court of Criminal Appeals in its 1999 rejection of the appeal likewise partially justified its action based on Seagraves' testimony, buttressed by that of Robert Gonzalez, Jr., Roel's brother.

Butcher's appeal also challenged the sufficiency of evidence for the finding of future dangerousness. He pointed out that the Court of Criminal Appeals had not reversed a case based on insufficient evidence for that finding in eight years, planting the implication that there was no meaningful appellate review in Texas of sufficiency claims on this point. He argued also that the court was violating state law by avoiding review of jury decisions in the punishment phase. He said that was "unfortunate because it appears to be a transparent attempt by the court to avoid a difficult responsibility that has the potential for being *politically incorrect* at this particular instant of time."[72]

In other words, there is no review in Texas of the jury decision in this part of the punishment phase. Perhaps this is because of the very subjective and political nature of the issue, which may be the heart of the "tough on crime" versus "bleeding heart liberal" debate that has cost political candidates their races in recent decades, should they be so bold as to challenge the prevailing mentality.

Habeas attorney: prosecutor in defensive pose

Jack Strickland is a former Tarrant County prosecutor who spent his last two years in the D.A.'s office fruitlessly trying to convict Fort Worth billionaire Cullen Davis of several murders and attempted murders for hire. He is the TCCA appointed attorney to write the writs of habeas corpus at the state and federal levels for Melendez.

Though appointed in August of 1996, while Butcher was in the process of the direct appeal, Jack Strickland didn't return the inmate's letters for a long time, according to Torres and Melendez. Once, when Melendez' mother went to his office to get some information, she was told he was no longer her son's attorney, leaving the family in confusion. But after Melendez wrote his attorney saying if he wouldn't respond to his letters or visit him he wanted him off the case, Strickland visited him in 1998, with a translator. Pablo told him "The facts are there. Do your job and you'll find them." Strickland didn't return to visit the condemned man until December 2000. He took a deposition in early 2001 from Mickey Ross, prior to filing the first federal appeal.

Strickland filed a motion in July 1998 for an evidentiary hearing on the newly discovered evidence of the state's withholding of information about Jeffrey Jackson from the defense. It alleged actual innocence and an unfair trial, which constitutes a Brady claim, which has been the basis for many reversals over the years across the nation.

Strickland filed the writ of habeas corpus with the state in September of 1999 pursuing the same issue. He mentioned Jett's testimony in the hearing on a Motion for a New Trial — that she had told Mike Parrish as well as Detective Tefft about Jeffrey Jackson, but Strickland also wrote that he:

... knows and respects Mr. Parrish and finds it difficult if not impossible to believe that a lawyer of Parrish's experience, knowledge, and integrity would violate his Brady obligations, either intentionally or through oversight.[73]

He let the prosecution off the hook, although he told this author that the note "explained offer – Jackson Barbecue"[74] came from the assistant prosecutor's desk by her own admission.

He wrote:

By withholding the Jackson evidence from Applicant and arguably, even from the prosecution, the police substituted their judgment for that of the State, the defense, the trial court, and the jury usurping the lawful responsibility of each of these trial entities.[75] The police assumed for themselves the role of the "exclusive judges of [what] the facts proved, the credibility of the witnesses, and of the weight to be given their testimony."[76] What more could the police in this case have done to undermine confidence in this verdict — conducted their own secret trial in the police lockup?[77]

Inexplicably, Strickland also claimed "the case certainly produced significant evidence of his guilt."[78]

That is odd given that the only evidence against Melendez came from: 1. A parole violator with a bad reputation in the community who had a lot to lose by crossing the prosecution; 2. A woman who says she was pressured by the prosecution during a time of extreme emotional duress; 3. People related by blood or marriage to the man who fit the description of the killer.

Why would Jack Strickland undermine a claim of actual innocence for his client if he thinks there is a better than even chance that his client is innocent? He also argues innocence strongly in light of Jeffrey Jackson's information, which he stresses came to the attention of the defense through the efforts of the "mother of the victim, not a person likely to harbor sympathy for the defendant."[79]

Why didn't Strickland pick up on the significance of the probation department photo or the interesting clues in Detective Tefft's files? He missed the existence of Jeffrey Jackson's girlfriend and information about conflicts and threats from several of Seagraves' acquaintances. He missed information about a possible third person in the truck with Sanders and Seagraves, who'd fled the scene. He missed Jett's testimony at the May 1995 hearing in which said she passed on to Tefft information from her own investigation, regarding Seagraves' involvement in other shootings. The medical report on Seagraves from the hospital says he had a "boxer's fracture" on his right hand, one received within two weeks of Sanders' murder. There is no indication that Strickland followed up on that either, although the appeal he filed is basically the last chance for investigation and pressing claims based on newly discovered evidence.

Not surprisingly, the Court of Criminal Appeals turned his appeal down about two weeks after it was filed. Presiding Judge Womack denied an evidentiary hearing to consider the merits of the argument. Strickland had some hopes for the same claim in the federal district court:

> Judge Means is a decent guy and that's whose court this is in, in federal court . . . if he has any feel that this needs to be explored through evidentiary hearings, he'll do it . . . the problem is at the state court hearing they never give you an evidentiary hearing, so you make these allegations, you raise Cain, and then there's no way to ever substantiate it because there's no way to ever get it in the record. But he says the big picture is that chances are never good of getting off death row, the system becomes a self-perpetuating, self-fulfilling system ... I think it's very unlikely that once a case gets as far along as Pablo Melendez' has, that anything is going to turn that around. But I do think that because of the nature of the issues Melendez has raised, he ought to be entitled to an evidentiary hearing, and if he can carry the day, he can carry the day. If he can't, he can't.... The Brady claim is a very persuasive claim, I believe.[80]

In the summer of 2001 Judge Means played it safe and denied the hearing Strickland was hoping to get for his client.

Jack Strickland is listed as one of the best attorneys in Fort Worth in the 1997-1998 issue of *The Best Lawyers in America*.[81] He coherently argues the law in his brief. An indigent Mexican-American former gang member is lucky to have him on the face of it.

But one cannot help wondering if being entrenched in a specific legal community, and having to evaluate the competency and integrity of fellows on both sides of the bar, could preclude a hard look at those issues because of unconscious assumptions or simply community loyalties.

If so, could one condemn a client to certain execution while maintaining on the surface, timeliness, diligence, and the rest of the obvious standards for effective representation? Strickland acknowledged in an interview that his heart may have stayed in the D.A.'s office: "I probably enjoyed my time as a prosecutor as much as any time I've ever practiced law ... there was a public purpose to be served. It was rewarding work intellectually, socially."[82]

Austin attorney Rob Owen, who teaches at the University of Texas law school's Capital Punishment clinic, was part of a team representing another inmate with claims of innocence from Tarrant County, Richard Wayne "Ricky" Jones, executed in August of 2000. Strickland not only was Jones' trial attorney, but in that case also wrote the direct appeal and the state habeas petition, a situation that couldn't happen today unless everyone involved in the case gave their permission. Strickland was removed from Jones' case after he wrote Jones that every man he'd sent to death row deserved to be there, a statement Jones and officials apparently interpreted to mean he wouldn't vigorously pursue claims of innocence

On another capital case that came to Owen on appeal, Strickland had served as trial defense attorney while simultaneously working as a special prosecutor in a death penalty trial in another county. Even more troubling to Owens was the fact that Strickland, as prosecutor, planned to use Dr. James Grigson, (the infamous psychiatrist known as "Dr. Death" for his role in sending over a hundred men to Texas death row), to testify against the accused, despite the fact that Grigson was scheduled to testify for the state against Strickland's defense client about the same time.[83]

Owen says what he's seen "over and over," when ex-prosecutors turn to the defense side of the game, is that they accept the investigation by the prosecution without questioning it. They try to beat the state "within the four squares" defined by the prosecution, instead of going outside that field of inquiry as a good defender would do, particularly in a case where guilt is questionable. Owen blames this mentality in Texas on the absence of a public defender system where defense attorneys would be trained from law school onward from the perspective of the defense. In Texas, an attorney with his sights eventually on defense often has to learn the game at the district attorney's office.

Strickland said he doesn't believe he needed to impugn the reputations of the trial attorneys who worked hard to defend Melendez. For that reason, he didn't file an ineffective trial representation claim, for example, regarding the puzzling fact that the probation photograph wasn't used in the guilt innocence phase at all and was barely referred to in the sentencing phase. Nor does he think Mike Parrish would risk losing his law license and his powerful post in the D.A.'s office by engaging in misconduct, so he blames Detective Tefft, although he acknowledges that legally the prosecutor bears responsibility if the detectives or others on his staff do wrong.[84] Defense investigator Larry Hickman agrees with him regarding Parrish, saying: "I cannot picture Mike Parrish being anything less

251

than professional. There's times when he's an a... hole, but as far as any misconduct, no. He plays hardball, and there's times when I thought maybe the D.A.'s office had got to a witness, but if you gave me a million dollars to name one person in the D.A.'s office who isn't ethical, I couldn't do it."[85]

On the other hand defense investigator Larry Hickman talks about the inequities of the resources available on capital trials for the defense as opposed to the prosecution. His pay has stayed at $35 an hour on these court appointed cases since he began doing the work in 1988, after walking off a 15-year career as a police officer when he was told to write more tickets. He says the most he's ever been paid on a capital case to investigate was $5200; he'd billed $5500 and they'd shaved some, as he was at the point where judges look askance at appointed defense investigators' invoices. He says he worked over a hundred hours on Pablo's defense, for about $3,800, but the prosecution could put two investigators on it and work them as much as they needed. On all other cases but capital to which he's appointed for the defense, including aggravated rape for which people can get 99 years, judges hold him pretty close to $500, including mileage — "that's 12.5 hours, girlfriend."[86]

Mike Parrish told the author there was no inconsistency in the testimony of the gang members and their relatives and girlfriends who testified against Melendez in the grand jury and at his trial.[87] Perhaps his memory failed him. Perhaps he didn't expect the author to have read the record. But the record was plain, and the contradictions were plentiful.

After Judge Means affirmed the conviction and sentence, Melendez had only the Fifth Circuit, which rarely reverses a state court decision, and the Supreme Court, which won't take a death penalty case unless it raises some constitutional issue it needs to address, between him and the gurney. Barring a return to the state court on a second habeas round, if new grounds of innocence arose, especially if attached to a strong constitutional violation, Pablo Melendez will be cut down in his youth.

Victims once again

Gracie Jett says she used to believe in the death penalty and when her son was killed, she wanted the killer on death row: "People don't realize what losing a child is like."[88] But now she is close to two young men she believes to be innocent who are there, and she feels like she should be included among families of the condemned inmates. "I just kind of dedicated my life to tryin' to help these two young men. I have plenty of love and shirt tail to hang onto."[89]

"They don't need to be killing a boy that didn't do it," Jett says, adding that neither her son nor Pablo were angels, but "six feet under is not the answer....It's going to drive me crazy – another young man dead for nothing, a wasted life. And the real killer is out there to put somebody's else's mother through what I've been through."[90]

Contemplating the death penalty looming over Pablo Melendez, a tearful Mickey Ross, sitting beside her husband Melvin who nods in agreement, says it will just do to the Melendez family what Michael's death did to theirs. And so they continue their investigation of what really happened that night, but now they have Pablo's sisters and mother to help them find the answer. The question is, with Texas and federal death penalty law and courts as they are, will it do Pablo Melendez, Jr. any good?

Chapter Eleven: Michael Toney

Michael Toney, a flamboyant cowboy con man, offered tickets to his execution on E-Bay, wrote scores of letters to newspapers, judges, attorneys, public officials, and international abolitionists, and then finally became despondent, exhausted by the ordeal of life on death row.

Was he an easy causality of the fervor to root out domestic terrorists so politicians could look like they were doing something in response to the 1996 Antiterrorist and Effective Death Penalty Act?

Photo by Susan Lee Campbell Solar.

Cowboy on death row

It was a cold Thanksgiving evening, November 28, 1985 in North Texas, just outside Fort Worth. Joe Blount, 44, a transmission mechanic, had returned to Texas earlier in the year from Washington state to care for his ailing father, who'd suffered a stroke. They had recently moved to the Hilltop Mobile Home Park near the Jacksboro Highway between Fort Worth and Wichita Falls. Blount's 15-year-old daughter Angela, his 16-year old son Robert, and a teenaged nephew, Michael Columbus, visiting from Seattle, had gone out for potato chips and soft drinks. When the three youths returned from the store around 9 P.M., they saw a briefcase on the steps leading to their mobile home.

Curious, Angela carried it inside to the living room where Joe Blount was watching television. After a few beers, Angela sat down with the briefcase on her lap and popped the latches. The detonation and fire that followed killed everyone in the room except Robert, who was badly burned from head to toe. It demolished most of the home. Susan Blunt, Joe's wife, asleep in a bedroom in the rear, was awakened by yelling and screaming and walked into the hall, where she saw someone on the floor burning. Repelled by the fierce heat on the floor as she started toward the living room, she exited through the bedroom door and later found her son propped up in an ambulance, his clothing melted into his skin.

Four months later, in late March of 1986, there was an interesting development. A businessman and member of the Optimist and Bass clubs in nearby Azle, Douglas Raymond Brown, a former candidate for mayor and owner of Azle Business Machine Products, a man described as an outstanding machinery repairman, was arrested. He had sold an undercover agent from the Bureau of Alcohol, Tobacco and Firearms (ATF) the second of two explosive devices, both delivered in a form they hadn't requested, a briefcase. The bombs were similar to the one that killed the Blounts. Firearms experts said detonation would have caused an explosion, then a fire. Explosives and chemicals were also discovered in Brown's office and rural home.

For a concurrent drug investigation, ten people were arrested for drug trafficking, which was why Azle police had been watching Brown for five months prior to his arrest. They were unaware until a week before the arrest that ATF agents had also been investigating Brown for firearms violations. The police believed his business served as an exchange for guns and drugs. However, Police Chief Richard Wilhelm told the *Fort Worth Star Telegram* that Brown, who was being held without bail in the Tarrant County jail, was "one of the last persons I'd suspect . . . ."[1] The Tarrant County Sheriff said he was "floored" by the news. Oddly, a federal agent dismissed the similarities in the cases as "coincidental."[2] Brown was never charged with the bombing, as there was no other evidence to link him to the crime. Two days after his arrest for possessing and delivering an explosive device, he was freed on $10,000 bond.[3]

For eleven years, the Blount family bombing remained an unsolved crime. After the Oklahoma City bombing prompted re-investigation of all domestic bombings, however, Special Agent in Charge of the Dallas Field Division of the ATF Bureau, Lester D. Martz, mounted a special initiative on the case. He directed agents to start from scratch to re-investigate the crime, working with a task force including representatives of the Tarrant County Sheriff's and District Attorney's Offices and the Texas Department of Public Safety. Amazingly, it did not lead them back to Brown — who'd sold undercover agents explosives in a briefcase the same year the Blount family was blown up in their trailer home.

Instead, the investigation led to a rodeo bullrider with a long criminal record for theft and forging checks, a man with a string of aliases which always ended with his real last name, Toney. He was indicted for capital murder on December 4, 1997. Conveniently Toney was already in custody.

Actually, Michael Roy "Cowboy" Toney led the agents to himself. A fellow convict, Charles Ferris, was suffering from liver disease and unable to get interferon. Toney says Ferris "had turned yellow and was real sick."[4] Toney urged Ferris to tell authorities he could give them information about a long unsolved bombing case in return for his freedom and access to the life-saving medicine. Toney then told Ferris what he'd learned from another inmate who'd been questioned in the re-investigation of the Blount bombing.

The sick inmate was released in August of '97 from the Parker County jail. Toney told him there could be no consequence to involving him because he was innocent, had been working in Alaska at the time of the crime, and knew only what he'd been told by another inmate. After what Toney describes as stunning betrayals by an ex-wife, friends, business partners and acquaintances, all of whom he thought would exonerate him, Michael Toney spent his 35th birthday on December 29th, 2000, on death row.

The California-born "cowboy" with the big grey-blue eyes, sad boyish face and one hell of a hard-luck story was riding for his life on a fearsome trail — the appeals process through state and federal courts that almost never reverse a capital conviction.

What he didn't know yet was that thanks to support organized by a woman in France and a lay minister from Texas and Louisiana named Edwin Smith, he might have a chance.

A long ride

Michael Toney, born in 1965, spent his early childhood on a small ranch in the Sacramento Valley, near Cottonwood, California, a town where he says everyone was either related to his family or knew them well. His parents had divorced when he was six. He arrived in Texas at the age of 15 as a result of serious family violence, directed at him. At age 15, he saw his mother's latest boyfriend kick a door shut which she was holding. It "skinned her fingers down to the bone." Toney jumped the man to "hurt him so he would stop."[5] After a few days at a girlfriend's house, Toney returned home. The boyfriend slugged him with a baseball bat smashing Michael's ankle. No one filed charges against the boyfriend in spite of the fact that Michael's hospitalization should have instigated at least some questions.

In fact, Toney's mother, an alcoholic to this day, chose the man over her adolescent son. She sent Toney off to Texas to live with his father, who instead of enrolling him in school, helped him for a month, then told him he'd have to find his own place to live. Michael, age 15, was expected to support himself doing construction work for his father. After a year of that, Toney found a job in Alaska, where he worked for a year. He was convicted of driving without a license in Anchorage in July 1984. By fall, he was back in Texas, working for his father again.

In 1985 his younger brother arrived in Texas and got the same treatment from their father. One day they both walked off the job. The brother returned to California. Michael stayed in Texas and met a man named Chris Meeks, who was to become his best friend and eventual betrayer. In November of 1985 the two young men began subcontracting small jobs.

About that time Toney met Kim. They began an intense affair which would eventually result in marriage and the birth of a daughter named after her. He maintains that he spent Thanksgiving day of 1985 in Keller, Texas with the Meeks family and Laura Brannigan, who was dating Chris Meeks. That night he says he spent with Kim in her apartment in Euless.

In early December of 1985 Toney and Meeks ran into trouble framing a house in Grapevine when neither knew how to cut rafters for the roof. They had to ask Toney's dad for help. According to Toney, his dad exacted half their pay. With what was left they bought a 1979 Chevy Silverado truck.

The truck played a big role in several ways in Toney's life. He fought with his brother over it and injured the brother's girlfriend, the conviction for which was brought up in his trial many years later to indicate a violent nature making him a future danger to society. The truck was also part of a story that tied him to the crime scene in testimony against him by his best friend and girl friend. Much later evidence was discovered that proved he didn't even own the truck until a month after the Blount trailer was blown up in 1985.

Michael Toney does not deny having had a string of problems with the law. He was arrested in Euless on a Midland County Sheriff's Department warrant for theft of $200 or less, possibly related to a dispute with Meeks who said their partnership fell apart after Toney wrote a series of hot checks forging Meeks' signature on their joint account. In May of 1986, Toney was also convicted of criminal trespass of a habitation in Tarrant County. In November of that same year, he was charged with injury to a child for the incident involving his brother, the Silverado and a coke bottle he threw either at his brother's girl friend, who was a minor, or at a dumpster. The bottle hit and injured the girl.

Toney says he fled with Kim to California, fearing arrest. In Flagstaff along the way, he picked up a conviction for theft, to which he pled in December and received a sentence in March of 1987. Out on bail in California, he deliberately flunked an exam for the Army, which his family was pressuring him to join. In November of 1988 he was back in Tarrant County, convicted of petty theft. A year later that charge, plus burglary of a habitation appear on his record.

In August of 1989 Toney was sentenced to eight years for one of the burglary convictions. That same year he and Kim were divorced and she joined the Army. Toney admits to driving Kim off with womanizing and brutality (which he says was always triggered by her reaction to numerous infidelities, which he has no idea why he was compelled to commit). He says after they divorced their relationship improved and they became friends.

It was in prison in 1990 that Toney met Bennie Joe Toole, who had been one of the early suspects in the Lake Worth bombing. Toole told him about the unsolved case.

By July 1991, he was evidently out of jail, because he was convicted of "unauthorized use of a vehicle" and "theft by hot check of $200 or less." That year he says he talked to Kim for the last time until after his capital murder trial, when he called her at her parents' home one time. He knew something had ended their post-divorce friendship by her tone and her refusal to let him speak to their daughter. During the Gulf War, she had met another man.

In April 1993 another Tarrant County hot check charge, followed by a Dallas County conviction for "theft of between $750 and $20,000," presumably pulled the Cowboy off the bulls and into the pen again. There's a gap in his record until April 1996, when he got five years for burglary.

He also got a DWI that year he says, but no jail time. In March 1997 Toney got bucked into the judicial system again with "credit card abuse," "burglary of a habitation," and "driving while intoxicated," In November 1997 he was charged with "burglary of a habitation," a second degree felony. It was while he was in the Parker County jail serving time for the credit card abuse that Toney met Charles Ferris.

Arrest and conviction

When Toney was arrested at the Wise County Jail where he'd been transferred some time after Ferris was freed, he was shown the *Ft. Worth Star Telegram* story about his impending arraignment. He was shocked and didn't believe it was real. It had been several months since he'd suggested the ruse. He told the authorities he wanted to take a polygraph. He was taken several days later, with his appointed attorney Roger Blair, to the Dallas office of a forensic psychologist. Polygraph examiner John Lehman had him fill out forms about medication, etc., and sign papers. Lehman told him he would get to the truth, which Toney said he welcomed, and left him in a room with a camera in the corner for 15 or 20 minutes. Toney says Lehman returned and said that though he thought Toney would be a fascinating subject, he couldn't give him the test. On the way back to jail, Toney was told he needed a doctor's release to take the exam. He obtained the release the next day, but was never tested.

Thinking they would exonerate him although they hadn't been in touch for years, because they were with him the day and night the bombing had occurred, Toney gave investigators the names of his ex-wife, Kimberley Toney, and his former best friend, Chris Meeks. Meeks was tracked down in New Mexico. Kim was a blackjack dealer at an Indian casino in Wisconsin. She was re-married to a man she had met in the Army. At first she told the ATF investigators she didn't know a bombing had occurred, much less anything about Michael's connection to it.

She admitted in court that afterward that she had gone to the library and read up on the case. Presumably she learned about the $50,000 reward offered for information regarding the crime. She contacted the agents saying she now realized the murders took place a few miles from the Fort Worth Nature Center on Lake Worth where they had gone fishing together that Thanksgiving night. In October of 1997, she met with several investigators in Tarrant County including Charley Johnson. Toney believes Johnson encouraged Kim Toney and Chris Meeks to commit perjury.

Meeks was first interviewed on October 21, 1997, in Dexter, New Mexico, where he was on probation for a fourth drunk driving charge. He'd been imprisoned for 18 months on an earlier charge. He was subpoenaed to Fort Worth to testify to a grand jury on November 6, 1997. He also at first denied any knowledge of the crime, then was given a polygraph, which he reportedly failed. After he was promised immunity for perjury to the first grand jury, he gave a statement on November 11 incriminating Toney and turned state's witness against his former partner and friend. To explain why he'd never mentioned what happened before, he implied that fear kept him from coming forward.

In mid-January of 1998, a little over a month after Toney's indictment for murder, Charles Ferris told the press that he and Toney had made the story up. He said "Toney was shocked when authorities believed the bombing story."[6] The *Dallas Morning News* reported ATF agent Bart McEntire, the lead investigator, said Ferris could "recant anything he wants. That doesn't change the facts that we know about . . . evidence that can't be explained away."[7]

At trial in May of 1999, Kim Toney and Chris Meeks told similar stories, involving their being together that Thanksgiving, the night of the crime. They said Michael Toney talked of going "on a mission," drove their recently-purchased Silverado truck to Lake Worth and parked near a propane tank, where he pressured Chris to scope out the scene of the crime in the trailer park, to see if someone was at home. They said Toney pulled a briefcase from under the toolbox in the pickup bed and headed off toward the trailer park, returning at a run without it. Allegedly the three then went to the nearby Nature Center to hang out until after midnight, during which time Michael shot and killed an endangered beaver with a .22 rifle. They said he then buried the animal, since he realized it was illegal to shoot it, before returning in the middle of the night to Euless.

Under cross examination, Kim admitted she didn't see a bomb or any emergency vehicles, didn't hear sirens or an explosion. According to Toney, Chris Meeks testified very nervously. At one point, under questioning about the location of a propane place where he claimed they'd parked the car when Toney delivered the briefcase, Meeks said he "was told it's directly beside it (the trailer park),"[8] suggesting that he'd had help creating his story.

Other testimony portrayed Toney as a danger to society. Dawn Gorcenski, a former girlfriend from 1990-1991, who is the mother of Toney's second daughter, testified he held a pistol to her head, threatened to kill her, that he beat her at least once weekly during the time they were together, and that he shot at one of her friends. Abusive relationships were the norm for him, as the psychiatrist for the defense testified. He also maintained Toney was not a sociopath. The prosecution, however, supplied for the benefit of the psychiatrist and the jurors a litany of horror stories about Toney waving weapons around, and about physical and emotional abuse of women. The stories included inflicting a hand-sized welt on the back of his toddler daughter and then leaving her in the house alone, and sending a girlfriend to the hospital in 1985.

The jury was convinced, and gave Toney the death sentence after answering "yes" to the questions of future danger and "no" to the issue of whether there was sufficient mitigating evidence to justify a life sentence instead of lethal injection.

Toney says he thought he was sitting through someone else's trial, watching them and hearing their testimony. Edwin Smith of Dove Prison Ministry International said about the Toney case:

> I am always skeptical of these "I'm innocent" stories. Many tell me that and it just doesn't ring true. Michael was convicted without any physical evidence, mostly on the word of his ex-wife, so called best fried, and a jailhouse snitch. Michael has a letter from the snitch admitting he lied to cut a deal with the state to reduce his sentence. His ex-wife all but committed perjury.[9]

Toney says the pain of Kim's betrayal was the worst, though he acknowledges he was an immature, cheating and abusive husband, and says she was and is a wonderful person to whom he feels gratitude for giving him a beautiful daughter. According to Toney, Kim told him when she visited him in jail after her testimony helped convict him, "I know you're not a murderer, I just assumed you did it because they said you did."[10]

Gracie Jett, mentor to death row inmate

Gracie Jett, who lost her only natural son to homicide in 1994, had taken on a mothering role toward Toney, after he learned about her from Pablo Melendez, also prosecuted by Mike Parrish. She says,

> Michael told me right from the start, "Gracie, I am far from being no angel, you name it, I've probably done it, with the exception of one thing, I am not a murderer; I will never take anybody's life. Life is too precious to me, I don't feel like it's my place to take anybody's life.[11]

Jett says Toney's mother called her up drunk one time and chewed her out for trying to "take her son" because Jett had talked to him like a mother, advising him.

Gracie said,

> I will never make apologies for sayin' whatever it takes just for your son to survive in there, until we can try to get him out. I'm doin' what needs to be doin'. I'll say whatever I have to say to get him to hang on to try to do something to get him out of there.[12]

Eventually Gracie Jett and Michael Toney began to understand there were other places to look for the perpetrator of the Blount bombing. Alexander Garcia Gonzalez, an inmate in the Clements unit in Amarillo, wrote a letter to Wise Country Sheriff Phil Ryan, regarding undercover work he'd done for the Tarrant County Sheriff's office in 1986. He had read a newspaper account of Toney's ongoing trial and wrote to point out he'd never been debriefed on what he knew of the case. Gonzalez wrote that while in a Texas prison he'd encountered a black man, Wesley Jones who claimed to have known who did the bombing.[13]

Gonzalez said that the *Fort Worth Star-Telegram* had printed articles saying the suspects were "methamphetamine distributors . . . some were now dead and some were currently doing time in prisons."[14] He added that, "a few months before I went undercover . . . I had seen Curtis Mackayea with numerous sticks of dynamite inside of a totebag and that he intended to take the explosives to . . . the north side of Fort Worth."[15]

Gonzalez finished the letter with a proposition: that he be hired to help narc out speed manufacturers which he'd read were spreading like wildfire in the Dallas/Fort Worth metroplex as well as the state as a whole, with the condition that he be given a full pardon once he'd helped close down a certain number of speed labs.[16] Apparently the law passed over the offer, as Gonzalez is still in prison, now in East Texas.

To Mike Parrish Gracie Jett may have been "a piece of work,"[17] but to Michael Toney on death row she was a friend and advocate.

Toney posts tickets to his execution on E-Bay, gets help instead

After he was sentenced, Toney worked hard to save himself, writing to the Blount family survivors, his ex-wife Kim, Chris Meeks and his mother, and other witnesses. His letters brought media attention, public wrath, scorn from the District Attorney's office and an order to the prison system to seize any letters addressed in the future to the offended parties. He directed allies to find receipts proving the truck toolbox and rifles weren't bought until almost a month after the bombing. He located weather history showing that Thanksgiving night was one of the coldest of the year, dropping to 31 degrees, not exactly ideal for hanging out several hours by a lake and shooting at beavers, as Kim had testified.

Suffering from the imposed isolation of the new quarters in the Terrell Unit where all death row inmates were transferred in early 2000, Toney went through profound depression. There was no opportunity for contact with anyone apart from guards and the occupant of the next cell, whom he couldn't see, could only communicate with by lying on his stomach and speaking through a vent near the floor on the side of the door. He watched inmates being led off to their death at the rate of three or four a month. He wasn't getting along with his attorney, and was thwarted in his attempts to get to the surviving Blunt family members to talk to him.

Jett didn't know it, but in the spring of 2000 Toney decided to waive all appeals and speed his death. He submitted an auction item to e-bay in the spring of 2000 selling tickets to witness his execution, an item which was hastily pulled by E-Bay when it came to their attention. Toney says he did it to raise money so he could leave something to his two daughters. The action garnered international media attention, but also the disdain of his first appellate attorney, Robert Ford, who felt such behavior could further damage his client with the justices who held his fate in their hands.

Not long after the incident, the intervention of lay prison minister Edwin Smith of Dove Ministries, who believed his story and garnered national and international support for him, seemed to revive the Cowboy's hopes for relief. Letters from penpals in Texas and abroad began pouring in, like life blood. Some of those letters came from a French abolitionist who had been involved with Texas death row cases before, Sandrine Ageorges. She understood the vital importance of serious investigation at the stage of the final state appeal, the writ of habeas corpus, and hired an able veteran investigator, Tena Francis. Francis and her team were eventually able to determine what hadn't been done regarding Toney's claims of innocence, and to supplement the investigation of writ attorney Jack Strickland in a significant way.

In mid-February Robert Ford pled Toney's case to the Court of Criminal Appeals, an event to which Toney was not invited, as is the custom in such hearings. Ford and Toney had been clashing even before Ford learned of Toney's E-Bay auction attempt. Toney had written the Court of Criminal Appeals asking them to ignore Ford's brief on his behalf. The inmate felt it did not sufficiently raise actual innocence claims. Toney was right. A judge interviewed several months after the hearing was unaware innocence was even an issue in his case.

Ford served as Toney's attorney for direct appeal, a process which is about establishing whether or not the trial was conducted properly, not about innocence or guilt. He found an error in the trial transcript, which he says in prior years, before the court was taken over by activist judges with an ax to grind that far outweighed their interest in case law or justice, would have resulted in almost automatic reversal. Now, Ford says, he rarely argues any of his appeals before the court because it's like "talking to the deaf, dumb and blind."[18]

The point of error was related to the prosecutor's charge of transferred intent. No one had ever been able to find any reason the Blount family would have been deliberately targeted for violence. Several sources had reported the wrong trailer had been bombed. Therefore, the argument to the jury to prove the murders were deliberate (necessary in a capital murder case) had to be handled through a "transferred intent" claim.

The prosecutor, Mike Parrish, a senior assistant D.A., had purposefully rejected the application paragraph. The Tarrant County D.A.'s appellate chief Chuck Mallin, arguing against Ford in February, admitted (as several of the justices chuckled) that Parrish's "transferred intent" action would have prompted him to take a baseball bat to the prosecutor had he been there at the trial.[19] Mallin acknowledged to Ford back home that the error was egregious. Ford argued powerfully that the justices either had to grant a reversal to his client or forget the case law they'd applied for years.

While things were bogged down on the legal front in the waning winter months of 2001, the investigation was breaking loose. Investigators hired by the French to check out Toney's story and follow his leads struck pay dirt in about two weeks.

Finis Blankenship, a jailhouse snitch, claimed to have been promised freedom (that never came) for testifying that Toney had told him he'd been carrying out a $5,000 contract which had something to do with four kilos of heroin when the Blounts were bombed.[20] The story went that Toney didn't receive half his pay because of blasting the wrong home.[21] Jett exchanged letters with Blankenship regarding Toney's case over a period of four months in 2000, letters which state several times that the witnesses against Toney committed perjury in exchange for cash and money.[22]

Chris Meeks, Toney's former partner, one of the two key witnesses against him, told an investigator who interviewed him in New Mexico an entirely different story than he'd told in court. When confronted by the investigator he couldn't remember or imagine why he would have told the story that he had.

Finally, investigators found state records proving what Toney had said all along — the truck which Meeks' and Kim's stories featured so prominently hadn't been purchased until December 13th, several weeks after the bombing. Toney had earlier unearthed records proving that the toolbox and rifles were also purchased considerably after the Blounts were bombed.

Toney was lucky that the investigation results came in before his writ of habeas had been submitted at the state level. His court-appointed attorney, Jack Strickland, was able to include some of this new evidence of prosecutorial misconduct and of innocence in that all-important appeal. Although there was no DNA to prove his genetic innocence, the prosecution's case was crumbling, and with the heat of the previous year on the Court of Criminal Appeals, Cowboy stood a fair chance of hanging onto the most important bronco of his career.

Terrorism and prisoner abuse

In a poem posted by Michael Toney on the Lamp of Hope website just after 9/11, Toney ponders the relationship between state sponsored murder of an innocent person and terrorism. Of course, anyone condemned to death might see himself as society writ large, as a symptom of a far greater problem. Maybe he's feeling sorry for himself. Maybe he has a point.

He challenged President George W. Bush — who rode to power on a tough-on-crime horse, bridled with tough rhetoric in favor of the death penalty, who presided over the execution of so many people in Texas he earned the name "Governor Death," who abandoned the essential relationship between evidence and consequence when he invaded Iraq — to stop state sponsored terrorism.

It's far from evident that Michael Toney blew up that trailer in North Texas in 1985. It's a fact that George W. Bush ordered, without letting United Nations weapons inspectors finish their work of gathering evidence, the pre-emptive "shock and awe" bombing of Baghdad. The civilian death toll in Iraq at the time this book went to print was between eleven and thirteen thousand people.[23]

Terrorism
by Michael Toney

Texas Death Row
October 11, 2001

If someone was to ask me how I feel about the death sentence that has been wrongfully imposed on me or how my impending execution by lethal injection makes me feel, I would say:

Extreme fear! Dread! Horror! I feel anxiety, dismay, consternation and trepidation. I am intimidated and in awe.

What one word did I leave out in describing how I feel about my impending execution? There's one word that describes my feelings perfectly.

TERROR! All of the words I used to describe the fear I have of being strapped to a gurney and injected with poison until dead are synonyms of TERROR!

The United States Government, President George W. Bush has vowed to stop terrorism both here in the United States and abroad.

Terrorism is defined by the Oxford and Webster as:
the use of terror
and intimidation to gain ones political objectives.

I have been wrongfully sentenced to death by the United States government and the government of the State of Texas. These governments are made up
of the people of both the United States and the State of Texas.

Terrorist is defined by Oxford and Webster as a person who uses or favours violent or intimidating methods of coercing a government or community.

Doesn't this analogy show that the United States government is acting as a terrorist in it's use of the Death Penalty?

When the Honourable President Bush vowed to stop all terrorism
worldwide, did he mean that the United States of America
is going to cease its use of the death penalty as a deterrent to crime?

Is the State of Texas going to stop terrorizing human beings
by sentencing them to the terrifying punishment of death
by lethal injection?

I agree with President Bush, terrorism must be stopped and I know
he is an Honourable President because if he wasn't
he wouldn't expect God to bless America.

For God to bless America the terror must cease!

Has the death penalty ever been used to gain one's political
objective? To answer this question we only have to reflect
on the last Presidential elections and the last gubernatorial election
in Texas. We don't have to look far.

May God bless humanity, America and every country of the world.
May God bless President George W. Bush with wisdom to
recognize terrorism and the compassion to stop it.[24]

Compassion isn't a common component of Texas death row. Inmates bake in temperatures that can top three digits four months of the year and fans are rare, though they do exist for some lucky inmates thanks to a fan project headed by Lois and Ken Robison and Texas Cure.[25] Inmate inflicted injuries are commonplace and churn out of a maelstrom of rage, rumor and dis-information. In a letter to this author in July of 2001, Toney wrote:

> . . . I have had terrible luck since the middle of June and what could go wrong has. I have second degree burns on the right side of my face and neck due to another inmate throwing boiling water mixed with oil and shaveless hair remover on me. After he did it he said, "that's for your mom and [B] but that ain't shit I'm going to burn your ass up." Someone has started a rumor that I was in prison for either "beating my mother to death or shooting her with a shotgun." On July 3rd my friend [B] came to visit me and the first things she did was start telling me my friends . . . are not trustworthy. I had already been having a hard time and I

didn't react well to this but rather than argue I terminated the visit. Things have really gone to shit since. [B] really has it in for me now and she has got some inmates to turn on me as well. One of them . . . and his buddy . . . have been sending threatening letters to the warden and to [B] but they have been putting my name and return address on them. So [B] is telling people that I am threatening her and the Inspector General visited me on Monday because of a threatening letter to the warden allegedly written by me. Thank God the mailroom ladies knew the letters were not from me and cleared me right aways but now there is an investigation into the burning and the letters and I have been moved for my safety. Now I'm near Pablo. He told me he didn't tell you about my face when you visited him today. On the 14th I got burned and then learned that my grandfather has had a massive stroke and is dying. I'm also afraid that [T] may be sending letters to the media with my name on them. . . .[26]

Oppressive heat, second degree burns, threats of anal rape, rumor, and dis-information were part of the package deal for Michael Toney on Texas death row. In an earlier letter he wrote about a problem even more troubling.

I'm as well as the situation and this Hell hole will allow. Today is a bad day for me because there was an execution a couple of hours ago. I just can't get used to people being killed on a regular basis. I know its wrong for anyone to ever take the life of another but I always wonder how many innocent people are executed.[27]

Chapter Twelve:
Odell Barnes

"I thank you for proving my innocence, although it has not been acknowledged in the courts. May you continue in the struggle and may you change all that's being done here today and in the past."
Odell Barnes last words, March 1, 2000

Photo by Susan Lee Campbell Solar.

A week before execution

The last interviews Odell Barnes, Jr. gave were a week before he died on March 1, 2000 at the hands of the state. The interviews in late February took place near Huntsville, down a two-lane road through the East Texas piney woods that led to the Ellis Unit where death row inmates were then housed.

I was the third journalist to arrive in the little guard room just outside a tall fence topped with razor wire. A young woman from the *Huntsville Item* was there when I arrived, along with a cameraman and anchorman from a Wichita Falls television station.

Odell Barnes, Jr., like proportionately too many men on Texas death row, was black. His great-uncle was the legendary bluesman, John Lee Hooker, who died the year after Barnes was put to death. As my own interview with Barnes reached past the details of his case into the human condition, I realized I was witness to the essential catalyst for a major American art form, the Blues.

I may have come in with an agenda. What occurred was a profound conversation with a man at peace with himself, and with death. He spoke about his spiritual journey, which began when someone finally believed him. He'd come to terms with a childhood wrought with alcoholism and violence, juvenile crime, then death row. He'd been jailed twice before he turned twenty. His first, of six children, was born when he was thirteen years old. He asked for drug rehab, didn't get it; asked for job training, didn't get it. He lived the life he knew until a frame landed him on death row. He died at thirty-one. Odell Barnes referred over and over again to "the situation."[1]

It was a situation — child abuse, racism, addiction, justice derailed — knotted completely against him. The fact that a large part of the world believed the DNA evidence against him had been faked opened a window in his soul. Because someone sided with him, he was able to make peace with the executioner, knowing he was innocent of the crime for which he was being killed. He said the state's killing of him proved the system wrong. He knew the world was watching, which gave meaning to his sacrifice, and he made peace with it. I can think of nothing sadder. And yet, standing in the parking lot outside the execution chamber the night he died, this reporter felt as if the tide against state sponsored homicide was turning.

Much of the world believed George W. Bush presided over the murder of an innocent man when he denied clemency to Odell Barnes, the 122nd person killed on his watch. The Board of Pardons and Paroles gave him a fast 18-0 vote of "No." International newspapers referred to the process as "Texecutions" and to Bush as "Governor Death." When asked about human rights violations, Bush once quipped that Texas didn't sign the Geneva Convention and didn't need to abide by it.

Mrs. Nicole Fontaine, President of the European Parliament made the following pronouncement on February 24, 2000:

> . . . the execution of Odell Barnes scheduled for 1 March . . in Texas, despite the grave doubts surrounding his actual guilt, can only create a profound sense of unease in the conscience of Europeans and the world at large. . . for several decades now all the countries of the European Union have totally outlawed the use of capital punishment. It is barbaric. It is widely accepted that it has no deterrent effect on criminals, because it has sent to their deaths too many victims later found to be innocent.[2]

In a final letter to the world in October of 1999 Barnes said:

> It is not until society looks at the injustice and seeks punishments and sanctions against such acts by prosecutors and judges that the very integrity of our legal system will be restored . . . I have written all of this because I have been the suspect, the convicted, the falsely accused and very much a victim.[3]

The issue is significant. Why does our justice system let prosecutors and judges avoid personal responsibility for egregious errors that result in the execution of innocent people? Governor George W. Bush presided over the execution of 152 people. Governor Ryan of Illinois, also a Republican, declared a moratorium because in his state the courts had been wrong fifty percent of the time. Is a governor responsible for the deaths he allows to occur? Governor Ryan thought so. Should Texas governors be allowed to continue to dodge responsibility when this Board of Pardons and Paroles gives rubber stamp denials to virtually all petitions for clemency?

The Barnes case as reported by the Grassroots Investigation Project is as follows:[4]

Allegation

On March 1, 2000, the State of Texas, with acquiescence by the federal government, executed Odell Barnes by lethal injection. The state and federal governments failed to ensure Barnes's right to a fair and impartial trial. The unfair trial resulted in Barnes's execution.

Crime

Helen Bass was murdered on November 30, 1989. She had been shot, bludgeoned, and stabbed. She was found face down on her bed, nude. A rifle butt was found in her room and a kitchen knife covered in blood was found on the floor just inside the door to her house. The room was in shambles. Her jewelry box and two purses appeared to have been dumped and scattered. Other belongings were discovered near a fence outside her house. Barnes was arrested, tried, and convicted for the murder.

Salient Issues

*The original defense attorneys appointed by the state failed to investigate, and thus failed to discover and present evidence of Barnes's innocence.

*The original defense attorneys failed to have evidence that was used to convict Barnes tested by defense experts.

*Counsel who took over the case for federal appeals sought analysis of the crime scene, fingerprint identification, DNA testing, and additional time to conduct a factual investigation. All these requests were denied.

*Counsel in federal appeals nonetheless carried out independently funded investigations that yielded substantial evidence that raised doubts about Barnes's guilt.

*Blood on Barnes's coveralls, part of the evidence used to secure his conviction, contained a preservative found in test tubes used to store blood. The expert opinion of the chemist, hired by the defense, was that it did not come from "original, legitimate crime scene evidence . . . deriving from natural bleeding from a normal human being."

*The primary eyewitness and his sister saw a man jump a fence near the crime scene one and one-half hours before the victim returned home. The witness told his sister that the man was not Barnes, but testified at trial that it was Barnes.

* The two main witnesses for the prosecution were implicated in the crime by independent witnesses.

*The fingerprint on the murder weapon was analyzed by the state and was found not to be Barnes's fingerprint. A defense expert identified the fingerprint as belonging to one of the state's main witnesses.

*A lamp on which Barnes's fingerprint was found, and that the state claimed had been recently acquired by the victim, had been in the victim's home for at least five years. Barnes had been in the house numerous times and had helped move furniture.

*Evidence suggests that one of the state's witnesses cut a deal with the District Attorney on two drug charges pending against him in exchange for his testimony, although this was not revealed to Barnes's original trial lawyers.

Trial

Barnes was convicted of Helen Bass' murder. The prosecution's case against Barnes consisted primarily of circumstantial evidence. Two witnesses were presented to link Barnes to the murder weapon. There was substantial evidence implicating one of these witnesses in the murder. [The evidence suggests] the other witness agreed to testify in exchange for a deal on two drug charges, despite a state policy prohibiting such deals. There was no other evidence that the gun had been in Barnes's possession or that he had used it. Two small spots of blood were found on coveralls in Barnes's car. The blood was consistent with the victim's blood type, which is also the blood type of 50% of the African-American population in the U.S. Another witness for the prosecution testified that he had seen Barnes jump a fence at the victim's house one and one-half hours before she returned from work, even though he had earlier told his sister that it was not Barnes. This witness admitted he was at least 45 yards away. Barnes's mother testified that she had brought the victim home that night and returned to her home whereupon her son arrived within five minutes.

Defense attorneys appointed by the state failed to carry out their own investigation or to test independently the forensic evidence. At trial, they did not present evidence of Barnes's innocence or challenge the prosecution's witnesses.

Appeals

Initial appeals at the state level were handled by Barnes's original state appointed lawyers. Both the District Court of Wichita County and the Court of Criminal Appeals affirmed the trial court's decision and upheld Barnes's conviction and sentence. Part way through the [Federal Writ] appeals process, new attorneys took over the case. Finding that independent investigations and forensic testing had never been done, they asked courts for funds and time to investigate. In Texas, new evidence must be introduced within 30 days of the original sentencing. They were repeatedly denied, but performed an investigation using volunteers and private funding, which uncovered substantial evidence of innocence. They also uncovered evidence of prosecutorial misconduct, perjury, and constitutional violations. Nevertheless, state and federal courts denied relief.

Conclusion

Odell Barnes was executed despite compelling evidence of his innocence that was never heard by any court in the United States. His original court-appointed defense attorneys failed to provide him with adequate legal counsel. They neither found nor presented evidence of his innocence or evidence challenging key prosecution witnesses. Once the opportunity had been missed at the trial level, state and federal appeals courts refused to hear new evidence – evidence that had been suppressed by the prosecution and that had gone undiscovered by the defense. In many cases, inflexible time limits and increasingly rigid thresholds for review, such as those imposed by the Federal Anti-Terrorism and Effective Death Penalty Act, lead to violations of constitutional protections and human rights. Odell Barnes's was one such case. Despite the fact that he did not receive a fair trial and in spite of evidence of his innocence, no appeals court would hear his case.

The "Situation"

The Wichita Falls television reporter, the first allowed to interview Barnes the day in February 2002 when I arrived to conduct my first death row interview, was white. It was obvious he didn't give much credence to the notion that Barnes might have been innocent of the murder of middle-aged black nurse Helen Bass. He focused on trying to get Barnes to admit guilt in an earlier rape case. The inmate politely declined to comment, saying the matter could still go back to the courts. The reporter from Wichita Falls pressed on, saying in effect, "Look, you're a dead man anyway, why not fess up . . . what do you have to lose?"[5]

Barnes calmly refused to be moved, though he seemed to be admitting guilt in the two aggravated rape trials in which he'd been convicted and found guilty during 1991, after getting the ultimate penalty for the murder of Helen Bass. He came back to the Bass case:

> My [trial] lawyers did nothing to investigate and the evidence was out there. Planted evidence should be enough to get the case reconsidered.[6]

Barnes also pointed out the deal between the D.A. and one of the key witnesses against him, a well-known local drug dealer, and the conflicting statements given by a prosecution witness shortly after the crime and at trial. The reporter seemed unconvinced.

A few days before my interview with Barnes, a lengthy two-part story ran in the *Times Record News* of Wichita Falls. The reporter, Steve Clements, was a high school classmate of Barnes. Odell's loyal younger sister Connie believes Clements harbored a grudge dating back a long time.[7] The lead paragraph of the front page story that Sunday read:

> In an era when crack cocaine fueled near-record homicide rates, open-air drug markets sprang up on previously quiet streets and a rising wave of crime nearly destroyed an entire neighborhood, Odell Barnes, Jr. was the baddest of the bad on the city's East Side.[8]

A summary of twelve acts of violence attributed to Barnes, beginning with shooting his father twice when he was a young teen, was enclosed in a box later in the story to reinforce the point.[9]

European allies, Barnes' final defense attorneys, and his family believe that portrayal and Odell's fate were generated by the deep-seated racism of the region. The East Side of Wichita Falls housed blacks and whites of lesser means. The D.A., Barry Macha, a Democrat who was first elected back in the mid-eighties is, according to Barnes' sister Connie, a member of the local country club in which she worked as hostess for some years. She said Macha had personal issues with Odell.[10] And that leads us to the final factor, perhaps the most fatal of all, the relative poverty of the defendant and his kin, which doomed him to a lackadaisical defense.

But the "situation" didn't stop at neighborhood, or class, or race, or even economic lines. Odell Barnes was raised in a violent, alcoholic home. The "shooting of his father" occurred in the context of family violence aimed at the mother and other children. Odell began drinking with family members when he was 8 years old. He stopped living at home by the time he was 13. As Barnes spoke of his early life to this reporter, days before he was to be executed, it was as if he was speaking to the world. He wasn't making excuses and admitted doing wrong in his life. He was explaining the "situation." I asked him how he had been able to come to peace with his impending death. He said he had learned to meditate, that the discipline of Siddha Yoga had helped him.

When after some discussion of the crime, the Huntsville reporter asked if he was anxious about his impending execution Barnes, smiling and at ease, replied:

> Yeah, at first, but ...once everything is in motion there's no going back. I haven't worried about it. I worry more about my friends and family. A lot of the things I've done in my life have been selfish acts. I'm not going to worry about myself. I'm pretty much at peace. I've accomplished . . . my biggest goals: to prove my innocence, that the evidence was fabricated and planted. If they kill me, it shows the system doesn't work.[11]

The execution of Odell Barnes focused world attention on egregious problems with the death penalty.

"Texecutions" draw international scorn: World sees Gov. Bush as cold-hearted killer[12]

(Here follows the complete text of an article about the importance of international attention to the Texas Death penalty, published by the author in June, 2000)

A disabled woman in Denmark and a young couple in Canada build websites for Texas death row inmates. In Paris, hundreds rally for a black former athlete and crack addict from Wichita Falls awaiting execution; the Pope, the European Parliament, and French President Jacques Chirac all plead with an immovable George W. Bush to save a life. From France alone, Bush received 7,000 letters pleading for one death-row inmate's life. The execution of Mexican nationals is a huge issue for our southern neighbor and NAFTA partner. Eighteen more Mexicans wait in various stages of Texas' death penalty proceedings for their date with the needle.

International attention is focused on the latest flurry of executions in Texas, which were described as "barbarous" in the French press. Pope John Paul II has appealed to Governor Bush to spare the lives of several inmates who were nonetheless dispatched with a lethal mix of chemicals. Texas Department of Corrections officials responsible for executions have been very busy, and that activity has drawn many foreign visitors to Huntsville who come to mourn or document the planned deaths of people who are important to these individual visitors, or to their nations. Texas executions have replaced South Africa's apartheid as a source of global moral outrage.

The roll call in the first three months of this year saw the execution of a woman in her 60s (Bettie Lou Beets), a man who was a juvenile when he committed murder, and at least one diagnosed mentally ill man (Larry Robison). Even more appalling to many ordinary French and Swiss citizens, one man (Odell Barnes Jr., a 31-year old drug addict from Wichita Falls) appeared to be innocent of the crime for which he was strapped to a gurney on March 1 and injected with chemicals. Barnes' attorney, Gary Taylor said the drugs "sucked the life out of him."

Although none of the gurney's victims drew worldwide attention comparable to that garnered by Karla Faye Tucker, these executions kept Huntsville, Texas, Governor Bush, and the Texas judicial system in the spotlight of criticism.

The Pope appealed to Bush to stay the executions of Robison, Beets, and Barnes, and to request that Bush's appointees on the Board of Pardons and Paroles, consider and grant clemency to the condemned. The Board ignored the pleas. They never meet in person to discuss appeals, but conduct business by phone or fax, thus generating the term "death by fax." Except for Henry Lee Lucas, who could have been an embarrassment if executed because he was out of the state when the murder was committed here, Bush's Board has never recommended clemency. To date, Bush has presided over, and thus condoned, 127 executions.

This year began with a national moratorium conference in Huntsville at Sam Houston State University, on a weekend sandwiched between executions. On Friday night, January 21, paranoid schizophrenic Larry Robison was put to death, believing he was going to be beamed up to the mother ship. He was killed despite the pleas of the Pope, Larry's agonized parents and attorneys, and angry articles and editorials from across the Atlantic, especially the British Isles.

Editorials, articles, and letters in England, Scotland, and Ireland, as well as in France, also denounced the killing of great-grandmother Bettie Lou Beets, and news stories about her appeared in Argentina and Mexico. (Media visits to her were cruelly limited, according to her attorney Joel Margulies, and a Spanish journalist was denied an interview on spurious grounds.) In the United States, groups opposing family violence agitated on her behalf, and Bush's office received 2,000 protesting phone calls and faxes on the day Beets was to be executed.

Nonetheless, as scheduled on February 24, Beets met her silent fate in the Walls Unit. The president of the European Parliament stated he was deeply angered that the governor of Texas didn't grant a stay in response to the many pleas from throughout the world; and that these executions are more outrageous in a democracy when they occur during elections, implying they were driven by politics rather than justice. *La Nación* of Buenos Aires reported that Beets' attorney described Bush as lacking compassion and her execution as an act of cowardice.

As the first of March neared, it seemed the entire nation of France, and pockets of Switzerland, the Netherlands, Scandinavia, and Australia were mobilized to prevent the execution of Barnes, who was convicted in 1991 of the murder of a black nurse. Thanks to European donors to his investigation, his new attorneys found strong scientific and testimonial evidence of his innocence and others' guilt. Unfortunately it was never admitted by appellate courts because of new procedural laws, which almost eliminate the admission of new evidence after conviction. Desperate calls by his attorneys and others in the months preceding his death by poison had inspired little US media interest in the case, despite the issue of possibly innocent inmates on Texas death row being highlighted in the presidential debates.

A rally in Austin supporting Barnes, Gary Graham, and others was organized by University of Texas students. They gathered outside the governor's mansion the weekend after Barnes was killed. Nearly 500 death-penalty protesters ringed the mansion, but the media again were absent; presumably they were with the governor campaigning in California.

The weekend before Barnes' death, a similar crowd rallied in Paris, trying to get the attention of the US media and of Bush, who had already been contacted by the European Parliament and visited by the French cultural minister about the case. Chirac pled with Bush's father via telephone for more than an hour on Odell's behalf.

One French university student attended both rallies. Houriya Berthes, with her mother Colette and fellow student Fabrice Guillot, had organized a group for Barnes' defense. The group raised money to hire a chemist, crime scene experts, and a videographer needed to prove and communicate his innocence. Three of the organizers came to Huntsville on the execution date they had worked for years to halt. Heartsick afterwards, Berthes vowed never to return to Texas. A French university canceled orders for 100 Dell computers as a posthumous protest.

Closer to home, while scattered pockets of Amnesty International members protest in Central and South America, there is less noticeable involvement or interest in the issue, unless a local is involved. A search of websites for newspapers from the region revealed significant coverage of Karla Faye Tucker's execution but little for anyone else (12 articles in one Argentine paper, but only two for Bettie Lou Beets, and nothing for Barnes or Robison). Several Hondurans are on US death rows. One is in Texas, and draws coverage in his native country. Similarly the Mexican media heavily covered the 1998 execution of a national here. Mexico officially protested to the US State Department over Texas' violation of internationally-recognized rights in that case, and was issued an apology by the feds, who apparently put no pressure on Texas to change. (Mexico ended the death penalty in 1926, following the earlier examples of Colombia and Venezuela.) Now 18 Mexican nationals sit on Texas' death row. As their appeals run out, we can expect the Mexican media to remind us again and again of our crimes against humanity, killings that no civilized society would ever permit.

Conclusion

I was afraid I was going to be late for my first death row interview at the Ellis Unit outside Huntsville, Texas, in the East Texas piney woods. If I missed it, there would be no second chance with this inmate, who was scheduled to die exactly a week and six hours later, on March 1, 2000. As luck would have it, being late gave me the chance to be with Odell Barnes, Jr. for over two hours, the last 40 minutes or so alone with him on one side of the glass and me on the other. I left the interview, deeply moved and impressed by this human being that society and the courts were ready to discard. Death certificates issued by the state after executions list the cause of death as homicide. At the end Odell Barnes worried more about his friends and family, than about himself. Later Odell's mother Mary Barnes said simply: "Bush is our president and my baby is dead."[13]

I thought of canaries in the mines that coal miners kept there, so far from the light, caged and helpless, their purpose — to die if the shaft filled up with poison. I thought Odell Barnes and others like him were canaries for justice in a system wrought with poison through and through.

Endnotes by Chapter

The Legend of Josefa "Chipita" Rodriguez

1 *San Angelo Times*, SHNS, 2/1/98.
2 Murphy Givens, "The day they hanged Chipita," *Corpus Christi Caller Times*, 3/22/98.
3 Ibid.
4 David M. Horton and Ryan Kellus Turner, *Lone Star Justice: A Comprehensive Overview of the Texas Criminal Justice System*, (Austin, TX: Eakin Press, 1999).

Introductory Remarks

1 *Dallas Morning News*, 9/10/00, cited in *The Death Penalty in Texas, Due Process and Equal Justice . . . or Rush to Execution? The Seventh Annual Report on the State of Human Rights in Texas*, (Austin, TX: Texas Civil Rights Project, 2000), p. 37.

Chapter One:
A Tilted Playing Field

1 Robert Jordan, Commentary, "Best way to protect our citizens is to keep ban on death penalty," *Boston Globe*, 3/28/99.
2 Randall Dale Adams, William Hoffer, and Marilyn Mona Hoffer, *Adams v. Texas* (New York: St. Martin's Press, 1991).
3 Charles Baird audio interview, 8/7/00, Susan Lee Campbell Solar Death Penalty Archives, Center for American History, The University of Texas at Austin.
4 Robert Ford notes from phone interview, 1/29/01, Susan Lee Campbell Solar Death Penalty Archives, loc. cit.
5 D. Dow interview notes, 2/1/01, Susan Lee Campbell Solar Death Penalty Archives, loc. cit.
6 Doug Robinson audio interview, 4/14/00, Susan Lee Campbell Solar Death Penalty Archives, loc. cit.
7 Brian Evans notes UT Law Forum on Death Penalty, 4/19/01, Susan Lee Campbell Solar Death Penalty Archives, loc. cit.
8 Author's analysis of statistics supplied by Lori Kirk, statistician, *Uniform Crime Reporting*, Texas Department of Public Safety, 5/01.
9 Author's analysis of figures supplied by the Texas Department of Public Safety on homicide arrests between 1982 and 1999.
10 Mike Tolson, "A Deadly Distinction," *Houston Chronicle*, 2/4/01.
11 Ibid.
12 Note 5, supra.

13 Austin Amnesty International Death Penalty webpage, quoting from the *"Dallas Morning News,"* 9/19/99.
14 Note 10, supra.
15 James W. Marquart, Sheldon Ekland-Olson, and Jonathan R. Sorenson, *The Rope, the Chair, and the Needle* (Austin: University of Texas Press, 1994).
16 Jack Greenberg, "Execution Pace Should Tell Us Something," *Los Angeles Times*, 10/18/88.
17 James Langton, "The Texas Terminator keeps death row busy," *The Sunday Telegraph*, (London), 7/18/99.
18 Note 10, supra.
19 Ibid.
20 Steve Brewer, "County has budget to prosecute with a vengeance," *Houston Chronicle*, 2/4/01.
21 Gary Taylor audio interview, 4/27/01, Susan Lee Campbell Solar Death Penalty Archives, loc. cit.
22 Sister Helen Prejean, *Dead Man Walking* (New York: Vintage Books, 1996).
23 Don Reid with Gurwell, John, *Eyewitness* (Houston: Cordovan Press, 1973).
24 Ibid.
25 Note 15, supra, pp. 118-119.
26 The illegal lynchings which occasionally swept up women and teenagers in their wide net are not included in this total number of women executed.
27 Note 15, supra, p. 107.
28 Note 8, supra.
29 The estimates of murders committed by women stemmed from the author's study of DPS statistics on homicides over the years 1982-99.
30 Nancy Mathis, "'Racial Justice' Provision for death penalty advances," *Houston Chronicle*, 4/21/94.
31 Texas Department of Criminal Justice webpage, death row statistics, gender and racial breakdown of death row offenders, 1/30/01.
32 Texas Department of Criminal Justice webpage, execution statistics, 4/10/01, also "Politics and Policy — Bush's Race Issue: What's the Role of the Death Penalty?" *Wall Street Journal*, 3/2/01.
33 Note 8, supra.
34 Population figures from Texas Health and Human Services Commission website, 5/01.
35 *Texas Tough? An Analysis of Incarceration and Crime Trends in the Lone Star State* (Washington D.C., Justice Policy Institute, 2000).
36 Ibid.
37 Eileen Poe-Yamagata and Michael A. Jones, "And Justice for Some: Differential Treatment of Minority Youth in the Justice System;"

and Jolanta Juszkiewicz, "Youth Crime/Adult Time: Is Justice Served?," *Building Blocks for Youth* (Washington D.C.: Youth Law Center, 2000-2001).

38 Jolanta Juszkiewicz, "Youth Crime/Adult Time: Is Justice Served?," *Building Blocks for Youth* (Washington D.C.: Youth Law Center, 2000-2001)

39 Ibid., Executive Summary, pp. 4.

40 Ibid, pp. 9.

41 Ibid., passim.

42 Note 15, supra, pp. 51-52 and footnote 30.

43 Ibid. pp. 51-52.

44 Amnesty International Austin webpage, 9/12/99.

45 Texas Bar Association webpage, 5/7/01.

46 Note 7, supra.

47 *A State of Denial: Texas Justice and the Death Penalty* (Austin: Texas Defender Service, 2000.) pp. 57.

48 Ibid.

49 Ibid., pp. 48-50.

50 Ibid.

51 Matthew Eisley, "Race of victims plays role in sentence: In NC, killing whites carries harsher penalty," Charlotte, NC, newsobserver.com 3/01.

52 Death Penalty Information Center webpage on race, updated 4/10/01.

53 David A. Vise, "Disproportions on U.S. death row," *The Washington Post*, 9/13/2000.

54 Note 7, supra.

55 Lori Dorfman, Vincent Schiraldi, *OFF BALANCE: Youth, Race & Crime in the News* (Washington D.C.: Building Blocks for Youth, Youth Law Center, 2001)

56 Ibid., pp. 19.

57 Ibid., pp. 17.

58 Ibid., pp. 13.

59 Ibid., pp. 15.

60 Ibid., pp. 27.

61 Ibid., pp. 10.

62 Ibid., pp. 11, 13.

63 Ibid., pp. 23.

64 Rick Halperin audio interview, 7/10/00, Susan Lee Campbell Solar Death Penalty Archives, loc. cit.

65 Note 15, surpa, pp. 47.

66 Stepen Keng e-mail, 2/01/01, Susan Lee Campbell Solar Death Penalty Archives, loc. cit.

67 Kerry Cook e-mail, 3/14/0, Susan Lee Campbell Solar DeathPenalty Archives, loc. cit.

68 Diane Jennings, "Defense of Indigents Criticized in Texas," *Dallas Morning News*, 7/16/00.
69 Allan K. Butcher and Michael K. Moore, *Muting Gideon's Trumpet, The Crisis in Indigent Criminal Defense in Texas, A Report Received by the State Bar of Texas from the Committee on Legal Services to the Poor in Criminal Maters* (Austin: State Bar of Texas, 2002).
70 Ibid.
71 George Haj, "Death-case lawyers 'ill-trained'; Study also says pay low, standards few", USA Today, 6/4/1990.
72 Mills et al., *Chicago Tribune*, 6/11/01.
73 John Curry interview, 7/12/00, Susan Lee Campbell Solar Death Penalty Archives, loc.cit.; also "DNA testing casts doubt in girl's slaying," *The Dallas Morning News*, 6/18/01, regarding the Michael Blair case.
74 *Texas Monthly*, 01/94.
75 Roy Allen Rueter interview 11/22/00, Susan Lee Campbell Solar Death Penalty Archives, loc. cit.
76 *The Death Penalty in Texas: Due Process and Equal Justice... or Rush to Execution? The Seventh Annual Report on the State of Human Rights in Texas* (Austin: Texas Civil Rights Project, 2000) pp. 38.
77 Gary Cartwright, *Texas Justice: The Murder Trials of T. Cullen Davis* (New York: Pocket Books, Simon & Schuster, 1979).
78 Note 23, supra, pp. 379.
79 *State of Denial*, pp. 54.
80 *State of Denial*, pp. 57
81 "Cold Blooded Killing," *Nokoa, The Observor*, 5/25/00.
82 Note 66, supra.
83 Note 4, supra.
84 Allan Turner, "Bloodthirsty image at odds with local poll," *Houston Chronicle*, 2/4/01.

Chapter Two:
Innocence in the Lone Star State

1 John Moritz, "New appeals rules pushed Texas executions to record," *Fort Worth Star-Telegram*, 12/10/00.
2 David Dow, *Christian Science Monitor*, 6/26/ 00.
3 Ibid.
4 Ibid.
5 Dorothy Otnow Lewis, M.D., *Guilty By Reason of Insanity* (New York: The Ballantine Publishing Group, 1998).
6 David M. Horton and Ryan Kellus, *Lone Star Justice: A Comprehensive Overview of the Texas Criminal Justice System* (Austin, TX: Eakin Press, 1999).
7 Ibid.

8 Ibid.
9 Ibid.
10 Jacquelyn Dowd Hall, *Revolt Against Chivalry: Jessie Daniel Ames and the Women's Campaign Against Lynching* (New York: Columbia University Press, 1979) pp. 142.
11 Ibid.
12 Steve J. Martin, Sheldon Ekland-Olson, and Harry M. Whittington, *Texas Prisons: The Walls Came Tumbling Down* (Austin: Texas Monthly Press, 1987).
13 James W. Marquart, Sheldon Ekland-Olson, and Jonathon R. Sorenson, *The Rope, the Chair, and the Needle* (Austin: University of Texas Press, 1994) pp. 59.
14 Marquart et al., pp. 59.
15 John Aloysius Farrell, "Report slams death penalty process in Texas," *Boston Globe*, 10/16/00.
16 David Atwood, "The tragic death of Ricky Jones: Executed in spite of innocence," *The Touchstone*, Vol. X - 4, Sept./Oct. 2000.
17 Terrence Stutz, "Freedom's embrace: 12-year prison ordeal ends for man cleared by DNA test," *The Dallas Morning News*, 1/17/01.
18 Morris, Errol, *Thin Blue Line*, Anchor Bay Entertainment, 9/26/00.
19 Adams, Randall Adams, William Hoffa, and Marilyn Hoffa, *Adams v. Texas* (New York: St. Martin's Press, 1991).
20 *CBS News*, "Deadly Diagnosis: Trying Testimony," 10/15/88.
21 Ibid.
22 Ibid.
23 Adams, pp., 120-121.
24 *Fuller v. State* (1992).
25 Adams, pp. 120-121.
26 Errol Morris, *Thin Blue Line*, 1988.
27 Adams, pp. 178.
28 Susan Lee Campbell Solar Death Penalty papers, loc. cit.
29 Ibid.
30 Ibid.
31 Peter Applebome, "The Truth is Also on Trial in a Texas Death Row Case," Special to the *New York Times*, 10/4/1987.
32 Jim Dwyer, Peter Neufield, and Barry Scheck, *Actual Innocence: Five Days to Execution and other Dispatches for the Wrongfully Convicted* (New York: Doubleday, 2000).
33 *Texas Lawyer*, 5/27/91.
34 Texas Civil Rights Project, "The Death Penalty in Texas: Due Process and Equal Justice – or Rush to Execution? The 7th Annual Report on the State of Human Rights in Texas" (Austin: Texas Civil Rights Project, 2000) pp. 15.
35 Christy Hoppe, "Death Appeals Changes Seen As Hindrance," *Dallas*

Morning News, 6/4/00.
36 Doug Robinson audio interview, 4/14/01, Susan Lee Campbell Solar Death Penalty Archives, Center for American History, The University of Texas at Austin.
37 Vanessa Curry, "Miscarriage of Justice: Mitchell Awaiting Possible New Trial for 1979 Murder," *Tyler Morning Telegraph*, 9/28/97.
38 Andrew Mitchell audio interview, 7/5/00, Susan Lee Campbell Solar Death Penalty Archives, loc. cit.
39 Ibid.
40 Note 37, supra.
41 Protected source, Susan Lee Campbell Solar Death Penalty Archives, loc. cit.
42 Kerry Cook audio interviews, 7/ 6 and 7/9 /00, Susan Lee Campbell Solar Death Penalty Archives, loc. cit.
43 "Former death row inmate seeks pardon," *Houston Chronicle*, 9/13/99.
44 Kerry Cook e-mail, 7/14/01, Susan Lee Campbell Solar Death Penalty Archives, loc. cit.
45 Texas Defender Service, *A State of Denial: Texas Justice and the Death Penalty* (Austin: Texas Defender Service, 2000), Ch. 2, pp. 3.
46 Carols G. Rodriguez e-mail, 4/01/01, Susan Lee Campbell Solar Death Penalty Archives, loc. cit.
47 Barry Scheck, Peter Neufeld and Jim Dwyer, *Actual Innocence: When Justice Goes Wrong and How to Make It Right* (Quoting 122 L.Ed.2d at 246) (New York: Signet Books, 2001).
48 Austin Bureau Staff, "Execution date set for convicted hitchhiker," *Houston Chronicle*, 6/16/94.
49 "Tug of War on Death Row", *St. Louis Post-Dispatch*, 10/23/93.
50 Jennifer Liebrum, *Houston Chronicle*, 6/25/1994.
51 Holmes v. Third Court of Appeals.
52 Mark Smith, "Vermont lawmakers move to halt Texas execution: Sanctions likely if 'innocent man' is put to death," *Houston Chronicle*, reprinted in *Phoenix Gazette*, 10/7/93.
53 Robert McDuff, letter to *New York Times*, 1/20/95.
54 Sam Howe Verhovek, "When Justice Shows Its Darker Side," *New York Times*, 1/8/95.
55 "Murderer Jacobs Put to Death," *Houston Chronicle*, 1/4/95 and *Austin American Statesman* (editorial) 1/4/95.
56 Rather, Dan. "Dead Wrong?" *Sixty Minutes*, May 30, 2000.
57 Ibid.
58 Ibid.
59 TDCJ website, former death row inmates list.
60 *New York Times*, 5/14/00.
61 Julian Borger, "Bush leads charge of death brigade: The candidates in the race for the White House all agree — when it comes to capital punishment, the more the better," *Guardian*, (Manchester) 1/20/

2000.
62 Note 60, supra.
63 Dallas Morning News, August 2000; State of Denial, 152 - 154; Summary of Jones Case by Tena Francis of Capital Investigation.
64 Moratorium News, Summer 1998.
65 Houston Chronicle, 5/1/98.
66 Dallas Morning News, 6/22/98.
67 "Death Sentence Again in Doubt in Texas: Lucas' confessions clash with facts," Washington Times, 6/23/98; and "One-eyed Murderer sets a precedent in Texas: they let him live," David Osborne, The Independent (London) 6/28/98.
68 Austin American Statesman, 3/13/01.
69 Marquart, et al.
70 Chicago Tribune, 1/00.
71 The Independent, 10/15/02
72 Discovery Channel, 3/00.

Chapter Three:
Appeals, The One Way Door

1 Coleman's statement before the Subcommittee on Crime of the Committee on the Judiciary of the U.S. House of Representatives, 6/20/00.
2 James S. Liebman, Jeffrey Fagan and Valerie West, "A Broken System: Error Rates in Capital Cases, 1973 - 95," study released 6/12/00.
3 Columbia University News, 6/12/00.
4 Richard Stengel, "The Man Behind the Message," Time, 8/22/88, pp. 29.
5 John Brady, Bad Boy: The Life and Politics of Lee Atwater (Reading: Addison-Wesley Publishing Co., Inc., 1997), pp. 173 - 182.
6 Richard Stengel, "The Man Behind the Message," Time, 8/22/88, pp. 29.
7 Kathleen Hall Jamieson, Dirty Politics: Deception, Distraction and Democracy (New York: Oxford University Press, 1992), pp. 30.
8 "The Incident; the Victims; the Candidates," USA Today, 10/12/88.
9 Eric Alterman, "Playing Hardball," New York Times Magazine, 4/30/89.
10 Kathleen Hall Jamieson, Dirty Politics: Deception, Distraction and Democracy (New York: Oxford University Press, 1992), pp. 16 - 27.
11 "The Incident; the Victims; the Candidates," USA Today, 10/12/88.
12 Time Magazine, 11/4/88.
13 Jamieson, pp. 16 - 27.
14 William Greider, Who Will Tell the People? (New York: Simon and Schuster, 1992), pp. 275.
15 Chris Matthews, Hardball: How Politics is Played Told By One Who Knows The Game (New York: Simon & Schuster Adult Publishing

Group, 1998), pp. 120.
16 Brady, pp. 173 - 182.
17 Mike Shropshire and Frank Schaefer, *The Thorny Rose of Texas: An Intimate Portrait of Governor Ann Richards* (New York: Birch Lane Press, 1994).
18 Rick Halperin audio interview, 7/10/00, Susan Lee Campbell Solar Death Penalty Archives, Center for American History, The University of Texas at Austin.
19 Brian Evans notes UT Law Forum on Death Penalty, 4/19/01, Susan Lee Campbell Solar Death Penalty Archives, loc. cit.
20 Anna M. Tinsley, "State Rejecting Most Paroles," *San Angelo Standard Times*, 7/28/97.
21 Molly Ivins and Louis Dubose, *Shrub: The Short but Happy Political Life of George W. Bush* (New York: Vintage Books, 2000).
22 Elizabeth Mitchell, *W — Revenge of the Bush Dynasty* (New York: Hyperion, 2000), pp. 302-304.
23 Note 20, supra.
24 Dudley Sharp, Op. ed., *Fort Worth Star Telegram*, 2/5/00.
25 Angela K. Brown, "Critics: Texas prison system too punitive," *Laredo Morning Times*, 1/29/01.
26 "Innocent People Executed, Group Suggests," *USA Today*, 10/27/00.
27 Eric Berger, "Two new stamps memorialize Tucker: Groups attempt to put face on those executed," *Houston Chronicle*, 3/16/98.
28 Ibid.
29 Sam Kinch audio interview, 5/00, Susan Lee Campbell Solar Death Penalty Archives, loc. cit.
30 *Austin American Statesman*, "Ensuring Justice: What if the State is Wrong?" 4/26/01.
31 Mark Smith, "Inmate's time on death row sparks debate: Killer's lawyers cite unusual punishment," *Houston Chronicle*, 5/7/95.
32 Larry J. Sabato and Glenn R. Simpson, *Dirty Little Secrets: The Persistence of Corruption in American Politics* (New York: Times Books, 1996), pp. 162.
33 Mitchell, pp. 302 - 304.
34 Texas Civil Rights Project, "The Death Penalty in Texas: Due Process and Equal Justice ... or Rush to Execution?" *The Seventh Annual Report on the State of Human Rights in Texas* (Austin: Texas Civil Rights Project, 9/00), pp. 36 - 37.
35 Doug Robinson audio interview, 4/14, 01, Susan Lee Campbell Solar Death Penalty Archives, loc. cit.
36 Note 35, supra.
37 Stephen B. Bright's Congressional Testimony regarding the Innocence Protection Act of 2000, before the Committee on the Judiciary, Subcommittee on Crime, United States House of Representatives, 6/20/00.
38 Note 2, supra, pp. 50.

39 Texas Court of Criminal Appeals, Capita; Appeals: statistics 1990-95, author analysis, Susan Lee Campbell Solar Death Penalty Archives, loc. cit.
40 Ken Armstrong and Steve Mills, "Gatekeeper court keeps gate shut," *Chicago Tribune*, 6/12/00.
41 Email, 4/01 from former Court of Criminal Appeals judge.
42 Stephen B. Bright, "Death in Texas," *The Champion*, 7/99.
43 *Frontline*, "What harm would there be in giving Roy Criner another trial?" PBS, Interview: Judge Sharon Keller, 1/00.
44 Note 40, supra.
45 Charles Baird audio interview, 8/7/00, Susan Lee Campbell Solar Death Penalty Archives, loc. cit.
46 Robert Hinton, *Dallas Morning News*, 8/27/00.
47 Ken Armstrong and Steve Mills, "Gatekeeper court keeps gate shut," *Chicago Tribune*, 6/12/00.
48 *Dallas Morning News*, 12/15/00.
49 Note 40, supra.
50 Stephen B. Bright, "Death in Texas," *The Champion*, 7/99.
51 Ibid.
52 Robert Ford interview notes, 1/29/01, Susan Lee Campbell Solar Death Penalty Archives, loc. cit.
53 Armstrong and Mills, 6/12/00.
54 Note 45, supra.
55 *The Death Penalty in Texas: Due Process and Equal Justice… or Rush to Execution? The Seventh Annual Report on the State of Human Rights in Texas by the Texas Civil Rights Project* (Austin: Texas Civil Rights Project, 2000) pp. 41.
56 Texas Defender Service, *A State of Denial: Texas Justice and the Death Penalty* (Austin: Texas Defender Service, 2000).
57 Ibid. pp. 130 - 131.

Chapter Four:
Gary Graham (Shaka Sankofa)

1 Mike Gray, *The Death Game: Criminal Justice and the Luck of the Draw*, (Monroe: Common Courage Press, 01).
2 James Ellroy, "Grave Doubt," GQ, 6/26/00.
3 David Dow, *Christian Science Monitor*, 6/26/00.
4 Ibid.
5 Richard Burr audio interview, 5/23/00, Susan Lee Campbell Solar Death Penalty Archives, Center for American History, The University of Texas at Austin.
6 *Texas Observer*, 10/85.

7 Jack Broom, "Execution down to a smooth, lethal routine in Texas," *Seattle Times*, 12/13/92.
8 Note 2, supra.
9 "High court limits federal death-row appeals; says new evidence not enough for stay," *Arizona Republic*, Phoenix, 1/26/93.
10 Michael Graczyk, "Pace of Texas Executions Steps up to one per week," AP report reprinted in *Seattle Times*, 9/19/93.
11 "Texas execution would be 200th," *Tucson Citizen*, 4/28/93.
12 The opinion was authored by Judge Charles Baird, a former criminal defense attorney from Houston considered a liberal on the court, and supported by Judges Sam Houston Clinton, Lawrence Meyers and Chuck Miller. Judge Bill White agreed with them regarding the jurisdictional issue with the Third Court of Appeals, but disagreed with eliminating the time limit on appeals. Clinton felt the stay should not have been lifted.
13 Charles Baird audio interview, 8/7/00, Susan Lee Campbell Solar Death Penalty Archives, loc. cit.
14 James W. Marquart, Sheldon Ekland-Olson, and Jonathon R. Sorenson, *The Rope, the Chair, and the Needle*, (Austin: The University of Texas Press, 1994), pp. 106.
15 *Austin-American Statesman*, 6/21/00.
16 "American Digest" column in the Sunday, 6/25/00, *Austin-American Statesman*.
17 Steve Mills, "Texas case highlights defense gap," *Chicago Tribune*, 6/18/00.
18 Note 2, supra.
19 Jonathan Alter, "A reckoning on death row," *Newsweek*, 7/3/00.
20 Richard Burr e-mail to Susan Bright, 2/26/04, Susan Lee Campbell Solar Death Penalty Archives, loc. cit.
21 Elnora Graham audio interview, 12/26/00, Susan Lee Campbell Solar Death Penalty Archives, loc. cit.
22 Ibid.

Chapter Five:
No Clemency, No Mercy

1 Napoleon Beazley's last recorded statement, Texas Department of Criminal Justice Website.
2 Charles Baird audio interview, 8/ 7/00, Susan Lee Campbell Solar Death Penalty Archives, Center for American History, The University of Texas at Austin.
3 Ibid
4 Ex parte Karla Faye Tucker, Application/Petition for Post-Conviction Writ of Habeas Corpus, No. 388,428-B, 180th Judicial District Court, Houston, Texas, located at: http://www.courttv.com/

archive/legaldocs/newsmakers/tucker/; see also, Michael L. Radelet and Barbara A. Zsembik, Executive Clemency in Post-Furman Capital Cases, 27 U. Richmond L. Rev. 289, 293 (1993) (describing "judicial expediency").

5 Walter Long audio interview, Jan. 12, 2001, Susan Lee Campbell Solar Death Penalty Archives, loc. cit., updated Sept. 12, 2004. The commutation of Henry Lucas' death sentence by Governor George Bush was supported by the Texas Attorney General's Office. The Board of Pardons and Paroles' first post-1973 recommendation for a death sentence commutation, in a case in which apparently no representative of the State also requested commutation, was for Kelsey Patterson in 2004. But Governor Rick Perry rejected the Board's recommendation and Patterson was executed on May 18, 2004.

6 Don Reid with John Gurwell, *Eyewitness* (Houston: Cordovan Press, 1973).

7 Amnesty International, Death Penalty Facts, Website: http://www.amnestyusa.org/abolish/mental_illness.html

8 Dorothy Otnow Lewis, M.D., *Guilty By Reason of Insanity* (New York: Ballantine Publishing Group, 1998).

9 Amnesty International, special report, 2/21/01, Susan Lee Campbell Solar Death Penalty Archives, loc. cit.

10 *Houston Chronicle*, 3/17/01.

11 Howard Swindle and Dan Malone, "Meanest man may have lied to get death penalty," *Dallas Morning News*, printed in *Florida Times Union* 11/9/97.

12 Ibid.

13 Malone and Swindle, *America's Condemned: Death Row Inmates in Their Own Words* (Kansas City: Andrews McMeel, 1999).

14 Lois Robison audio interview, 3/1/01 and 3/5/01, Susan Lee Campbell Solar Death Penalty Archives, loc. cit.

15 Jim Yardley, "Bush to Decide on Stay of an Inmate's Execution: Case Puts Focus on Mental Health Policies," *New York Times*, 8/17/99, pp. 10.

Chapter Six:
Larry Robison

1 Lois Robison audio interview, 3/1/01 and 3/5/01, Susan Lee Campbell Solar Death Penalty Archives, Center for American History, The University of Texas at Austin.

2 A poem, speech, or song of lamentation, esp. for the dead.

3 Note 1, supra.

4 Note 1, supra.

5 Note 1, supra.

6 Note 1, supra.

7 Note 1, supra.
8 Note 1, supra.
9 Note 1, supra.
10 Note 1, supra.
11 Note 1, supra.
12 Note 1, supra.
13 Note 1, supra.
14 Note 1, supra.
15 Note 1, supra.
16 Note 1, supra.
17 Note 1, supra.
18 Note 1, supra.
19 Note 1, supra.
20 *Psychological Services* 49: pp, 483-492.
21 Ibid.
22 Amnesty International, special report, 2/21/01, Susan Lee Campbell Solar Death Penalty Archives, loc. cit.
23 Note 1, supra.
24 Note 1, supra.
25 Anthony G. Hempel, *Journal of the American Academy of Psychiatry and the Law*, V. 27, 213-225, 1999.
26 Ibid.
27 Ibid.
28 Note 1, supra.
29 Note 1, supra.
30 Note 1, supra.
31 Note 1, supra.

Chapter Seven:
Anthony Graves Story
Part One: Crime and Conviction

1 Texas Department of Public Safety, Criminal Law Enforcement Division, Offense Report, File Nr RF092294, 09-21-92, pp. 4., Susan Lee Campbell Solar Death Penalty Archives, Center for American History, The University of Texas at Austin.
2 Ibid., pp. 3.
3 Ibid.
4 Texas Depatment of Criminal Justice, website: Last words, Robert Earl Carter, 5/31/00.
5 Burleson County Grand Jury Proceedings August 26, 1992, Susan Lee Campbell Solar Death Penalty Archives, loc. cit.
6 Charles Sebesta audio interviews, 7/13/00, 12/ 20/00, 12/21/00, 12/29/00, Susan Lee Campbell Solar Death Penalty Archives, loc. cit.
7 Graves v. Johnson, C.A. G-00-221, S.D. Tex.-Galveston, Oral

Deposition of Robert Earl Carter, May 18, 2000, Susan Lee Campbell Solar Death Penalty Archives, loc. cit.
8 Note 6, supra.
9 Graves v. Johnson, C.A. G-00-221, S.D. Tex.-Galveston, Oral Deposition of Robert Earl Carter, May 18, 2000, p. 35., Susan Lee Campbell Solar Death Penalty Archives, loc. cit.
10 Note 6, supra.
11 Note 9, supra.
12 Note 6, supra.
13 Center for American History, Graves trial, Carter testimony.
14 Bill Torey interview transcript 2/1/01, Susan Lee Campbell Solar Death Penalty Archives, loc. cit.
15 Bertha Meith interview transcript, 12/23/01, Susan Lee Campbell Solar Death Penalty Archives, loc. cit.
16 Ibid.
17 Kerry Cook audio interview, 7/9/00, Susan Lee Campbell Solar Death Penalty Archives, loc. cit.
18 Roy Allen Rueter audio interview, 11/22/00, 11/23/00, Susan Lee Campbell Solar Death Penalty Archives, loc. cit.
19 Ibid.
20 Dick DeGuerin audio interview, 1/26/01, Susan Lee Campbell Solar Death Penalty Archives, loc. cit.
21 Doris and Author Curry interview transcript, 1/25/01, Susan Lee Campbell Solar Death Penalty Archives, loc. cit.
22 Anthony Graves audio interview, 11/00, Susan Lee Campbell Solar Death Penalty Archives, loc. cit.
23 Ibid.
24 Ibid.
25 Graves family audio interviews, 7/01, Susan Lee Campbell Solar Death Penalty Archives, loc. cit.
26 Ibid.
27 Ibid.
28 Roy Allen Rueter audio interview, 11/22/00, 11/23/00, Susan Lee Campbell Solar Death Penalty Archives, loc. cit.
29 Note 12, supra.
30 Note 28, supra.
31 Doris and John Curry audio interview, 7/12/00, Susan Lee Campbell Solar Death Penalty Archives, loc. cit.
32 Note 18, supra.
33 Yolanda Mathis audio interview, 7/01, Susan Lee Campbell Solar Death Penalty Archives, loc. cit.
34 Dietrich Lewis audio interview, 7/01, Susan Lee Campbell Solar Death Penalty Archives, loc. cit.
35 Note 15, supra.
36 Doris and John Curry audio interview, 7/12/00, Susan Lee Campbell

Solar Death Penalty Archives, loc. cit.
37 Texas Department of Public Safety, Criminal Law Enforcement Division, Offense Report , File Nr RF092294, 09-21-92,Susan Lee Campbell Solar Death Penalty Archives, loc. cit.
38 Ibid.
39 Note 22, supra.
40 Ibid.
41 Ibid.
42 Note 8, supra.
43 Anthony Graves letter to Patrick McCann, 1/98, Susan Lee Campbell Solar Death Penalty Archives, loc. cit.
44 Note 18, supra.
45 Note 22, supra.
46 Ibid.
47 Burleson County, Texas Grand Jury Proceedings August 26, 1992, Susan Lee Campbell Solar Death Penalty Archives, loc. cit.
48 Ibid.
49 Ibid.
50 Note 22, supra.
51 Louise Addison, Jennings Bryant and Travis Bryan audio interviews, 1/7/01 – 1/9/01, Susan Lee Campbell Solar Death Penalty Archives, loc. cit.
52 Note 1, Supra.
53 Richard Surovik audio interview, 1/9/01, Susan Lee Campbell Solar Death Penalty Archives, loc. cit.
54 Note 6, supra.
55 Note 53, surpa.
56 Ibid.
57 Dick DeGuerin audio interview, 1/26/01, Susan Lee Campbell Solar Death Penalty Archives, loc. cit.
58 Graves Jurors interviews transcripts, 1/14/01 and 1/15/01, Susan Lee Campbell Solar Death Penalty Archives.
59 Hank Paine, Frank Rush, Tengon, audio interviews, 1/8/01, Susan Lee Campbell Solar Death Penalty Archives, loc. cit.
60 Texas v. Carter, No. 10,764 (Dist. Ct. of Burleson County, 21st Judicial Dist. of Texas, June 3, 1993) Statement of Facts (Pre-trial Hearing) p.6, Susan Lee Campbell Solar Death Penalty Archives, loc. cit.
61 Judge Tom McDonald, Roland Searcy and Brooks Cofer audio interviews 2/06/01, Susan Lee Campbell Solar Death Penalty Archives, loc. cit.
62 Texas v. Carter, No. 10,764 (Dist. Ct. of Burleson County, 21st Judicial Dist. of Texas, June 3, 1993) Statement of Facts (Pre-trial Hearing) p.39, Susan Lee Campbell Solar Death Penalty Archives, loc. cit.

63 Note 59, supra.
64 Dain Whitworth audio interview, 1/8/01, Susan Lee Campbell Solar Death Penalty Archives, loc. cit.
65 Bill Whitehurst transcribed interview, 7/17/01, Susan Lee Campbell Solar Death Penalty Archives, loc. cit.
66 Note 8, supra.
67 Ibid.
68 Note 18, supra.
69 Ibid.
70 Note 6, supra.
71 Note 18, supra.
72 Barbara Taft, founder of People of the Heart, Lacresha's defense committee, audio interview, 7/15/01, Susan Lee Campbell Solar Death Penalty Archives, loc. cit.
73 Christopher Goodwin, *The Sunday Times*, U.K., " 'Black Louise' case ignites justice row," 11/23/97.
74 Robert Jensen, "Justice goes unserved for a Texas girl; Class, race emerge in a child's conviction for a toddler's death," Baltimore Sun, 9/13/1998.
75 Note 18, supra.
76 Ibid.
77 Ibid.
78 Ibid.
79 Ibid.
80 Charles Sebesta phone interview, 12/29/00, Susan Lee Campbell Solar Death Penalty Archives, loc. cit.
81 Walter Prentice phone interview, 1/17/01, Susan Lee Campbell Solar Death Penalty Archives, loc. cit.
82 Note 22, supra.
83 Note 25, supra.
84 Note 20, supra.
85 Note 18, supra.
86 Lydia Clay-Jackson audio interview, 12/23/00, Susan Lee Campbell Solar Death Penalty Archives, loc. cit.
87 Note 6, supra.
88 Calvin Garvie transcription of interview, 11/20/00, Susan Lee Campbell Solar Death Penalty Archives, loc. cit.
89 Note 25, supra.
90 Note 18, supra.
91 Note 22, supra.
92 Note 61, supra.
93 Note 86, supra.
94 James Harrington audio interview, Susan Lee Campbell Solar Death Penalty Archives, loc. cit.
95 Note 25, supra.

96 Note 86, supra.
97 Center for American History, interview with Jay Burnett.
98 Note 20, supra.
99 Note 25, supra.
100 Texas v. Graves, No. 28,165 (Dist. Ct. of Brazoria County, 23rd Judicial Dist. of Texas), Statement of Facts Jury Trial, pp. 3543-3547.
101 Ibid.
102 Ibid.
103 Ibid.
104 Ibid.
105 Ibid.
106 Note 86, supra.
107 Note 6, supra.
108 Note 18, supra.
109 Ibid.
110 Note 61, supra.
111 Note18, supra.
112 Victor Leeper and Theodore Hohn audio interviews 1/14/01, Clarence Sasser audio interview 1/15/01, Susan Lee Campbell Solar Death Penalty Archives, loc. cit.
113 ABC interview, Charles Sebesta, 2000.
114 Original Petition for Writ of Habeas Corpus, #23165-A, Patrick McCann, 1998, p. 11.
115 Rick Carroll phone interview, 1/23/01, Susan Lee Campbell Solar Death Penalty Archives, loc. cit.
116 Center for American History, Graves court records.
117 Note 25, supra.
118 Clarence Sasser, Hahn, Kilsby audio interview, 1/ 15/01, Susan Lee Campbell Solar Death Penalty Archives, loc. cit.
119 Note 100, supra.
120 Note 25, supra.
121 Note 86, supra.
122 Note 25, supra.
123 Note 22, supra.
124 Note 86, supra.
125 Calvin Garvie letter to Anthony Graves, 12/6/92, Susan Lee Campbell Solar Death Penalty Archives, loc. cit.

Anthony Graves Story
Part Two: Railroad Justice

1 Richard Surovik audio interview, 1/09/01, (on Sebesta family), Susan Lee Campbell Solar Texas Death Penalty Papers, Center for American History, University of Texas at Austin.
2 Charles Sebesta audio interviews, 7/13/00, 12/ 20/00, 12/21/00, 12/29/00, Susan Lee Campbell Solar Death Penalty Archives, loc. cit.
3 Protected source, Susan Lee Campbell Solar Death Penalty Papers, loc. cit.
4 Richard Surovik, Carey, Boethel audio interview, 1/10/01 and 1/11/01, Susan Lee Campbell Solar Death Penalty Archives, loc. cit.
5 Tom Torlincasi audio interviews, 12/4/01, 2/13/01, 12/22/01, Susan Lee Campbell Solar Death Penalty Archives, loc. cit.
6 Ibid.
7 Dick DeGuerin audio interview, 1/26/01, Susan Lee Campbell Solar Death Penalty Archives, loc. cit.
8 Judge Tom McDonald, (with Roland Searcy and Brooks Kofer) transcription of interview by author, 2/6/01, Susan Lee Campbell Solar Death Penalty Archives, loc. cit.
9 Note 5, supra.
10 Ibid.
11 Ibid.
12 Ibid.
13 Ibid.
14 Richard Surovik audio interview, 3/26/01, Susan Lee Campbell Solar Death Penalty Archives, loc. cit.
15 Stephen Keng audio interview, 2/4/01, Susan Lee Campbell Solar Death Penalty Archives, loc. cit.
16 Ibid.
17 Robert Kuhn audio interview, 1/09/01, Susan Lee Campbell Solar Death Penalty Archives, loc. cit.
18 Stephen Keng audio interview, 1/5/01, Susan Lee Campbell Solar Death Penalty Archives, loc. cit.
19 Brooks Kofer audio interview, 2/6/01, Susan Lee Campbell Solar Death Penalty Archives, loc. cit.
20 Note 17, supra.
21 Ibid.
22 Ibid.
23 Pat Holloway audio interview, 1/10/01, Susan Lee Campbell Solar Death Penalty Archives, loc. cit.
24 Ibid.
25 Ibid.
26 Ibid.
27 Ibid.

28 Center for American History, source withheld.
29 Ibid.
30 Eric Perkins (with Judge Tom McDonald and others) 1/17/01, Susan Lee Campbell Solar Death Penalty Archives, loc. cit.
31 Ibid.
32 Steve Brittain audio interview, 1/10/01, Susan Lee Campbell Solar Death Penalty Archives, loc. cit.
33 Ibid.
34 Ibid.
35 Ibid.
36 Ibid.
37 Travis Bryan audio interview, 1/6/01, Susan Lee Campbell Solar Death Penalty Archives, loc. cit.
38 Ibid.
39 Ibid.
40 Stephen King audio interviews, 12/6/00, 1/5/01, 2/4/01, Susan Lee Campbell Solar Death Penalty Archives, loc. cit.
41 Richard Surovic audio interviews, 1/08/01, 1/09/01, 1/10/01, 1/11/01/, 1/12/01, 12/13/01, Susan Lee Campbell Solar Death Penalty Archives, loc. cit.
42 Ibid.
43 Ibid.
44 Ibid.
45 Ibid.
46 Richard Surovic audio interview, 3/30/01, Susan Lee Campbell Solar Death Penalty Archives, loc. cit.
47 Note 40, supra.
48 Note 41, supra.
49 Ibid.
50 Ibid.
51 Ibid.
52 Stephen Keng audio interiew, 1/5/01, Susan Lee Campbell Solar Death Penalty Archives, loc. cit.
53 Note 41, supra.
54 Note 46, supra.
55 Note 8, supra.
56 Ibid.
57 Ibid.
58 Ibid.
59 Ibid.
60 Ibid.
61 Ibid.
62 ibid.
63 Ibid.
64 Ibid.
65 Ibid.

66 ibid.
67 Texas Department of Criminal Justine Website, Robert Earl Carter, last words.
68 Charles Sebesta audio interview, 3/30/01, Susan Lee Campbell Solar Death Penalty Archives, loc. cit.
69 Tom Torlincasi audio interviews, 12/22/00, 12/4/00, 2/13/01, Susan Lee Campbell Solar Death Penalty Archives, loc. cit.

Anthony Graves Story
Part Three, Post-conviction Chances

1 Texas v. Graves, No. 28,165 (Dist. Ct. of Brazoria County, 23rd Judicial Dist. of Texas), Motion for New Trial..
2 Ibid.
3 Texas v. Graves, No. 28,165 (Dist. Ct. of Brazoria County, 23rd Judicial Dist. of Texas, Jan. 13, 1995). Motion for New Trial, Statement of Facts, pp. 50-54.
4 Ibid., pp. 37-39.
5 Ibid., pp. 42.
6 Ibid., pp.15.
7 Doris Curry, Bertha Mieth, et al. audio interview, 2/6/01, Susan Lee Campbell Solar Texas Death Penalty Papers, Center for American History, University of Texas at Austin.
8 Note 3 supra, pp. 64.
9 Ibid., pp. 58.
10 Ibid.
11 Jay Burnett audio interview, 11/17/00, Susan Lee Campbell Solar Texas Death Penalty Papers, loc. cit.
12 Graves v. Texas (Tex.Cr.App. No. 72042, 1996) Appellant's Brief.
13 Graves v. Texas (Tex.Cr.App. No. 72042, 1996) State's Appellant Brief
14 Note 12, supra.
15 Note 13, supra.
16 Ibid.
17 Ibid.
18 Ibid.
19 Ibid.
20 Ibid.
21 Ibid.
22 Graves v. State (Tex. Cr. App. No. 72042, delivered April 23, 1997) (unpublished).
23 Note 13, supra.
24 853 S.W.2d 558 (Tex.Crim.App. 1993).

25 Note 22, supra.
26 Ibid.
27 Ibid.
28 Ibid.
29 Ibid.
30 Ibid.
31 Texas v. Graves, No. 28,165 (Dist. Ct. of Brazoria County, 23rd Judicial Dist. of Texas), Findings of fact and Conclusions of law.
32 Ibid.
33 Ibid
34 Rick Carroll audio interview, 1/23/01, Susan Lee Campbell Solar Texas Death Penalty Papers, loc. cit.
35 Ibid.
36 Note 22, supra.
37 Texas v. Graves, No. 28,165 (Dist. Ct. of Brazoria County, 23rd Judicial Dist. of Texas), Walter Quijano testimony, pp. 4414-4440; Jerome B. Brown, affidfavit, Harris County Texas, Jun. 20, 1998.
38 Note 22, supra.
39 Ibid.
40 Ibid.
41 Ibid.
42 Charles Baird audio interview, 8/7/00, Susan Lee Campbell Solar Texas Death Penalty Papers, loc. cit.
43 Ibid.
44 Ibid.
45 Ibid.
46 Roy Greenwood audio interview, 1/11//01, Susan Lee Campbell Solar Texas Death Penalty Papers, loc. cit.
47 Ibid.
48 Ibid.
49 Anthony Graves letter to Patrick McCann, 1/98, Susan Lee Campbell Solar Texas Death Penalty Papers, loc. cit.
50 Ibid.
51 Ibid.
52 Oral Deposition of Robert Earl Carter, June 19, 1998, Huntsville, Texas, p. 32, included in Supplemental Transcript, Cause No. 28, 165-A, District Court No 23rd, Anthony Charles Graves vs. the State of Texas, Harold Towslee presiding, 26, ll. 1-3.
53 Ibid.
54 Bill Whitehurst and Michelle Cheng transcribed audio interview, 7/17/01, Susan Lee Campbell Solar Texas Death Penalty Papers, loc. cit.
55 Ibid.
56 Ibid.
57 Note 52, supra, pp. 56-57.

58 Note 54, supra.
59 Roy Greenwood email to editor, Susan Bright, 8/5/03, Susan Lee Campbell Solar Texas Death Penalty Papers, loc. cit.
60 Ex Parte Anthony Graves, No. 28, 165-A (Tx. Cr. App, Dist. Ct. of Brazoria County, 23rd Judicial Dist. of Texas) Original Petition for Writ of Habeas Corpus, pp.4-5.
61 Jay Burnett phone interview, 11/17/00, Susan Lee Campbell Solar Texas Death Penalty Papers, loc. cit.
62 Ibid.
63 Ibid.
64 Patrick McCann letter to Graves, 1/95, Susan Lee Campbell Solar Texas Death Penalty Papers, loc. cit.
65 Note 59, supra.
66 Ibid.
67 Note 54, supra.
68 Robert Earl Carter letter to Roy Greenwood dated 11/22/99, included in Graves' writ file related to Cause No. 28, 165-A.
69 Ibid.
70 State's Response to Applicant's Motion to file a Supplemental Application for Post-Convicition Writ of Habeas Corpus, 1/99, 3.
71 Townslee findings of Fact and Conclusions, 1999.
72 *Drew v. State*, 743 S.W. 2d 207,Tex. Crim. App 1987.
73 Towslee cited the Supreme Court's 1993 decision in *Herrerra v. Collins* to justify this argument, ignoring the fact that the state habeas is the appropriate vehicle until exhausted.
74 Note 71, supra.
75 Ibid.
76 Ibid.
77 Patrick McCann brief in opposition of Judge Townslee Findings of Facts and Conclusions, 3/99.
78 Ibid.
79 Ibid.
80 Ibid.
81 Note 46, supra.
82 Roy Greenwood letter to Anthony Graves, 6/99, Susan Lee Campbell Solar Texas Death Penalty Papers, loc. cit.
83 Note 46, supra.
84 ibid.
85 Ex Parte Anthony Graves (Tx. Cr. App. No. 73,424, delivered Feb. 9, 2000) (unpublished).
86 Note 46, supra.
87 Ibid.
88 Ibid.
89 Note 46, supra.
90 Ibid.

91 Richard Burr phone interview, 5/22/00, Susan Lee Campbell Solar Texas Death Penalty Papers, loc. cit.
92 Charles Sebesta audio interview, 7/31/00, Susan Lee Campbell Solar Texas Death Penalty Papers, loc. cit.
93 Note 61, supra.
94 Ibid.
95 Ibid.
96 Ex Parte Anthony Graves (TX. Cr. App. No. 73,927) Petitioner's Brief in Support of Amended Second Subsequent Habeas Corpus.
97 Graves v. Johnson, No. G-00-221 (S.D. Tx. - Galveston) Oral Deposition Robert Earl Carter.
98 Dorris Curry audio interview, 2/6/01, Susan Lee Campbell Solar Texas Death Penalty Papers, loc. cit.
99 Ibid.
100 Graves Family inc. Yolanda Mathis; Dietrich Lewis; Dorothy Cloud, and others, 7/01, Susan Lee Campbell Solar Texas Death Penalty Papers, loc. cit.
101 Roy Allen Rueter audio interview, 11/22/00, Susan Lee Campbell Solar Texas Death Penalty Papers, loc. cit.
102 Charles Sebesta audio interview, 12/20/00, Susan Lee Campbell Solar Texas Death Penalty Papers, loc. cit.
103 Graves Jury audio interviews inc. Clarence Sasser, Hahn, Kilsby, 1/15/01, Susan Lee Campbell Solar Texas Death Penalty Papers, loc. cit.
104 Ibid.
105 Roy Allen Reuter audio interview, 11/22/00, Susan Lee Campbell Solar Texas Death Penalty Papers, loc. cit.
106 Note 103, supra.
107 Rick Carroll audio interview, 1/23/01, Susan Lee Campbell Solar Texas Death Penalty Papers, loc. cit.
108 Note 54, supra.
109 Note 107, supra.
110 Ibid.
111 Charles Sebesta audio interviews, 12/20/00, 12/21/00, 12/29/00, Susan Lee Campbell Solar Death Penalty Archives, loc. cit.
112 Anthony Graves letter to Susan Lee solar, 8/22/00, Susan Lee Campbell Solar Death Penalty Archives, loc. cit.
113 Anthony Graves letter to Susan Lee solar, 9/9/00, Susan Lee Campbell Solar Death Penalty Archives, loc. cit.
114 Anthony Graves letter to Susan Lee solar, 1/24/01, Susan Lee Campbell Solar Death Penalty Archives, loc. cit.
115 Roy Allen Rueter audio interview, 11/22/00, 11/23/00, Susan Lee Campbell Solar Death Penalty Archives, loc. cit.
116 Ibid.
117 Note 100, supra.

118 Added posthumously by editor, Susan Bright, based on notes from Roy Greenwood, autumn, 2003, Susan Lee Campbell Solar Death Penalty Archives, loc. cit.
119 Roy Greenwood email to editor, Susan Bright, 8/7/03, Susan Lee Campbell Solar Death Penalty Archives, loc. cit.
120 Ibid.
121 Ibid.
122 Ibid.
123 Ibid.
124 Ibid.
125 Ibid.
126 Ibid.
127 Ibid.
128 Ibid.
129 Roy Greenwood email to Susan Bright, 8/6/04, Susan Lee Campbell Solar Death Penalty Archives, loc. cit.

Chapter Eight:
Remedies

1 Eden Harrington audio interview, 4/24/01, Susan Lee Campbell Solar Texas Death Penalty Papers, Center for American History, University of Texas at Austin.
2 Ibid.
3 Ibid.
4 Ibid.
5 Ibid.
6 Ibid.
7 Ibid.
8 Texas Defender Service. *A State of Denial: Texas Justice and the Death Penalty*. Austin, TX: Texas Defender Service, 2000.
9 Carol Byers, audio interview, MVFR, Houston, 6/14/00, Susan Lee Campbell Solar Texas Death Penalty Papers, loc. cit.
10 Ibid.
11 Ibid.
12 Rick Halpern audio interview, 7/10/00, (SMU), Susan Lee Campbell Solar Texas Death Penalty Papers, loc. cit.

Chapter Nine:
Reconciliation, Not Retribution

1 Tag Evers, "Restorative Justice", *Yes!*, fall 1998. (Positive Futures Network: Bainbridge Island, WA).
2 Ibid.
3 Video, Thomas Ann Hines.
4 Carol Byers audio interview, MVFR, Houston, 6/14/00, Susan Lee Campbell Solar Texas Death Penalty Papers, Center for American History, University of Texas at Austin.
5 Ibid.
6 Ibid.
7 "Interfaith Group Applauds Texas Governor for Courageously Signing Hate Crimes Act," Interfaith Alliance Press Release, Washington DC, 5/15/01.
8 "Byrd Son Fights for Life of Father's Murderer," *Houston Chronicle*, 7/4/02)
9 Journey of Hope website, Carol Byer's page. http://www.journeyofhope.org/people/carol_byers.htm

Chapter Ten:
Pablo Melendez, Jr.

1 Gracie Jett letter to Governor, George W. Bush, TDCJ Director Wayne Scott, the Texas Attorney General, and the Texas Board of Pardons and Paroles, Susan Lee Campbell Solar Death Penalty Archives, Center for American History, The University of Texas at Austin.
2 Gracie Jett audio interview, 2/8/01 and 2/24/01, Susan Lee Campbell Solar Death Penalty Archives, loc. cit.
3 Ibid.
4 Crime Report, Sept. 13, 1994 by Det. Dian L. Tefft and analyst Diane Swearingen, Susan Lee Campbell Solar Death Penalty Archives, loc. cit.
5 Note 2, supra.
6 Ibid.
7 Melendez case audio interviews (Torres, Pablo, Ross, Sanders) 3/20/01, Susan Lee Campbell Solar Death Penalty Archives, loc. cit.
8 Ibid.
9 Ibid.
10 Ibid.
11 Ibid.
12 Ibid.
13 Ibid.

14 Ibid.
15 Ibid.
16 Ibid.
17 Ibid.
18 Ibid.
19 Mickey Ross audio interview, 3/20/01, Susan Lee Campbell Solar Death Penalty Archives, loc. cit.
20 Ibid.
21 Ibid.
22 Larry Hickman audio interview, 3/30/01, Susan Lee Campbell Solar Death Penalty Archives, loc. cit.
23 Gracie Jett audio interview, 2/8/01, Susan Lee Campbell Solar Death Penalty Archives, loc. cit.
24 Ibid.
25 Tarrant County District Attorney website, 2004, http://www.tarrantcounty.com/eDA/site/default.asp.
26 Note 22, supra.
27 Note 2, supra.
28 Ex Parte Pablo Melendez, Jr. (Tex.Cr.App., No. C-372-3756-0580494-A, V. XXXVIIp. 647), Susan Lee Campbell Solar Death Penalty Archives. loc. cit.
29 Mike Parrish phone interview, 7/30/01, Susan Lee Campbell Solar Death Penalty Archives, loc. cit.
30 Gloria Torres audio interviews, 3/20/01 and 2/13/01, Susan Lee Campbell Solar Death Penalty Archives, loc. cit.
31 Note 2, supra.
32 Ex Parte Pablo Melendez, Jr. (Tex.Cr.App., No. C-372-3756-0580494-A, V. XXXVIIp. 711), Susan Lee Campbell Solar Death Penalty Archives, loc. cit.
33 Ibid., p. 717.
34 Note 22, supra.
35 Ibid.
36 Note 2, supra.
37 Ibid.
38 Note 29, supra.
39 Note 22, supra.
40 Jack Strickland phone interview, 3/26/01; and Ex Parte Pablo Melendez, Jr. (Tex.Cr.App., No. C-372-3756-0580494-A), State's Reply to Applicant's First Application for Writ of Habeas Corpus, p. 14, Susan Lee Campbell Solar Death Penalty Archives,
41 Note 2, supra.
42 Note 29, supra.
43 Ibid.
44 Ibid.

45 Ibid.
46 Ex Parte Pablo Melendez, Jr. (No. C-372-3756-0580494-A,, 372nd Jud. Dist. Ct. Tarrant County, Texas) Michael Parrish Affidavit, 10/2/1998, Susan Lee Campbell Solar Death Penalty Archives. loc. cit.
47 Note 2, supra.
48 Ibid.
49 Ibid.
50 Note 30, supra.
51 Note 29, supra.
52 Ibid.
53 Ibid.
54 Ibid.
55 James Teel phone interview, 3/06/01, Susan Lee Campbell Solar Death Penalty Archives, loc. cit.
56 Warren St. John audio interview, 3/26/01, Susan Lee Campbell Solar Death Penalty Archives, loc. cit.
57 Ibid.
58 Gloria Torres phone interview, 2/13/01, Susan Lee Campbell Solar Death Penalty Archives, loc. cit.
59 Note 7, supra.
60 Ibid.
61 Note 2, supra.
62 Written confession, Pablo Melendez, April 13, 1995.
63 Note 30, supra.
64 Ibid.
65 Note 22, supra.
66 Note 2, supra.
67 Pablo Melendez letter to Gracie Jett, 7/16/00, Susan Lee Campbell Solar Death Penalty Archives, loc. cit.
68 Pablo Melendez letter to Gracie Jett, 9/10/00, Susan Lee Campbell Solar Death Penalty Archives, loc. cit.
69 Note 2, supra.
70 Ex Parte Pablo Melendez, Jr. (No. C-372-3756-0580494-A,, 372nd Jud. Dist. Ct. Tarrant County, Texas) Memorandum 7/30/1998, Susan Lee Campbell Solar Death Penalty Archives, Center for American History, loc. cit.
71 Seagraves is as of 2001 back in prison in Texas for burglary.
72 Allan Butcher audio interview, 4/12/01, Susan Lee Campbell Solar Death Penalty Archives, loc. cit.
73 Strickland writ, 9/99, Motion for a New Trial, p 19.
74 Jack Strickland audio interview 3/26/01, Susan Lee Campbell Solar Death Penalty Archives, loc. cit.
75 Ex Parte Pablo Melendez, Jr. (Tex.Cr.App., No. C-372-3756-

0580494-A First Application for Writ of Habeas Corpus, pp. 16-29, Susan Lee Campbell Solar Death Penalty Archives, loc. cit.
76 Ibid.
77 Ibid.
78 Ibid.
79 Ex parte Melendez, 9/27/99, p 17.
80 Note 74, supra.
81 Steven Naifeh and Gregory White Smith, *The Best Lawyers in America, 1997-1998,* (Woodward/White: Aiken, S.C.).
82 Note 74, supra.
83 Email from Rob Owen to Susan Bright confirming comments, 1/27/04, Susan Lee Campbell Solar Death Penalty Archives, loc. cit.
84 Note 74, supra.
85 Note 22, supra.
86 Ibid.
87 Note 29, supra.
88 Note 2, supra.
89 Ibid.
90 Ibid.

Chapter Eleven:
Michael Toney

1 Orville Hancock, "Suspect in bomb sale is well-known in Azle," *Fort Worth Star Telegram,* 3/28/86.
2 Ibid.
3 "Suspect in bomb delivery case freed on bond," *Fort Worth Star-Telegram,* 3/29/86.
4 Michael Toney letter to Susan Lee Solar, 10/05/00, Susan Lee Campbell Solar Death Penalty Archives, Center for American History, The University of Texas at Austin.
5 Michael Toney letter to Susan Lee Solar, 11/20/00, Susan Lee Campbell Solar Death Penalty, loc. cit.
6 Dave Michels, "Man says he made up story . . . ", *Dallas Morning News,* 1/17/98.
7 Ibid.
8 No. 137B, In Grand Jury A of Tarrant County, Texas, Testimony of Christie Meeks November 6, 1997, p. 30.
9 Edwin Smith email to Susan Lee Solar, 1/28/01, Susan Lee Campbell Solar Death Penalty, loc. cit.
10 Note 5, supra.
11 Gracie Jett audio interview, 2/24/01, Susan Lee Campbell Solar Death Penalty, loc. cit.

12 Ibid.
13 Alexander Garcie Gonzalez letter to Phil Ryan, Wise County Sheriff Department, 4/22/99, Susan Lee Campbell Solar Death Penalty, loc. cit.
14 Ibid.
15 Ibid.
16 Ibid.
17 Mike Parrish phone interview, transcription, 7/30/02, ,Susan Lee Campbell Solar Death Penalty, loc. cit.
18 Robert Ford audio interview, 1/29/01, Susan Lee Campbell Solar Death Penalty, loc. cit.
19 Ibid.
20 State v. Toney, No. 0676220D (Dist. Ct. of Tarrant County, 297th Judicial Dist. of Texas , May 21, 1999)Testimony of Finis Blankenship, Susan Lee Campbell Solar Death Penalty Archives, Center for American History, The University of Texas at Austin
21 Ibid.
22 Note 11, supra.
23 Iraq Body Count website, http://www.iraqbodycount.net/.
24 Michael Toney website link, 2004, http://www.lampofhope.org/drj16k.html.
25 Texas Cure Indigent Prison Fan Project, http://www.txcure.org/fans.htm.
26 Michael Toney, letter to Susan Lee Solar, 7/27/01, Susan Lee Campbell Solar Death Penalty Archives, loc. cit.
27 Michael Toney, letter to Susan Lee Solar, 10/05/00, Susan Lee Campbell Solar Death Penalty Archives, loc. cit.

Chapter Twelve:
Odell Barnes

1 Odell Barnes audio interview, 2/23/00, Susan Lee Campbell Solar Death Penalty Archives, Center for American History, The University of Texas at Austin.
2 Nicole Fontaine appeal from European Parliment to spare the lives of Betty Lou Beets and Odell Barnes, Brussels, 2/24/00, Odell Barnes website, http://ccadp.org/EU-bushplea.htm.
3 Odell Barnes final letter to the world, 10/11/99, Odell Barnes website, http://membres.lycos.fr/odell/lettreodellangl.html
4 Grassroots Investigation Project, Quixote Center, PO Box 5206, Hyattsville, MD 20782, 301-699-0042, quixote@quixote.org. Report quoted in entirety from website: http://www.lairdcarlson.com/grip/Barnes/Case%20Summary.htm.

5 Odell Barnes audio interview, 2/23/00, Susan Lee Campbell Solar Texas Death Penalty Papers, loc. cit.
6 Ibid.
7 Steve Clements, "Barnes: 11 days remain; European group aids killer's lawyers," *Times Record News*, 2/20/2000.
8 Ibid.
9 Ibid.
10 Connie Barnes audio interview, 7/12/00, Susan Lee Campbell Solar Texas Death Penalty Papers, loc. cit.
11 Odell Barnes audio interview, 2/23/00, Susan Lee Campbell Solar Texas Death Penalty Papers, loc. cit.
12 Susan Lee Solar, "Texecutions" draw international scorn, World sees Gov. Bush as cold-hearted killer," Asheville Global Report, No. 72, June 1-7, 2000. Ashville, North Carolina. (Article printed in entirety.)
13 Mary Barnes audio interview, 7/7/00, Susan Lee Campbell Solar Texas Death Penalty Papers, loc. cit.

Bibliography

Books

Adams, Randall Dale, Hoffer, William and Hoffer, Marilyn Mona. *Adams v. Texas*. New York: St. Martin's Press, 1991.

Berthès, Colette avec Fillaire, Bernard. *La Machine à Tuer*. Paris: Les Arènes, 2000.

Brady, John. *Bad Boy: The Life and Politics of Lee Atwater*. Reading MA: Addison-Wesley Publishing Co., Inc.,1997.

Cartwright, Gary. *Texas Justice* (Formerly titled: *Blood Will Tell*). New York: Simon & Schuster, Pocket Books, 1994.

Cartwright, Gary. *Texas Justice: The Murder Trials of T. Cullen Davis*. New York: Pocket Books, Simon & Schuster, 1979.

Davies, Nick. *White Lies: The True Story of Clarence Bradley, Presumed Guilty in the American South*. London: Chatto & Windus, 1991.

Dwyer, Jim, Neufield, Peter and Scheck, Barry. *Actual Innocence: Five Days to Execution and other Dispatches for the Wrongfully Convicted*. New York: Doubleday, 2000.

Ekland-Olson, Sheldon, Marquart, James W., and Sorenson, Jonathon R. *The Rope, the Chair, and the Needle*. Austin: University of Texas Press, 1994.

Ekland-Olson, Sheldon Martin, Steve J., and Whittington, Harry M. *Texas Prisons: The Walls Came Tumbling Down*. Austin: Texas Monthly Press, 1987.

Foucault, Michel. *Discipline & Punish: The Birth of the Prison*. New York: Random House, 1979.

Glenn, Lon Bennett. Texas Prisons: *The Largest Hotel Chain in Texas*. Austin: Eakin Press, 2001.

Gray, Mike. *The Death Game: Criminal Justice and the Luck of the Draw*. Monroe, ME: Common Courage Press, 2001.

Greider, William. *Who Will Tell the People?* New York: Simon & Schuster, 1992.

Hall, Jacquelyn Dowd. *Revolt Against Chivalry: Jessie Daniel Ames and the Women's Campaign Against Lynching*. New York: Columbia University Press, 1979, 1993.

Horton, David M. and Turner, Ryan Kellus. *Lone Star Justice: A Comprehensive Overview of the Texas Criminal Justice System*. Austin, TX: Eakin Press, 1999.

Ivins, Molly and Dubose, Louis. *Shrub: The Short but Happy Political Life of George W. Bush*. New York: Random House, Vintage Books, 2000.

Jamieson, Kathleen Hall. *Dirty Politics: Deception, Distraction and Democracy*. New York: Oxford University Press, 1992.

Lewis, Dorothy Otnow, M.D. *Guilty by Reason of Insanity*. New York: Ballantine, 1998.

Lifton, Robert Jay and Mitchell, Greg. *Who Owns Death? Capital Punishment, The American Conscience, and the End of Executions.* New York: HarperCollins, 2000.

Malone, Dan and Swindle, Howard. *America's Condemned: Death Row Inmates in Their Own Words.* Kansas City: Andrews McMeel, 1999.

Matthews, Chris. *Hardball: How Politics Is Played Told by One Who Knows the Game.* New York: Simon & Schuster, 1998.

Mitchell, Elizabeth. *W — Revenge of the Bush Dynasty.* New York: Hyperion, 2000.

Naifeh, Steven and Smith, Gregory. *The Best Lawyers in America, 1997 - 1998.* Aiken, SC: Woodward/White.

Prejean, Sister Helen. *Dead Man Walking.* New York: Random House, 1996.

Protess, David and Warden, Rob. *A Promise of Justice.* New York: Hyperion, 1998.

Reid, Don with Gurwell, John. *Eyewitness.* Houston: Cordovan Press, 1973.

Rhodes, Richard. *Why They Kill: The Discoveries of a Maverick Criminologist.* New York: Alfred A. Knopf, 1999.

Sabato, Larry J. and Simpson, Glenn R. *Dirty Little Secrets: The Persistence of Corruption in American Politics.* NEW YORK: Times Books, 1996

Scheck, Barry, Neufeld, Peter and Dwyer, Jim *Actual Innocence: When Justice Goes Wrong and How to Make It Right.* New York: Signet Books, 2001.

Shropshire, Mike and Schaefer, Frank. *The Thorny Rose of Texas: An Intimate Portrait of Governor Ann Richards.* New York: Birch Lane Press, 1994.

Texas Civil Rights Project. *The Death Penalty in Texas, Due Process and Equal Justice . . . or Rush to Execution? The Seventh Annual Report on the State of Human Rights in Texas.* Austin: Texas Civil Rights Project, 2000.

Texas Defender Service. *A State of Denial: Texas Justice and the Death Penalty.* Austin: Texas Defender Service, 2000.

Wright, Donald Delano. *To Die Is Not Enough: A True Account of Murder and Retribution.* Boston: Houghton Mifflin Company, 1974.

Vaughan, Genevieve. *For-Giving: A Feminist Criticism of Exchange.* Austin: Plain View Press, 1997.

Periodicals

Alter, Jonathon. "A reckoning on death row," *Newsweek*, 7/3/00.

Anthony G. Hempel. *Journal of the American Academy of Psychiatry and the Law*, V. 27: 213 - 225, 1999.

Associated Press. "Innocent People Executed, Group Suggests," in *USA Today*, 10/27/00.

Associated Press. "Judges Say Clements Stepped on Judicial Authority," *Houston Post*, 10/01/81.
Armstrong, Ken and Mills, Steve. "Gatekeeper court keeps gate shut," *Chicago Tribune*, 6/12/00.
Associated Press. "Azle men held in bomb sale," *Dallas Times Herald*, 3/28/86.
Associated Press. "Bombing case yields suspect 12 years later" *Houston Chronicle*, 12/07/97.
Atwood, David. "The tragic death of Ricky Jones: Executed in spite of innocence," *The Touchstone*, X (4): Sept./Oct. 2000.
Austin American Statesman, "Ensuring Justice: What if the State is wrong?" 4/26/01.
Austin American Statesman, editorial, 1/4/1995.
Austin American Statesman, March 13, 2001.
Austin-American Statesman, American Digest (Sunday), 6/25/2000.
Austin Bureau Staff. "Execution date set for convicted hitchhiker," *Houston Chronicle*, 6/16/94.
Berger, Eric. "Two new stamps memorialize Tucker: Groups attempt to put face on those executed," *Houston Chronicle*, 3/16/98.
Borger, Julian. "Bush leads charge of death brigade: The candidates in the race for the White House all agree — when it comes to capital punishment, the more the better," *The Guardian*, Manchester, 1/20/2000.
Brewer, Steve. "County has budget to prosecute with a vengeance," *Houston Chronicle*, 2/4/01.
Bright, Stephen B. "Death in Texas," *The Champion*, 7/99.
Broom, Jack. "Execution down to a smooth, lethal routine in Texas," *Seattle Times*, 12/13/92.
Brown, Angela K. "Critics: Texas prison system too punitive," *Laredo Morning Times*, 1/29/01.
Chicago Tribune, January, 2000.
"Cold Blooded Killing," *Nokoa, The Observer*, 5/25/00.
Crist, Gabriel. "Lake Worth briefcase bomber sentenced to death; 1985 explosion killed three people: *Fort Worth Star Telegram*, 5/6/99.
Curry, Vanessa. "Miscarriage of Justice: Mitchell Awaiting Possible New trial for 1979 Murder," *Tyler Morning Telegraph*, 9/28/97.
Dallas Morning News, 12/15/00.
Dallas Morning News, 8/00.
Dallas Morning News, 6/22/98.
"Death Sentence Again in Doubt in Texas: Lucas' confessions clash with facts," *Washington Times*, 6/23/98.
"Death Penalty for bombing," *Houston Chronicle*, 5/26/99.
Dow, David. *Christian Science Monitor*, 6/26/00.
"DNA testing casts doubt in girl's slaying," *The Dallas Morning News*, 6/18/2001.

Eisley, Matthew. "Race of victims plays role in sentence: In N.C., killing whites carries harsher penalty," Charlotte, N.C., newsobserver.com 3/01.

Ellroy, James. "Grave Doubt," *GQ*, June 2000.

Farrell, John Aloysius. "Report slams death penalty process in Texas," *Boston Globe*, 10/16/2000.

Fennell, Molly and Hancock, Orville. "2 Tarrent men linked to bombs: 1 arrested." 3/28/86.

"Former death row inmate seeks pardon," *Houston Chronicle*, 9/13/1999.

Givens, Murphy. "The day they hanged Chipita," *Corpus Christi Caller Times*, 3/22/98.

Goodwin, Christopher. " 'Black Louise' case ignites justice row," *Sunday Times*, London, 11/23/97.

Graczyk, Michael. "Pace of Texas executions steps up to one per week," AP report reprinted in *Seattle Times*, 9/19/93.

Greenberg, Jack. "Execution Pace Should Tell Us Something," *Los Angeles Times*, 10/18/88.

Greer, N. Press Release: "Suspect arrested in 12-year-old bombing," 12/4/97.

Haj, George. "Death-case lawyers 'ill-trained'; Study also says pay low, standards few," *USA Today*, 6/4/1990.

Halpern, Rick. "Toney Letters," *Death Penalty News*, 11/28/99.

Hancock, Orville. "Suspect in bomb sale is well-known in Azle," Fort Worth Star-Telegram, 3/28/86.

Hancock, Orville. "Suspect was mayoral candidate," Fort Worth Star-Telegram, 3/27/86.

"High court limits federal death-row appeals; says new evidence not enough for stay," *Arizona Republic*, 1/26/1993.

Hinton, Robert. *Dallas Morning News*, 8/27/00.

Hoppe, Christi. "Death Appeals Changes Seen As Hindrance," *Dallas Morning News*, 6/4/2000.

Houston Chronicle, 5/1/98.

Houston Chronicle, 3/17/01.

Jennings, Dianne. "Defense of Indigents Criticized in Texas," *Dallas Morning News*, 7/16/00.

Jensen, Robert. "Justice goes unserved for a Texas girl: Class, race emerge in a child's conviction for a toddler's death," *Baltimore Sun*, 9/13/98.

Jordan, Robert. Commentary, "Best way to protect our citizens is to keep ban on death penalty," *Boston Globe*, 3/28/99.

Kelso, John. "Capitalizing on Capital Punishment," Austin American Statesman, 6/2/00.

Langton, James. "The Texas Terminator keeps death row busy," *Sunday Telegraph*, London, 7/18/99.

Liebrum, Jennifer. *Houston Chronicle*, 6/25/1994.

Malone, Dan and Swindle, Howard. "Meanest man may have lied to get death penalty," *Florida Times Union* 11/9/97.

Malone, Dan. "Azle man held without bond on bomb charge" Fort Worth Star Telegram, 3/28/86.

Mathis, Nancy. "'Racial Justice' Provision for death penalty advances," *Houston Chronicle*, 4/21/94.

Mills, Steve. "Texas case highlights defense gap," *Chicago Tribune*, 6/18/00.

Moratorium News, Summer 1998.

Moritz, John. "New appeals rules pushed Texas executions to record, *Ft. Worth Star Telegram*, 12/10/2000.

Murderer Jacobs Put to Death," *Houston Chronicle*, 1/4/ 1995.

New York Times, 5/14/00.

Osborne, David. "One-eyed Murderer sets a precedent in Texas: they let him live," *The Independent*, London, June 28, 1998.

"Politics and Policy – Bush's Race Issue: What's the Role of the Death Penalty?" *Wall Street Journal*, 3/2/01.

Ross, John. "Awaiting Death at El Norte," *Texas Observer*, 9/12/1997.

Sharp, Dudly. Editorial, *Fort Worth Star-Telegram*, 2/5/00.

Smith, Mark. "Vermont lawmakers move to halt Texas execution: Sanctions likely if 'innocent man' is put to death",*Houston Chronicle*, reprinted in *Phoenix Gazette*, 10/7/1993.

Smith, Mark. "Inmate's time on death row sparks debate: Killer's lawyers cite unusual punishment," *Houston Chronicle*, 5/7/95.

Stengel, Richard. "The Man Behind the Message," *Time*, 8/22/88.

"Suspect in bomb delivery case freed on bond." *Fort Worth Star-Telegram*, 3/29/86.

"Texas execution would be 200th, *Tucson Citizen*, April 28, 1993.

Texas Lawyer, 5/27/91/.

"The Incident; the Victims; the Candidates," *USA Today*, 10/12/88.

Tinsley, Anna M. "State Rejecting Most Paroles," *San Angelo Standard Times*, 7/28/1997.

Tolson, Mike. "A Deadly Distinction," *Houston Chronicle*, 2/4/01.

Turner, Alan. "Bloodthirsty image at odds with local poll," *Houston Chronicle*, 2/4/2001.

"Tug of War on Death Row," *St. Louis Post-Dispatch*, 10/23/93.

Verhovek, Sam Howe. "When Justice Shows Its Darker Side," *New York Times*, 1/8/1995.

Vise, David A. "Disproportions on U.S. death row," *Washington Post*, 9/13/2000.

Yardley, Jim. "Bush to Decide on Stay of an Inmate's Execution: Case Puts Focus on Mental Health Policies," *New York Times*, 8/17/99.

Public and Legal Documents

Texas Department of Public Safety Criminal Law Enforcement Division. Master File: Capital Murder.
Tucker (Finnis) Blankenship vs *Tim Curry* et al, 6/29/00.
Fuller v. *State* (1992).
Holmes v. *Third Court of Appeals*
United States House of Representatives. Bright, Stephen B. Congressional Testimony regarding the Innocence Protection Act of 2000, before the Committee on the Judiciary, Subcommittee on Crime, 6/20/00.
Texas Court of Criminal Appeals, Statistics: Capital Appeals, 1990-95.
Furman v. *Georgia*
Lyles v. *US*, 1957.
Hot Check Division, Tarrant County District Attorney. Records for Michael Toney and Chris Meeks.
Affidavit of Christie Meeks, 3/13/01.
Affidavit of Alexander Garcia Gonzales, 4/9/01.
Bureau of Alcohol, Tobacco and Firearms, disposition of Remington rifle, etc to Chris Meeks, Hurst, TX 12/18/85.
Bureau of Alcohol, Tobacco and Firearms, disposition of Ruger rifle, etc. to Chris Meeks, Hurst, TX 12/19/85.
State of Wisconsin vs. *Kimberley E. Toney*, 4/14/99.
Michael L. Radelet and Barbara A. Zsembik, Executive Clemency in Post-Furman Capital Cases, 27 U. Richmond L. Rev. 289, 293 (1993) (describing "judicial expediency").

Published Reports

Eileen Poe-Yamagata and Michael A. Jones. *And Justice for Some: Differential Treatment of Minority Youth in the Justice System.* Washington D. C.: Building Blocks for Youth, Youth Law Center, 2000) www.buildingblocksforyouth.org.
Juszkiewicz, Jolanta. *Youth Crime/Adult Time: Is Justice Served?* Washington D. C.: Building Blocks for Youth, Youth Law Center, 2000). www.buildingblocksforyouth.org.
Justice Policy Institute. *"Texas Tough? An Analysis of Incarceration and Crime Trends in the Lone Star State.* Washington D. C., fall, 2000.
Butcher, Allan K. and Moore, Michael K. *Muting Gideon's Trumpet, The Crisis in Indigent Criminal Defense in Texas, A Report Received by the State Bar of Texas from the Committee on Legal Services to the Poor in Criminal Maters.* (Austin: State Bar of Texas, 2002).
Summary of Jones case by Tena Francis of Capital Investigation. Ch.4, # 68.

Liebman, James S., Fagan, Jeffrey and West, Valerie. "A Broken System: Error Rates in Capital Cases, 1973-95," (study) (NEW YORK: Columbia University,6/12/00.)

Texas Civil Rights Project, "The Death Penalty in Texas: Due Process and Equal Justice… or Rush to Execution?" The Seventh Annual Report on the State of Human Rights in Texas. (Austin: Texas Civil Rights Project, 9/00).

Amnesty International, Death Penalty Special Report, 2/21/01.

Websites

Amnesty International
Austin Texas Bar Association
Building Blocks for Youth
Texas Defender Service
Texas Health and Human Services Commission
Texas Department of Criminal Justice
Justice Policy Institute
Texas Department of Criminal Justice website, former death row inmates list.
Death Penalty Information Center
Northwestern University: Center for Wrongful Convictions
   www.law.northwestern.edu/wrongfulconvictions
Texas Civil Rights Project
Victim Offender Reconciliation Services (VOMS): http://www.vorp.com/
Journey of Hope: http://www.johgriefsupport.org/
Susan Lee Solar Memorial: http://www.aimproductions.com/SusanLee/

Media

Morris, Errol, *The Thin Blue Line*, Anchor Bay Entertainment, 9/26/2000.
C.B.S. News, "Deadly Diagnosis: Trying Testimony," 10/15/1988
Rather, Dan. "Dead Wrong?," *Sixty Minutes*, May 30, 2000.
Special on Odell Barnes, *Discovery Channel*, March 2000. *Frontline*,
   "What harm would there be in giving Roy Criner another trial?"
   PBS, Interview: Judge Sharon Keller, January, 2000.
Sebesta in an ABC interview in 2000.

Unpublished Materials housed at the Susan Lee Campbell Solar Texas Death Penalty Papers, Center for American History, University of Texas at Austin

Interview Tapes *(Author tapes which include multiple interviews and dates are listed alphabetically by name.)*

Addison, Louise, 1/7/01 – 1/9/01; Allensworth, Thomas, 7/13/00; Baird, Charles, 8/7/00; Barnes, Connie, 7/12/00; Barnes, Mary, 7/7/00; Barnes, Odell, 2/23/00, (Ellis Unit); Boethel, Cary 1/10/01 and 1/11/01; Brock, David, 7/11/00; Bryan, Travis, 1/7/01 – 1/9/01; Bryant, Jennings, 1/7/01 – 1/9/01; Burr, Richard, 5/23 /00; Butcher, Allan, 4/12/01; Byers, Carol, (MFVR) 6/14/00; Carey, 1/10/01 and 1/11/01; Ceoco, Chris, (on Sebesta), 3/30/01; Clay-Jackson, Linda, 12/23/00; Cook, Kerry. (Plano) 7/9/00; Dorris Curry, 7/12/00; DeGuerin, Dick, 1/26/01; Dow, David, 2/1/01; Ellis, R., 6/ 2/00; Glass, Marta. (ACLU) 6/15/00 ; Graham, Elnora, 12/26/00; Graves Case: Tootsie, Doris, Felicia, Arthur, Bertha Mieth, 1/24/01; Graves Family: Yolanda Mathis; Dietrich Lewis; Dorothy Cloud 7/01; Graves Jury: Clarence Sasser, Hahn, Kilsby, 1/15/01; Greenwood, Roy, 1/30/01; Hall, Steve, 3/01; Halpern, Rick, (SMU) 7/10/00; Harrington, Eden, 4/24/01; Harrington, Jim, (no date); Hatfield, Ralph, 3/6/01; Hearon, Genevieve, 10/3/00 and 10/26/00; Hickman, Larry, 4/2/01 (Melendez); Jennings, Steve, 2/01/01; Jett, Gracie, 2/24/01; Jett, Gracie, 2/8/01; Jones, Edith, (and students) UT Law School 1/30/01; Keng, Stephen, 2/4/01; Keng, Stephen, 2/5/01; Kinch, Sam, 5/00; Latimer, Steve, 4/24/01; Lindemann, J., 5/01; Long, Walter, 1/12/01; Long, Walter, 1/31/01; Lourcey, Lou, Police Chief Cameron (no date); Macha, Barry, 7/13/00; McDonnald, Tom, (Judge) and others, 2/6/01; Meads, Wayne, 1/5/01; Megirern, Jim, 9/9/00, (History of Death Penalty); Melendez Case: Torres, Pablo, Ross, Sanders 3/20/01; Melendez, Pablo, 7/27/01; Meyers, Laurence, (TCCA), 4/12/01; Mitchell, Andrew, 7/5/00; Montoya, Irineo, 6/19/00; Moratorium Bill: Dutton, Adams, Harrington, Hubbarte; Moratorium Rally, 4/16/01; MVFR Conference, Dallas, 8/26/00; Paine, Hank, 1/8/01; Pierce, Pierce, 1/8/01; Rivera, Geraldo, 1/01 (from broadcast); Robinson, Doug, 4/14/01; Robison, Lois, 3/1/01 and 3/5/01; Ross, Mickey, 3/6/01; Rueter, Roy Allen, 11/22/00 and 11/23/00; Rush, Frank, 1/8/01; St. John, Warren, 3/26/01; Schulman, David 2/01; Schultz, Jo Ann, 11/22/00 and 11/23/00; Schuraldei, Vincent, 1/01; Sebesta, Charles, 12/20/00 ; Sebesta, Charles, 12/29/00; Sebesta, Charles, 2/5/01; Sebesta, Charles, 7/13/00; Sebesta, Charles, 7/31/01; Sebesta, Charles. 3/30/01; Shuvalov, Andy, 4/30/01; Slade, Marilyn, 3/6/01; Sloyan, Wanda, 1/8/01; Smith, Edwin, 11/8/01; Stoker, Danny, 4/12/01; Strickland, Jack, 3/26/01; Surouik, Richard, 1/10/01 and 1/11/01; Surovic, Richard, 2/6/01; Surovik, Richard, 1/09/01; Taylor, Gary, 8/9/00; Teel, James, 3/6/01; Tengon, 1/8/01; Torlincasi, Tom, 12/22/00; Torlincasi, Tom, 12/4/00; Torlincasi, Tom. 2/13/01; Torres, Bernice 6/19/00; Torres, Gloria, 2/13/01; Whitworth, Dain, 11/08/01; Wilson, Reggie, 7/13/00.

Interview Transcriptions: *(Interview transcriptions include highlights from interviews and are listed alphabetically, by interviewee.)*

Addison, Louise, 1/7/01; Boethel, Carey, 1/11/01; Brittain, Steve, 1/10/01; Bryan, Travis, 1/6/01; Bryant, Jennings, 1/08/01; Burnett, Jay, 11/17/00; Burr, Richard, 5/22/00; Carroll, Rick, 12/23/01; Curry, Arthur, 1/25/01; Curry, Doris, 1/25/01; Dilsby, Marvin, 1/14/01; Ford, Robert, 1/29/01; Garvie, Calvin, 11/20/00; Graves Jurors: 1/14/01 & 1/15/01; Graves, Felicia DeSharon, 1/25/01; Holloway, Pat, 1/10/01; Holn, Theodore, 1/14/01; Jackson, Lydia Clay, 12/23/00; Jennings, Steve, 2/1/01; Keng, Stephen, 1/5/01; Keng, Stephen, 12/6/00; Keng, Stephen, 2/4/01; Kilsby, Marvin, 1/14/01; Kuhn, Robert (Bob), 1/09/01; Leeper, Victor, 1/14/01; Maca, Barry, 7/13/00; McDonald, Tom (Judge) and others (Eric Perkins) (Brazos County), 1/17/01; McDonald, Tom (Judge) with Searcy, Roland and Brooks Kofer, 2/6/01; Meads, Wayne, 1/05/01; Meith, Bertha L., 12/23/01; Orozco, Robert, 1/12/01; Paine, Hank, 1/08/01; Parrish, Mike, 7/30/01 Prentice, Walter, 1/17/01; Rueter, Roy Allen, 11/17/00; Rueter, Roy Allen, 11/23/00; Rueter, Roy Allen, 2/1/01; Rush, Frank, 1/10/01; Sasser, Clarence, 1/14/01; Sasser, Clarence, 1/15/01; Sebesta, Charles, 7/31/00; Sebesta, Charles, 12/20/00; Sebesta, Charles, 12/29/00; Slloyan, Wanda Bird, no date; Smith, Charlie, 1/09/01; Surovic, Richard, 1/08/01, 1/09/01, 1/10/01, 1/11/01/, 1/12/01, 12/13/01; Taft, Barbara, 715/01; Taylor, Jerry, 5/30/01; Torrey, Bill, 2/1/01; Wallenhurst, Denise, 2/2/01; Wallenhurst, Denise, 2/2/01; Whitehurst, Bill; 7/17/01; Whitworth, Dain, 11/08/01; Wilson, Reggie, 7/13/01.

Notes:

Brian Evans' notes from UT Law School Forum on the Death Penalty, 4/19/01.
Notes for and drafts of articles gathered from personal interviews of persons involved in the James Byrd Jr murder, 1998-99.
Journal entry, Christmas Day, 2000, by Michael Toney.

Letters and emails:

Burr, Richard, emails to editor Susan Bright, 2/23/04, 2/27/03; Carter, Robert Earl letter to Roy Greenwood, (included in Graves writ file: Cause No. 28, 165-A); Cook, Kerry, email, 3/14/01; Gonzales, Alexander Garcia letter to Phil Ryan, Wise County Sheriff Department, 4/22/99; Gonzales, Alexander Garcia letter to Susan Lee Solar, 2/25/01; Gonzales, Alexander Garcia letter to Susan Lee, 2/5/01; Gonzales, Alexander Garcia letter to Susan Lee, 4/19/01; Gonzales, Alexander Garcia letter to Susan Lee, 4/29/01; Graves, Anthony, letters to Susan Lee Solar, 8/22/00, 8/30/00, 9/9/00, 5/23/01, 1/24/01, 6/17/01, 3/27/01; Graves, Anthony, letter to Patrick McCann, 1/98; Calvin Garvie letter to Anthony Graves, 12/06/92; Greenwood, Roy, email to editor, Susan Bright, 8/5/03; Greenwood, Roy, emails to editor Susan Bright, 8/7/03, 6/10/03; Jett, Gracie, letter to Governor, George W. Bush; TDCJ Director, Wayne Scott; the Texas Attorney General; and the Texas Board of Pardons and Paroles; Keng, Stephen, email 2/01/01; McCann, Patrick letter to Graves, 1/95; McCann, Patrick, letter to A. Graves, 2/21/98; McDuff, Robert, letter to *New York Times*, 1/20/95; Melendez, Pablo letters to Gracie Jett, 7/16/00; Rodriguez, Carlos G., email, 4/01/01; Greenwood, Roy to Anthony Graves, 6/99; Smith, Edwin, email to Susan Lee Solar, 1/28/01; Toney, Michael, "To Whom I Hope and Pray It Concerns," from Michael Toney's website, reference to trial transcript at outlawzzz.com; Toney, Michael, email to Judge Everett Young, 287th Judicial District Court, 10/27/99; Toney, Michael, letter to Mike Parrish, 6/23/01; Toney, Michael, letter to Susan Lee Solar, (2 emails enclosed re. Bomb maker) 12/02/00; Michael, letter toSusan Lee Solar, (bio of events) 10/05/00; Tortella, Wayland Tim, letter to Michael Toney, 7/21/99 ; Tortella, Wayland Tim, letter to Tony's grandmother, Ms. Ross, 6/21/99; Tortella, Wayland Tim, letter to Tony's mother, Marty, 7/9/99

About the author

Susan Lee Campbell Solar was born, Susan Lee Campbell, on December 30, 1941 in Houston, Texas and grew up near Rice University. In 1964 she graduated Cum Laude from the University of Texas Plan II Honors Program with Special Honors in English. Following this she earned a Master of Arts in Teaching from Vanderbilt University. She earned a *Diploma in Sculputre at L'Academie Royale des beaux arts de Bruxelles* in Belgium in 1967. Her first art work consisted of large fiberglass sculptures which later evolved into goddess jewelry forms which have gained international recognition under the name *Ssymbols* by Susanna Libana. In the 60s she was active in the civil rights movement and in anti-Vietnam war efforts.

In the late 60s and early 70s, two daughters were born to Susan and Hoyt Purvis. The family lived in Washington, DC and then in Austin, Texas on Wheeler Street. Their back gate opened to the Wheatsville Food Coop, where she was an early member and nutrition activist. She helped found InterArt Works, which employed more than twenty artists to accomplish a wide range of public art programs in Austin and performed with the improvisational, myth-based performing group Pandora's Troubadours. She was the mother of the Energy Dragon, a giant puppet built by Ric Sternberg which focused attention on environmental and energy issues and "spoke" at Austin City Council hearings.

In late 70s Susan worked as an educational consultant at Region XIII Education Service Center in Austin, co-creating an art-based, gender equity curriculum. She was also a founding producer at ACTV in Austin. In the 1980s, Susan moved from Austin to Fayetteville, Arkansas to be with her children and to work on a Master of Science Degree in Anthropology at the University of Arkansas where she also taught English at the University of Arkansas.

Susan lived in Dallas in the late 1980s and early 1990s, and was Director of the Dallas Peace Center, a consultant for diversity at Richland College, and a trainer for peer mediation in the public schools.

In Austin in the 1990s, she worked at The Foundation for a Compassionate Society, creating and touring with "The Earth and Sky Women's Peace Caravan for a Nuclear Free Future," a sky blue, second-hand, rebuilt RV, which served as a travelling museum and anti-nuke organizing tool. One project involved purchasing a share of stock in an area nuclear facility so she could attend stockholder meetings with the Radiation Rangers, a group of protesters in comic costumes.

She also worked for Greenpeace and gathered members for the Volt-Revolters, a citizen group who refused to pay the percent of their utility bills that went to nuclear power. She organized Grandmothers and Others for a Nuclear Free Future and SMART – Sensible Mothers Against Radio Active Transport.

In 1994 she traveled to Guatemala to serve as body guard for Jennifer Harbury, who conducted a hunger strike in front of the *Politénica* in Guatemala

City to obtain information about her husband Everado, who had been captured and executed by government forces.

In 1998 she was a write-in candidate for Governor of Texas for the Green Party, changing her name to Susan Lee Solar for the occasion. In the fall of 2001 she began work as an elementary bi-lingual teacher at Pickle Elementary School in Austin.

In addition to her activist work for peace, gender equity, the environment and social justice, Susan was a video artist, dancer, and avid advocate of sustainable building. She was a land owner at *La Tierra de los Pedernales*, where a group of people are creating sustainable homes and a residential nature preserve. She generously helped others build straw bale homes, and designed a straw bale house for her land along the Pedernales River.

Her first book *You Ask What Does This Mean, This Interest in Goddesses, Prehistoric Religions?* was published by Plain View Press in 1985.

Susan Lee Campbell Solar died on Feburary 13, 2002 unexpectedly of systemic pneumonia.